As Easy As That

Mary O'Sullivan

POOLBEG

This novel is entirely a work of fiction. The names, characters and incidents portrayed in it are the work of the author's imagination. Any resemblance to actual persons, living or dead, events or localities is entirely coincidental.

Published 2007
by Poolbeg Press Ltd
123 Grange Hill, Baldoyle
Dublin 13, Ireland
E-mail: poolbeg@poolbeg.com
www.poolbeg.com

1 3 5 7 9 10 8 6 4 2

A catalogue record for this book is available from the British Library.

ISBN 978-1-84223 -270-5

Typeset by Patricia Hope in Bembo 10.75/14

Printed by
Litographia Roses, Spain

Note on the author

Mary O' Sullivan lives in Carrigaline, County Cork, with husband Sean and her two dogs, Schumi and Dougie. Her first novel *Parting Company* was also published by Poolbeg.

Acknowledgements

The road from writing school essays to being a published author has been long. Luckily it was not a journey I had to make alone. I have been privileged to have had help and support from very many people and I would like to take this opportunity to thank them.

Thank you to Paula, Niamh, Lynda and all the staff in Poolbeg Press. Your support and encouragement are much appreciated.

Gaye Shortland deserves thanks for her commitment, and admiration for her skills as writer and editor.

To Karen Kinsella, Olive O'Hare and Phillip Ryan, my heartfelt thanks for reading the fledgling manuscript of *As Easy As That*. Your comments and encouragement were a big help along the way.

For their friendship and encouragement, thanks to Claire Vickery, Karen Aherne, John and Regina Byrne and fellow-author Mary Malone.

I would also like to thank David Collins and Joan Hilton of Collins SuperValu, Carrigaline, Jerome O'Leary of Carrigaline Bookshop and everybody who helped to make my first novel *Parting Company* a success.

To my family: Sean, Owen and Vera in Carrigaline, Paul in New Zealand, Annie and Emmett in Bonn. For the support and encouragement, for always being there when I need you, for being a safe haven in stormy weather, the biggest thanks of all goes to you.

For Sean

Köszönöm szépen

Chapter 1

The contrast had a certain beauty. Warm blood on cool silk. Kate threw the stained scrap of fabric into the laundry basket. She sat on the side of the bath and waited for the tears to come. Her eyes remained dry. She was beyond crying. Getting up she opened the cabinet drawer, took out her pristine pregnancy-testing kit and threw it against the mirror. It bounced off the glass and tumbled into the washbasin, then lay there, taunting her, mocking her failure. Their failure.

The front door opened. She heard Fred drop his briefcase on the hall table with a thump. He called up the stairs.

"Kate! Sorry I'm running so late! Are you nearly ready?"

She stared at the battered pregnancy-testing kit, then picked it up and put it back into the drawer. With eyes closed, she whispered, "Next time. Please let it be all right next time!" When she heard him walk up the stairs, she quickly plastered some cleanser onto her face. She smiled at him as he came to the door.

She was playing the game. His rules, his game, where work was priority and a family happened. Or not.

"Just about to shower now. Your clothes are ready in the bedroom. Busy day?"

"The meeting with Super Store went on and on. Pernickety crowd. But I think we just about clinched the contract. It's small but I can't afford to turn it down."

"Well done, Fred! You'll feel like celebrating tonight then."

He took a step towards her and slipped his hand inside her robe. "Want to know what I feel like doing tonight?"

"Not really," she smiled as she pushed him gently away.

Kate stood under the shower and tried to make her mind as empty as her belly felt, tried to stop the grieving for a baby that had not been conceived, tried to wash away the fears and doubts. It was party time and her party-time husband was waiting.

The Cochranes' house spoke of a need to advertise their new-found wealth. Everything from the electronically controlled gates to the porticos and pillars on the house displayed an abundance of spending power and a terrible lack of taste.

"No doubt about it, there's money in muck," Fred remarked as they parked the car in Cochranes' courtyard.

Kate flipped down the mirror and checked her hair and make-up. She peered at her reflection, trying to find some connection with the sophisticated image. From the carefully made-up brown eyes to the sleek dark hair, she seemed every inch the sophisticate. A look of effortless elegance achieved through heroic efforts with hair-straighteners and an armoury of cosmetics. A mask. Snapping the mirror back into place, she looked at her husband.

"We've got to talk, Fred. We –"

He kissed her on the lips and smothered her words. She gave up. He was probably right. Now was not the time. But there just did not seem to be a right time for Fred to discuss . . . their problem. How could he be so insensitive? So selfish?

She slipped into her role as beautiful wife of the advertising executive and linked his arm as they made their way towards the vast foyer of the Cochrane mansion.

"Fred! Kate ! Welcome. You look wonderful, Kate!"

Sheila Cochrane grabbed their hands, kissed their cheeks and dragged them into the lounge all at the same time. It was as if she had read rules one to ten of hostess etiquette and was trying to apply all of them at once.

A quick glance around the huge reception room told Kate all she needed to know. Carefully arranged on and around the state-of-the-art furniture were the same tanned faces and honed bodies that had peopled the last party. And the one before that. And probably the next twenty.

Drawn to potential business like a magnet, Fred zoned in on the retail group. Nigel Greenway, the car-sales supremo, owner of a string of garages, was holding court in front of the bay window. A circle of respectful disciples surrounded him.

Kate watched as Fred slipped into a slot which seemed to have been reserved for him. He shook hands, smiled, struck a pose halfway between subservience and assertiveness and suddenly became the moon orbiting the retailing super-planet. His handsome features were animated, his body tensed, the hunter ready to pounce on any business prey. This was his milieu; this was what Fred was about.

"Kate Lucas! How do you do it?"

Kate turned around and smiled when she saw Patty Molloy. They touched cheeks and stood back to look at each other.

"You're always perfection itself, Kate. Not a hair out of place or a spare ounce of flesh!"

Kate smiled at the petite woman standing in front of her. So tiny and yet she had produced three children in quick succession. Number four was obviously well on the way.

"You look great yourself, Patty. When's the baby due?"

"The next, and last, baby Molloy is due in a month's time. I love them all dearly but enough is enough. I feel like a baby-making machine at the moment. Anyway, I'm boring. Tell me about life in the fast lane. I see a lot of your boss on television these days. Must be exciting in your office."

Exciting? Yes, there had been a lot more work to do lately in Richard Gordon's law office. Research, cross-referencing, press releases. Being personal assistant to the leading trial lawyer in the country was demanding, especially since he was defending in the highest profile case in years. But exciting?

"It's very busy in the office, Patty. A lot of nose to the grindstone and very little else. How are the children?"

"They all take after Brian so they're a handful. And stop changing the subject. Did he do it? Did our sainted minister murder his mistress?"

Trust Patty to put the question everyone else only hinted at. She looked like the others, tanned and toned, but she had a directness unique in their circle.

"I've no idea what the man did or did not do," Kate replied with a smile. "Anyway, I couldn't tell you even if I did know."

Patty shrugged. "Worth a try! I believe he strangled the poor girl and thought he could get away with it. You could tell me the results of the DNA tests. It'll be in the papers soon anyway. Was the baby his?"

A bell rang.

"My God! A dinner-gong!"

They both laughed and then changed their expressions to suitably solemn as they joined the procession into the dining-room and the lavish buffet.

Sheila Cochrane knew how to choose a good caterer. The food was delicious, as was the wine, and conversation flowed.

It would have been a good party except that the host, Gus Cochrane, became coarser and louder with each drink. Sheila was visibly nervous. She knew her husband's veneer of culture was alcohol-soluble. When his voice reached a certain pitch, it signalled the end of the party and people began to gather themselves together to leave.

"I think it's time I went home," Patty said, standing up

from the comfortable couch she and Kate had found for themselves.

Kate stood and kissed Patty on the cheek. "Take care, Patty. And do tell Brian we were asking for him."

Patty replied with a little wave as she waddled off to thank her hosts. Kate glanced around and noticed that Fred was still talking to Nigel Greenway. Or at least he was still listening to the great man. She flopped back onto her seat again. Fred would not thank her for interrupting the sermon. She began to get the uncomfortable feeling that somebody was staring at her. Then she noticed Gus Cochrane weaving towards her, at great speed considering his condition. Immediately she got up from her seat and beckoned to Fred but he was too engrossed in Nigel Greenway to see her. Then she was smothered in a wave of alcohol fumes as Gus Cochrane stood unsteadily in front of her.

"Katie Lucas!" he roared. "When're we going to see little Lucases? Are you afraid to ruin your figure or's Fred shooting blanks?"

The loud comment stopped all conversation. The room fell silent.

Sheila went to her drunken husband and grabbed his arm. "Time to go to bed, Gus. Party's over."

"Let me go, woman!" he snapped. "I just asked a civil question. Maybe they've a problem I could help with!"

Fred crossed the room quickly and took Kate's hand. He squeezed her fingers and she could feel some of his strength transfer to her. Ignoring Gus, they turned to Sheila.

"Thank you very much for the evening," said Fred. "It was very nice."

"The meal was beautiful. Thank you," Kate added.

Little beads of sweat were gathering on Gus's forehead and trickling down the creases of his porky face. Kate and Fred walked away from him.

"Fred! Fred! Listen to me!" the drunk man spluttered.

"Good night, Gus."

"No. Listen! If you can't do the job, I'll do it for you. I'd no trouble getting Sheila pregnant. A favour to a friend so to speak and . . ."

Kate clung onto Fred's hand as they headed for the door, praying that she could control the tears until she got to the car.

Suddenly Fred let go her hand.

"I won't be a minute. You go on ahead," he said casually.

In panic, Kate watched her husband make a beeline back to Nigel Greenway. Then she ran and did not stop until she reached her car. She leaned against the door, shaking with embarrassment and anger. Gus Chocrane! That big ignorant pig! The foul-mouthed lout! He might have made money from his waste-disposal empire but he was still a piece of filth! And why was Fred taking so long? Why was he making her wait here alone?

Patty came walking towards her.

"Are you okay, Kate? I saw what happened."

"I thought you'd gone."

"I had to go back to use the bathroom. I was passing the reception room when Gus Cochrane started shouting at you. I hope you're not going to let that drunken oaf upset you. God! The man is vile!"

Kate straightened herself up and smiled. "No, of course

not. He's not worth bothering about. Did you see Fred? Is he on his way?"

Patty took Kate's hand and squeezed it. "Why don't you sit into my car for a few minutes? I saw Fred talking to Nigel Greenway. He'll probably be a while."

Without saying a word Kate went with Patty. She did not trust herself to speak. There were no words for the hurt she felt. No decent words. They sat in silence.

"Like some music?" Patty asked, moving her hand towards the stereo.

Kate nodded. The soundtrack of *The Lion King* filled the emptiness.

"The kids love it," Patty explained.

At that, Kate lost her control over the tears which needed so badly to well up and spill over. Would she ever be able to say something like that? *The kids love it.* Would she ever feel the warmth of her baby snuggling into her, guide tiny feet towards their first step, buy school uniforms, help with homework, read bedtime stories? Month after month and still the pregnancy-testing kit remained sealed.

"Fred doesn't care. He's too busy building up his client accounts to worry about having children."

Kate sat bolt upright in shock. How had these words left the safety of her head? "The Circle of Life" played on. And on. What must Patty think? What would Patty say and to whom would she say it? She saw Fred approach the car, keys in hand.

Patty turned to her. "I hope it works out for you, Kate. Remember Fred is no different from other men. They define themselves by their careers. It doesn't mean he cares less."

"Thanks, Patty."

"And don't worry. I won't say anything to anyone else."

Kate gave her a grateful hug and got out of the car.

Fred talked non-stop all the way home. He had almost secured a big advertising campaign with Nigel Greenway.

"This could be one of our biggest yet. He'll be opening two new garages up-country in the spring and he wants a national campaign for the launch. Multimedia. Television, radio, press, the lot!"

He was still talking about the Greenway contract as they got ready for bed. Kate nodded every so often but he really did not need her input. Gus Cochrane's insult obviously had not hurt him at all. Nor did he seem to realise how much it had pained her. So she just listened to his enthusiastic babble until she could take it no more.

"Night, Fred."

"Night, sweetheart. Aren't you glad now that we went to Cochrane's dinner party?"

She turned her back on him and tried to sleep.

Chapter 2

Kate smiled as she typed her dictation. She was remembering her conversation with Patty Molloy a week before at the Cochranes' party. The DNA tests were back. How Patty would love this little snippet. The ex-Finance Minister was indeed the father of the baby the murdered woman had been carrying. So now Henry Hennessey had motive as well as opportunity. It was beginning to seem that even the renowned legal defence skills of Richard Gordon would not save this politician from a guilty verdict. But then that is what Kate had thought in many previous cases and Richard had found some technicality, some obscure piece of legislation, some long-forgotten precedent which left the courts with no option but to free his client.

She switched off the Dictaphone, took out her earphones and walked to the window. On the street below, lunch-time traffic was beginning to build. She checked her watch. The morning session in court would be winding up by now. Going back to her desk she picked up the checklist. No one was ever in any doubt about what Richard Gordon needed. He wrote everything down in meticulous detail. She ticked his requirements off one by one and put the necessary documents into her briefcase. Just one remained outstanding. She picked up the internal phone and rang Len Murphy. He was in her office within a minute, carrying a huge leather-bound volume of case histories.

"Good timing, Mrs Lucas. I've just found it."

He put the volume down on her desk and opened it at the bookmark. Kate glanced at it and immediately knew how her boss was going to defend his famous client. Richard had his precedent. The case was the State vs O'Brien 1956. This trial had been sensational in its day because the evidence had such sexual content. Bondage, to be exact – at a time in Irish history when any random thought about sex called for purging in the confessional. O'Brien had claimed that his girlfriend's death by strangulation had been accidental, the result of over-zealous lovemaking. In the absence of any proof that she had attempted to defend herself, the inference was drawn that the sex – including the bondage – had been consensual. There had been outrage and scandal but in the end a verdict of Death by Misadventure had been returned. O'Brien had walked free. Maybe he was still around, feeble and senile, tying old ladies to the bed with silk scarves.

"Right, thanks, Len. I'll photocopy this and give it to Richard at lunch."

As she listened to the photocopier whirring, she mulled over what she could remember of the medical reports on the victim in the minister's case. The girl's neck was bruised but a case could possibly be made for the accidental theory, the momentary application of pressure on the jugular. A horrible accident. Richard would make sure that reasonable doubt was well planted in the jurors' minds. She slammed down the lid on the photocopier. Public sympathy was huge for the victim and her family. The girl had been used and abused by this high-ranking politician. Some had sympathy for him. A great career in ruins, his family destroyed. But there was no mention, no thought, no sympathy given to the baby. Just a four-month foetus, a collection of cells. Another life over before it had a chance to be lived.

She put the photocopy into her briefcase along with the other documents and picked up her handbag and keys. She had to hurry then because Richard did not tolerate tardiness.

She would not allow herself to think about her plan until later. After work. She must have it all organised in her head before she spoke to Fred. And this time he would have to listen.

Shopping after work, rushing home, peeling, chopping and cooking had been exhausting. Kate stood in the middle of her kitchen and inhaled deeply. It was worth all the frantic effort now. The blend of aromas was heady. Garlic, oregano, basil. She should cook more often. Really cook as opposed to reheat. She went into the dining-room and looked at the table. It was beautiful. Stephen Pearce tableware, John Rocha glassware, candles and one simple red rose in a bud vase. A well-laid trap. She shook off that thought and went upstairs to bathe and dress.

She was just getting out of the bath when the phone rang. It was Fred. He would not be home until later.

"How much later? I've cooked for us now. Dinner will be ruined."

"Don't bother about me. Have your own. I'll probably eat out."

"Fred! I've something important to discuss with you! I need you to come home!"

His short, sharp sigh was full of impatience. He knew what she wanted to talk about and he was wriggling out of it again.

"Give me a break, Kate. I'm going to the golf club with Nigel Greenway. If I get this contract it could set us up for life. Put us in the big league. I don't need this hassle from you now."

A thousand angry words sprang into Kate's head. Hassle! Starting a family was just a hassle! His precious advertising company was his baby. Bastard! Bastard! Bastard! She counted slowly to five before answering.

"Right, Fred. See you later."

She did not bother dressing. Throwing on her robe, she went downstairs and took the lasagne out of the oven. It looked delicious with a golden cheese and yoghurt crust. She heaped some onto a plate and tasted. Perfect! Sitting at the kitchen table she ate her lonely meal. After clearing the dining-room table and tidying up, she poured herself a glass of wine and got her new book. Then she went to bed with just her glass of wine and her book for company. After reading two chapters of *Infertility and How To Overcome It*, she turned off the light and went to sleep. Fred did not wake her when he crept into bed in the small hours of the morning.

Chapter 3

"Kate! I'm talking to you. Trying to give you dictation. You're a million miles away."

Kate started. Richard Gordon was in a very impatient mood. It did not help that the jury in what had become known as the 'Minister's Mistress Case' had been out for the past two days. The introduction of the DNA evidence a week ago had sent the trial into a tailspin. Now that the jury were sequestered in a hotel mulling over the evidence, everyone in the office was jumpy. Richard's closing speech had been brilliant but so had the prosecutor's. The politician's fate and Richard Gordon's professional reputation still hung in the balance.

"I'm sorry," she muttered. "You were saying?"

"I was saying that I'm going to take a break when all this is over and I think you should take one too. Are you all right? You look very pale."

She smiled at him. "Actually I'm going to the doctor this evening for a check-up. I feel fine really. Just a precaution."

"Hmm. And how's Fred these days? I heard he's doing a bit of business with Nigel Greenway."

How was Fred indeed! Who was Fred? Where was Fred? By Nigel Greenway's side, at his beck and call, panting after him, probably even carrying his golf bag. She may as well be married to Nigel-fucking-Greenway. She cleared her throat to shift the hot ball of anger lodged there.

"Yes. Fred's going to handle a national advertising campaign for the Greenway chain. He's excited about it and very busy."

Richard gave her one of his piercing stares, the one he usually used to intimidate prosecution witnesses. She sat up straight and stared right back. Richard Gordon was her employer, not her counsellor. How dare he try to see inside her head, inside her marriage!

"I'd advise Fred to be careful. Double-check everything. Greenway is a slick character. He's –"

The phone rang and Richard grabbed it. He jumped up.

"The jury's about to come in. Grab your case. C'mon!"

Kate shoved two sheets of paper into her briefcase. One was the press release for a guilty verdict, the other for a not-guilty result. Everyone in the office wished Richard good luck as he strode through but he swept past without acknowledging them. His focus was totally on the courtroom and the verdict of the jury. Following in his wake, Kate tried to focus her own thoughts. Court case now. Think about the doctor later. By the time she took her place at the back of the courtroom her strategy had worked. She had no other thought but witnessing the closure of this case. Reprieve for the politician or justice for his mistress.

The crush outside the courtroom was frightening. The dingy corridors in the old courthouse had not been built to accommodate a mob. Kate clutched her bag to her chest as she was pushed along with the forward motion of the crowd. Richard was taller than average and she could see his distinguished white hair rising above other heads in front of her but she could not reach him. The crush began to ease as they approached the front doors and people spilled out onto the steps. Television cameras from five different networks were trained on the doorway. She saw Richard look over his shoulder and she managed to move towards him. Opening her briefcase, she handed him the appropriate page. He smiled at her and moved forward to stand in front of a bank of microphones and cameras.

Richard's speech was precise and to the point. A just verdict had been reached. Death by Misadventure. No triumphalism. His client was truly sorry about the tragic death of the young woman and the baby she was carrying but was gratified that the court had exonerated him of any blame. Kate gave a little smile of satisfaction. She had suggested, as strongly as her terms of employment allowed, that the baby be mentioned in any press statement. When Richard had finished speaking, the journalists all began shouting at once.

"Minister, are you going to stand for office again?"

"Mr Gordon, is the verdict going to be appealed?"

"Minister, is it true that your wife is filing for divorce?"

Attention turned to a small group now emerging from the courthouse. A middle-aged couple, flanked by their lawyers, walked slowly up to the cameras. The woman was crying, the man pale and drawn. The parents of the girl who had died. The pain on their faces was so intense it seemed to stab Kate in the stomach. The flipside of Richard's triumph. She looked away.

Glancing at her watch, she saw that her doctor's appointment was in thirty minutes' time.

She managed to get Richard's attention. "I'm going now," she mouthed.

He came over to her.

"Congratulations, Richard."

He shook her hand. "Thank you, Kate. I appreciate all the work you put in on this. It's your victory too."

She looked at him but did not smile. She wasn't sure if he was patronising her. He knew her opinion on the verdict. It was unjust. Wrong. Minister Henry Hennessey should be locked up. He should suffer just as his mistress and baby had suffered; he should feel the humiliation his wife and family felt, the grief that had destroyed the girl's family.

"We're having a little get-together at our place tonight. You know how Cora is for organising parties."

Kate smiled. Richard Gordon's wife was certainly a party person. Cora was as vivacious and extrovert as her husband was solemn and measured.

"Think Fred will be able to make it?" Richard asked.

"Fred's in Belfast at the moment. But I'll be there anyway. See you later. Eightish?"

Richard was again surrounded by media before he could reply. Kate hurried away. The doctor's surgery was on the other side of town and she did not want to be late.

Kate clasped and unclasped her handbag nervously. The click was loud in the otherwise silent waiting room. Just one other patient was queuing ahead of her. An elderly woman who smelled of lavender. The door to the surgery opened and a woman carrying a crying toddler came out. The doctor put his head around the door and his secretary went over and handed him a file. A name was called out. The old woman got up and shuffled towards him. The door closed and there was silence again.

The clicking of Kate's handbag must have been getting on the secretary's nerves because she switched on the radio. The evening news bulletin came on and the only topic of discussion was the trial. Legal experts from all over had been raked up and they were giving their opinions on the result.

"My God! He got away with it!" the secretary said.

Kate nodded. Richard Gordon paid her salary, so she couldn't do more than nod. Richard's statement was read out, then the statement on behalf of the girl's family. Minister Henry Hennessey was staying very quiet.

The surgery door opened again and the old woman emerged. Then the doctor's head appeared and his secretary went and handed him another file.

"Mrs Lucas. This way, please."

Kate followed him in and sat on the edge of her chair. Her book said there was no need to be nervous. Doctors dealt with cases of infertility all the time. God damn their blasé attitude! She had never dealt with this before and she felt like getting up and running out the door.

"How are you, Kate? It's been quite a while since I last saw you."

"Very well, thank you. I'm not sick. At least I don't think so."

The doctor sat back and looked at her. He began to swing his swivel-chair from side to side. She found the movement hypnotic. Fear and the motion of the chair lulled her into a near trance. The words she had rehearsed were lost. She sat in silence.

"How's Fred?"

"Busy. He'd be here with me today except that he had to go to Belfast. He's as concerned as I am."

The words began to tumble out now, falling over each other in an incoherent mess.

"We've been trying for twelve months. We don't use protection. We have a normal sex life. And nothing. Month after month, nothing. I'm thirty-two. I'm running out of time. Everyone else my age has a family. All my friends, my work colleagues. Even the minister's mistress got pregnant. Why can't I? What's wrong with me?"

The doctor stopped swinging in his chair, leaned forward, put his elbows on the desk and looked steadily at her.

"First things first, Kate. Calm down. I understand that this must be nerve-racking for you but we can deal with it a lot better if we are calm. You may feel now that the whole world is producing babies without a bother but that's far from the truth. Lots of couples have difficulty getting pregnant but there's plenty of help available."

"But can't you see I'm worried about my age? If I was in my twenties I'd have plenty of time to try this and that – but I'm thirty-two! I can't afford to wait and see."

"We'll have to establish some solid information first. For instance, we must know if you are ovulating, if there are any blockages, if Fred's sperm count is within the normal range. We have a long road ahead, Kate, and must start with small steps."

Kate sat back and sighed. Her reading had told her this would be the situation. Nice and easy does it. One step at a time. Relax. Don't worry.

"Fine, doctor. So what's the first small step?"

"I'll give you a general check-up now and do a blood and urine test."

He examined her, gave her temperature charts to fill in, a talk on diet and a lecture on patience.

"I'll send these off," he said, pointing to her urine and blood samples. "You keep your charts and that will help us pinpoint your fertile time. See me again in two months."

"Two months!"

"Yes. And maybe Fred could come with you next time."

Maybe Fred would come with her next time. If he was not too angry at her for starting the process he had tried so hard to avoid. And if the problem was hers, not his.

Chapter 4

Cora Gordon obviously had great confidence in her husband's ability to win court cases against the odds. The party was so well organised that she must have been working on it for days, maybe weeks. Not even Cora could have whipped up this spread in an afternoon. What would she have done if Richard had lost? If the minister was now behind bars as many still believed he should be?

Kate looked around and was glad that she had put on her black dress. Every designer label known to credit cards was at this party. This was far more than just a few friends. It was a gathering of the elite. An opportunity lost for Fred.

"Over here, Kate!"

Patty Molloy was waving at her from across the room. Her stomach was so distended by now that she seemed almost the same width as height. Kate walked over to join her.

"How are you, Kate? Congratulations. I know you had

your part to play in today's victory. I still think the minister did it deliberately though."

Kate laughed. Typical of Patty to stand here in Gordon's home and say that.

Patty beckoned for Kate to follow and they went out through the patio doors into the garden. A marquee sprawled the width of the lawn and fairy lights hung from the trees. Violin music wafted over trees and flowers and guests.

"Well, well!" said Patty. "An orchestra. Or at least a violinist anyway. Sheila Cochrane will eat her knickers!"

"Pity she won't see it. The Cochranes don't make it onto Cora's guest list."

They strolled down to inspect the marquee. It was lined with tables of fabulous food and hung with lanterns and garlands. At the centre was a dance floor and on a dais a girl was playing violin.

Kate and Patty looked at each other.

"My God!" said Patty. "This is lavish, even by Cora's standards! I know Richard had a great victory but isn't this a bit much?"

Kate nodded. It was strange. Understatement was more the Gordons' style. Strange too that Patty was on her own yet again. It was quite a while now since Kate had seen Brian Molloy by his wife's side.

"Brian busy?"

Patty frowned. "Oh! He had to go. Again. He was here earlier but they called him from the hospital. Some emergency or other. Someone should have warned me about marrying a heart surgeon. Too late now," she laughed, patting her stomach. "And Fred? He couldn't make it either?"

"He's in Belfast."

At least that is where Kate assumed he was. She had not heard from him since yesterday. She had tried contacting him several times today but his mobile phone was switched off. He must have a lot of meetings. She opened her bag and checked her phone to make sure it had reception here. The bars were full.

"Kate! Patty! Welcome! You both look great!"

Cora Gordon embraced them and then led them to the bar.

"I know you can't drink alcohol, Patty, but I don't want to see any empty glasses tonight. Kate, Richard told me how hard you've all worked on the Henry Hennessey case. He's lucky to have a team like you around him."

"Where is Richard? "

"He has just gone to the airport to collect a friend of his. He won't be long. Pity Brian had to go, Patty. That husband of yours works too hard."

"Try telling him that!" Patty laughed but there was no mirth in the sound.

Cora spotted Richard arriving back. He was walking towards them, a very tall, dark-haired man by his side.

Cora offered her hand to the tall man. "Martin! Welcome! So nice to see you again. Did you have a good flight?"

"Hi, Cora. Great to be here. Looking forward to settling in. Nice party."

He looked over towards Patty and Kate and smiled. He

had the whitest teeth Kate had ever seen. His skin was tanned. A real tan, redolent of sun and surf. For one shocking moment Kate imagined him in swim trunks, astride a surfboard, his muscles rippling, water glistening on his skin. She shook her head to rid herself of the adolescent image and realised that Richard was talking to her.

"Just a quick word, please, Kate. We'll go to the library."

She followed Richard back into the house. There were people everywhere, trampling over thick carpets and polished floors, sitting, standing, laughing, talking. A good party. It was a relief to get into the peace of the timber-lined library. Richard waved her to a chair.

"You must be wondering if Cora has lost her head completely. She's a great entertainer but this is above and beyond."

Kate smiled. "It's extravagant. But it's wonderful."

"The reason why Cora pushed the boat out on this one is that I'll be making a special announcement tonight. I wanted to tell you myself before the public announcement. I've sold the practice, Kate. I'll be retiring with immediate effect."

She stared at him in shock. How? Why? God, she was his PA and she hadn't had the faintest idea that he had retirement on his mind!

"I'm sixty now. Neither of our children has any interest in the law practice, as you know. Cora and I would like to enjoy what time we have left together. See a bit of the world maybe while we still can."

"But who bought your practice? And what about our jobs?"

"You've just seen the new owner. Martin Burke. A brilliant criminal lawyer. He's been in the States for the past six years but he's ready to come home now. And don't worry. I made it a condition of sale that all staff are retained."

Kate fiddled with the belt on her dress. She felt like crying. She had not realised the depth of her emotional dependence on Richard. Reliable, quick-thinking, capable Richard! Yes, he could be ruthless. He had to be to protect his clients. But he was loyal. If you were in Richard's camp, he looked after you. Tears welled in her eyes.

"I'll miss you, Richard."

He leaned across and squeezed her hand. "We'll still see each other, Kate. I'm very grateful to you for everything you've done for me. Putting up with my impatience and moods. Your efficiency. Your loyalty. We've had an interesting seven years, haven't we?"

"I can't believe it's been seven years. That's right. I joined your firm the year I got engaged to Fred. Time flies."

"Indeed. That's why I made this decision now. The older you get the quicker it seems to pass." He stood up and offered his arm to Kate. "Let me introduce you to Martin. Then I'll make my announcement. At least I'm going out on a high. The minister is probably partying now too."

Kate looked at him but could not discern anything from his expression. Maybe he genuinely believed in Henry Hennessey's innocence. Maybe not.

Martin Burke's handshake was warm and firm. Kate

felt a little shy, a little intimidated by his good looks, his deep blue eyes and long dark eyelashes, his imposing height. Richard's announcement surprised everyone. Like Kate, the general opinion had been that Richard would work while there was a case to be defended. Well, there was Patty's theory about men's self-esteem hit on the head! Richard was one man, at least, who did not define himself solely by his job. Surprising as it was, quality time with his wife seemed to be his priority now.

The mood of the party became even more frenetic. The centre of the floor in the marquee was cleared and dancing began. Kate danced with Richard and then with Martin. She even took to the floor with Patty, who somehow managed to move her bulk to the rhythm of the music. It was a very happy night, a night full of celebration and hope for the future.

Until the phone call came.

Cora's face was white when she put the phone down. She went out to the marquee, crossed the dance floor, caught Richard by the hand and pulled him away from the group he was with. They huddled together whispering.

"What do you think's going on there?" Patty asked.

Kate shrugged. "I don't know but they both seem pretty upset. Looks like we'll find out soon. They're coming this way."

Richard reached them first. He was pale. Cora seemed ready to cry.

"Come into the house, please," he said to Patty. "We've got something to tell you."

He led Patty away and nodded at Kate and Cora to follow. They went into the library again but this time the silence was not comforting. It was full of threat. Cora fussed around Patty and sat her on the large leather armchair. Richard cleared his throat. Patty pulled herself to the edge of the chair and stared into his face.

"Look, what is going on? What is it? Just spit it out, Richard."

"I'm afraid it's bad news, Patty. The hospital's been on the phone. Brian has had an accident."

Patty slumped slowly back into the chair. She looked like a waif enfolded in the big leather seat. The colour began to leave her face and even with make-up she was ashen. "What happened? Has he been badly hurt?"

"He was involved in a car accident. He has significant injuries. I'm sorry, Patty."

With one incredibly swift movement for somebody almost nine months pregnant, she was out of the chair and on her feet. "I must get to him! Will you drive me, Kate? I must see him!"

Cora put her arm around Patty. "The hospital has arranged a police escort for you. They're on their way now."

"A police escort! Jesus! He's dying. Maybe he's dead. Oh, my God!" Patty began to pace and murmur: "Please let him be all right! Please let him be all right!"

There was a tap at the door and a policeman came in. As he introduced himself, Cora went to get the coats.

"If you want us to drive you, Mrs Molloy, we will. Or we'll escort whoever is taking you. We estimate twelve minutes to the hospital."

Somehow they organised themselves. Kate would drive Patty. Richard and Cora would follow on as soon as they had told their guests what was happening. Kate led Patty to her car and tied her seat belt. Patty was beyond taking care of little details. The squad car switched on their blue light and siren and led them down the driveway.

The twelve-minute journey seemed endless. Patty kept up her continuous murmur of "Please let him be all right!". Kate tried to focus only on the squad car speeding ahead but Patty looked so ghastly in the reflected spinning blue light that she kept glancing at her. They were not taking the direct route to the hospital and Kate guessed that the police were sparing them the sight of the accident scene. Richard had whispered to her before they left that Brian had had a head-on crash with an articulated truck. It had seemingly taken the rescue service quite some time to cut him free.

As they approached the hospital they could see two people waiting at the doors for them.

"His registrar and his senior house officer," said Patty.

Kate went cold. The doctors' presence at the hospital door was ominous.

They were a very grim group as they stood in the foyer, waiting for the lift to the fourth floor. Kate thought it arrived too soon. It would never be the right time to take this trip to the Intensive Care Unit.

When they arrived at Intensive Care, they paused for a moment outside the door. Through the glass Kate could see banks of tubes and wires connected to the still figure in the bed. The registrar took Patty's arm and led her in. He indicated to Kate to stay outside.

"May I get you tea or coffee, Mrs Lucas?"

Kate looked at the young man beside her and saw the answers to her unasked questions in his face. "He's not going to make it, is he?"

He clenched his teeth and his jaw muscles quivered. He found the control he was struggling for. He shook his head.

"There's nothing we can do. It's just the life support now."

Through the glass, Kate watched Patty leaning over the inert figure in the bed. She was rubbing her husband's face, kissing him, begging him to wake up. Kate looked away. The pain was too raw. Too intense.

"Have the rest of his family been informed? His parents and his brothers?"

"They're on their way. At least Mrs Molloy won't have to make the decision on her own."

"To switch off the life support?"

He nodded. The ifs began to torment Kate. If Brian had not answered the call to the hospital, if he had stayed at the party, if he had driven more carefully. God! What that split second had done to Patty and her children!

"The baby! She's almost due. Will she be all right?"

"We have the gynaecologist standing by. He'll see her when she's ready. The baby's full term now anyway. Their last, Brian said."

Kate remembered Patty saying that too and wondered if we write the script for our own destinies. The lift doors opened and Brian's family emerged, his parents frail and elderly, his brothers tense and shocked. The registrar saw them arriving and came out to meet them.

Kate slipped away towards the lift. She was drowning in the waves of pain and grief. Going to the foyer she took out her phone, dialled Fred's number and listened as it rang out. Her tears fell then, for Patty and her children, for Brian and his brilliant career cut short, for his parents and brothers. And for Kate. For the pain and loneliness she was feeling, for the emptiness of childlessness and for the huge distance that separated her from Fred, even when he was by her side.

Martin Burke sat alone in the darkened office of Richard Gordon & Co and wondered just what in the hell he had done. He could have stayed in the States, set up his own practice there, prosecuted criminals until he was white-haired and flabby, then retired to Florida to shrivel up in the sun. An ambulance siren wailed in the street below and he shivered. His tenure as Richard Gordon's replacement had had an inauspicious start – the party to mark the handover marred by news of a horrible accident. A heart surgeon, Cora had said. Husband to that very pretty, pregnant woman. And it seemed his injuries were critical. What a fucking start, Martin thought, and then felt guilty for his selfishness.

He glanced around. The street lighting cast a yellowish glow on the office. It was peaceful here. He could turn on the lights and start some work, begin his orientation course. He remained sitting in the gloom. He was already familiar with the work involved. The detailed CD-ROM Richard had made for him had given him ample time to study all the active files. His weekend visit a month ago had been enough to familiarise himself with this small but lucrative practice. Besides, Richard had a very competent workforce in place. The takeover should be seamless. Martin's concern was not with the future. It was thoughts of what he was leaving behind which bowed his head and kept him sitting in the semi-darkness of his new office into the small hours of the morning.

He must have dozed, his body clock confused. He woke with a start, acutely aware of danger. The office door was opening. Somebody, a man, was walking through. He was tall, his hair colouring difficult to discern in the yellowish dimness. The man's head was lowered, his hands patting his pockets. The distinct rattle of keys clinked as the intruder pulled a bunch from his pocket and walked towards the largest filing cabinet in the office. The property files.

Martin stood and the man twirled around, the keys dangling from his fingers.

"Jesus Christ! Who's there?" the intruder shouted in panic.

Recognising the voice, Martin flicked on his desk lamp. Richard Gordon stood by the filing cabinet, pale and shocked.

"What in the fuck are you doing here at this hour, Martin?" he asked. "You frightened the life out of me."

"I could say the same," Martin replied. "And how come you still have a set of keys?"

Richard did a shuffle with his feet. An uncomfortable little shift. He seemed to be giving himself time to calm down. To make up a plausible reply.

"I'll give you these when you start. I assume that won't be for a few days yet. You'll need time to acclimatise, to settle up accommodation. Things like that."

Martin held out his hand. "The keys, Richard, please. I've already started."

Richard's eyes flicked from the filing cabinet to the younger man with hand outstretched. Martin watched in puzzlement as first defiance, then anger were reflected on Richard's face.

"There are some files I want to look over. A few things I wanted to wrap up before I leave."

Martin walked towards him, hand still outstretched. "Don't worry about it, Richard. If I have any questions, I'll contact you. But as of now, I'm in charge here. The keys, please."

The bunch of keys was handed over reluctantly. Richard walked slowly to the door and stood there, his back to Martin.

"Brian Molloy died," he said softly and then he walked out and closed the door behind him.

Martin went over to the property filing cabinet and unlocked it. If it took all night he would find out why Richard Gordon had needed to access that cabinet. Even shock from the death of a man who had obviously been a friend of his had not stopped him creeping into the office under cover of darkness. A quick examination of the files in the top three drawers revealed nothing much of note.

When the bottom drawer did not run smoothly on its tracks, Martin emptied out the files and examined the mechanism. A page from a notebook, the type a child might have, had got stuck on one of the runners. Martin freed the page and smoothed out the creases. Then he brought it over to his desk and read it with increasing disbelief.

The sun was lightening the sky by the time he returned the files to the bottom drawer. The page from the notebook he put in his briefcase. He walked through the empty streets back to his hotel. All his tiredness was gone now, chased away by his awful suspicion. He needed a shower. Then he needed to get back to the offices of what used to be Richard Gordon & Co.

Chapter 5

It was the following morning before Fred contacted home. Kate was in no mood for sensitivity.

"Where've you been? I've been trying to contact you. Brian Molloy is dead."

"What! How? When?"

"He was in a car crash. Severe head injuries. When are you coming home?"

Fred was silent then and Kate regretted her brusqueness. Fred and Brian had not been friends but they knew each other socially. The Lucas way. No close friends but many acquaintances.

"There are two more people I must see here. I'll be home tonight. When's the funeral?"

"Tomorrow."

"See you tonight. Love you."

Then he was gone. Kate stood there, phone in hand, wondering just what he felt, if anything, about Brian Molloy's death, about their marriage, about their future. He would come home tonight, make love to her, be by her side at the funeral tomorrow, do and say all the right things. But what was he feeling? She had lived with this man for six years and at this moment she felt she did not know him.

The phone rang again and she felt a guilty pang. It would be Fred, wondering why she had been so abrupt, wanting to know if she was all right. She was smiling as she said hello.

"Good morning, Kate, Martin Burke here. Hope I didn't wake you."

He need not have introduced himself. He had a very distinctive accent. Lilting Donegal with an undertone of American drawl.

"Not at all, Martin. I'll be leaving for the office shortly."

"That's why I rang. I understand you were at the hospital last night. I'm very sorry about your friend. It was a terrible tragedy. If you feel like taking a few days off, I have no problem with that."

"The funeral's tomorrow so I'll have Sunday to rest. But I'm fine today."

"See you soon, then. If you're sure."

"I'm sure. Thank you."

As she was getting ready for work she wondered at the irony of a stranger showing her the type of consideration of which her husband seemed incapable. Her new boss seemed like a very nice person. Maybe she would not miss Richard Gordon that much after all.

Martin examined the notebook page for the umpteenth time. He was almost sure now. No. He was sure. He dropped it into his pocket in disgust. The discreetly hidden Post-its he had discovered in the bottom-drawer property files had confirmed his suspicions. This was the last thing he had expected. Or wanted. There was a tap on the office door and Richard Gordon came in. He looked pale and tired, his age showing in the morning light.

"Good morning, Richard. I wasn't expecting to see you in here to-day. My sympathies on your friend's death."

Richard nodded acceptance of Martin's condolences and sat down at the desk.

"It's tragic," he agreed. "Poor Patty. You met her last night. The pregnant lady. I wish there was something we could do to help her. You always feel helpless in these situations, don't you?"

Martin agreed and then waited for Richard to go on. When the older man just sat there, darting glances around the office, Martin asked him bluntly what he wanted.

"I just want to have a last check. A run through the files to make sure everything's in order."

"Didn't we already discuss this last night? Our arrangement was that when I arrived here, you left. Immediately."

"Yes. But . . ."

"Fine," Martin agreed. "All right. Go ahead. You don't mind if I get on with some work?"

Martin logged onto his computer as Richard went from shelf to shelf, from press to press, searching with increasing agitation. Eventually he went to the filing cabinet and tried to open it.

"This is locked. Do you have the key, Martin? I want to look over the property files."

"Sorry. I left the key in my coat pocket. It's in my hotel. Have you mislaid something?"

"No. No, I'm just making sure everything's in order."

So am I, Martin thought, as he wondered how long he would let Richard sweat.

Kate felt restless when she went in to the office. Her mind kept drifting back to Patty Molloy and wondering how she was coping. She banished all thoughts of Patty and even of Fred with a determined effort. They were after-work concerns. The atmosphere in the office didn't help either. It was always downbeat after a big case. The thefts and drink-driving defences seemed so mundane after the excitement of the minister and his mistress.

Richard Gordon and Martin Burke had been in conference all morning. Obviously handing over a business like this was not as simple as saying you wanted to retire.

Coffee break in their little canteen was subdued. They were a small group. Six in all: receptionist, secretary, conveyancing lawyer, contract lawyer, personal assistant and over them all, the boss, the title that had fitted Richard Gordon so well.

"Who's this new guy?" asked Len Murphy.

It was obvious from his tone that he was peeved at the suddenness of the change and at the fact he had not been informed beforehand. He glared at Kate.

"You must've known. Why didn't you tell us?"

"It was as much of a surprise to me as to you."

"Yeah, sure. And what do you know about Martin Burke?"

"He's gorgeous," Eileen, the receptionist, said. "What else do you need to know?"

Before the break was over they decided to make a collection for a retirement gift for Richard. Kate got the job of shopping for something appropriate.

Back at her desk she picked up the phone and started to dial Patty's number. Halfway through she put down the receiver. Patty's family would be with her. Ringing would be an intrusion. Patty Molloy was the closest she had to a friend. But not that close. Not confiding close. She texted a message of concern to her and then went to lunch.

Richard and Martin Burke were still in their office at closing time. Kate tapped on the door and opened it at Martin's impatient "come in". Martin was sitting behind the desk while Richard was sitting on the windowsill behind him. The desk was strewn with files and folders. Both men looked exhausted.

"Sorry to disturb you but I just wanted to let you know I'm going home now. And, Martin, I wanted to remind you that I won't be in tomorrow."

"Oh, yes. The funeral. See you on Monday so. Thanks, Kate. And sorry I didn't get a chance to really introduce myself to staff today. I promise to be better organised when you come back."

"These returned Yanks!" Richard laughed.

Richard's attempt at a joke did nothing to ease the tension apparent between the two men. It made Kate wonder about what type of arrangement they had or when and how they had struck this deal. They appeared to be having problems now. What did they expect with such a lightning turnaround? Best let them get on with whatever it was they were trying to sort.

She handed Richard the box she was holding. "This is from the staff, Richard. To wish you good luck in your retirement. I hope you like it."

He took the gift-wrapped Waterford Crystal vase from her and smiled. She had agonised today over what to buy but now she really did not care whether he liked it or not. She just wanted to be out of this tension-filled room. Before she had even closed the door they had returned their attention to the reams of paper that littered the desk. She forgot about them instantly. There were more important problems, more delicate situations, to cope with at home.

Kate switched over from the late news and checked the teletext for the third time. The last plane from Belfast was on schedule and due in twenty minutes from now. The least she had expected from Fred was a phone call to let her know which flight he was taking. He must have been so caught up in his self-important round of meetings that he had forgotten about her. She felt foolish now in the new dress she had impulsively bought at lunch-time.

She went to the bathroom and looked in the mirror. She did not look thirty-two. Slim, taut and unlined, the reflection in the mirror could pass for twenty-six or seven. Impatiently she grabbed a wad of face cleansers and swiped off the make-up she had so carefully applied in anticipation of a cosy dinner with her husband.

She had planned for tonight so well. First she would listen to Fred waffle on about prime-time television advertising, radio slots, billboards, press coverage, the sainted Nigel Greenway and his chain of motor garages. Then they would talk about Patty and Brian Molloy and he would say how awful it must be for them all. Of course they would discuss the surprising news of Richard Gordon's retirement and speculate a little on Martin Burke. Then, as she served coffee, she would tell him about her visit to the doctor, about the help available for infertile couples, about the numbers of people who found themselves in the same situation. Now he had ruined her carefully laid plans. Fuck him! The self-obsessed would-be advertising mogul!

She ripped off her jewellery and her new dress. He was not going to have the satisfaction of seeing that she had been all dressed up, waiting for him. "It's midnight, Cinderella," she muttered as she put on her dressing-gown over her nightdress. The phone rang. Kate felt the blood drain from her face. Suppose it was the police, just the same as last night? Suppose Fred, like Brian Molloy, had had a terrible accident? Suppose he lay dying while she had been cursing him? Her hand shook as she picked up the receiver.

"Hi, Kate. I've just arrived in at the airport now. Hope you didn't wait up for me."

"Are you all right, Fred? Is everything OK?"

"Yes. Yes, I'm fine. Just tired. You sound a bit shaky though. Anything wrong?"

Anything wrong! Of course not, you idiot! It's just that last night I watched a woman hold her dying husband in her arms, I don't know why my boss has suddenly decided to retire and I can't understand why my husband thinks an advertising contract is more important than starting a family. Otherwise, dickhead, I'm fine. She took a deep breath.

"Of course I'm all right. See you in about thirty minutes then."

"Kate, there's something else. Could you make up the guest bed, please? I'll explain when I get home."

And with that little bombshell, he was gone. Thirty minutes to make up the bed, hoover and dust. Who in the hell was he bringing home? A quick look in the fridge told her she had barely enough milk to make breakfast for two. Grabbing bed-linen from the hot press, she spent the next half hour in a flurry of activity. The car pulled into the driveway as she was putting out clean towels. She was on her way down the stairs when Fred came into the hall, standing aside to usher in a stunning blonde girl. Kate stood with her hand on the banister, painfully aware of her unmade-up face and her dressing-gown. She walked towards them. Fred kissed her on the cheek.

"Kate, meet Adele Sheehan. Our new graphic designer. Adele, my wife Kate."

The two women looked at each other and shook hands.

"Mrs Lucas, I hope this is not too inconvenient for you. It was a last-minute decision to fly down here tonight."

"No problem," Kate said as convincingly as possible. "And please do call me Kate. Would you like some supper before I show you to your room?"

Adele shook her head and her long blonde hair shimmered. "No, thank you. Sleep's what I need now. I'll go straight to bed if you don't mind. We have a big day tomorrow."

The girl smiled at Fred and he returned the smile.

Kate stood there, pasty-faced and frumpy, and felt as if she were an intruder. She turned her back and began to walk up the stairs. "This way, Adele, please."

Light and graceful, the girl seemed to float up the stairs.

When Kate got back down, Fred was pouring a glass of wine for himself. "Want one?"

She shook her head. "No, thank you. But I do want to know how long our houseguest is going to stay. A very temporary arrangement, I hope."

"Sorry about the short notice but she's in big demand and I had to grab her now. You know that commercial for Low Cal Yoghurt, she did that. "

"Expensive?"

"Since when have you been interested in the finances of Lucas Advertising?"

Kate looked into his face and saw a childish petulance there. She used to find that attractive. So boyish that she had wanted to cuddle him. She found it irritating now. Miss Blonde Low Cal Yoghurt must be arriving at the firm with a big price-tag attached.

"Your business, Fred, but remember no matter how big the Greenway contract, it's still just one contract. If you get it. Nigel still has to approve your proposals, doesn't he? Besides, you already have a graphic designer."

"Jim Grant? He's fine for the locals. We're moving onto the national stage now. Anyway, I'm tired, Kate. I'm off to bed. What time is the funeral tomorrow?"

"Twelve o'clock service."

"I'll meet you there."

"Richard Gordon has sold his practice. He's retiring."

"Really?"

Fred stooped and pecked her on the cheek. Then he was gone upstairs, leaving behind an empty wineglass, a waft of after-shave and a furious wife. He was sleeping soundly by the time she was calm enough to lie down beside him.

As Kate got ready for church the following morning she found it hard to believe that she was going to Brian Molloy's funeral. Old people died, peacefully in their beds. Just as her mother and father had. Young men, at the peak of their careers, were not supposed to die.

Traffic was heavy because of the funeral. By the time Kate had found a parking space the chapel was full to overflowing. Patty sat in the front pew, surrounded by her children. Her eldest son, who was only eight, already reached to her shoulder. Big, just like his father. People shuffled along the seats, trying to make room for arrivals. Kate could not keep a seat for Fred any longer. She pushed to the end of the pew and allowed an elderly man to sit. The huge attendance was a reflection of the esteem Brian had earned in his community. It would have been a consolation to Patty if she could have seen it but her attention was focused exclusively on the casket at the altar.

Patty's gaze never wavered. It was as if she needed to memorise every grain and knot in the oak coffin, every bloom in the wreaths.

The ceremony was halfway through before Kate saw Fred make his way into the chapel. He stood at the back with other latecomers and by his side stood Adele Sheehan. What in the hell was she doing here? Fred nodded in Kate's direction and Adele smiled. Turning back towards Brian's coffin, Kate did not acknowledge either salute. She put her puzzlement and her rising anger aside, in a hidden place to be accessed later. There was no room now for anything except sympathy and pity and grief for the very pregnant young widow and her children, who walked slowly down the aisle behind the coffin of husband and father.

In true Irish tradition Patty had brought friends and relations back to the Grand Hotel for a meal after the funeral. The children ran around playing with their cousins, relieved for the moment at least of the burden of tragedy. The adults talked about Brian, everyone adding their own anecdote. Kate was surprised to learn that he had been so skilful a rugby player in his youth that he had been offered a place on a professional team. What a loss to the medical profession that would have been! She learned too that Patty had been a nurse. Theirs had been a stereotypical doctor-nurse romance. Patty had fitted so well into the role of wife and mother that it was hard to imagine her in any other capacity. Kate looked around at the crowd of mourners and wondered how many more of them had a hidden persona. They were all very image-conscious and very protective of what lay behind their public face. The type of people to whom the young Kate had aspired to belong. What a shallow aspiration that had been!

Kate excused herself from the table and made her way towards the ladies' room. The anger she had hidden away surfaced again. But not the puzzlement. She knew now why Fred had brought Adele Sheehan along to the funeral. She and Fred were sitting at a corner table in conversation with Nigel Greenway.

Fred saw her approaching and came to meet her.

"Sorry I didn't make the service on time, Kate."

She shrugged. "Never mind. The best business opportunities are here now anyway."

He leaned close to her and caught her elbow. "Whatever bee you have in your bonnet, now's not the time to air it. We'll talk later."

"Will we? You mean you'll be home early tonight with nothing else on your mind but a discussion with your wife?"

Fred shuffled his feet and put on his best little-boy look. "Adele and I may be a little late getting back."

"She's back again tonight? God! Will I have to cater for her too?"

"Don't bother. We'll be having dinner with Nigel Greenway. See you later."

He turned quickly and walked back to the corner table. Adele waved to Kate. Kate waved back and smiled.

She did not cry until she got home.

Chapter 6

Kate lay in bed and listened to the sound of breakfast ware clattering in the kitchen. Monday morning was bad enough without having to look at a hung-over Fred and Adele's blonde prettiness. She did not want to see either of them. It must have been at least two o'clock before Fred had fallen into bed last night, reeking of alcohol. In fact he and Adele seemed to have spent the weekend out drinking. They said they had been having meetings with Greenways but short of waiting up for him with a rolling pin in her hand Kate had not been able to have a private chat with her husband. In the short time since she had arrived, Adele seemed to have completely taken over Fred's time. And he appeared to be enjoying that. Too much. As soon as she heard the front door close, Kate got out of bed and began to get ready for work.

It was a relief to go in to work. Kate had always been good at compartmentalising. Once she crossed the door of the office, she usually set aside her home worries. Experience had taught her they were always waiting at the close of the working day. She was surprised to see Richard here again this morning.

"Is this an active retirement, Richard, or do you just miss us?"

"Amazing how like Cora you sound, Kate. She's threatening to come in and drag me out today if I'm not home by early afternoon."

Martin Burke came in and Kate was struck again by his dark good looks. She decided to look at him, to really examine him from the top of his sleek black head to the toecaps of his shiny shoes. That should still the little gasp she felt each time she saw him. So what if his teeth were sparkling, his shoulders broad, his eyes deep blue? He was her new boss and she would have to evolve a sensible working relationship with him. She would have to learn his habits and moods, as she had with Richard. From scratch.

Ignoring Richard, he said a general good morning and disappeared into his office.

Richard winked at her and stood up to follow Martin. "Better go into the lion's den."

Len Murphy made his way over to Kate. He pushed aside some paperwork and sat on her desk, his big feet parked on the chair on which he should have been sitting.

"Why are there raised voices from inside the Holy of Holies?"

"Are there?"

"Come on, Kate! I saw Richard wink at you. You know all. Spill the beans. Why are those two at loggerheads? Is the deal between them really signed and sealed or could it all fall through?"

"If you get off my desk and sit on the chair like any civilised person, I'll tell you what I know, Len. Deal?"

He immediately jumped up and seated himself in front of her, his young face anxious. Kate felt a little of his anxiety too. The tension she had witnessed between Richard and Martin in the short time she had seen them together was intense. They had seemed fine at the party. Then some problem, some serious difference of opinion appeared to have arisen.

"Well, Kate?"

"Honest answer, I don't know. No matter what you think, I had no inkling that Richard was planning retirement. And I know nothing about Martin Burke except that he was a hot-shot criminal lawyer in the States for six years."

"He's not married," came Eileen's voice.

Kate and Len both laughed at the receptionist's contribution. Eileen had a talent for information gathering. She probably knew Martin's favourite food and his birthday date by now.

"Maybe it's Eileen you should be talking to, Len."

"Well, whoever, I think it's time someone told us exactly where we stood and who's going to pay our salaries."

She agreed. This was a busy office. Pressurised when a big case was pending. But the atmosphere had always been friendly, the staff united. Now there was an air of uncertainty. Unease. She switched on her computer.

"Early days yet with the new boss. I'm sure it'll all sort out. We'd better do some work now or we'll definitely have no jobs."

Len went reluctantly back to his own desk. It was obvious that his mind was not going to be fully on his work this morning.

When Martin Burke saw Richard come into his office he knew the time had come to bring the charade to an end.

"What in the hell are you doing here again today, Richard? This company's been bought and paid for. By me. I'm getting a bit annoyed, to say the least, by your constant presence."

Richard sat without being invited. Leaning his arms on the desk he treated Martin to one of his well-practised sincere gazes.

"No wonder you're so stressed, Martin. This whole changeover has been too quick. I really underestimated the time I'd need to wind things up."

"Bullshit! There's no winding up to be done. Nothing's changed except that it's going to be my name over the door instead of yours. We sorted everything on my last visit. So, the truth. Why are you here? "

The two men eyed each other. Richard was the first to blink.

"The truth? I wasn't expecting you to start work straight away. I thought you'd take at least a few days to settle in before you came to the office. It's not easy letting go the reins, you know. I built this company, this client list."

"I see. So I caught you unawares, did I? You were too busy with your big ministerial case to clear the decks. Is that it?"

Richard sat up straight. He was alert now. On his

guard. Martin stooped down and, picking up his briefcase, put it on the desk between them. He took out the notebook page and placed it on the desk.

"Would this be what you're looking for?" he asked.

The shock on Richard's face was fleeting. Just a momentary glazing of the eyes, a slight catch of his breath. It was enough to tell Martin what he needed to know.

"Don't be so ridiculous, Martin!" said Richard. "Why would I want a tatty little piece of paper?"

He reached out quickly and tried to grab the page but Martin's reflexes were quicker. Richard's expression changed to cunning. He smiled at Martin. There was a challenge in the smile. A dare.

Martin frowned as he examined his options. Accuse Richard Gordon of cheating? On the basis of suspicion? On the strength of a crumpled page with some numbers and letters written on it? The old pro would laugh in his face. But yet Martin trusted his gut instinct. The instinct that had stood him in such good stead in his career. The instinct which had helped him break the Ciccerone money-laundering scam in the States. The initial evidence in that case had been just as tenuous. And very similar. This page was what Gordon had been searching for and somewhere in the jumbled script lay a plan, a history.

"It was in the filing cabinet. Stuck at the back."

"Really?" Richard said, his tone seemingly uninterested. "The cabinet with the property files? The one you've kept locked since you arrived here?"

"Yes. Would you care to tell me what it's about. What do the numbers and letters mean?

"Don't know." Richard shrugged. "Never laid eyes on it before. I think it belonged to one of the young people I had here on work experience. Why don't you shred it if it's annoying you that much? "

Underneath the casual demeanour, Martin detected confidence in Richard. If he had something to hide, he was obviously satisfied that it was well concealed. He felt safe, even with this page in Martin's hands. That could be his vulnerable point.

Richard stood up and stretched. "I'm in your way here, Martin. I do apologise. Please let me take you to lunch. I'd like to invite the staff too, if I may?"

"As long as it's a farewell lunch."

Richard nodded agreement. There was nothing more he could do here now. It was indeed time for a farewell lunch.

Kate had kept herself busy all morning sending out client notices to inform them of the change in ownership. As she put the circulars into envelopes she was struck by just how big the customer base was. While Richard had built up a peerless reputation as a defence lawyer, he had, at the same time, been quietly and very efficiently building a healthy practice in Probate and Conveyancing. The list contained all the big players. Nigel Greenway, Gus Cochrane, even Fred's name hopped up. When she had got as far as the M's she stopped. Brian and Patty Molloy were on the contact list. She set their envelope aside and continued on. And on. The stack of post was vast. Why had Richard sold out of this lucrative practice? Could he not have appointed a deputy to do the work but still remain in control of the company? Kate shrugged as she sealed the last envelope. Maybe he had got an offer he could not refuse. Just as this thought struck her, the door to the main office opened and the two men came out. Richard was smiling. Martin was not.

"Come on, folks," Richard said. "Lunch is on me. I've booked the Italian. Last Supper type of thing. Everybody ready to go?"

There was a scatter as computers were put on standby and coats were gathered. For the first time since Martin Burke had appeared on the scene, the mood in the office seemed to be picking up.

Romano was the Italian restaurant of choice despite the décor. The floor was covered in mismatched tiles, the walls in garish prints and the tables were small and placed closely together. Romano's secret weapon was about twenty stone in weight, very temperamental, very loud and an extremely talented chef. Somehow, it all came together to make dining there a much sought-after experience.

Richard busied himself pushing several tables even closer so that they could all sit together. Eileen managed to manoeuvre herself beside Martin. Kate found herself sitting directly opposite him. The menus were brought along and there was a lot of chat while dishes were being chosen. But all the chatter was underscored with tension. Richard was in his 'let's all be jolly' mode. Kate had always found that annoying. It seemed to her that he believed he could control people's moods. To a large extent, he did. He called for the wine list now and ordered a bottle of red and a bottle of white.

"Looks like we're going to have a happy little work force this afternoon," Martin remarked. He picked up his glass, which had just been filled by the waiter. "We'll drink to you, Richard. Here's wishing you a long and happy retirement!"

They all raised their glasses in the toast. It was only at that moment Kate truly realised that Richard was leaving. He had been a demanding boss, intimidating until you got to know him. She had been young, full of hope, when first she had become Richard Gordon's PA. In fact, she had been so eager to please, so unsure of herself for the first year that she had been terrified of the Big Boss. But he had grown less intimidating and she more confident with the years. Until he had announced his surprise retirement, she felt she had known everything about the man. She was going to miss him.

"Don't cry, Kate. I'm sure Martin won't be too fierce."

Eileen's joke had focused attention on Kate. She blushed. "I can cope with fierce. Richard taught me that. But the unknown scares me."

Martin laughed, a deep musical sound which filled the little dining area. "I've been called many things, Kate, but scary isn't one of them. Let's make a deal. We'll all meet up here this time next year and you can name the unknown qualities that scare you now. And see how you feel then. Agreed?"

Kate had not meant to blurt out her fears. It had not

been fair to Martin. She smiled at him and raised her glass. "To new beginnings!"

"To new beginnings!" they all echoed and the little group seemed to gel as they settled down to eat their food.

It may have been the wine, or the delicious food, or Eileen's none too subtle quizzing of Martin, but whatever the reason the Burke/Gordon lunch party was relaxed and in good humour. Richard had kept them amused with stories of court cases past, while Martin had them laughing heartily at some of the more outrageous litigation claims his law firm dealt with in the States.

"What made you come back here, Martin? Surely you'd have better opportunities in the States?"

There was an embarrassed silence when Eileen asked the question but yet everybody wanted to know the answer.

"I just wanted to come home."

"But it must have taken ages and loads of study to get your licence to practise in America and now you have to learn Irish law all over again. You must have been very homesick."

"Like riding a bike, Eileen. I assure you, I know Irish law very well." He glanced at his watch. "As far as I know Richard is the only one retiring. We'd better weave our way back to the office. Clients may be –"

He stopped mid-sentence. He was looking towards the entrance. The white smile that so attracted Kate flashed across his face. He stood and pushed back his chair. Kate had her back towards the door and had to turn to see who had come in. Then she, too, stared in surprise.

Fred was standing there, flanked by Adele Sheehan and Jim Grant.

"Lucas! Fred Lucas!" Martin called.

Fred looked towards the person calling him and a huge grin appeared on his face. He made his way over to their table and grasped Martin's outstretched hand.

"I don't believe it! When Kate said her new boss was Martin Burke, I never guessed it could be Burkey himself!"

Martin looked from Kate to Fred and shook his head in disbelief. "Well, I'll be damned! My new PA is married to Lippy Lucas! What a turn-up!"

He turned to the group to explain that he and Fred had been in university together. They had sat different courses but had both belonged to the same debating society.

"That husband of yours can talk up a storm, Kate! I bet your career involves convincing people over to your point of view, Fred?"

"Advertising actually. Takes a lot of convincing at times." Fred turned and waved Adele and Jim over to the group. "I'd like you all to meet my design team, Adele and Jim."

There were nods and smiles all around but Kate sensed that Martin's gaze lingered a little longer than necessary on Adele. Then she noticed Richard and Len. And Fred. They were all staring at the beautiful willowy blonde. Martin began to button up his coat.

"Fred, we've a lot of catching up to do. Give me a call and we'll arrange to meet."

"Sure," Fred answered. "How about you come around

to our house for dinner? Kate can organise a time to suit you. And do bring your wife. We'd love to meet her."

Eileen kicked Kate underneath the table. Richard picked up a fork and began to fiddle with it, head bowed so that his expression was hidden. Eileen's eyes were wide. She had never got her facts so wrong before.

Martin seemed uncomfortable. He shuffled from one foot to the other before answering. "I'd be very pleased to accept the invitation, Fred, but I'll be alone. I don't have a wife."

"I'm sorry. I obviously got the wrong end of the stick. I thought somebody told me you had married. We'll look forward to seeing you then, won't we, Kate?"

Kate smiled but she really felt like screaming at Fred. She could not imagine anything more awkward than a dinner party with the new boss. Typical Fred. 'Lippy Lucas' indeed!

Richard called for another bottle of wine and invited Fred's group to join him. "I've a few things to discuss with you, Fred. May as well do it now."

Kate raised an eyebrow. What did Richard want to discuss with Fred? Hardly advertising.

It took another few minutes for the office staff to thank Richard for lunch and to wish him well. Kate was the last to leave. She looked back from the door and saw that Adele was seated beside Fred. The light was dim but there was something very intimate about the way Fred had his arm draped over the back of her chair. Kate's stomach did a little twist and her risotto churned. She swallowed hard.

When she stepped out, the sun was shining and there

was a light breeze. She turned her face up to the sky and closed her eyes. Traffic sounds and petrol fumes vanished. She was Katie again, young and free, roaming the fields and hills, cosseted and adored by her elderly parents. Their miracle child. She felt a longing for the warmth of her mother's arms around her, for the security of her father's quiet pride in her every achievement.

"Hey, Kate! How much of that wine did you drink? Are you going to start singing or something?"

Kate opened her eyes and laughed at Eileen's comment. True, she must look odd standing on this city path, her face turned up to the sun, blocking busy, busy people in their hurry to be somewhere important.

"Just thinking about home. About where I came from. And about my parents." Then she added before Eileen could ask, "They're both dead."

She need not have worried. Eileen's only topic of conversation on the walk back to the office was the new boss and his marital status.

"You must ask Fred. Martin was definitely uncomfortable at the mention of a wife and Richard knows something too. Fred said somebody told him Martin was married, didn't he? Could he find out? Could he check?"

She waffled on and on until they reached the office. At the door she stood in front of Kate. "You will ask Fred, won't you? Promise."

"I promise," Kate said.

And she meant it. But it would not be Martin Burke's marriage she would be asking him about. The only marriage she needed to discuss now was her own. Yes. She had plenty of questions for 'Lippy Lucas'.

The warmth of sunshine and memories stayed with Kate for the rest of the day. She went shopping after work and bought a fillet of lamb to roast. She would make a dinner tonight just like her mother used to cook. Roast lamb, roast potatoes, carrots and parsnip. Even gravy.

The kitchen was stuffy from the heat of the oven and the house was filled with the appetising aroma of roasting meat by the time Fred and Adele arrived back.

Fred kissed her on the flushed cheek. "Pushing the boat out tonight, are we?"

"Oh! You're just like my mum," Adele announced. "She's a great believer in a good plain diet too."

Kate felt her shoulder muscles knot with tension. The little bitch had managed to insult her and the food while still smiling. Just like her mother indeed!

"Maybe you'd like to wash. I'll have served up by the time you're ready."

They both headed up the stairs while Kate stirred the gravy with far more vigour than was necessary.

They all felt mellow, and full, after the meal. And Adele had one piece of news that made Kate feel even more satisfied.

"You'll be glad to know that tonight is my last night here. Jim Grant's sister has bought a new apartment and is looking for someone to share it with her. I met her this evening and we got on well. You two will be glad to have your own space back again."

"No. Not at all. We loved having you here. Didn't we, Kate?"

Kate hesitated only a fraction of a second before agreeing with him. Long enough for him to pick up on it and want to hit back at her.

"It was nice to have a bit of life around the house for a change. If things don't work out with the apartment, you'll be more than welcome to come back here."

Kate excused herself and went to the kitchen to make coffee. When she came back Adele had a sketchpad out and, as she was drawing, Fred was looking over her shoulder. Kate had to manoeuvre around them to put their coffee cups down.

"Greeenways?" she asked.

They both nodded but did not reply. Maybe she should tip over their coffee. Or get up on the table and dance. Nude. They would probably still just nod. It was clear that Adele was as passionate as Fred was about this advertising campaign. It had been silly to think that their relationship could be anything but work-related. And that thought reminded her.

"Fred, who told you Martin Burke was married? He told Eileen he's not."

"Oh, yes. I meant to tell you. I made a few phone calls since lunch. I really put my foot in it with your new boss. He was married to one of the Pages. *The* Pages, the electrical appliances people. There's not a home in the States without some Page appliance in the kitchen. Seems like there was a messy divorce. She's with someone else now and she has custody of their son."

"Oh! So he has a child."

"A three-year-old, or so I'm told."

"So he didn't lie to Eileen. He's not married. Not currently anyway."

Adele looked up from her sketchpad and smiled. "I'm glad to hear that. He's one gorgeous man."

Kate got great satisfaction when she saw the hurt look cross Fred's face. Maybe she could grow to like Adele after all.

Chapter 7

Eileen too, was very pleased when Kate passed on the results of Fred's research the following morning.

"So, Martin Burke's available then. Just the kind of news I like to hear first thing in the morning. Sounds like he needs some consolation."

"He's out of your league, Eileen," Len said in passing and his comment ruined the light mood because they all knew it was true.

It was after ten o'clock when Martin called Kate into his office. She grabbed notepad and pen on her way. He was standing with his back to her, looking out the window. The view of rooftops and trees in the distant park seemed to have him enthralled. She tapped lightly on the desk and he twirled around.

"Sorry. I didn't mean to startle you."

He grinned. "I'm still jet-lagged. This fast turnaround from America to Ireland is taking its toll. Sit down, Kate, please."

She sat herself on the chair that always creaked, making yet another mental note to have it oiled or whatever it took to stop that infernal squeaky sound when anyone sat into it. Seating himself opposite her, he pushed a page towards her. It was wrinkled, as if it had been crumpled up and then smoothed out.

"What do you know about this?"

She picked it up and glanced at the meaningless lines of letters and numbers. The neat handwriting was familiar though. She shook her head. "Sorry, Martin. This means nothing to me. Should it?"

He began to move his swivel-chair from side to side and for a moment Kate was reminded of her visit to the doctor. It had been four days since she had her blood and urine tests done. Maybe she would ring the surgery this afternoon to see if her results were back.

"You're sure?" Martin asked, forcing her to refocus on his silly piece of paper.

"Of course, I'm sure. It's gibberish to me. Where did you get it?"

He leaned forward and stared at her, as if trying to decide whether to answer her question or not. There was silence as he appeared to hesitate and then suddenly made up his mind to speak.

"I got it in the property filing cabinet. Stuck behind one of the drawers."

"Ask Richard about it then."

"I did ask."

"And?"

"He says he's never seen it before. That maybe it

belonged to someone who had been here on work experience. What do you think?"

Kate picked up the page and looked at it again. It was covered in Richard's distinctive handwriting. Nobody else formed f's and r's quite like he did. Why had Richard denied having seen it before when he had obviously written it? Maybe he had just forgotten. Or maybe he didn't want to tell Martin Burke about it. They certainly didn't appear to have a warm relationship. It could not be of any significance anyway. What was wrong with this man?

"But if he didn't want you to know about it, why was it in the office?" she asked. "Richard knew you were going to go through everything."

"He'd expected a few more days to tidy up loose ends. He assumed I wouldn't start into work until next week. Or maybe he removed the notebook it belongs to, and didn't realise until later that a page was missing?"

"So you think you were never meant to see this?"

Martin stood up and walked over to the window again. He looked outwards, his back turned to her. His broad shoulders were raised. He seemed tense, angry. This was getting silly. Why should Richard deny this page of mumbo-jumbo and why should Martin Burke be so concerned about it? Just when she thought the silence was going to last forever, he turned back to face her.

"Yes, Kate. I know I was never meant to see this notebook page. It contains some very private information. I've a suspicion what it's about but I must be very sure before I say anything. Len Murphy's the conveyancing lawyer here, right?"

"Well, at the moment, yes."

"What do you mean, at the moment?"

Kate sat back, wondering how that had slipped out. The staff turnover here had always puzzled her. She herself, at seven years' service, was the longest serving staff member with the practice. Eileen was next and even she had been with the company for less than two years. Richard seemed to have had a policy of employing newly qualified people on short-term contracts. Six months, maybe a year. They were glad of the experience and obviously the arrangement had suited Richard too. The standard joke was that he could never get rid of Kate because, as his PA, she knew too much. How much should she say to Martin Burke? She cleared her throat.

"Well, Len's contract has only two more months to run. I can let you have the details about the recruitment agency we use if you like. Unless, of course, you want to offer him a renewed contract."

"I see," he said, walking back from the window and seating himself opposite her. "So only one person deals with all property transactions here. And that's whoever the current conveyancing lawyer happens to be?"

"Well, I'd be involved too. I'm always aware of what title deeds are going to the Registry Office and I know the identities of vendors and buyers. What are you getting at, Martin, and what does this have to do with your page of jumble?"

Martin leaned forward and stared at her with an intensity that was unsettling. His eyes were such a deep blue they were almost navy. Then he sat back suddenly, as if he had just reached a decision.

"Kate, I was in this very office one month ago. I spent a whole weekend going through files and accounts. It was after this I decided to quit my post in the States and take over from Richard Gordon here. Now, tell me honestly, did you know anything about that? Had you any inkling that a stranger spent many hours here, going through all the documents and accounts?"

"I'd no idea the practice was for sale, never mind who was creeping around the office at the weekend."

"I wasn't creeping around. I was here with Richard. I was just trying to make the point that there may have been a lot going on that you didn't necessarily know about."

Kate was beginning to be uncomfortable with this conversation. She could not quite figure where it was going. Was Martin Burke making an accusation against her? Or was he saying something negative about Richard? Whichever it was, he was certainly making her feel very defensive but she did not know what she was supposed to defend herself against. They would never be able to work together if this was his idea of good staff relations. Enough of the pussyfooting.

"I don't understand what you're getting at, Martin. You'd obviously satisfied yourself that everything about this company was above-board before you bought it. What's the problem now?"

"Aha! This is the point, Kate, where we have to make some decisions."

This man was mad. He was making no sense at all. What she would give now for Richard's take-charge attitude! At least you knew where you stood with him.

"Decisions?" she prompted.

Getting up, he walked around the desk and stood in front of her. She felt intimidated by his height so she too stood to face him.

"We need to trust each other," he said. "I must know that anything I tell you in here will remain strictly confidential. You must never repeat any of our discussions outside this office."

"Richard would not have kept me as his PA for seven years if I didn't take my confidentiality clause seriously."

Martin rubbed his hands across his eyes and she could see that he was very tired. He indicated to her to sit and he perched on the corner of the desk.

"Right. I can see I'm making you angry. We'll start again. I've uncovered a potential problem here. It must be sorted and I need your help to do it. I'm not questioning your professional integrity. I just have to assure myself that we can work together with total trust."

"It would help if I knew what the problem was."

He tapped the notebook page on the desk in reply.

"This is a problem?" she said. "This little piece of paper?"

He nodded. "I believe the letters refer to properties and their owners. The figures represent sums of money being shifted back and forth between different accounts. I've dealt with something very similar in the past."

A cold shiver ran down Kate's back. She did not like the direction this was taking. Serious allegations were being made. Secret files. Double accounts. My God! This was Richard Gordon's practice. The great and respected

Richard Gordon! How dare this stranger float in here and start throwing accusations around!

"If I understand you correctly, Martin, you're saying that Richard is involved in some shady dealings. That's what you're saying, isn't it? "

He directed his intense stare at her. "I'm saying, Kate, that I was sold this business without being given the full picture and I'm trying to find out why."

"What proof do you have that this has anything to do with here? I don't see anything to link it with this office. Maybe it's a private investment. Maybe it is nothing important at all and you're overreacting."

"That, Kate, is why we're having this conversation. I must investigate. Richard refuses to give me the reassurance I need. I was hoping you would know something about it but the fact you don't makes me even more uneasy. I must find out who's involved and why Richard is so reluctant to talk about it. I need your help to do that. I want you to think about it and come back to me tomorrow with your decision as to whether you can support me in this or not."

Kate stood up. She certainly had a lot to think about. Was her loyalty going to be to her new boss or to Richard, whom she had trusted and admired for the past seven years?

"I'll let you know in the morning, Martin."

He was already back at his desk, examining the files. She closed the door quietly as she left and went straight to the canteen to make a very strong cup of coffee.

The afternoon dragged on. Just as well her workload was

light because Kate could not concentrate. Her dilemma kept drifting around in her head. Of course she had the option of leaving. Maybe that would be best. How reliable could Martin Burke be? There was something slightly manic about giving up your job and rushing across the Atlantic to buy a business. By his own admission, he had made his decision after spending just one weekend examining the records of the practice. And now he was throwing accusations around the place on the flimsiest of evidence. If you could call that scrap of a notebook evidence of any sort. She got up from her desk and went over to the water dispenser.

"You're very fidgety today, Kate. Are you missing Richard?"

She turned around and smiled at Len. Maybe she was. Or at least she was missing the man she had perceived Richard to be. She stood, polystyrene cup in hand, and looked around at the little group. Just suppose Martin Burke was right? Everybody here would be under suspicion if there had been any illegal conduct. Len, their property expert; Anna, the quiet withdrawn solicitor who dealt with contracts brilliantly and with people as little as possible; Eileen, receptionist and gatherer of gossip; Rose whose job it was to deal with the day-to-day clerical work. And of course, Kate. What made him think she had known anything about . . . about what? A jumble of letters and numbers. For God's sake! He must be paranoid. Paranoid delusional. Idiot! She squashed the cup and enjoyed the crackling sound as it buckled. Tossing it in the bin, she began to walk over to Eileen. Five minutes' chat about Eileen's love life, or lack of it, was just what she needed now. But her phone rang before she got to reception. She ran back to her desk and grabbed the receiver.

"Kate. Dr Shorten here. I have your test results. Is it convenient for you to talk now?"

She sat down slowly. He would not ring her at work unless it was bad news. "Yes. Yes, it is. What's wrong, doctor?"

"Don't worry, Kate. Nothing serious. I'd like you to make an appointment to see me though. We can talk then."

"Can't you tell me, please? I'll just worry now that I know something has shown up."

"Well, we can't have you worrying, can we? It's just that your blood count is low. Quite low in fact. I'd like to start you on a course of iron injections as soon as possible."

Kate sighed with relief. This was not the first time she had been anaemic. And she had been feeling quite tired lately. She should have known.

"Nothing else? Nothing that would explain . . . you know what?"

"Make that appointment, Kate, and we'll talk things over then. I'll put you through to my secretary now and she'll give you a time. Bye bye."

The appointment was made for next evening. At least she would not have to ask for time off work. If she still had a job by then.

Thinking she would get a head start on her iron intake,

Kate bypassed the frozen meals cabinet and bought liver and bacon for the dinner. Not Fred's favourite dish but then he would not be the one cooking. Just to reassure herself, she went upstairs when she got home and checked the guest-room. It was empty, the bed stripped and everything neatly in place. She did a little pirouette of triumph and then ran downstairs to start dinner.

As she braised and boiled, her mind kept wandering back to her parents. Strange. She had not thought about them for so long. Yet the touch of sunshine on her face yesterday after the lunch in Romano had brought back a yearning to see them. So strong was the need that it pushed Martin's mysterious page and her suspicions about Fred's interest in Adele to the back of her mind. How different her life was now, compared to the struggle her parents had endured! Year in, year out, clinging onto their smallholding on the side of the Kerry Mountains. They did it for her and never begrudged the sacrifices they made. Because she was their child. Their precious child. They would have loved their grandchild with the same quiet passion. Kate squeezed her eyes shut and made them a solemn promise. She would do whatever had to be done to give them their child's child. They would know, wherever they were.

"Kate! Why are you standing there with your eyes closed?"

Kate jumped with fright and then laughed as she realised how odd she must have appeared to Fred.

"Just thinking about Mam and Dad. I'm suddenly missing them so much."

"Well, here's something to cheer you up then." He handed her a beautiful bouquet of flowers.

She put the flowers down on the draining-board and threw her arms around him. "Thank you! They're beautiful. And very welcome. I've had a horrible day. I love you so much."

"I love you too, Kate, but I hope you won't be disappointed in me when I tell you the flowers are a thank-you from Adele. Read the card."

"Oh!"

"Is dinner nearly ready? Have I time to make one call?"

"Five minutes."

He was gone before she had answered. She picked up the flowers and put them in a vase but they seemed to have lost some of their beauty.

All through dinner Fred spoke about the ad campaign for Greenways and how brilliantly Adele was handling it. Kate tried to look interested as he waffled on. He was so enthusiastic that he did not even notice he was eating liver and bacon. Eventually Kate got fed up of hearing about Adele's brilliance.

"But she's only been with you a few days. How can you be so sure about her work?" She should not have said that. He launched into an Adele-for-Graphic-Designer-of the-Year speech. Kate half listened and got her thoughts together.

"Dr Shorten rang me today. I must get iron injections."

"I didn't know you'd been feeling unwell. Why didn't you tell me? When did you see the doctor?"

"I'm not feeling sick. Just a little tired. I went to see him about . . . our problem and he did blood tests."

"Our problem? What problem?"

Anger and resentment gushed geyser-like from inside her. How could he have forgotten? Or pretend to have forgotten.

"For God's sake, Fred! We spoke about this. About starting a family. About having a baby. We agreed that if I wasn't pregnant after twelve months trying, then we would have medical investigations."

"We spoke about it, yes. I don't remember agreeing to anything. Are you telling me now that you went to the doctor behind my back? Discussing my private business without my permission?"

"How in the hell can I discuss it with you when you're seldom here? And I can see this Greenway contract is going to eat into what little time we have together."

Fred threw his napkin on the table and pushed back his chair. His anger matched hers.

"I've worked my fucking fingers to the bone to get my company up and running. It's starting to happen. This is my opportunity, my chance to get into the big time. The least I could expect from my wife is a little support. But not you. Not Kate. Kate wants a baby. And Kate must get what Kate wants!"

His face was blotched with red patches and his eyes glittered with anger. She looked at the foul-tempered man standing in front of her and for a split second she hated him.

"I'm thirty-two, Fred. You're thirty-four. How long do

you think we can wait? Until you're a millionaire? A billionaire? When?"

"Certainly not now. I've commitments to meet."

"You sure have! You made a commitment to me."

"And have I ever let you down? I've given you a good life. Better than you ever thought you'd have."

Kate took deep breaths to control her anger and the tears that threatened to spill. What was going on here? Twelve months ago he had wanted a baby as much as she did. Or so she thought. All she knew now was that shouting at each other was not going to solve anything.

"Sit down, Fred. Let's talk this over like adults. I know the thought of fertility tests is embarrassing but Dr Shorten said that you –"

"He said that I what? How dare you! How dare you discuss the intimate details of my life with anybody else!"

She reached out to touch his hand but he pulled away. He was sulking now, his mouth shaped in a childish pout. All the words tumbling around Kate's head were bitter, hurtful ones, best kept silent.

She got up to make coffee. The kettle was just boiled when the phone rang. Fred answered it and called her.

"For you. It's Patty Molloy."

Kate listened to the distraught woman on the other end of the line. Then she put down the phone and turned to Fred.

"I've got to go. Patty's in a terrible state. We must finish our conversation when I come back. We have to discuss this, Fred. It won't go away."

The sulky look was replaced by an expression of

defiance. "I'm not, did you hear, *not* getting involved in visits to doctors and clinics. I need all my concentration to pull everything together at work. If I succeed, Lucas Advertising will be a force to be reckoned with. But if I fail, Kate, then you will suffer the consequences too. So forget it. I'm going back to work now."

He slammed the door on his way out. Kate stood there, the echoes of the bang and his words thundering in her head. Fred's ambition had been one of the traits which had attracted her to him. Now that ambition was like a cancer, gnawing away at their relationship. What if she had got pregnant a year ago? What if there had been no problems with conception and she was holding their baby in her arms? Would he still be slamming doors in her face, running back to work rather than have a conversation with her? She grabbed her coat and car keys. The answer to that question, like her decision for Martin Burke, would have to wait. However troubled she felt, Patty had sounded right on the edge.

Chapter 8

The Molloys lived almost two miles outside town. They had bought the old rectory some years ago and spent a fortune refurbishing. It was a beautiful home now, stylish, yet comfortable and welcoming. Kate smiled as she drove up the stately tree-lined avenue. The grandest old oak had a tree-house perched precariously in it and there were child-sized goalposts on the perfect lawn. So Patty! But her call for help had not been. It could even be seen as a breach of the unspoken rule in their circle. They shared the fun things. The parties, the chitchat. The rest, the dross of relationships and living, they kept to themselves.

Patty opened the front door before Kate had even switched off the engine. Her face looked haggard, tiny in comparison to the bulk of her body. She reached out for Kate's hand and took it in both of hers.

"Thank you for coming over, Kate. I'm sorry for dragging you out at night like this. I hope Fred wasn't too upset?"

"He's gone back to work actually."

Patty's mouth tightened, giving her face a bitterness Kate could never have imagined on those elfin features. "I know that story well. Tell him to slow down. While he still has time."

She led the way into the kitchen and they sat at the big pine table while the kettle boiled. Patty just sat there, twisting her wedding ring round and round on her finger. Kate began to wonder if she even knew she was not alone.

"I'm so very sorry, Patty. I really don't know what else to say to you."

"That's the trouble, isn't it? None of us really talks to each other."

She got up and waddled over to the kettle. Kate did not want to drink coffee this late at night but she took the cup Patty placed in front of her. Was Patty rebuking her for not calling? At first Kate had decided not to intrude and then she had got caught up in her own worries. Her marriage problems, her work problems. Excuses. Excuses.

"I'm sorry I didn't ring you. I thought you might like some privacy."

"To hell with privacy! I need help, Kate. I need somebody to lean on, somebody with real feelings and real compassion. Not the shake-hand, can't-look-you-in-the-eye, don't-ruin-the-party type of sympathy. Was I wrong? Are you one of them? Have we both come so far from our roots that we can't talk honestly to each other?"

Kate frowned. What a coincidence that she had spent so much of the day thinking about her parents, her roots in the Kerry hills! And yes, she had moved very far away from that time and place and suddenly the distance seemed like a step too far. She reached her hand across the table to Patty.

"You're right, Patty. The best part of Kate Lucas is the little bit of Kate O'Hanlon from Kerry that still survives."

Patty smiled. "Delighted to meet you, Kate O'Hanlon. I'm Patty Cleary. One of the Clearys from Marble Street. Not a place most of our friends would be familiar with. My father worked in an abattoir. I can still remember the horrible stink from his clothes when he came home from work. He went to football matches, had a few pints at weekends and that was the sum total of his life. Except for his daughters. There were two of us and he slogged in the blood and guts to educate us. I'm the eldest and was the first in my family to have third-level education. There were tears in his eyes the day I graduated as a nurse."

"I hadn't known you were a nurse until –"

"Until the funeral. Yes. Very few people did. I worked hard at becoming Mrs Brian Molloy, wife of the eminent heart surgeon."

"Your parents? Are they still alive?"

"Mum is. Well, she's not dead. She has Alzheimer's disease. She's in a nursing home. My father died a long time ago. And my sister now lives in Canada. So that's my family. Now tell me about yours, Kate O'Hanlon."

"You're looking at it." Kate laughed. "I was an only child. Mum and Dad are both gone. Not even a cousin to call my own."

Patty got up from the table and walked around the kitchen, her hands supporting the small of her back. Kate began to feel panic. Suppose Patty went into labour. Her panic must have been very evident on her face because Patty laughed.

"Don't worry. This is my fourth baby. I'll know exactly what to do if things kick off."

Kate sat back and watched the other woman pacing. There was something else, something Patty was finding difficult to say. "Why did you call me over here, Patty?"

Patty pulled out her chair and sat down. She looked steadily at Kate. "Because I'm going insane with worry. Yes, of course I'm grieving for Brian. But I'm very angry with him too. I can't say that to his family, can I? And my sister is too far away. Anyway we've grown apart."

"Of course, you're angry, Patty. You've every right to be but it's not Brian you're angry with. It's karma or whatever cruel fate decided that Brian should die the way he did. And when he did."

"You think so? What if I told you I think Brian has left us penniless and maybe even without a roof over our heads?"

"Good God, Patty! What are you talking about? That couldn't be true. What makes you say so?"

Patty sat there nervously twisting her wedding ring and staring at the table as if the answer to Kate's question was written there.

Kate frowned. She was trying to put the pieces together so that she could understand how Patty had got the silly idea into her head that she was broke. Surely the next best thing to being a heart surgeon's wife was to be a heart surgeon's widow? Ashamed of the cynical thought,

Kate reached across the table and put her hand on Patty's arm.

"Money is the least of your problems now, Patty."

Patty looked directly at her. "Do you know the last thing Brian said to me?"

Kate shook her head.

"We were in the Gordons' garden. You remember – Richard's party, lights, music, marquee. We were listening to the violinist when Brian told me, quite casually, that he had re-mortgaged our home two months ago. He explained that he had needed money for an investment. Something to do with a property-development syndicate. It had never crossed his mind to consult me or ask my opinion. It was a done deed. I kept smiling, like we do when in public, but I let him have it. I was furious with him. When he told me that he'd also cashed in his pension and our savings to fund this investment, I nearly forgot where I was. I wanted to hit him. Then his phone rang."

She paused and the pain on her face was so intense that Kate could see she was reliving the awful events over again.

"So then he said, 'Sorry I've got to go – there's an emergency at the hospital'. He leaned across to kiss me but I turned my cheek to him. He whispered into my ear: 'I don't want you to worry. This is a solid investment. It leaves us pretty broke now but we'll be in clover when it matures. And I have an appointment with Gareth Owens in the bank tomorrow to sign an insurance policy to cover the re-mortgage. Just in case.' Then he was gone. For ever."

Patty stared at Kate, reading the confusion on her face.

"You think I'm crazy, don't you? Maybe gone mad with grief. But the fact is Brian has no pension, no savings and the house is mortgaged to the hilt. And, as I told you, he hadn't got around to increasing the mortgage-protection insurance."

"But I don't see how he could have increased the mortgage without increasing the protection policy. That's standard, isn't it?"

"He used to play rugby with the bank manager. Gareth Owens. Good old Gareth. Old boys' network. I can just imagine the conversation. 'Drop by, Brian, whenever it suits you to sign up. Just to keep the paperwork straight.' Kate picked up the coaster from underneath her cup and began to twirl it around in circles. She had thought at first that Patty was overwrought and overreacting but she was not so sure any more.

"What do you know about this investment scheme? How much did he invest? You said a syndicate. Who's involved?"

"I've told you all I know. I've torn the house asunder, searched it from cellar to attic and I can't find any information about the property investment. I went to the hospital too. Searched Brian's office there and went through all the contacts on his phone. Nothing. It's as if he begged, borrowed, stole the roof from over our heads and threw it all into a black hole!"

"Have you spoken to his accountant?"

"Of course. Brian didn't tell him either. He would have advised against it. Our mortgage repayments were high and the maintenance on this house is huge. Anyway he knew nothing about the syndicate. Neither did Richard Gordon."

"Richard?"

"Yes. You know he's – I mean he *was,* Brian's solicitor. I thought Brian might have given him some paperwork. Contracts for the deal or something. But he didn't. Brian's family are in the dark too."

"And the bank? They must know. This Gareth Owens. He gave him the re-mortgage, didn't he?"

To Kate's surprise Patty laughed but there was an edge of hysteria to the sound. "I'm trying to avoid the bank as long as possible. Even the current account is already running low. I'm afraid to draw attention to myself there."

"But you must go see them. Maybe it's not too late to reverse this deal that Brian made? And could he have had other accounts that you may not have known about?"

"It's possible. Shagging was our thing, not communicating."

Snap, Kate thought. She excused herself and went to use the bathroom. She needed a moment alone to absorb her sense of shock and helplessness. My God! What had Brian Molloy been thinking of? He must have been, he undoubtedly had been, a very intelligent man. Yet he seemed to have committed himself to a very stupid course of action. Worse still, he had condemned his wife and children to a very uncertain future. Unless, of course, Patty had got the story all wrong. Which was a possibility too. Whatever the case, Patty was expecting some help, some advice from Kate now. What could she say? She splashed water on her face and hoped for inspiration. None came.

Patty was sitting in the exact same position when Kate got back to the kitchen. It was as if the weight of pregnancy, worry and grief had immobilised her.

Kate put her arms around her and hugged her. "We'll figure this out, Patty. What about Brian's family? I'm sure they'd help you go through his paperwork again. You're so upset now you could have missed out on something."

"Yes, they probably could but first they would have to let me know, yet again, that they were so disappointed in Brian's choice of partner. They've never forgiven me for being from the wrong side of town. But I suppose, for the children's sake, I'll have to eat humble pie. I hate them knowing that Brian did all this without telling me. I hate anyone knowing. It's humiliating."

"I wish there was something I could do."

Patty smiled at her and squeezed her hand. "Oh, but you have! I really appreciate you being here for me tonight. Bleak as things look now, I feel better for having talked. Thank you, Kate O'Hanlon."

Kate put on her coat. It was almost midnight and she had work in the morning. Patty walked with her and stood, a lonely figure silhouetted in the wide doorway, as Kate got into the car and started the engine.

Kate put the car in gear and waved at Patty. But Patty did not wave back. She was bent over, clutching her stomach.

Heart pounding, Kate jumped out and ran to her.

"It's time," Patty gasped. "Brian's last child is on the way."

Jonathan Alan Molloy was born at 2.46 that morning. A magnificent seven-pounds-and-nine-ounce triumph of life over death.

Chapter 9

Patty and baby Jonathan were both sleeping. Kate bent over and kissed the top of the baby's head. He bunched up his fists and flailed at the air. A little fighter with a big battle ahead. She tiptoed out of the room. Too exhausted to drive without a caffeine boost, she went to the cafeteria.

Fred was getting ready to go to work when she arrived home.

"How are they?" he asked as she flopped down on a chair.

"Great. Both sleeping like babies when I left."

"You look shattered, Kate. Do you want me to ring your office for you?"

"No, thanks. I'll give them a call myself before I go to bed. I'll probably go in after lunch."

Fred came over to her and put his arms around her. She leaned her head against his shoulder, closed her eyes and allowed the safe, protected feeling to flood through her. This was the Fred she knew and loved, the Fred she needed.

"You must come to see Jonathan," she whispered against the cool cotton of his shirt. "He's so beautiful. We could make an even more beautiful baby. I just know it."

He pulled away from her. "Call me if you need anything," he said abruptly.

Then he was gone. Another door banged in her face. Her eyelids began to droop. She prised herself off the chair, rang Eileen to say she would be late and then fell into a deep, deep sleep.

Eileen had been busy doing what she always did best. She had spread the news. Everybody knew about Patty's new baby boy by the time Kate got into the office at two o'clock.

"Does he look like Brian?" she asked.

Kate had to think about that. He was as dark-haired as Patty but his features were stronger. "Yeah. He's like his dad."

There were tears in Eileen's eyes. Kate went to her desk before she too cried for the child who was destined never to meet his father. She switched on her computer.

There was an email from Martin: *In court this morning. Expect to be back about two. Talk then.*

Shit! Today had been his first day representing clients at the District Court. She should have been here to help him prepare, to fill him in on the backgrounds. One way and another, she and Martin were not getting off to a very good start. The expression on his face when he came in confirmed that it was not going to get better any time soon.

"Give me five minutes, then I'll see you in my office, please, Kate."

Eileen pulled a face behind his back. When he closed his office door, she came over to Kate's desk.

"I put a call from the States through to him early this morning. It was a woman. He's been in vile humour since. Do you think it was his wife? His ex-wife?"

Kate shrugged. She had enough problems with her own relationship without worrying about Martin Burke's as well. She put her head down on her hands and squeezed her forehead tight. There were so many thoughts swirling around, bashing off each other, blending together, that she thought her head might burst. Control over her life and the predictability she found so comforting seemed to be drifting away from her. It was as she was lifting her head again that she remembered the decision Martin Burke expected from her today. To work with him on his silly page of jumble or not. What a petty life he must have, turning a scribbled page into a major incident!

"He's probably ready for you now," Eileen reminded her.

"And I'm ready for him, Eileen. More than ready."

She picked up notepad and pen and marched into his office. He was standing gazing out the window again.

"You want to see me, Martin?"

He gestured to her to sit and he walked over to his chair. "How are you, Kate? I believe you had an interesting night."

"I'm sorry about this morning. I didn't get to bed until after eight o'clock so there was no way I could come in to work."

"That's no problem. Just two speeding charges and a shoplifting case at court so I had no difficulty. Are mother and baby doing well?"

"As well as can be expected without husband and father. It's really difficult for Patty."

"Yes, I'm sure it must be. She's lucky to have a friend like you."

Kate had to bite her lip. How glibly that comment had tripped off his tongue. The fact that he did not know either woman, let alone be in a position to judge the quality of their friendship had not stopped him offering up his pious little platitude. Martin Burke seemed to have quite a habit of jumping to conclusions.

"Well?" he asked. "Have you thought about what we discussed yesterday?"

"I haven't had time to properly consider the matter."

"I see. But I would appreciate as speedy a reply as possible. The sooner we get on the trail the better. We don't want to give people too much time to cover their tracks."

"Are you sure you want a PA? Wouldn't a private detective suit you better?"

"Kate, it's your choice. Either we work together on this or not. If you find it too uncomfortable, you do have an alternative."

Well! So he was issuing an ultimatum! All get up and go, this blow-in from across the Atlantic! He seemed to believe he could storm in here and make accusations and allegations and expect her to support him. Kate felt her temper rise. She opened her mouth to tell Martin Burke what she thought of him and his ridiculous suspicions. Then the predominantly cautious side of her nature intervened. She closed her mouth and began to think the situation through. She liked working here and had studied hard and spent a long time getting to this position. The pay was good, the location convenient, the work interesting and varied. If she resigned, she would have to start job-hunting. Besides, she would be giving up anyway when she got pregnant. Not worth changing jobs now. This business of the page was so silly. He was blowing it all out of proportion. Why not let him go ahead with his Boy Wonder investigations? They would come to nothing. Then the established routine would return to normal. Calm efficiency and everything under control. She looked across at Martin, at the troubled dark blue eyes and the little lines around his mouth. This man was so controlled that he was rigid with suppressed energy. Efficient and successful, yes. But calm? This was one quality she would have to learn not to expect from her new boss.

Her new boss! She seemed to have made her decision. She smiled at him.

"Right, Martin. Let's get down to work. Where do you want to start?"

Satisfied now that he had her agreement, he handed her a copy of the notebook page that seemed to be obsessing him. "I've highlighted some letters. I think they're initials representing the people involved in a syndicate.

Take it and study it. See if the combinations ring any bells."

She glanced at the highlighted pairs of letters. If they were initials, they certainly were not of people familiar to her. She looked more carefully and realised the pairs of letters were oddly but very regularly placed. Martin had just taken the first and last letter on each line and highlighted them, ignoring the other letters and numbers in between. Surely initials should be side by side? And how did he intend her to read them? Last letter in a line followed by first letter in the next line? Or the first letter in a line followed by the last? Either way they meant nothing to her. He was obviously pairing letters up to suit his own purpose. Which for some reason seemed to be to catch Richard Gordon out.

She shook her head. "Nothing immediately familiar to me here, Martin. Can I keep this? It might help if I look over it several times. I'll make sure nobody else sees it."

"Remember, this is for your eyes only."

Kate nodded and decided her handbag would be the safest place for this piece of paper. Eileen could not, as yet, see through leather. To her relief, they then started on the routine work of the day. The page lay forgotten as she got on with doing the job for which she was paid.

Kate glanced at her watch. She had already been sitting in Dr Shorten's surgery for over half an hour. It was crowded this evening. Judging by the coughing and sniffles, a flu epidemic was doing the rounds. She buried her head in a magazine and hoped that none of the germs would fly in her direction. She tried to concentrate on an article on yoga but her mind kept wandering back to her recent conversations with Fred. How was she going to explain to the doctor that her husband would not be attending for fertility testing? Maybe she should just get up and go. Save her pride.

"Mrs Lucas, please."

Too late now. Kate smiled at the receptionist and followed her to the door of the surgery. Dr Shorten was reading her file as she went into the room.

"Kate. Sit down. We must talk about your diet. It's some time since you had this anaemia problem last. Have you been looking after yourself? Are you eating properly?"

Kate relaxed. At least this was one problem for which she had the answer. "To be honest, Dr Shorten, I've been very busy. I've been skipping meals and then relying a lot on ready-prepared foods. It's easier to open a packet rather than start cooking after work."

He tutted and looked at her from over his glasses. "You know you must not skip meals, Kate. We've been through this before. I want you to ensure that you have a good balanced diet. Meat, fish, fruit, vegetables, especially green leafy veg. Because your count is so low, I'll give you a course of iron injections but you can make sure this doesn't happen again by being sensible about your diet. Make the time to eat and cook. Your health is more important than anything else."

He was wrong. Having a baby was more important than anything else. Could this be the answer? If her blood count was as low as he said. Her heart began thumping.

She blurted out the question. "Is this why I'm not pregnant?"

He waved her over to the examining couch and began to prepare an injection. "No. It's not that simple, I'm afraid. Being anaemic would not prevent you from conceiving. But it would certainly make pregnancy and labour a lot more difficult for you. Better you get yourself into good shape first. Now turn over on your side, please."

Kate bit her lip as the needle plunged into her buttock. True, she was very tired. Maybe that was why her life suddenly felt so out of control.

Dr Shorten walked back to his desk as she settled her clothes.

"I'm going to give you a prescription for a folic acid supplement. I'd prefer to take this precaution in case you get pregnant soon."

"Is that the protection against spina bifida?"

"Amongst other things. Folic acid reduces the risk of a number of foetal neural tube defects. How's Fred? Still busy?"

He had caught her off guard with that question. She sat down on the chair in front of him and just nodded her head.

"Not easy getting a business up and running these days," he said.

"He'll come to see you as soon as he can."

"I see."

Kate blushed. The wise old eyes looked at her and knew she was desperate for a baby but that her husband was not. Humiliation piled on top of her embarrassment. She jumped up from her chair.

"Next week again, Kate. And remember. Meat and veg."

Muttering her thanks she rushed out of the surgery. Without noticing, she broke the speed limit several times on her way across the city. Pulling into the hospital grounds, she parked, unaware that she was in an invalid space. She sat there for a full ten minutes, staring ahead, wondering just why things were going so badly wrong between herself and Fred. And how her doctor had noticed, when she had not.

Worried that mother and baby might be asleep, Kate tapped lightly on Patty's door and walked in. The atmosphere was so tense she almost took a step back. Patty was lying in bed, Jonathan in her arms and Brian's brother was sitting in a chair beside them. Both adults looked towards the door and frowned.

"I'm sorry." Kate said, without being sure why she was apologising. "I'll call back later."

Brian's brother stood. "Don't go on my account. I'm leaving now."

Patty had been crying. Her face seemed even smaller and tears streaked her cheeks. She wiped them with the back of her hand and nodded towards the tall man towering over the bed. "Kate, this is David, Brian's eldest brother. My friend, Kate Lucas."

He nodded to Kate and turned back towards his sister-in-law. "We'll talk again at a more appropriate time, Patty. Have your bank manager check things out for you."

Then, without another word, he turned and walked

out. Kate put the magazines she had brought on the bedside locker and sat down on the chair.

"Prick!" Patty said and then both women laughed. "I told you what my in-laws are like. I tried to talk to him again about Brian and his investment but he jumped to the conclusion that I was begging for money. He lectured me. Said I would have to consider a different lifestyle for the children and me now that Brian was no longer here to support us. He just wouldn't listen. The pompous ass!"

Patty's eyes were filling with tears again. Jonathan stirred in her arms. She held him out towards Kate.

"Will you hold him, Kate, please? I need to wash my face. Brian's parents will be here soon and I don't want them to see me like this."

She eased the warm bundle into Kate's arms. He opened his eyes. They were inky blue and full of shadows. What was he thinking, this little scrap of death-defying life? He wrinkled his nose and then those tiny fists began flailing around again. Kate put out her finger and he gripped on to it with surprising strength.

"You're such a clever boy, Jonathan," she said. "When you grow up you're going to be such an important person. You'll change the world."

Kate began to rock from side to side. The baby snuggled into her body and they both closed their eyes. She started to hum, a lullaby her mother used to sing to her, a memory teased from her subconscious by the warmth of the moment. When Kate opened her eyes again, Patty was standing there, smiling at both of them.

"I was going to ask you to be godmother to Jonathan

but it looks like he's asked you himself. Did you say yes?"

"Oh, Patty, I'd love to! Thank you. You're sure? What about family?"

"You practically delivered him. Who else would I ask?"

Kate kissed her godson-to-be and put him into his cot. He was happy and content for now. His mother was the one who looked fragile and in need of attention.

"Did you think about Brian's investment?" Patty asked.

A flood of excuses rushed onto Kate's tongue. She had been busy at work, had to see the doctor, had to sleep. She kept her mouth shut. The truth was she had done nothing to help Patty. She had not even thought about what she could do.

She looked, shamefaced, at her friend. "Patty, I'm sorry. I'm not sure what I can do for you anyway. Have you thought about speaking to Gareth Owens at the bank?"

"Gareth Owens? Yeah. I've thought about it. I've even considered asking him to be Jonathan's godfather. That's how desperate I am. I figured he might be slower to take the roof from over his godchild's head. Kate, are you listening to me?"

Kate was sitting there, a faraway look on her face. Her thoughts were not too distant though. They were focused on the photocopied page still in her bag, where she had put it today for safe keeping. Gareth Owens. GO? Hadn't she seen those letters side by side in the jumble of letters? Could Martin Burke be right? Did this notebook represent the blueprint for a property syndicate? The one for which Brian had re-mortgaged his home? It would make sense that a banker should be involved. But why all the secrecy and why did Richard deny his own writing on the silly little scrap of paper? Kate's fingers itched to take it out now and check the other letters. Was BM there? Was Brian Molloy on the list? Surely she would have noticed if it was?

"Well, Kate? Are you going to tell me what's the matter?"

Kate could not tell Patty about Martin Burke's suspicions. On the other hand if she could tell Martin about Patty's problems, then maybe he could make some sense of it.

"Would you mind if I spoke to Martin Burke about your situation? I think he may know what to do."

"What could he do? He's only just arrived here. But if you think he could help, go ahead. Anyway, I suppose he'll be handling Brian's will since Richard has so suddenly retired. He'll find out everything then. Everybody will."

There was a tap on the door and Brian's parents came in. They both seemed to have aged in the past few days. The loss of their brilliant son had taken a terrible toll on them.

Kate stood and put on her jacket. "Mr and Mrs Molloy, I'll leave you to enjoy your new grandson in peace."

Kate went over to the cot. Jonathan was still sleeping soundly, even his fists at rest. She kissed her fingers, touched them gently to his silky cheek and prayed that the tragedy surrounding his birth would not follow him into life.

The phone was ringing as Kate was going in the door at home. She grabbed it.

"Hi, Kate. I've been trying to contact you for ages. Did you have your mobile switched off?"

As soon as she heard Fred, she knew he would not be home until very late. She could hear a woman's voice in the background and recognised it as Adele's.

"I've been at the hospital to see Patty and the baby. I forgot to switch my mobile on again. So, I assume you're working late."

"I'm sorry, Kate, but we have a deadline for proposals on the Greenway contract. They must be ready by tomorrow afternoon. I'll grab a bite to eat here. You look after yourself."

"I'm getting used to doing just that. See you later."

"Don't wait up for me. You need your rest. I love you, Kate."

She put down the phone without answering him and then wondered why. She loved Fred Lucas. Loved everything about him. His sense of humour, his boyish good looks, his drive and ambition, his strength, the way he made her feel safe and protected. The way he used to make her feel safe and protected. There was a shift in their relationship and his precious company was usurping her central role.

Going into the kitchen, she stored away the dinner ingredients. She put on the kettle and opened a tin of beans, convincing herself that there was plenty of nourishment in beans on toast.

When she had finished eating, she took the photocopy out of her bag and opened it up on the counter top. Her memory had served her correctly. GO was indeed one of the letter sets. Buried in the middle of a line, untouched by Martin's highlighter. Gareth Owens? Could it be? There was no BM, nothing to link Brian Molloy to this puzzle. She folded the page carefully and put it into her bag. Tomorrow she would discuss her GO theory with Martin. And tomorrow she would forget her own problems long enough to try to help Patty. Was Fred right? Maybe she was too focused on her own needs and wants. Her own overwhelming desire for a baby. With that thought, her body ached for the fragrant warmth of Jonathan in her arms. For one moment, she envied Patty. Then she grimaced in total self-disgust.

She did not fully wake when Fred came home but she was aware that he had slipped into bed beside her. Cuddling into his strong body she fell back into a deep sleep.

Chapter 10

As she sat at her desk the following morning Kate thought she saw a pattern begin to emerge in the law offices of Martin Burke. Martin came into work each morning, dour, withdrawn and preoccupied. By lunchtime he had thawed a little and by evening, when everyone else was on their way home, he was charming, effusive and full of energy. The night porter in the building had told Eileen that Martin worked into the small hours of the morning. No wonder he was cranky at the start of each new day.

Kate switched on her computer to find a message from her new boss. He had obviously planned her next day, as well as his own, while working during the small hours. She read through it quickly.

Kate, please check though all correspondence relating to property transactions for the past year. See if there is perhaps any link to the confidential matter we discussed yesterday. I would also like you to check any correspondence you may have taken on Dictaphone and examine for the same parameters. I remind you that discretion is vital. Will talk later. Martin.

Kate felt her face flush with anger. *"I remind you that discretion is vital!"* Did he think she was going to go around the office, asking people to produce copies of client correspondence with certain initials? Perhaps he feared she might jump up on her desk and announce he was trying to tie Richard Gordon into some sinister plot. Maybe she should! And how in the fuck could she find links to something when she didn't even know what she was supposed to be looking for?

Getting her bunch of keys, she went to her filing cabinet and unlocked the drawer where she stored her Dictaphone and tapes. As she took out the Dictaphone machine, she suddenly remembered with a flash of guilt that there should really be two machines in this locked cabinet. A tape had got wound up in the other machine after she had accidentally left it running all night. She had brought it home for Fred to fix and had given Richard the second one instead for his dictation. Richard had not noticed and she had seen no reason to tell him. She had also completely forgotten about it. For six months!

Going to her desk, she scribbled a reminder note to herself to find and fix the Dictaphone at home and bring it back to where it belonged. It too would have to undergo the Martin Burke scrutiny in relation to the 'confidential matter'. She popped the note in her bag and read Martin's email again. Checking the time on the email she noticed that it had been sent at 2.35 a.m. God, what a prat! Well, at least there would be a little peace this morning. Not even Martin Burke could work around the clock. She went to the canteen to make herself a nice mug of coffee.

When she arrived back at her desk, Martin was standing there waiting for her.

"Good morning, Kate. Busy?"

Sarcastic prick! Kate placed her coffee on the desk as casually as she could manage. "Yes, I am, Martin. Trying to figure out what your email's about."

Martin frowned at her, then turned abruptly around. "My office," he said as he walked away.

Abandoning her cup of coffee, Kate walked after him, feeling like she should be saying something assertive. Instead she followed in his wake and sat in front of his desk. His dark eyebrows drawn together made him look peevish. Handsome peevish.

"Now, Kate, which part of my email are you telling me you can't understand? Is it the bit about correspondence or the bit about discretion? What's your problem?"

Having decided so recently that she wanted to keep this job, Kate managed to grit her teeth. "I never said I can't understand the content, Martin," she said as calmly as possible. "It's your intention I'm puzzled about. Just what am I supposed to be looking out for? Signposts? Clues?"

"Assuming that was not meant as sarcasm, Kate, I sympathise with what you're saying. I know the instructions are vague. I want you to look for any pattern, any names that may be recurring with unusual frequency. Anything out of the ordinary. I'm sorry I can't be more specific."

Kate nodded acceptance of his explanation. It was probably as good as she was going to get. "Do you want me to look up the archives?"

"I thought I explained to you that this is very sensitive.

What's the secretary's name? Rose, isn't it? Well, she'd know there was something afoot if you started going through records. We don't know as yet whom we can trust. Charming as your naiveté is, you must lose it if we are to solve this puzzle."

Kate could not control her angry exhalation of breath. How had this man earned himself such a glowing reputation? Was he even competent? It seemed as if he was going to turn a few letters and numbers into a major incident. It must have suited Richard to get a quick sale for his practice but he could have been a little more discerning in choosing a buyer. But just why had Richard Gordon sold so quickly and so secretly anyway? Each man was as perplexing as the other. She glared across the desk at Martin. The furrows and frowns disappeared and his face shone with his lovely white smile.

"You really think I'm mad, don't you?" he said. "Paranoid!"

Kate shook her head in an unconvincing denial.

He leaned forward towards her. "I don't like being duped. Nobody does. And despite what you think, there are good grounds for suspicion. I've got experience and expertise in this area."

"Just what area would that be, Martin?"

"Fraud and deception. And we've had this conversation before. Can we move on from here, please?"

Kate knew she was being very unprofessional. It was not as if he was asking her to do something unethical. He was just reminding her to keep her work confidential and that was the basic requirement of her job anyway. Maybe she feared the outcome of an investigation. What if Richard Gordon was guilty? What if GO stood for Gareth Owens?

"I think I might know who GO on the list refers to."

He was immediately alert. "Good. Who?"

Kate took a deep breath and then launched into Patty's story. Martin listened attentively.

"Interesting. Very interesting."

"I doubt that is the word Patty would use to describe her situation."

"I'm not trying to minimise the woman's suffering. But you must admit that what you've told me is intriguing. Somebody told Brian Molloy about an investment scheme that was tempting enough for him to put his home at risk. He must really have trusted whoever told him. What is his property worth, do you think?"

"Given the area it's in and the grounds it's on I'd imagine it must be worth a lot of money. At least a million, I'd say."

"If he cashed in his pension, re-mortgaged and topped that up with savings, then he has made a very substantial investment indeed. Somebody must have been *very* convincing. And you think Brian Molloy's bank manager may be the GO on our list? Gareth Owens."

"I think it's a possibility. Maybe. I don't know. I'm still not sure why you're so determined to attach importance to some mindless scribbles."

Martin sat back in his chair and stretched his arms behind his head. He was looking in Kate's general direction but she knew he did not even see her. He had an expression of intense concentration on his face. Kate sat there, silently, waiting for his next comment.

"I'm sorry, Kate but I think you're wrong. Gareth Owens may very well be involved but those letters are not his initials. The letters won't refer to names. Secrecy is the number one rule in this type of operation."

Jesus! He was the one who had mentioned that the letters represented people's names! He was beyond weird. She would not entertain his stupid notions any more than she had to.

"What about Patty? What should she do?" she asked.

"She should speak to the bank. It sounds to me as if she has only a vague idea of what deal her husband made. She's traumatised now. Maybe her recollection's not accurate. He was a very successful and obviously intelligent man. I'd find it hard to believe that he left his family so exposed."

"When's Brian's will due to be read? I know it's filed in this office. Richard handled it himself."

Martin glanced down at his diary. "Actually his brother rang this morning. David, his eldest brother. He's executor of the will. The family will be coming here for the reading as soon as Patty feels strong enough. Maybe the best advice to her is to let David handle all the financial details. That's his role as executor anyway."

Kate frowned. Not very helpful advice since she had already heard David Molloy telling Patty to see the bank manager herself. Executor or not, that man was not going to be much help to his sister-in-law.

"Forget about the correspondence for the time being," Martin said suddenly. "I want you to go through the property files. Very discreetly. Make a list of the people dealing with this office on a regular basis for conveyancing. Auctioneers, developers, builders, architects, engineers. Anyone associated with buying, selling or developing property. OK?"

"OK." Kate stood up to go and as she did, she remembered something. "There's a second Dictaphone. I had forgotten about it. I know there's a tape in that because it's stuck there."

"Oh! Could you pass it in to me?"

She shuffled uncomfortably from one foot to the other. Somehow Martin Burke always seemed to put her on the defensive. "Actually, it's at home. I accidentally left the Dictaphone switched on overnight and the tape got jammed. I brought it home to get Fred to fix it but he has been very busy. I don't usually bring office property home. In fact I never before –"

He put his hand up. "Stop, Kate. Enough. It's all right. Just bring the Dictaphone back and we'll try to salvage the tape. When was it recorded?"

"About six months ago, I think."

"Right. We'll leave it at that now. We'll talk more tomorrow when you've researched the property files. We're dealing with a sophisticated operation here. Every little detail will need to be investigated."

Kate stared at him. Was this man a lunatic or a genius? She made a quick wish that it was the former – because, if he was a genius, then Richard Gordon could be a criminal. She shied away from wondering what that would make her.

Kate felt very virtuous after lunch. She had gone to the

market café for Greek salad. As she'd waded through the mounds of greenery on her plate she wondered how Fred's presentation was going. There had been a time, not too long ago, when they had phoned each other several times a day. She tried to remember now when the need to stay in contact had stopped. Or which one of them had stopped it. She finished the last piece of feta and olive and took her phone out of her bag. She quickly tapped in her message. *Good luck with presentation. Hope it goes well.* Her finger hovered over the send button. She added, *I love you*, then sent the message.

She kept her phone switched on all afternoon but when it rang it was not Fred. It was Patty to say that she had been discharged from the hospital and had made an appointment to see Gareth Owens in the bank the following day.

Kate could not keep the concern out of her voice. "Are you crazy, Patty? You've just had a baby as well as . . . on top of everything else. You can't go racing around like that. You'll make yourself sick. The children really need you now. Think of them."

"Why else do you think I'm going to the bank? The children need me but they need a roof over their heads too."

There was no doubting the determination in Patty's voice. The only thing Kate could do was offer to go with her.

"Would you, Kate? I was hoping you'd offer. The appointment is for 1.15 so you'll be at lunch then. No need to get time off. Would you mind?"

It was not that Kate minded but she wondered if her presence would be any help. Well, at least she could keep an eye on Patty.

"Of course, I don't mind, Patty. I'll meet you outside the bank at ten past one. How's Jonathan?"

"Happy. All it takes is a full tummy and a dry nappy. Lucky Jonathan. See you tomorrow then. Thanks, Kate."

Kate put her phone back into her bag and looked at her watch. Almost going-home time. She was tidying her desk when she saw the lights go off in Martin's office. Surprise! Surprise! The big man must be suffering burnout and was opting for an early night. He passed by her desk on his way out.

"I'm looking forward to seeing you later. About eightish OK with you?"

Kate stared at him. What was he talking about?

"Dinner," he reminded her. "Fred said we'd meet for drinks about seven and then go to yours for around eight. He did tell you, didn't he?"

"Yes. Yes, of course, he did. See you around eight then."

"Bye for now."

She waited until he had left the office before frantically dialling Fred's number. It was engaged.

Eileen was beaming at her from behind the reception desk. "Oh, nice! 'Looking forward to seeing you later! Bye for now!'"

What a gem this piece of eavesdropping was for Eileen!

Kate swung her chair around to face the grinning girl. "Eileen, what in the fuck am I going to do? Fred never told me. He must have –"

Her phone rang and she grabbed it.

"Fred! I've been trying to get hold of you. What've you done? Martin Burke thinks he's coming to dinner in our house tonight. What did you say to him?"

"Shit! I'm sorry, Kate. I just remembered a few minutes ago. I met him yesterday and it seemed like a good idea. You can rustle something up, can't you? For four."

"Four?"

"I've asked Adele to come along too. A celebration. We sealed the contract. Greenways loved our presentation. They've given us the go-ahead!"

"Congratulations! I'm very pleased for you, Fred. But that still doesn't solve my problem. How am I going to have dinner ready by eight? I don't even have any shopping done."

"Look, I've got to go now. I'll take them for drinks. Delay them as long as possible. You'll manage. You always do."

"I might call by the chipper on my way home. Butcher's paper, plastic forks and all. That would teach you to remember, Fred Lucas!"

"I'll try to get them drunk enough not to notice the plastic forks! Must go."

Eileen had abandoned all pretence at not listening now. She came over and sat on Kate's desk. "Steak," she said. "It's quick and easy to cook. Chargrilled steak, salad and baked potatoes."

Kate nodded. She could not think now so any suggestion seemed like a good one. "What about dessert? How in the name of God am I going to get a dessert together?"

"Strawberries and cream. Marinate the strawberries in a little liqueur, sprinkle with castor sugar. Serve with cream and shortbread biscuits. Hey presto! Auntie Eileen's emergency dessert."

"And would Auntie Eileen care to come to dinner?"

"Yes. I'd definitely love to be there. How I'd enjoy seeing Mr Big getting tiddly! But I promised my flatmate that I'd go out with her tonight. We're going speed-dating. Desperate measures for a desperate situation! I've time to do the shopping with you though, if you could do with a hand."

Kate grabbed Eileen by the arm and dragged her off to the shops before she changed her mind. The speed-shopping would be good practice for her speed-dating later.

Somehow it all came together. At ten minutes to eight Kate stood back and looked at the table. It was perfect. Simple and stylish. Elegant. The Parma ham and melon starter was ready to serve, salads tossed, steaks and strawberries marinating, potatoes baking. Thank God for Eileen. Kate flopped down on a chair and drew her hand across her forehead. She was exhausted. Where was she going to find bubbly hostess energy? Glancing up she caught sight of her reflection in the plate glass of the patio door. She was as dishevelled as her table was elegant. Running to the shower she ducked in and out, grabbed the first dress that came to hand, tied her wet hair back and sprayed some perfume onto her wrists. Just as she was about to put on lipstick she heard the car pull into the driveway. She dashed downstairs and was waiting in the hall to greet them when they opened the door.

"Adele, Martin. You're both welcome. Come in!"

Martin handed her a bottle of wine. "Thank you for inviting me, Kate. Lippy and I will try not to bore you girls too much with our reminiscences."

Both men laughed and Kate could see that they were already rekindling their student bond. Adele stood between them, blonde and beautiful and very sexy in a miniskirt and strappy top. It was only then, as she looked at the young girl, that Kate realised the dress she had jumped into was the one she normally wore for funerals and sombre occasions. That's why it had been nearest to hand. She'd worn it to Brian Molloy's funeral. Black, long-sleeved, high-necked. Drab. Fuck!

"You look lovely, Kate. So sophisticated."

Kate looked suspiciously at Adele when she spoke but could see no mockery on the girl's face. She smiled and thanked her for the bouquet of flowers which had so disappointingly not been from Fred.

"Come through to the dining room, folks. Fred, would you look after drinks, please?"

Fred put his arm around her shoulder as they walked through the hall. "Lovely smells from the kitchen. Are we nearly ready to eat?"

She nodded. There was quite a strong smell of alcohol from his breath and she could tell from the glint in his eye that he was already slightly drunk.

He leaned towards her and whispered in her ear. "Knew you could do it. That's my Kate!"

The warm glow his words gave her lasted right through to dessert.

As she put on the percolator in the kitchen Kate realised the people in the dining room were drinking too much. Well, Fred was anyway. She could hear him now, filling up the glasses again and proposing yet another toast to his success with the Greenway contract.

"Here's to Adele, without whom we would still be fighting for the contract. Beautiful and talented! Adele!"

Kate poured coffee and decided to bring this party to an end very soon. She put the cups on a tray and carried them into the dining room.

"You always had an eye for the blondes, Lucas. Remember the Rag Ball our first year in college? You went with one blonde and came home with a different one. Kept them both on a string for quite a while as far as I remember."

Kate put the tray down on the console and subconsciously patted her dark hair. Martin turned around and looked at her. His eyes were glittering but otherwise he seemed none the worse for drink.

"Oh! Kate. Didn't see you come in there. That was the old Fred Lucas I was talking about. Long before he met you."

She glared back at him. He could be so fucking smarmy. And so reticent about his own history.

"So tell us then, Martin. Where did you meet your wife?"

Martin's expression instantly changed. The peevish

look was back. "I did some work for her father. He introduced us and then spent six years trying to get her away from me. He succeeded very well. Anything else you'd like to know?"

Kate thought she would like to know how he still hurt so much, why the mention of the woman he had married made him defensive and angry, why he had not yet spoken about his son. But remembering that he was a guest in her home, she just smiled at him.

"Sorry if you think I'm prying, Martin. Maybe you've been away too long to remember how curious we Irish are."

"No. It's I who must apologise for my snappy answer. I think I might've had a bit too much to drink. If you don't mind I'll call a taxi now."

As soon as Fred heard the word taxi he began to make a nuisance of himself. He was at that stage of drunkenness where he believed he was invincible. He was insisting on driving Adele and Martin home. Kate found his car keys and put them in her pocket. Fred was embarrassing and beginning to frighten her. Adele also was very unsteady on her feet when she went to walk. They must both have been drinking long before dinner.

For one horrific moment Kate looked at Fred and saw his father. Maybe she was just being silly. Fred rarely drank and when he did, it was in moderation. He was very aware of his family history and of the hereditary element in alcoholism. She had to allow that today was an exception, a celebration of the biggest contract Lucas Advertising had ever won. Or else he had planned on getting Adele drunk and just succeeded in making an asshole of himself. In front of Martin Burke!

Kate managed to keep smiling as she said goodnight to her guests. She had to stand between Adele and Fred because he looked like he was going to lunge at the blonde girl. It was ten minutes before they heard the taxi pull into the driveway. And all the while Martin just observed with his superior gaze from his superior height. People must be very nasty to him. He invited it.

"Our cab at last," he said. "Thank you for a lovely evening, Kate. And just so that your Irish curiosity won't be too deprived, I'd like you to know that you can meet my ex-wife in person soon."

He stooped then, kissed her on the cheek, caught Adele's arm and walked out the door. Kate whispered a prayer of thanks to the wise men who organised High Court sittings. They would be occupying Martin Burke's time tomorrow. At least she would be spared the humiliation of facing him at work.

Chapter 11

Standing on the pavement in front of the bank, Kate felt as if she was the one with the hangover. Her head was aching and her mouth dry. Just as well it was Patty's bank manager she was going to see and not her own. She opened her bag and took out her bottle of mineral water. The bottle was almost empty by the time Patty came rushing along.

"Sorry, Kate! Have you been waiting long? The baby-sitter was late and Jonathan wouldn't settle. Sorry!"

"I haven't been here long. Now calm down. You need to have all your wits about you for this visit. Deep breaths. Close your eyes – I find that helps."

Patty stood still and closed her eyes. She did not move for a whole minute. People were beginning to stare at the small, well-dressed woman, standing at the entrance to the bank, meditating. Kate felt she should not interrupt this calming process but she wished it could have been more private.

Patty suddenly opened her eyes and smiled. "I've just been talking to Brian. Told him to get his act together and come back from wherever he is to help me. D'you think I'm mad or is he still there? Somewhere."

"Of course, he is. You've had four children, built a home, built a life together. He'll always be part of you, Patty. He'll always be there for you."

Kate was surprised at the strength of her own conviction. Those words were not just empty consolation. She meant them. And she had no idea until now that that was how she felt.

Patty linked her arm. "C'mon then! The two of us will face Mr. Gareth Owens. Maybe Brian will appear and frighten the life out of the pokerfaced old fart!"

They were laughing as they entered the bank but the subdued atmosphere inside soon had them in a more sober mood.

"Mr Owens will be with you shortly. Take a seat, please."

They did as they were told. There were several queues for the cashier desks. Kate noticed how furtive and silent the people in the queues seemed. Almost reverent. Lodging or withdrawing money was a serious business. 'Shortly' turned into five, then ten minutes. Patty was just suggesting that they should remind the girl at the desk they were still waiting, when Gareth Owens appeared and came towards them. He shook Patty's hand and looked at Kate with raised eyebrow.

"This is my friend, Kate Lucas," said Patty. "I asked her to accompany me."

"This way, please."

Without further acknowledging Kate's existence, he led them into his office. He sat ramrod straight in his chair.

Pokerfaced was a good description of him. Kate was very surprised that he had played rugby. She could not imagine him in the rough and tumble of a mucky scrum. As if to prove her point he picked a minute piece of lint off the sleeve of his immaculate suit and flicked it away in annoyance.

"How are you, Patty? I believe I should congratulate you on the birth of a son."

"Thank you. Brian would've been very pleased with another boy. I'm sorry now that we didn't allow them to tell us the baby's sex from the scan. He always joked about producing his own rugby team."

"We did tease him a bit about that at the club. He'll be missed."

Kate wondered how long the polite chat was going to continue before the business of the meeting was mentioned.

Patty was obviously wondering the same. "I've come to see you, Gareth, because I need to know our financial situation. Unfortunately, I left all the money management to Brian and now I'm not really aware of where we stand in relation to our bank balance."

He pulled a file towards him and raised an eyebrow in Kate's direction again.

Patty answered his unspoken question. "You can talk freely in front of Kate."

"If you say so. Are you sure you want to go through this? Why not let Brian's executor deal with it? You've so much on your plate at the moment."

"Are you trying to tell me that our bank account is going to add to my burden?"

He cleared his throat and opened the file. He pushed read-outs towards Patty. "This is the closing statement on your savings account. Here's your current account and this one relates to your mortgage."

Patty picked up the pages and read them. She went so white that Kate thought she might faint. Gareth Owens just watched, making no attempt to explain. The pages fell out of Patty's hands and fluttered to the desk. Gareth Owens' silence was grating on Kate's nerves. What was he waiting for? Tears?

Kate met his icy gaze. "Needless to say Brian and Patty discussed money matters but I'm sure you understand that Patty's still in shock after the accident and not very clear on details. Could you outline them for her, Mr Owens, please?"

He shifted his attention from Kate to Patty and that eyebrow rose again.

Patty nodded for him to go ahead.

"Certainly, if that's what you want. But my best advice is still to leave all these matters in the executor's hands. But if you insist."

"She does."

His glare told Kate exactly where he rated her. It was somewhere just below idiot. He turned towards Patty.

"As you know, the mortgage on The Rectory is with this bank. It's a twenty-five-year term loan, secured by the title deeds. When Brian first approached me about re-mortgaging I advised him against it. His loan, which included renovations to the house, was quite sizeable, even with Brian's earning capacity."

Patty gave an involuntary shiver at the mention of

renovations. The Rectory had an insatiable appetite for money. In the beginning, no sooner had one structural problem been sorted than another presented itself. Even now, after all the rewiring, re-plumbing, re-plastering, the whole building needed redecorating. Their dream home had come at a nightmare price. But Brian had never told her how much he was borrowing. His house, his debt. Until now. She swallowed hard and tried to concentrate on what Gareth Owens was saying.

"Brian came to me two months ago, quite excited about a business plan put to him by a trusted friend. He'd been offered a share in a property-development company for seven hundred and fifty thousand and he was quite determined to be part of it. I agreed to give him four hundred thousand on re-mortgage on condition that he provided the rest out of his own funds and also that he revise his mortgage insurance to reflect the increased debt."

"So he took his savings and cashed in his pension at the hospital in order to finance this share. Did you give him the rest of the money?"

Gareth Owens showed the first flicker of unease. He squinted and nodded, waiting for the next question from Patty.

"And the revised mortgage insurance? When did he sign that?"

"I'm afraid events overtook him before he got the opportunity to sign the policy."

"But not before you allowed him to plunge us into terrible debt. Did you check out this development company?"

To say that Gareth Owens was uncomfortable would have been wrong. That would have required a sensitivity this man did not possess. Nevertheless, his tone was defensive when he spoke.

"That company has nothing to do with my bank. It wasn't my business to investigate it."

"But it was your business to ensure my husband's loan was secured by an insurance policy."

"It was indeed secured from my perspective. We hold the title deeds to The Rectory. With increasing property values that's well over one million worth of security. Probably two."

Patty stood up and leaned across the desk. She was so angry that flecks of spittle sprayed onto Gareth Owens' suit when she shouted at him.

"It might represent a security bond for you! But it's my home! It's the children's home! How dare you play monopoly with it!"

"You think of it as your home but it was Brian's house. In his name. His collateral."

Patty sank back onto her chair. The fight had drained from her. This was one battle too many.

Kate felt confused. She wanted so much to help but she was completely out of her depth here. But she must try. "How can you justify taking such a risk? Surely it's good banking practice to have all insurance in place before sanctioning a loan?"

"This is very irregular, Ms Lucas. I don't wish to discuss a client's financial affairs with you. While I respect Patty's decision to have you party to her private business, I refuse to justify my bank's policies to you."

Pushing back her chair, Patty stood up. She walked around the desk to Gareth Owens and leaned towards him until she was almost nose to nose with him.

"Don't bother fixing me with your disapproving stare!" she said. "That doesn't scare me. Losing my home does. I can read a balance sheet. You must be trying to decide which auctioneer to use for the sale of The Rectory. I know that whatever you did, you're sure to have your prissy ass covered legally. But there's such a thing as a moral obligation. You failed Brian in that and you've failed his children."

Kate rose and, taking Patty gently by the shoulders, led her back to her chair. She whispered to her to be calm.

If only the pristine suit sitting across from them would give them information, they might find the situation was not as bad as they thought.

Seated again, Kate surreptitiously crossed her fingers before asking her question. "I assume the initial insurance policy is still in place? That must cover the bulk of the loan."

Kate's heart skipped a beat as she saw Gareth Owens' perfectly manicured hands reach for his cuffs again and give them a little tug. She knew that he was giving himself time to formulate nice words for nasty truths.

"That may be somewhat of a problem area. Brian stopped payments into that policy some time ago. Said he was going to deal with a different insurance company. If you check his correspondence, Patty, you'll find that we sent him several reminders. We're talking to the insurance people about it. We hope for a satisfactory outcome."

Patty was still, staring straight ahead. She seemed to have withdrawn into herself – the only protection she had left. Kate felt a most un-Kate-like urge to punch Gareth Owens in the face. Her nails bit into her skin as she clenched her fists underneath the desk.

"I'm wondering, Mr Owens, at what level of competence your bank operates. Would you care to tell Patty just where her money has been invested? What's the name of the property development company?"

Gareth Owens looked at his watch and stood up. "I'm sorry to bring this meeting to a close now but we've run over. I have an urgent appointment."

He reached out to shake Patty's hand. She ignored it.

"Why didn't you answer Kate's question?" she asked. "Which property development company did Brian invest with?" It seemed she had been listening after all.

There was a knock on the door and the girl from the reception desk came in.

"Your next appointment is waiting, Mr Owens."

The thought crossed Kate's mind that this girl had come in by pre-arrangement. She could almost hear Gareth Owens instruct her to knock on the door if the widow and her nasty friend were not gone in ten minutes.

"Show Mrs Molloy and Ms Lucas out, please."

It was an order not a request.

Patty pulled herself up to her full height of five foot one and walked out, head in air. She maintained the dignified pose until they had left the bank premises. Then the tears began to flow. Kate put her arms around her but she knew she was not helping. Patty was crushed, destroyed by a horrible accident, a foolish investment and a soulless bank manager.

Chapter 12

Kate got the vibes from the doorway of the office. Eileen was bristling with news. She had a way of tossing back her hair when she was onto something and there was a lot of hair-tossing going on now. Needing the balm of harmless gossip after the confrontation with Gareth Owens, Kate smiled at Eileen.

"Bet you're going to tell me that two of your speed dates from last night have rung you. They're lining up."

"I wish! No, it's *you* have the admirer. Look! On your desk."

Kate glanced over at her desk and then laughed. Fred must be very, very sorry for his drunken episode last night. He must have known too she had been disappointed that the last bouquet he brought home was from Adele Sheehan and not from him. He was certainly making up for his peccadilloes now. The bouquet of flowers practically covering her desk was magnificent.

"I told you Fred was a little tipsy last night," she said to Eileen. "Look what it's cost him now!"

"But they're not from Fred."

"Eileen! You read the card. You'd no right!"

Eileen blushed and tossed her hair a bit more. "It sort of fell out when I took the bouquet from the delivery boy. I couldn't help seeing it."

Kate went to her desk and picked the card up. It was in an unsealed envelope. A seal would not have challenged Eileen anyway.

Thank you so much for a lovely evening. I enjoyed the home cooking and the company – Martin.

She picked the bouquet up and sniffed. How had he guessed that tiger lilies were her favourite flower?

"I thought you said the dinner was a bit of a disaster?" Eileen was hanging over her shoulder, rereading the card. "That you were glad he wasn't here today."

"Eileen! Stop exaggerating. I never said the word 'disaster'. Your menu worked a treat and most of the evening was pleasant. It just got a little messy later on. That's all. Besides, I knew he was going to the High Court today so I'd no worries about facing him. You'd make a very unreliable witness!"

Eileen managed to look ashamed. "Sorry. I do get carried away. I s'pose I thought it unfair that I have to go trawling the depths for a boyfriend while you have two men running after you."

She scurried back to reception before Kate could say anything. Just as well. Kate was upset. Not alone at the silly allegation about Martin Burke but especially about the fact that the flowers were not from Fred. Yet again. It seemed these days everybody except her husband was sending her flowers. She picked up the phone and then put it down. Let him contact her. Fred was the one who needed to apologise. And the more she remembered his drunken behaviour last night, the more she needed that apology. Helping him upstairs had been disgusting – undressing him, putting him to bed, listening to his drunken snores. She wished him a very painful hangover. She put the flowers in water before going back to her research on property files.

Len Murphy was hovering. Kate sensed his unease. He found a reason to pass by her desk at least once every ten minutes, always glancing down at her files. The files that Martin had taken out of the bottom drawer of the cabinet in his office. Richard had always kept that drawer locked and Kate had often wondered what he hid there. Now she knew. Eventually, Len could contain his curiosity no longer.

"Is there something wrong with my work? Are you checking up on me?"

Kate looked at his anxious face and felt some sympathy. Since property was his area of expertise, it was natural that he should think himself to be under scrutiny. She smiled at him. "Just a routine audit. You're fine."

Some of the anxiety disappeared. But not all. "Is there anything I could help you with? Any questions?"

"I'll call you, Len, if I need to double-check on anything. Thanks."

Kate waited until he had gone back to his desk to continue her scrutiny of property sales and purchases for the past seven years. Opening the top folder she saw Gus Cochrane's name. She shivered, remembering the recent party in his home where he had humiliated her. Pig! She had forgotten how active the waste-disposal mogul had been in the property market at one time. She lined several of his files up side by side. His first purchase, at least through the office of Richard Gordon, had been a two-storey terraced house in an area of the city near the largest university college.

Her mind began to wander back to that time. Seven years ago. She had been newly engaged to Fred. New job, new life partner. Hope and expectation of happy ever after. And the belief that she would leave this job when the time was right. When she and Fred decided to have a family. She could hear her mother's voice now almost as clearly as if she was sitting beside her, muttering the saying which had encapsulated her life's philosophy. "Man proposes, God disposes." Unquestioning faith had given Kitty O'Hanlon the strength to continue on with dignity and hope, even when the crops failed, even when the herd developed TB and had to be slaughtered. Total acceptance. Abrogating responsibility for her happiness to a theory.

Kate shook her head to clear it. This was not the time or place for the big Does-God-Exist question. She went back to Gus Cochrane's files again. He had been less corpulent in those earlier years. His suits had been expensive and well cut but he had never seemed to fit comfortably into them. Kate realised now that she had disliked him from the beginning. Something about his meaty fists and the body hair which sprouted from his ears and nose held a threat of barely suppressed violence. She had not been surprised to find out that he made his money shovelling other people's shit. He had started his business at the right time. Just when waste disposal was about to become a big issue. A big money-spinner. He had started his property portfolio around that time too.

She picked up the file on the two-storey house and discovered copies of rental agreements. He had renovated the building and divided it into two apartments. Very astute. It was in a prime student letting area. She flicked through the pages, anxious to get on with this ridiculous job. A flash of colour caught her eye. She flicked the pages again and found a Post-it. The little yellow slip was tucked between the last page and the cover. It was handwritten in the Richard's distinctive style. The contents of the note were brief: *Title trans. Landform Securities.* She frowned. She must be losing her touch. She could not remember ever having heard of this company. She jotted the name down and then opened Gus Cochrane's next property file.

This was a site on what had been the outskirts of the city at that stage. Five acres of waste land. Cochrane Waste Disposal had bought it for a pittance and let it sit until urban development reached that far. It was a textbook clever investment. When the area was rezoned for commercial development, as Gus Cochrane had correctly assumed it would be, the price per acre increased a hundredfold. He sold to a company which developed it as a suburban shopping centre. No wonder he could afford the pillars and porticos in his palatial home. Kate knew that shopping centre well. It was thriving. Nigel Greenway also had a showroom and forecourt on the site. A huge display of glass and chrome and shiny cars. That had been Nigel's first venture from backstreet repair shop to super motor garage. It seemed as if the five acres of wasteland had produced a lot of millionaires. She checked to find out who owned the purchasing company. She searched through all the documents but could find no information. On instinct, she searched the space between the last page and the cover. It was there. Another Post-it. Another company name: *International Leaf Ltd.* She had never heard of this one either. Did the muck merchant have a network of companies? Why had she never heard of them before and why was Richard sticking notes in files?

Kate frowned as she looked at her notes. She already had two companies which she was certain she had never heard of before. She should have heard of them. Why had she not come across them in correspondence or in her dealing with the Register of Deeds? Or had she simply forgotten?

Landform Securities: LS. *International Leaf*: IL. She glanced around and saw that everybody was busy. Reaching into her bag she took out the copy of the notebook page Martin had given her. Would there be a match?

"Richard! How nice to see you. Are you missing us?"

Kate jumped guiltily as Eileen greeted Richard Gordon. Then she quickly closed the opened files.

"I just dropped by to see how you're all doing. Cora and I are off on holiday tomorrow and I wanted to make you jealous!"

"Oh, we are!" Eileen said. "Make us suffer more. Tell us which paradise spot you're going to."

"Here and there. We'll be visiting a few cities." He turned around to Kate. "And how're you, Kate? Is Martin Burke treating you well?"

He began to walk towards her. She felt a blush begin to work its crimson way from underneath her collar. Shit!

"I'm fine, Richard, thank you. How're you?"

He sat on the corner of her desk and stared at her, his eyes seeming to follow the course of the blush. "Hmm," he said as he always did when he was mulling over a problem. His eyes went from her red face to the files and back to her face again. He knew what she was looking at from the file numbers on the covers. He had not alone devised the filing system but he also possessed a photographic memory. "Doing some work on the property files, Kate? Going back a bit, aren't you?"

"Just an audit for Martin. He needs an overall picture of the range of conveyancing services we offer."

"Funny thing is that I did exactly the same exercise for him. Why do you think he needs it done again?"

"Maybe he's just trying to keep me occupied while he's away."

The blush had got so hot by now that little beads of sweat were beginning to form on Kate's hairline. Richard was playing with her. If he wanted to know why she was looking up Gus Cochrane's records, let him ask her. Or better still let him answer some questions himself.

"If you're still so interested in the business, Richard, why did you sell it?"

Richard laughed, but the sound came out more as a sneer than amusement. "How very upfront American of you! I can see Martin Burke's having a big influence on your attitude."

Kate bit back the reply that sprang to mind. She examined the words she had not allowed herself to say. They were bitter, vengeful words and they shocked her. How had she resented Richard's patronising attitude towards her so much and for so long and never allowed herself to acknowledge it? She had respected him, deferred to his superior knowledge, served him faithfully, and what had she got in return? A patronising pat on the head every so often. She took a deep breath. This was silly. He was no longer her boss so why upset herself about him? She forced herself to smile at him.

"Well, I hope you and Cora have a nice holiday. Are you going to the sunshine?"

Richard stood up and nodded towards Martin's office. "Not so quick, Kate. You asked me a question and I want to answer it. In private. Follow me."

Seven years of following where Richard led kicked in. Kate trotted after him and sat in her usual chair while he sat in the chair which now rightfully belonged to Martin Burke.

"Now tell me what's wrong, Kate. And don't try to pull the wool over my eyes. We know each other too well for that."

He sat confidently in Martin's chair, in Martin's office, as if he had every right to be there. Why had he come here today? Certainly not just to tell them he was going on holiday. Her blush was changing from embarrassment to anger.

"We had a good working relationship, Richard. That doesn't give you the right to question what work I'm doing for my new boss. You wouldn't have tolerated me discussing one of your assignments with somebody else. And you still haven't answered my question. Why did you sell out so suddenly?"

His rising colour matched hers now. He was very angry with her. Putting his elbows on the desk, he leaned towards her. "I'm disappointed, Kate. I considered that we were personal friends. Your defensive attitude is puzzling. Makes me wonder what Martin Burke's been saying. Has he been influencing you with his negativity, his overactive imagination, his – ?"

"I can think for myself, Richard. I don't need –"

"It's Cora. She's not well."

Cora? What was he talking about now? His head was bowed, so she could not gauge his expression.

"What's wrong with her? She seemed fine at your party."

He raised his head and looked straight at her. The angry frowns were gone. He looked sad. Hurt.

"You asked me why I sold the practice. I'm telling you why. Cora is sick. We just don't know how much time she has left but we're going to spend that time together. Enjoy it while we can. So you see, there's no sinister motive for selling up."

"I'm very sorry, Richard. She looks so well, I just couldn't have guessed. How much time, I mean, when? How long?"

"It's in the lap of the gods. We've done everything possible medically. It's just wait and see now."

They were both silent. Kate waited for Richard to talk more about Cora's illness but he did not seem to want to discuss the specifics. A weight of guilt bowed Kate down. Firstly she had gone readily along with Martin Burke's paranoid suspicions about Richard and then she had practically accused him of having a sinister ulterior motive for selling up so quickly. And, yes, she had turned her back on their seven-year relationship.

"It hurts that you've lost trust in me so quickly, Kate."

She reached across and caught his hand. The man sitting opposite her was no longer her ex-boss. He was a heartbroken husband devastated by his adored wife's terminal illness. She squeezed his fingers, trying to impart the depth of her sympathy in the physical contact.

"I'm very, very sorry. Everything has changed so quickly, I'm a bit adrift. One minute you were here, the routine so ordered and predictable, then you were gone. One minute Brian Molloy was at your party, laughing and chatting, then he was gone. And now Cora. It's sad and confusing."

"Yes. To paraphrase, it's the worst of times. That's why I'm taking Cora away on holiday. A change of scene will probably do her more good than any medication." He looked at his watch. "I must collect my new passport. Luckily I noticed in time that my old one was due for renewal. Before I go, Kate, I want to ask you a favour. Don't get all huffy again, please, but I must ask you to swear that you will not repeat this conversation. And I mean complete secrecy. Not even Fred. I'm not asking for myself. Cora doesn't want anybody to know. She doesn't want sympathy or pity. You know her. You know how independent and self-contained she is. She must be allowed to handle her illness the way she chooses."

Kate did not feel huffy or resentful. She just felt a deep sadness that such a vibrant woman should be losing her hold on life. "I promise, Richard. I will never repeat a word of this conversation."

He stood and walked around the desk to her. He stooped and brushed away the tear which trickled down her cheek. "Thank you, Kate. I know I can trust you."

There was a gentle click as he closed the door on his way out. Then silence. Kate went over to the window and looked out on Martin Burke's view. What fascinated him so much about the rooftops and the distant park? What made him so suspicious about Richard Gordon? What was any of it about? Struggling to survive and then being smashed against a lorry or having the life slowly squeezed out of you by a vicious disease. "Man proposes, God disposes" indeed! How wise her mother had been!

She stalked back out to her desk, closed the property files, stored them away, picked up her bouquet of flowers, announced that she had a headache and walked out. She felt eyes staring at her back as she left but she did not care. She was in no mood for pandering to Martin Burke's paranoia now. She needed a bit of fresh air, a walk and some quiet space to think.

Chapter 13

As Kate soaked in the bath, she realised her mistake had been to go for a trot rather than a walk. She had gone to the park. There, she had quickly passed the children's playground and headed off to where the wooded area sloped down towards the river. Then, head down, she had set off along the river path at a relentless pace. She should not have gone to the park in the first place. It was the one Martin Burke kept gazing at from his window. Well, at the treetops anyway, which was all he could see from across town. He could have come back early from the High Court. Awareness that Martin could have been standing at his window, staring at the canopy of oaks under which she was walking at an increasingly brisk pace, robbed her of the relaxation she had gone to the park to find. When she got back to her car, she was drenched in sweat and her thoughts were still knotted inside her head.

It was not until she got into her bath that her mind began to slowly let go of its burden. She had put on one of her classical compilation albums and lit a bank of candles before sinking into the warm, jasmine-scented water. She closed her eyes and breathed in the aromatic steam. The harmony of scent and sound and sensation seeped inside her skin, inside her head. She relaxed into her cocoon and felt safe.

The water had gone cold when she woke up. She jumped out of the bath and checked the time. It was after six. Fred would be home soon. Unless, of course, he was working late again. She must get dinner on anyway. She threw on some clothes and was halfway through her dash downstairs before she slowed herself down. What was the point in dissipating her little store of relaxation on rushing and racing to cook a meal that might not even be eaten? She deliberately slowed her pace. Potatoes were peeled and carrots scraped with serenity. The calm remained until the phone rang. Fuck him! He was going to be late again. She grabbed the receiver.

"Yes?"

"Kate, is that you?"

Shit! It was Patty. "Sorry, Patty. That was a bit abrupt. How are you?"

"How in the hell do you think I am after the debacle in the bank today?"

Kate squirmed with guilt. "You must feel awful, Patty. I should've rung you earlier only –"

"No, Kate. Stop. I'm not getting at you. I don't know what I would've done without you today and I want to thank you for that. But I need to ask another big favour of you."

"Yeah?"

"David Molloy, you remember Brian's eldest brother, has arranged to have the will read on Monday. I need to see him tonight to explain the bank situation to him."

"Really? I'm surprised. I didn't see the reading of the will in Martin's diary."

"The appointment was made just today. Martin gave David his mobile number. Arrangements were made over the phone. I've got a baby-sitter for the older lads tonight but I'm not comfortable with leaving Jonathan with her. Would you mind, Kate, if I brought him over to you? Would you look after him for an hour or so, please?"

Kate smiled as she recalled Jonathan's perfect little face, soft skin and flying fists. She could almost feel the warmth of him in her arms now.

"I'd love to look after Jonathan. You know that. But really, Patty, you must rest. Do you absolutely have to see the Molloys tonight?"

"Absolutely," Patty answered with a determination which left no doubt that she was going to meet her in-laws no matter who tried to advise her against it.

"Right then," Kate agreed. "I'll see you in about half an hour."

Kate spent the half-hour waiting time turning the heating on and off, opening windows and closing them again. She began to get very nervous. She knew nothing at all about baby care. How hot or cool should the house be for Jonathan? What temperature should his bottle be if he needed a feed? When she heard the doorbell ring, she jumped with fright. She took a deep breath. Patty did not need a hysterical baby-sitter and Jonathan did not need a neurotic godmother. She was smiling as she opened the door. Patty handed her the baby carrier and went back to the car for his travel bag. Jonathan's luggage was twenty times his size.

Kate placed the baby carrier securely on the middle of the kitchen table. Patty unzipped the bag and showed her where nappies and a change of clothes were. She put a prepared feed into the fridge.

"Don't panic, Kate. He won't be staying for a month. These are all just in case. I shouldn't be more than an hour. Two at most. David Molloy will be anxious to get rid of me anyway."

"We'll be fine. Don't worry, Patty. Take your time. Don't leave until he fully appreciates the seriousness of the situation."

"I believe he already knows and won't admit it. We'll see. Thank you so much, Kate. You're a good friend."

She hugged Kate, kissed Jonathan and went.

Kate tiptoed over to the table and looked down on the sleeping baby. Was his breathing very fast? Was he too hot? She eased down the blanket Patty had placed loosely over him. He stirred. Shit! She had woken him now. He wrinkled his nose and snuggled up again. She stood there watching him sleep until the smell of burning potatoes sent her dashing to the cooker. She dumped them in the bin, left two frozen pizzas out off the freezer and went back to her vigil by Jonathan's side.

When she heard Fred's key in the front door, she ran

out to the hall, fingers up to her lips. He was standing at the hall table, looking at Martin Burke's bouquet of flowers, the card in his hand.

"Smarmy."

"Ssh! You'll wake Jonathan."

"Jonathan?"

She explained to him in whispers about Patty's visit to her brother-in-law. She caught Fred's hand and led him into the kitchen.

"Isn't he beautiful?"

Fred shrugged. "He's a baby. They all look the same to me. What're we having for dinner?"

She nodded towards the pizzas.

"I couldn't face that rubbish now," he said, putting on the kettle. "I'll just have tea."

Kate was getting the feel of where this conversation was heading. Fred was hung over and tired and he wanted her to make a fuss of him. He wanted sympathy and a dinner on his kitchen table. Not a baby.

"Whatever you like," she said.

"I'd *like* you to get a grip on your obsession with babies and –"

"I told you, I'm just helping Patty out."

"And I'd *like* to know why Martin Burke is sending you flowers."

His voice was rising and he was going to wake Jonathan. Kate caught his arm and dragged him out into the hall.

"Will you go easy? I got those flowers because Martin has manners. Just a thank-you for the trouble I went to last night. It was very nice of him."

She was standing close enough to Fred to hear his angry breathing and to smell the alcohol on his breath.

"He has a way with women, all right. Always had. And you're all falling for it."

"What're you talking about, Fred? And why have you been drinking again?"

He picked his coat up off the hallstand and shrugged it on. "I couldn't finish what I wanted to do at work because Martin Burke has taken my designer away from her job. I'm paying her a fortune but she drops everything just to meet him. I come home for a quiet night in and what do I find? A baby parked on my kitchen table and a big bunch of flowers from Martin fucking Burke in my hall!"

If she understood him right, he was saying that Adele had got off work early to meet Martin Burke. Interesting! Adele and Martin! How Eileen would love to get her tongue around that little piece of gossip. Kate looked at Fred. He had his pouting expression on. He was jealous. It was written on every pore of his face. Jealous because another man was taking Adele out. What was his involvement with this girl? Why was he so upset because she had a social life outside of Lucas Advertising, outside of Fred Lucas?

She turned her back on him and went into the kitchen. She heard a bang as he slammed the front door on his way out.

The bang of the door woke Jonathan and he began to whimper. She picked the baby up and cuddled him. He fell asleep again in her arms, the restorative, guiltless sleep of infancy. The remnants of relaxation from her jasmine bath drained away. She sat in the silence of her kitchen watching the baby sleep, the pizzas thaw and her marriage slide towards crisis.

Chapter 14

By the time Patty thought of switching on the windscreen wipers the shower had developed into a downpour. She had been steering, changing gears and keeping the car moving by instinct. In her rush to put distance between herself and her brother-in-law, she had now driven five miles in the wrong direction. Jamming her foot on the brake, she pulled over to the side. The road was narrow, twisty and tree-lined, more suited to horses and carts than the four-wheel drive she was guiding between the ditches.

Leaning her head on the steering wheel, she tried to silence the noise in her head, the incessant playback of David Molloy's tirade. No. That was wrong. It had not been a tirade. There had been no shouting or swearing, no tears or unseemly tantrums. His words had been measured, calmly delivered and as sharp as a scalpel. They had cut into her heart, into her soul, into what remnants of hope she had left. God damn the snotty Molloys! God damn their dignity and snobbery! God damn their cruelty!

She wrenched open the door and jumped out into the downpour, welcoming the coldness of the rain on her head. A sudden gust of wind swept through the branches of the trees and dumped a cascade of water on top of her. The final indignity. Strengthening wind joined forces with the echoes in her head and Patty could no longer hold the sounds inside. She screamed. Desperate and hopeless, her shouts rose and fell on the swirling wind. She began to run, chased by the sounds of her own despair.

When she could run no more, when her muscles ached and her throat was hoarse, she threw herself down on the ground. There was a new sound now. It was the swish of rushing water, the lap of the river against the bank. She sat up and looked around, discerning nothing in the darkness except the black bulk of the woods behind her and the moving shadows of the river ahead. How had she ended up here? How far had she run? Stupid Patty! Ignorant, vulgar Patty!

David Molloy had chosen his words so well. His mission tonight had been to make her understand why the Molloys had never approved of her. And he had succeeded. She understood now. What would a girl from Marble Street know about etiquette, about dignity, about family pride, about the golden circle of privilege and wealth in which Brian had grown up? He should have had an affair with her, his little bit of rough, and then married one of his own kind.

"How much have you sunk into The Rectory? No wonder Brian was desperate to invest in a moneymaking scheme. You just didn't know where to stop with that house, did you? You had the man driven to despair with your spendthrift ways. And if he had spent twice as much again, he would never have succeeded in turning you into a lady. That's inherited, not bought."

David's words came back to her now and fresh tears fell at the unfairness of it all. She had tried to explain to him that The Rectory was Brian's passion, that he was the one who had wanted the gardens landscaped, the sauna installed, the games room built. David would not listen. He could not admit that his brother had made his own contribution to the vulgarity of his union with Patty Cleary from Marble Street.

"What about the children?" she had asked. "What'll happen to them if I have to sell their home to pay Brian's debts?"

"That's your business. The debts are yours now."

Patty stood and walked towards the river's edge, bringing those hateful words with her. The teeming rain had swollen the river so much that water was spilling over the bank. She watched, mesmerised, as the black, freezing swell lapped over her shoes, numbing her feet. The craving for numbness crept from her feet, through her body and into her head. Nothingness. No debts to repay. No bills. No humiliation and shame. No children.

The children! Jonathan! Kate was nervous about giving him a feed. And Helen Long, the baby-sitter she had for the older boys, was a stickler for time. Helen would be very annoyed if she was delayed. Patty thought of her four sons and felt strength rush back into her. It was as if they had surrounded her with their warm little bodies. She closed her eyes and drew on their energy, their love of life, their need of her. To hell with David Molloy and his quasi-royal family, to hell with Gareth Owens and his grabbing bank! It was just her and the boys now. She whispered a solemn promise to look after them, to always be there for them. She opened her eyes and smiled. How had she managed to be standing with her feet in a flooded river, in pitch darkness, on a windswept night? Definitely un-Molloy-like behaviour.

When Patty found that her numb feet would not move, she leaned down to pull one foot free. That is when she toppled over into the water. That is when she discovered that she was still weak after giving birth, when she discovered that the current was too powerful for her. That is when she learned how desperately she wanted to live.

Kate felt mildly nervous when Jonathan began to whimper. She rocked the baby-carrier gently and he fell back to sleep for another five minutes. The next time he woke, he made it perfectly clear he was not going to be fobbed off with a little rocking. She picked him up and cradled him close to her. He stiffened his body and made a noise impossibly loud for such a tiny person. Walking slowly, she went to the fridge, gingerly balancing the baby in her arms as she got out his bottle and boiled the kettle to heat it up. She dripped some of the contents of the heated bottle on her wrist at least five times before she was satisfied with the temperature of his milk. She offered him the bottle. He clamped his little rosebud mouth around the teat and sucked. She laughed with relief as he made slurping sounds.

"You were hungry, little man. You'll feel better when your tummy's full."

Together they got through the feeding, burping and changing routine without disaster. Then they shared a very special, very solemn five minutes. Jonathan was full and comfortable, cosy and safe in Kate's arms. She was relieved and at ease. Kate's heart reached out to the fatherless scrap in her arms. When she was sure he was in a deep sleep, she placed him back into his carrier and tucked his blanket around him. She had just finished washing out his bottle when the phone rang. It was Patty's baby-sitter, very irate.

"Are you Kate Lucas? Patty Molloy gave me your number."

Kate did not need to answer. The woman just rambled on.

"I told her I needed to be home by ten o'clock. It's 10.30 now. I can't stay."

"I'm sure she won't be much longer. Are the children all right? Any problem with them?"

"They're fine. Sound asleep. It's my own I'm worried about. I have teenagers. I need to be home to make sure they come in at a decent hour."

Kate wondered for a minute if she should try to contact Patty. She had not noticed that it was getting so late. Maybe she was working something out with the Molloys. Something to her benefit. Patty had mentioned that this woman was less than obliging. Best try to appease her for now.

"I'll tell you what, Mrs – Mrs –?"

"Long. Helen Long. Call me Helen."

"Right, Helen. If Patty's not here by eleven, I'll phone her."

"Don't bother ringing her mobile number. There's no reply. I've tried umpteen times."

"I know she'll be back soon. I'll give you a ring as soon as she arrives here to collect Jonathan. OK, Helen?"

Kate put the receiver down and crept over to check on the sleeping baby. She shivered. Refusing to accept that the coldness creeping up her back was caused by anything other than anaemia, she turned up the temperature on the thermostat. Then, afraid that Jonathan would be too warm, she rolled his blanket down. He should be in his cot. David Molloy's house was only six miles from here. What was taking Patty so long? Why hadn't she rung? Was she too upset to talk on the phone, too upset to drive?

Kate boiled the kettle and put a camomile tea bag into a cup to infuse. Some calm inside, that's what she needed. As she sipped her tea and watched the sleeping child, she tried to think herself into a positive frame of mind. Why did she always fear the worst? Expect things to go wrong? Almost invite disaster by recognising the possibility of failure?

Had she really believed she would conceive a baby just because she decided the time was right? Had her little voice inside, that nagging, whining sound which had travelled with her from the Kerry hills, not told her the timing was not up to her, that she would be punished for trying to control and order what was not hers to decide?

Man proposes, God disposes. She shook her head now and sent her Catholic conscience back to the inner recesses, back to where it belonged, with her childhood memories. One of them, either she or Fred, had a fertility problem. Prayer and penance would not solve that. And what about Richard Gordon? Look how readily she had accepted Martin Burke's accusations against Richard. She blushed in the dimly lit kitchen as she remembered Richard today, the suffering etched on his face, forced into telling her about Cora's illness. Against his wife's wishes. What suspicious streak in her nature prevented her from trusting? How could she have believed that Richard would jeopardise his reputation and career? And even more silly, how had she suspected Fred of having an affair with Adele Sheehan? Negative! Negative! Negative! Thoroughly selfish and introspective. Fred was right. She was suffering from the great 'Me' complex. She took a deep breath and pulled back her shoulders. "I will be more positive. I will trust in people." She whispered her mantra several times. She felt stronger and more self-assured until she looked at her watch.

It was 11.15. Patty had been gone for nearly four hours. She went to the phone and dialled Patty's mobile. It rang out. The cold was creeping along her spine again. Hoping that Patty had gone back to her own house first, she rang there. Helen Long answered the phone after one ring.

"No. She's not here. I feel very sorry for her because of the accident and everything but I will never baby-sit for her again. When I say two hours, I mean it. I really want to go home."

The positive reinforcement of the camomile tea and the mantra disappeared as Kate put the phone down. There was something wrong and all the meditating techniques in the world could not warm the cold knot of fear in her gut. She got the telephone directory and looked up David Molloy's number. It rang for a long time before he answered.

"David, this is Kate Lucas. We met at the hospital. I know Patty Molloy was calling to see you tonight. I'm just wondering if she's still with you?"

"She left here two hours ago. I've no idea where she went."

"Did she mention that she was calling somewhere else?"

David Molloy's sigh made it very obvious that she was being a nuisance. He certainly had none of the easy charm which had made his brother Brian such a popular person.

"I assume you've tried her home number. If she's not at home with her children, I don't know where she is. You're Martin Burke's secretary, yes?"

"His PA, actually."

"Well, then you know Brian's will is being read tomorrow. I hope his widow turns up on time for that. Goodnight."

Kate was left holding the phone in her hand, seething with anger. She understood now why Patty must have gone for a walk or a spin to clear her head after her meeting with that ogre. For all his snobbery, he was an ignoramus.

What in the fuck was she going to do now? She took

deep breaths to quell the panic. It did not work. She was beginning to shake, to have half-formed thoughts of disaster when she heard a car pull into the driveway. Thank God! Patty was safe! Just as she got to the hall door she heard a key being placed in the lock. She almost ran back to the kitchen, knowing in her heart that Fred would be drunk and that something terrible had happened to Patty. She stood staring at Jonathan, willing everything to be all right for him, wanting to protect him from the awful event that was casting a cold, black shadow ahead of it. A warm arm reached around her waist.

"Still baby-sitting? I thought this little man would be gone home by now. Where's Patty?"

She turned to look at Fred. He was exhausted. And sober.

"I thought that . . ."

"You thought I was going out to get drunk. To be honest, I was, but I ended up taking the taxi to work instead. Tried to get some of the paperwork out of the way. I'm sorry about earlier, Kate. Sorry about the way I spoke to you."

She leaned against his chest and closed her eyes. She was sorry too. Sorry that she had not had more faith in her husband, sorry that her suspicious mind had not allowed him the benefit of the doubt, sorry that she was not more supportive of his ambitions for Lucas Advertising. They needed to talk, to really communicate. Some time. Not now. Now they must find Patty.

"There's something wrong, Fred. Patty went to see David Molloy tonight but she left his house over two hours ago. She's not answering her mobile and she hasn't contacted home either. What're we going to do? Should we ring the police?"

"You're sure she wasn't calling somewhere else? A friend maybe? Did you ring around?"

"She would have told me. She said two hours tops. And she knows the baby-sitter she had for the older children needed to get away. God knows what she's done. She's under terrible strain. Just after a baby, Brian's funeral, the bank."

"The bank?"

"I'll tell you later. What're we going to do now?"

"Put on the kettle. I'll ring around. Maybe she's just chatting, not realising how late it is."

Kate went through the motions of making coffee but her ears were straining to hear Fred's side of the telephone conversation. She knew when he came back into the kitchen that he had failed to get any news of Patty's whereabouts. Fred poured two mugs of coffee and handed one to her. Her worry was reflected on his face now.

"We'll have to think this through calmly, Kate. No point in ringing the police about someone who has been missing for such a short length of time. OK. We know she left David Molloy's house over two hours ago and that she has not turned up in any of our friends' homes."

"So?"

"So how about you put the baby in your car and take him home. Then you can let the anxious baby-sitter go. I'll drive the route to David Molloy's. It's pretty remote there and it's a bad night. Maybe her car just broke down."

"She's not answering her phone."

"Well, maybe there's a good reason for that too. No point in anticipating trouble, Kate."

Kate smiled. It was as if Fred had seen inside her head. She silently repeated her mantra once more. *I will be more positive. I will trust in people.*

She kissed him with a passion that said all the things she did not have the time to put into words.

Helen Long wasted no time in courtesies. She disappeared out the door of The Rectory as soon as Kate entered. Kate brought Jonathan upstairs and put him into his cot. He was a little restless but did not wake. She checked on the other children. They were all fast asleep.

On her way back to the kitchen, she passed a group of photographs on the landing wall. There was a wedding portrait, Patty radiant in white, Brian tall and handsome. Then a collection of family photos, starting with Patty and Brian with one child up to the last family portrait. Patty, still radiant, obviously pregnant with Jonathan, Brian still handsome, surrounded by their three strong and healthy boys. This had been how the world had seen them, how Kate had always seen them. The smiling perfect family. And that is how they would have stayed except that Brian had driven too fast, braked too late, died too young. Talked to his wife too little.

Kate took her phone out of her bag and placed it on the table. Fred would probably ring her mobile if he had any news. Dependable Fred. What a mistake to think she could talk to him later, sort things out when they had time! She would tell him tonight how much she loved him. She would outpace fate and not allow it to do to them what it had done to Patty and Brian.

Even though she had been expecting the call, she jumped when her phone rang. Fred had retraced Patty's route and had found no sign of her.

"There's an alternate road back. It's the old route by the river. Not many people use it. I'll go that way just in case. The storm's bad now. She could be stuck somewhere. I'll ring you soon. Everything OK at The Rectory?"

"Yeah. Fine. All the children are asleep. I really think we should contact the police. It's after midnight now."

"You're right, Kate. We'll do that when I get back. Unless, of course, I bring Patty with me. Talk soon."

Kate wrapped her arms around herself and tried to pray, tried not to think. She failed on both counts.

Fred stopped the car. He had already driven over four miles along this narrow, rutted road with the overhanging trees. It seemed to be getting narrower and the line of grass growing in the middle was testament to the fact that it was little used. He checked his rear-view mirrors. He was stuck now. No room to turn so his best choice was to forge ahead and eventually meet up with the main road. The trees on his left-hand side grew more dense and thickened into a forest. The wind was whipping sheets of rain and broken twigs and leaves against the windscreen. He slowed the car down, afraid that a tree might fall across his path. Then he speeded up, afraid that a tree might fall on top of him. He regretted coming here now. Patty would never have driven this way. His knuckles were white as he gripped the steering wheel tightly and admitted to himself that he was terrified. There was an evil in the strength of the storm, the intensity of the darkness, the whine of the wind audible even above the engine noise. He had to slow again as he approached a hairpin bend. Panic began to set in. Suppose he had got it wrong? Suppose access to the main road had been closed off? Suppose there was a steep drop into the river around the hairpin bend? He inched around the corner and jammed on the brakes. He had almost crashed into a four-wheel drive. Patty's four-wheel drive.

Leaving the engine running he jumped out, calling to Patty as he ran towards her car. He almost stopped, terrified at what he might find. What he found when he looked inside was the most terrifying of all. Patty's phone was on the dash, her bag on the floor, a baby seat and some toys in the back. But no Patty. He stood there, rain streaming down his face, pushed and pulled by the swirling wind, terrorised by the whine of the gale. His mind went blank.

What to do now? Jesus! Ring the police? Get a search party together? There was a tearing sound as a branch overhead snapped. He ran to save his life, clearing the low ditch in one leap. He landed on a mucky slope and lost his balance. He half skidded, half rolled down the sheer incline, aware that he was getting nearer to the river all the time but unable to stop. The thunder of raging water was pounding in his ears when his feet finally found a grip. He had stopped on the edge of the raging torrent that was the river. He became aware of his heartbeat, his breathing, the coldness of his feet and the heat of sweat on his back. With eyes closed he whispered a prayer of thanks to whoever or whatever had held him back from certain death in the flooded river.

He looked back up the steep muddy slope he had slid down. It would be stupid to attempt to climb it again in these conditions. He began to walk upriver, stumbling over the rough ground as he scanned the sheer slope to his right, looking for a way to climb back to the road.

He almost fell over her. She was sprawled on the riverbank, barefooted and half-dressed, clinging to an overhanging branch. Fred stooped down beside her. Her teeth were chattering and her skin felt deathly cold. Her eyes were closed.

"Patty! Patty! It's Fred!" She didn't respond. He slapped her face gently and to his relief her eyes slowly opened. "You're OK now, Patty. I've got you. I'll get help for you."

"D-d-don't go, Fred!" she whispered, so faintly he could hardly hear the words.

She was gripping the branch as if her life depended on it. Fred tried to assess her injuries but it was too dark to make any judgement.

"Where are you hurt, Patty? It might be better not to move now."

She forced out some words with difficulty between her blue lips. "N-not hurt . . . f-fell into the river . . . swept along . . . grabbed the branch . . . g-get me out of here . . . I want to see my ch-children."

Fred understood her feverish grip on the branch now.

She grabbed at it as she was being swept past and used it to haul herself onto the bank. He could see the whites of her eyes shining in the dark as she looked in terror towards the river. She tightened her hold even more on the branch. He put his hands over hers.

"I've got you, Patty. You can let go. I'm holding you."

Fred heard her take a shuddering breath and then she transferred her grip from the branch to his hands. Her fingers were like a touch of death they were so cold.

Suddenly released, the branch sprang back towards the tree, scraping Fred's cheek en route. He put his arms underneath Patty and lifted her up. She was light. He would be able to carry her to the car. She clung onto him as they made slow progress back up the muddy slope. The angle of the climb seemed even steeper to him than the incline he had slipped down such a short time ago. He clambered over the ditch and then back along the road to Patty's car. Laying her across the back seat, he peered at her in the light from his own car. She looked ghastly. Blue-white skin and purple lips. He ran to his car, switched off the engine, got out the spare jacket he kept in the boot and brought it back to the four-wheel drive. He tucked the jacket around her and then jumped into the driver's seat. He'd decided it would be faster to continue along the river to the point where it joined the main road again rather than go back, and they would have a better chance of getting through in the four-wheel drive if there was any flooding. He put the car in gear and turned to check on Patty. A little colour was beginning to come back into her face.

Her eyes focused on him. "The ch-children?"

"The children are fine. Kate's with them at The Rectory. I'm taking you to the hospital. You're suffering from shock and hypothermia."

Patty tried to sit up. "No! Not the hospital! *Home.* Please, Fred!"

Fred stared at the tiny bedraggled woman, at the fear in her eyes, at the stubborn line of her purple mouth. He smiled at her.

"Tell you what. We'll go to The Rectory. You can see the children for yourself. Then we can decide whether you need medical attention or not. Deal?"

Exhausted again, she muttered her agreement and sank back onto the seat. She closed her eyes and gritted her teeth against pain as life began to creep back into her limbs. She embraced the sensation. Life, even the painful part of it, was precious to her.

Kate went to grab the phone when it rang and then hesitated. It could only be bad news. Her hand shook as she pressed the receive button.

"Kate, make sure the house is warm. Run a bath. Get some dry clothes ready. I'm bringing Patty home."

"Is she all right? Where did you find her? Is she hurt?"

Fred laughed and Kate thought she heard a little edge of terror in the sound. "Questions! Questions! She's very wet and cold. Otherwise I'm not sure. I'll see you in about ten minutes. I'm just heading onto the main road now."

The next ten minutes were a flurry of following Fred's

instructions. She found a heavy dressing-gown and fleecy pyjamas and put them on a radiator to heat. Turning on the bath taps, she tipped in some oils. Patty must have been out in the storm. Her car must have broken down.

She would need a hot drink. The kettle was just starting to boil when the car pulled into the driveway. Kate ran to open the big double doors of The Rectory for them. Her stomach knotted with fear when she saw Fred stride up the steps, Patty like a rag-doll in his arms. It was even worse when they came into the light. Patty's face was colourless, eyes huge and staring, what clothes she had on underneath Fred's jacket were mud-spattered and soaking wet. He had a gash on his cheek from which blood was seeping. Kate stood there, staring helplessly, as Fred brought Patty into the lounge and laid her down on the settee.

"The children?" Patty whispered.

Kate knelt down beside her and caught her icy cold hand. "They're all asleep upstairs, Patty. They're safe. You mustn't worry about them. It's you who need looking after now."

Patty sat bolt upright with an energy that seemed impossible from her frozen, drenched body. "I'll be all right. I'm just cold. Promise me no hospital. No doctor. I don't need them. Promise! Promise!"

Kate saw the fear and panic, the plea in Patty's eyes. "What happened, Patty? Are you hurt? Can you walk?"

"I'm cold. And shocked. I fell into the river."

"Well then, you need to go to the hospital."

"No! No! I won't go. I won't give those black-hearted

Molloys the satisfaction. They must never know anything about this."

Fred came in with a cup of strong, sweet tea and handed it to Patty. Fred and Kate exchanged looks. Neither of them knew what to do. It was obvious that Patty needed medical attention but equally obvious that she would refuse to be seen by a doctor. Fred shrugged his shoulders.

Maybe he was right, thought Kate. Maybe playing along with Patty for now was best.

She whispered in Patty's ear. "You're just after having a baby, Patty. Are you losing blood?"

Patty's teeth were rattling against the cup as she sipped the tea. She felt her strength come back as the scalding brew trickled down her throat. She looked at the people hovering over her, so concerned, so worried. She smiled at them.

"No, Kate," she said weakly. "I'm not bleeding to death. I'll be fine when I heat up. I need my children around me. I need a bath and I need to thank both of you from the bottom of my heart."

Kate put a fleecy blanket she had found in the hot press around Patty and then hugged her friend close to her, trying to impart some of her body heat to the shivering woman in her arms.

"I have a bath and warm clothes ready for you. Finish your tea and have your bath. We'll talk then."

She helped Patty upstairs. They looked in on the four sleeping children first, then she left Patty soaking in the hot water and went downstairs to tend to Fred's injured face. The cut was superficial. It would most probably heal without leaving a scar. Kate hugged him close to her when she had finished cleaning the wound.

"Thank you, Fred. I don't know what Patty and I would have done tonight without you."

He kissed the top of her head and stroked her hair. She cuddled into him, feeling closer to him than she had for a long time. The love bringing them together seemed so much more powerful now than the things pulling them apart. She pushed thoughts of Lucas Advertising and infertility treatment to the back of her mind. This was what she and Fred were about.

She could have stayed in his warm embrace forever but after a time Fred spoke, breaking the spell.

"She needs professional help."

Kate had to drag her attention from her oasis of calm. What were they going to do about Patty? She stood back and looked into Fred's worried face.

"I can't understand what she was doing down by the river in the first place. If you saw where I found her, Kate! I know I ended up there too by accident but I'm –"

"I'll tell you exactly what happened and why I was there. Then you can decide what type of professional help I need."

They both whirled around at the sound of Patty's voice. Even though she was still pale, her colour was more natural now. She looked cosy, wrapped up in her outsize dressing-gown. She had a bottle of brandy in her hand.

"Three glasses, please, Kate. I think we all need this."

They sat around the big kitchen table. Patty talked. Kate and Fred listened. Jonathan woke for a feed and Patty continued to talk as she made up his bottle and then fed him. It was into the small hours before the Lucases left The Rectory, satisfied that Patty and the children were safe. For now.

Chapter 15

Kate forced herself to jump out of bed at the first sound of the alarm on Monday morning. Still exhausted from the turmoil of Friday night, her body ached to stay between the sheets. At least Patty seemed to have recovered over the weekend from her brush with death. She had looked stronger yesterday. Physically anyway. She would need all the strength she could muster to sort the financial mess Brian Molloy had left behind.

Fred was already up and about. Coffee was made when she went downstairs. He handed her a cup and then opened the patio doors and went out into the garden. The morning was bright and sunny, the antithesis of the drenching storm which had almost cost Patty her life. It was as if the weather had done its worst and was now trying to compensate.

Kate made some toast and watched Fred as he stood still at the bottom of the garden. He appeared to be staring at the shrubs but she knew his interest in the garden started and finished with mowing the lawn. He must be feeling the after-effects of all the rain-soaked drama. She went down to join him, needing to reassure herself that he was well enough to go to work.

"You could take the day off. You need the rest after all that's happened. Are you listening, Fred?"

He started and when he looked at her it was as if he was coming back from a long way off.

"Has Patty any idea who exactly is involved in the property syndicate that Brian bought into? Any names?"

Kate frowned. They had spent hours talking about this with Patty over the weekend. Did he not remember? "No. She told you all she knows. It's an international development company. Gareth Owens either doesn't know or isn't saying. David Molloy claims to know nothing about his brother's financial affairs. Patty is completely in the dark. Why? Do you know something?"

Fred drained his coffee and looked at his watch. "I must go. I want to pin Adele down to her work today before your boss decides to steal her off again. She'd do well to remember who's paying her exorbitant salary."

"Just how much is this girl costing? Is she worth it?"

"That remains to be seen."

He stooped, kissed her on the cheek and went, leaving her to take her turn staring at the shrubs.

If Martin Burke had enjoyed his night out with Adele Sheehan, it did not show in his mood. He was his usual morning grouch. Not alone that, but when Kate switched on her computer she discovered he had been in the office last night at 1.30. Sunday night! Had the man any sense? Kate frowned as she read the terse note: *Please write a report on property file research and send it to me ASAP. Comment on Post-it notes attached to files.* So! He had already gone through these files himself and had a new obsession with Post-its. She regretted now that she had abandoned her research Friday afternoon. Martin was not going to let up on his mission to uncover a scam. Prat!

Needing to cobble together something to give to Martin, she got out some files. Her hand fell on the bulkiest one. It was Nigel Greenway's. Fred's hero. Nigel, the super garage, super businessman. Now here was a person who relished the buying and selling of property. Or at least he had at one time. There had been a period in this office when the conveyancing section of the company had worked almost exclusively on Nigel Greenway's deals. Not any more. Lately he seemed to be concentrating more on consolidating what he had rather than acquiring more. At least that was what Kate had assumed. She had not seen Nigel Greenway here for some time and had not dealt with any paperwork on his behalf. Which is why she was very surprised to notice two property purchases within the past twelve months. The details were sketchy. Even before she turned to the back of the folder, she knew she would find the Post-it stuck discreetly between the back cover and last page, just as she had in Gus Cochrane's files. The only difference was that this time it was a green slip. Again in Richard's hand. Again noting transfer of the two newly acquired properties to companies named International Leaf Ltd and Landform Securities respectively.

She got out Gus Cochrane's files again. Quickly glancing through the remainder of his property portfolio, she found two more commercial properties which had been bought by Gus Cochrane, the conveyancing handled by Richard Gordon's office. All signed, sealed and delivered in the accepted fashion. Except that to both had been attached the now familiar little note indicating transfer to International Leaf Ltd and Landform Securities. That made a total of four properties bought by Gus Cochrane which now appeared to be owned by either Landform Securities or International Leaf Ltd. And Nigel Greenway had transferred title deeds to the self-same companies. She should have asked Richard. He could have cleared up the mystery. She blushed as she remembered her fumbling attempt at hiding her research from Richard. Too late now. She could not bother him with business while his wife's life hung in the balance. Anyway, he had probably left the country by now. She felt someone hovering behind her and turned around to face Len Murphy.

"Len, have you ever handled conveyancing for Nigel Greenway?"

He grabbed a chair and sat beside her, his face creased with worry. "I knew it! I knew you were checking up on me. What've I done wrong?"

"Well, did you? Do work on Nigel Greenway's properties?"

Len seemed to shrink as he let out a big sigh of relief. He smiled at her. "No. Thank God. Whatever's wrong isn't down to me. I believe he had a fairly active file before I came here but he hasn't done any buying or selling in the past twelve months."

Kate smiled back at him. She hoped her puzzlement was not showing. "That's fine then. Thank you, Len."

Kate was just about to search more files for discreetly placed Post-it notes when her internal phone rang. Martin wanted to see her. Now. She locked all the client files away and went into what she also was coming to regard as the lion's den.

"Sit down, Kate. Do you have some information for me?"

She had. She would love to tell him he was so wrong about Richard Gordon. That Richard was driven by no motive other than spending what little time his wife had left by her side. But a promise was sacred so instead she thanked him for his flowers. He waved his hand dismissively.

"You're welcome. To business. Did you bring in the Dictaphone you have at home?"

Shit! It had completely slipped her mind. How could she be expected to remember a triviality like that when her life seemed to be turning into a series of tragedies? The glowering man sitting in front of her was making no excuses for her.

"Am I to understand that you have no tape and no report for me?"

Kate felt a childish urge to mimic him and stick out her tongue. This whole detective game was so silly in the face of real problems. Still, he was her boss.

"I'll bring the Dictaphone in tomorrow. Sorry I don't have it today. And I may have come across something interesting in the property files."

"Yes? How do you mean interesting?"

Kate frowned. What had she talked herself into now? What exactly could she tell this taciturn man? That some of the stick-on notes were green and some yellow? That should help to improve his opinion of her. Fuck! She cleared her throat nervously.

"Your email mentioned the Post-its attached to some of the property files. Obviously you know then that private ownerships of a number of properties have been transferred to International Leaf Ltd or Landform Securities. The odd thing is, I've never heard of these companies before."

"Should you have?"

"Well, yes. I think so. I should've been aware of deed transfers. But the business of transferring does not seem to have been handled through this office. Not to the best of my knowledge."

He stared at her and she clearly read the message in his eyes. Martin Burke had little regard for the extent of her knowledge on anything.

He looked at his watch. "The Molloy family will be here shortly. There's some routine correspondence I need you to handle. It's on Dictaphone. Don't take it home."

Kate had blushed an unbecoming shade of red before she saw the twinkle in his eye. She stood up. "I promise to have Dictaphone and report for you tomorrow."

He smiled at her and she was struck yet again by the attractiveness of the flash of white teeth in the tanned face. What an enigma this man was!

As she walked towards the door there was a gentle tap on the other side. Eileen stuck her head in.

"The Molloy family's here, Martin. Are you ready for them?"

Kate went out to reception and saw Patty, pale and drawn, seated between Brian's brother and father. They surrounded her, yet she seemed apart, lost. Eileen came over and led the Molloy group towards Martin's office. Kate smiled encouragement at Patty as she passed by. She sat at her desk, upset for Patty, feeling that there should be something more she could do to help.

"At least she won't have to worry about money," Eileen said. "He must've been insured for a fortune. And that big house will be hers now too. The Molloys always had pots of money."

Kate examined Eileen's face. She saw nothing there except genuine concern. "She'll have plenty else to worry about besides money," she remarked.

Eileen nodded solemnly. They were both silent then, their thoughts with the young widow in Martin Burke's office.

Patty was sitting across from Martin Burke. She appeared to be calm and attentive as the solicitor explained the legalities of probate and the responsibilities of the executor. She was not listening. She was remembering, thinking back to the day when Brian had made this will. It was the day her first pregnancy had been confirmed. They had felt so happy, so complete, so full of hope.

"We're going to have the most beautiful child," he had said, "and we'll be the best parents in the world."

They had kissed and hugged and laughed.

"I'll always be here for you, Patty, and for our precious family. But just in case I have to leave unexpectedly, I'm going to make my will now."

She shivered as she recalled his prophetic words. He had left unexpectedly all right. But he had neglected to protect his precious family. How ironic that a man who had devoted his life to coronary care should leave behind so many damaged hearts.

Chapter 16

Exhaustion hit Kate by mid-afternoon. She was not helped either by the sense of helplessness she had felt as she had watched Patty leave the office earlier, white-faced and shaken, after the reading of Brian's will. Kate's eyelids drooped as she ploughed through work. She drank cup after cup of coffee in order to stay awake. Seeing her snooze at her desk would hardly improve Martin Burke's opinion of her.

When Martin called her into his office at four o'clock, she sighed in resignation. It would have been nice just to relax until five and then to slip quietly home. Fat chance of that with Mr Burke in charge. He was standing at the window, his back to her, staring towards the park. Again.

"Tell me, Kate, are there swings and slides in that park way over there?"

"Yes. There's a play area. It's for children."

"Play areas normally are."

Fuck you too, Kate thought as she stood there staring

at his back. Why was he asking anyway? His son was in the States. Odd.

"I told you that you'd be meeting Lee, my ex-wife, soon. Actually it's sooner than I expected. She's flying in today. I'm going to collect her now."

"Oh! I see."

"Do you? She's bringing our son with her. That's why I was asking you about a playground. Still think I'm odd?"

"I never said –"

"You didn't have to."

Kate frowned in annoyance. She would have to stop allowing this man to embarrass her. He had a knack of making her feel foolish. Or was it that she had a knack for allowing him to? Whichever, this was a situation that would have to change.

"I hope they enjoy their visit. How long will they be staying?"

"I'm not sure. Anyway, I'd like to invite you and Fred to meet Lee. I've often spoken to her about Fred and told her of our antics during our college days. She'd enjoy meeting him. I was wondering if you could both come by my hotel tomorrow night for dinner? I'll book a table for us."

He was making this sound like a job assignment. As if she was under an obligation to go. A picture of what the evening would be like flashed across her mind and she searched desperately for an excuse.

"Thank you, Martin, for the invitation but I'd feel we were intruding. I'm sure you and Lee have lots of catching up to do."

"Lee and I don't have that much to catch up on any more. We covered most things in the divorce court. I'd really appreciate if you and Fred could make it. I know it's short notice but that's Lee for you. Full of surprises."

He had tried to keep the tone light and casual but Kate picked up on an undertone of desperation. Was he afraid to spend time alone with his ex-wife? Is that why he was trying to railroad herself and Fred into this dinner? All the more reason not to go. If they had unfinished business left over from their divorce they could keep it to themselves.

"I'm not sure about Fred. He may not be free. I'll have to check."

He walked around the desk and stood in front of her. She could smell his aftershave and wondered which expensive brand it was. Armani? Mont Blanc?

"OK, Kate. You win. The truth is Lee needs to be entertained. She has a low boredom threshold. I know from experience that when she's bored, she can be a very awkward person to be around. I'd prefer not to have to cope with a Lee tantrum. I'm taking her to a club tonight. So will you please help me keep her amused tomorrow night?"

He smiled his nice smile and Kate could see her hope of a restful few days going down the drain. Maybe she was just being her selfish self again. And how could she not respond to his honesty, to the plea in his voice? To the flash of snow-white teeth in the tanned face. This man was such an enigma and worse still she was allowing his moods to influence her response to him. She returned his smile now.

"When you put it like that, Martin, the answer's yes. Dinner would be very nice. I'll have to check with Fred, of course, but I'm sure he's free."

"I'd appreciate if you'd let me know as soon as you can. Thanks, Kate."

Then he checked his watch and dashed towards the door. It was the first time Kate had seen any nervous characteristic in Martin Burke's behaviour. She had judged him to be the epitome of self-confidence. Mrs Page-Burke must be a most unusual woman.

Kate left his office with the knowledge that she and Fred were being used. Martin Burke was dragging them to the hotel because he did not want to spend time alone with his wife. His ex-wife. Then she shrugged her shoulders and began to plan. She would have to spend time making herself presentable for meeting Lee Page-Burke. 'One of *the* Pages,' in Fred's words. What did one wear when having dinner with a millionairess? Shit! At least they should be guaranteed an interesting night.

Sure that Fred would decide to work late, Kate had delayed making dinner,. She had not been wrong. She fumed as she listened to his enthusiastic voice on the phone.

"We're on a roll now. The television ads are shaping up really well. Adele is surpassing herself. It's way better than her Low Cal series."

"That's good, Fred. I'm glad it's working out. But don't overdo things. You need time off too."

"Time is money, Kate. I can't afford to waste either."

Kate gritted her teeth. Her husband was beginning to

sound more like Nigel Greenway every day. He was obviously being well indoctrinated in the Greenway school of successful business. Every minute not devoted to making money was a minute wasted.

"I've got to go. I'm taking the team out for a bite to eat before we settle down to work again. Don't wait up for me."

She was just about to say goodbye when she remembered Martin Burke's invitation.

"Fred, don't make any arrangements for tomorrow night. Martin has invited us to meet his wife."

"His wife?"

"I'll tell you the full story later but just remember we're meeting them in the Grand for dinner. Don't make any other plans."

"Interesting."

That is exactly what Patty had said too when Kate rang her. It was the only light note in their conversation. Patty sounded exhausted.

"Will I drop over, Patty? Look after the children for you. Let you get some rest."

"Thanks but the children are what I need now. I'll go to bed the same time as them tonight. The gathering will be easier to face after a good sleep."

"The gathering?"

"The Molloy clan have called an emergency meeting for tomorrow. Damage limitation. I think they're afraid that having dragged Brian down so low, I'm now going to compound the disgrace by letting people know he died in debt."

"Oh Patty! I'm so sorry you've to go through all this. I wish I could do something to help."

"Just having someone to talk to is great. You enjoy dinner tomorrow night. And take note of everything. I'll ring you for the low-down."

Kate thought about Patty as she made herself a toasted sandwich. Where was Patty's strength coming from? What had given her the strength to fight the freezing waters of the flooded river? It was for the children, of course, for their future, for their survival. What greater motivation could there be? That thought brought her back to brooding about her own childless state and Fred's indifference.

Feeling restless, she went out into the garden. It was dusk. Too dark and too cold and the wrong time of year to do any gardening. Coming back into the house, she switched on the television and flicked from channel to channel, from one boring programme to another. Enough of that. She picked up her book and began to read. When she found herself going over the same paragraph twice and still not knowing what it was about, she gave up on the reading and wandered aimlessly around the house. It was then she spotted the Dictaphone. The one she had brought home six months ago for Fred to fix.

She had to stand on a chair to get it down from the top shelf where it had been hiding. It was dusty. She wiped it and began to examine it. The tape was knotted inside the machine. She went to the garage to get a screwdriver. If she could get the cover off, then maybe she could release the tape. Fuck Fred! She would fix this herself.

There was a little click when the cover finally popped

off. It was much easier to see the microtape now and to see how it had somehow come off the spool and wound itself into knots. Gently, very carefully, she began to loosen the knots. Tape spilled over the table and onto the floor as she released more and more of it, amazed at the volume that had been packed into such a tiny space. Head bowed, tongue between her teeth, she worked patiently until the tape was unwound and knot free. Now all she had to do was get it back onto the spool again. Shit!

Thinking that some wine might help her concentration, she poured a glass of red and regarded the mess of tape as she sipped. She could put it all into a bag and bring it to the electrical shop to be repaired. She could leave it for Fred to fix. She put down her glass with a thud. She could, and would, fix it herself. Pushing the smallest screwdriver into the centre of one of the spools, she managed to get it to turn. A tiny piece of tape wound on. She turned the screwdriver again and another centimetre of tape slithered from the table onto the spool.

Ten minutes later Kate sat back, a satisfied grin on her face. Not alone was the tape knot-free and rewound but the cover was back on too. She poured another glass of wine and toasted herself. She would shove this in Martin Burke's face along with her report on the property files. Remembering her report brought a frown to her face. She had uncovered ten properties in total with little slips inserted into their files. In Richard's handwriting. Each slip indicated that the property had been 'trans', which she assumed to be transferred, to either Landform Securities or International Leaf Ltd. Why had Richard dealt with these transactions himself? He was a criminal lawyer. That is why he employed other people with expertise in property law. And why had she never heard of these two companies until now? She was breaking one of her own cardinal rules, thinking about work at home, but the tape had forced her thoughts in the direction of Gordon's – or Burke's as it was now.

Casting her mind back she tried to guess what might be on the tape. Six months ago the main focus in the office had been the infamous case of the minister's mistress. Richard had been preparing the defence then. Kate remembered the girl's parents and how devastated they had been on the last day of the trial. The day the minister had been set free. He was no longer a minister, of course, but had slipped quietly onto the backbenches, ready to build up his profile again. And why not? Richard had, after all, proved that the man was innocent. On the other hand, the girl known as the Minister's Mistress was still dead and her parents were still grieving.

Kate sipped her wine and remembered her instinctive dislike of Finance Minister Henry Hennessey. He had been much respected and admired in political circles. In fact, he had wormed his way from the grassroots to the upper echelons of political power in record time. An effective media man. He was good-looking, suave, very articulate. Part of the new wave of forty-something, sophisticated, cosmopolitan representatives. Parish-pump politics was as alien to him as tweed caps and brogues. She had always seen him as a caricature, the perfect image of the new-look politician. Not that she knew him. She had escorted him into Richard's office on his visits there but that was the extent of her contact with him. His business with Richard Gordon had not begun with the trial. He had been a client long before that scandal. She had hated the way he always expected deference.

She looked at the Dictaphone again. This one ran on either battery or mains. The mains adapter was in the office but maybe she could find batteries for it. She went out to the garage and poked through the masses of tools. Fred owned every DIY tool known to man, most of them unused since his enthusiasm for new projects usually died as soon as he had the equipment together. She found a box of batteries, brought them back to the kitchen and fitted two into the Dictaphone. As she switched it on, she kept her fingers crossed. *Alleluia!* Richard's voice filled the kitchen. Kate stood, took a bow and laughed as she realised she was getting a little tipsy. Never one for half measures, she filled her glass again, swigging now instead of sipping. She turned up the volume on the Dictaphone.

"Just type those up and have them sent out as soon as possible, Kate. Handle them yourself, would you? They're important."

She listened with interest as she heard her own voice, compliant and somehow reverent, reply to Richard.

"Of course. I'll look after that first thing in the morning."

Yes, sir. No, sir. Three bags full, sir. Good old Kate. Obedient, obliging, nothing-is-too-much-trouble kind of Kate. She took a swig of wine and leaned towards the machine, listening intently to Richard.

"Would you mind getting a tray ready before you leave?

Henry Hennessey's coming in. It'll be a long session so I would appreciate some sandwiches with coffee."

Ah! Here she was again. Even before she heard her own voice Kate was miming the words.

"Of course. No problem. Anything else?"

"Not unless you know how I'm going to defend our minister against a murder charge."

Her laugh sounded silly on tape. Was it that she did not know what to say or had it been that she believed Richard expected a silly laugh in reply? On tape there was a rustle and then a door banged. She closed her eyes and pictured the scene. The rustle was when she had picked up her notepad, the bang when she went out the door, forgetting to turn off the tape, forgetting to take the Dictaphone with her. Maybe she had been angry at being asked to make sandwiches for a client. Maybe she had intended collecting the tape when she brought the tray in. Ten minutes of whirring tape passed by, with just the odd rustle as Richard turned pages. She filled her glass again and waited for the skivvy Kate to bring in the tray. Door opening. Here she comes.

"Ham and cheese all right, Richard? I left some coleslaw and mayo on the side."

Oh, fuck! Kate blushed with embarrassment. Judging by her deferential tone, she must have crept into the office on hands and knees, bearing the loaded tray on her back. With mayo on the side, of course.

"Fine. Just leave it over there. Goodnight."

And so she had been dismissed. She had probably backed out of the holy presence. The door closed again.

That was Kate, ready for home, another day full of job satisfaction at an end.

To the accompaniment of the whirring tape, she thought back over her time with Richard, the progression from terrified newcomer, overanxious to please, to experienced PA, still overanxious to please. Swirling the wine around in her glass, she wondered what it would have been like if she had stayed on at college, if she had done a law degree. If, if, if! She finished her drink and emptied what was left in the bottle into her glass. Suppose, just suppose, she was the one with the law practice and Richard was *her* Personal Assistant. She laughed out loud at the thought of getting Richard, or Martin Burke, to make coffee and sandwiches for her clients. How well Martin would look in a butler's uniform!

Standing up to turn off the tape, she almost fell over. She took a deep breath and straightened up. The wine had somehow gone to her legs and made them wobbly. Just as she reached her hand towards the off switch she heard new sounds on the tape. The door was opening. She heard Richard greet someone. The deep, rich voice replying was unmistakable. It was the minister. She listened as Henry Hennessey and Richard Gordon chatted as easily as if they were discussing a game of golf.

"Sit down, Henry. Just arrived from Dublin now, have you? How did things go?"

There was a creak and Kate knew Henry Hennessey had thrown himself onto the chair she usually sat in to take dictation. She made a mental note, yet again, to have someone fix whatever was making the annoying squeaky sound. She heard him wriggle himself into a comfortable position before answering.

"Well, apart from the Press, it went OK. The Boss called me in and we had a heart-to-heart. I followed your advice, Richard. Apologetic and humble."

"How did he take it?"

"You know what the prick is like. Nothing matters to him except his own image. He doesn't give a fuck whether I twisted her neck or not. He's just furious at the bad publicity and how it is reflecting on him and the party."

"Coffee?"

There was a series of clicks and hisses as Richard switched on the percolator. His voice had an anxious edge to it when he spoke again.

"How do you mean 'apart from the Press'? I hope you kept your mouth shut around the media?"

The minister laughed and to Kate's ears, the sound was much the same as her own laugh earlier on the tape. Richard seemed to inspire nervous, silly laughter.

"What do you think I said, Richard? 'Yes, lads, I did it! I wanted rid of her and the brat she was carrying!' What kind of an idiot do you take me for?"

"How about the kind who would murder his bit on the side instead of paying her off like any sensible man would do? That puts you high up on the idiot stakes as far as I'm concerned."

Jesus! Kate flopped onto a chair, her legs weakened by wine and a suspicion that the most shocking was yet to come.

On the tape the chair creaked loudly. Henry Hennessey must have leaned forward very suddenly or else he had stood up.

"I told you over and over, she wouldn't listen to reason. She wouldn't go quietly. She wanted the full nine yards. Marriage, admitting paternity. The lot. What in the fuck was I supposed to do?"

"Talk her out of it, of course. My God! Convincing people into your way of thinking is your career. You never had to strangle anyone before this to get them to agree with you."

"I had to shut the bitch up. She was going to go to my wife, to the papers. She would've ruined me. I had to do it."

Kate jumped up and hit the pause button. Fuck! That slime ball of a minister *had* murdered the girl and her baby. The prick was guilty! She picked up the wine bottle to refill her glass. It was empty. Coffee! She staggered over to the kettle, her legs weak from too much wine and shock. Not at Henry Hennessey's guilt. She had always realised that he was a louse. It was the fact that Richard had known all along and still had defended the indefensible. But wasn't that his job? He had been retained to defend Hennessey against the murder charge. The guilt or innocence of his client was something to be decided by the jury, not by him. Yet how could he have used his skills to deliberately hoodwink the twelve jurors, to deprive the dead girl and her baby of justice, to free the murderer to maybe kill again? Why hadn't he gone for a plea bargain? There would have been some justice in that. Henry Hennessey would at least have had to serve time. She made her coffee strong and black. After two mouthfuls, she realised she was overreacting. Richard Gordon had just done his job. Brilliantly, as usual. That was why both guilty and innocent paid him such exorbitant fees. She restarted the tape and sat back with her cup of coffee. Richard was speaking again.

"Anyway, this line of conversation is pointless. The fact is you did it but we must convince the jury."

"Exactly," Henry agreed. *"Except that you can drop the 'we'. You must convince the jury. That's what I'm paying you to do."*

"Do I hear 'or else'?"

Hennessey laughed again but this time there was no trace of nervousness in the sound.

"Do I have to spell it out, Richard? Yes. Maybe I should. If I lose this case, if I don't come out of the High Court an innocent man, then I may be forced to talk to the press about certain offshore accounts, about a certain high-profile defence lawyer who has a way with tax evasion and offshore companies, about –"

"All right! All right! I get the picture. If you go down, you'll drag me down with you. Not to mention all the other people involved in the scheme. You're a ruthless prick, Hennessey. Why in the fuck didn't you keep your pants on? This is turning out to be a very expensive shag."

Kate gulped the last of her coffee. She was shaking. The tape ran on but she was not hearing. Her head was replaying the last exchange over and over . . . *"about certain offshore accounts, about a certain high-profile defence lawyer who has a way with tax evasion and offshore companies" . . . "if you go down, you'll drag me down with you . . ."*

Suddenly the possibility that Richard Gordon was involved in a tax-evasion scam was very real. To whom else could Henry Hennessey have been referring? The 'certain high-profile defence lawyer' had to be Richard

Gordon. But why would Richard jeopardise a brilliant career, a peerless reputation, for financial gain when he already had so much? But he had. He had said so on the tape. Martin Burke had been right all along.

Realising that the tape had been running on, she paused it again. She began to pace the room unsteadily, feeling dizzy and sick. Henry Hennessey deserved to suffer, to be brought to justice, to be punished for what he did. But could he be retried? And would the tape be admissible evidence anyway? She knocked her shin against the coffee table. She sat, rubbed her smarting shin and admitted to herself that she was just making excuses. It was not her place to decide whether the tape had significance as evidence or not. It was her duty to hand it over to . . . to the police? To Martin Burke? And what else, what other admissions were on the tape?

With shaking fingers Kate rewound to the Richard's 'expensive shag' comment. Then she sat and listened as the sound of her creaking office chair filled the room.

Henry Hennessey was preparing to leave the office.

"You'll let me know as soon as you have the date for the hearing, Richard?"

"Of course. And you'll manage to keep your pants on and your mouth shut, won't you?"

Henry Hennessey did not reply. There was a loud bang as he slammed the door on his way out. Shortly after, the door closed again. Richard had gone home.

She sat listening as the tape played on, the silence broken only by the whirr of the machine. Suddenly there was a new sound. Kate leaned forward to listen to the high-pitched noise. It was seconds before she realised the tape had snapped. She hit the off button but it was too late. The tape had re-knotted itself around the inside of the machine. And this time it was in bits. She took the batteries out and returned them to the garage. Dragging a chair over to the high shelf, she stood on it and put the Dictaphone back where she had found it. Then she turned off the lights and went to bed. But not to sleep.

She tossed and turned, made one decision and then another, alternated between acceptance and denial. She was furious at Henry Hennessey, at Richard Gordon, at the system which allowed guilty people walk free . . . but most of all she was furious at herself. How had she allowed Richard to dupe her for so long? She'd had so much respect and admiration for him. There had been a certain amount of fear too and resentment of his superior attitude but never, ever had she doubted his integrity. No wonder he had kept her as his PA for seven years. She must have scored very highly in gullibility. She looked at the clock and noticed that it was quarter past two in the morning. She thumped her pillow in rage. No more naiveté! No more malleable, stupid Kate! Having a deceitful, conniving boss was one thing. Having a cheating husband was an entirely different matter. She cried herself to sleep.

Chapter 17

Kate looked in the mirror the following morning and regretted her bottle of wine last night. How was she going to get herself together for this command performance in the Grand Hotel tonight? Her eyes were puffy from crying and her hair was witness to all the tossing and turning she had done during the night. Fred was still asleep. She stood over him and watched his chest rise and fall to the rhythm of his breathing. He was peaceful. Innocent-looking, his mouth soft in rest, his lovely long lashes casting shadows on his face. She flexed her fingers and then locked them together to prevent them from reaching out to touch him. She wanted so much to stroke his hair, to touch his skin, to feel his bristly chin. To strangle him. Tough call. She turned her back on him and went downstairs.

Coffee and toast did not make her feel any better. She did not yet know what time Fred eventually came home last night and her head still reeled from the tape revelations. Goddamned men! Were they all the same or was it just the shower of chauvinists it was her luck to know?

On top of all that angst, she also faced the prospect of meeting Mrs Martin Burke tonight. Lee Page-Burke. Millionairess. Shit! Kate walked out to the hall mirror and examined her face. It hadn't improved any since she had woken up. An emergency plan began to form in her mind. Martin had said he would not be in the office today. Obviously too busy catering to Lee's low boredom threshold. With a little forward planning, a long lunch break and an early finish she could maybe be some way prepared for her meeting with Martin's wife. Kate picked up the phone and began to make appointments. The works. Wash and blow-dry, manicure and facial. Maybe something new to wear. Why not?

Fred came into the kitchen just as she put the phone down. He was at his tousled most appealing. Boyish and cuddly.

He smiled at her. "Morning, Kate. Is the coffee made?"

She turned her back as she filled his cup. It was easier to maintain her anger when she was not looking at him. Still silent, she put two slices of bread into the toaster. Fred walked up behind her and slipping his arms around her waist, kissed her on the nape of the neck. She stiffened, sickened by the thought that his lips might have kissed someone else. Someone young and beautiful. Someone named Adele Sheehan.

Fred sighed and walked away from her.

"Right, Kate. Shoot. What's going on?"

Slamming his plate of toast down in front of him, she stared at him. What was wrong with this man? He had been out most of the night with no explanation let alone apology and he had the cheek to ask what was wrong?

"Where were you last night? What time did you come home?" Even to her own ears, she sounded shrewish but his casual attitude was infuriating her.

"I told you I was working. Then Nigel Greenway rang. There were some people he wanted me to meet. It just ran on a bit. Sorry."

"And I s'pose these important people had to be met in a club and, of course, Adele had to be met too?"

"Yes. Right on both counts."

Kate blinked her eyes to clear the image burned onto her brain. She saw Adele, young, beautiful and very sexy, dancing cheek to cheek with Fred, his hand gently stroking her bare back. She always wore tiny little tops that exposed her midriff, showing off her pierced, tanned and very flat stomach. Kate took a deep breath.

"Couldn't you have rung me to let me know? Or wouldn't Nigel Greenway give you permission?"

Fred banged his cup onto the table, splashing coffee onto the polished surface. Kate automatically got a cloth and began to mop it up. She was good at mopping up messes. He caught her wrist.

"Stop that and listen to me. You've got to understand that this contract with Nigel Greenway's vital to our future. And so is he. If he says jump, I ask how high. And if you remember, I did tell you that I'd be late. Do I have to keep reporting on my every move?"

"When the move involves clubbing with a young girl, yes, I think I should know."

"Kate! Are you jealous? Adele's nothing more than an employee to me. A very talented employee, a person with the ability to get Lucas Advertising where I want it to go. But nothing more than an employee just the same. I love you, Katie O'Hanlon. There never was and never will be anyone else."

He smiled at her and Kate felt every cell in her body respond to the curve of his mouth and the warmth in his eyes. He looked tired. She reached out and stroked his face.

"And I love you. It's just that you always seem to be so busy these days. I get lonely. And there are so many things we need to talk about."

"If you're going to start the baby conversation again, Mrs Lucas, I have a suggestion to make."

Her heart did a flip. He was going to agree to see Dr Shorten! At last! She raised an eyebrow at him, afraid to threaten the promise of the moment with words.

"Forget about doctors and fertility clinics. Let's go make a baby now!"

He grinned at her. She glanced at the clock and saw that she was already late. She should be ready to leave for work by now. But Martin wouldn't be there, would he?

"Think you could produce a reasonable model in half an hour?" she asked.

"If I tried very hard. Did my very best work!"

She ran towards the stairs and Fred chased her. It was not until she was seated at her desk two hours later that

Kate realised they had never discussed an appointment with the doctor and that Fred had not agreed to fertility testing.

Martin Burke walked across the foyer of the Grand Hotel to greet the Lucases. Kate assumed the tall, auburn-haired, very beautiful woman by his side was his ex-wife. Only one word could describe her. Expensive. Everything about her from her silky suit to her delicate fragrance was top drawer. The perfume must be Chanel, Kate thought as she discreetly sniffed the air. Lee's smile was as glisteningly white as her husband's. They obviously shared the same dentist. Kate glanced down and noted that Lee's stockings were sheer silk and her shoes must have cost at least a week's wages. The confidence that Kate had walked in with evaporated, burned off in the radiance of the other woman's aura. The new dress she had agonised over buying, the hairdo, the facial, all the self-indulgent little confidence-boosters she had managed to fit in today, seemed tawdry and cheap in the face of such high-class elegance.

"Kate, I'd like you to meet Lee. Kate's my new PA. I told you about her."

Mrs Page-Burke was tall but Kate felt this was not the real reason she looked down her nose. She offered her hand and, for a second, Kate was not sure whether she was meant to kiss it or not.

"So nice to meet you, Kate. I'd have thought you were much older from what Martin has said. But that's my ex-husband for you. Never one to flatter."

Kate took the hand with the diamond rings and long,

graceful fingers. She smiled inanely and could not think of a single word to say.

"Of course, I've already met your husband," Lee said, retrieving her hand and turning towards Fred. "You've recovered from last night, Fred? As I recall, you were still dancing rather energetically when we left the club. That assistant of yours is some gal to go!"

Kate felt her breath catch in her throat. Her head snapped up and she glared at Fred. He was smoothly kissing Lee on the cheek, exchanging pleasantries, smiling, deliberately ignoring his open-mouthed wife. Not one word, not a hint had he given that he had already met Martin Burke's ex-wife. What else was he keeping secret?

Kate felt a hand on her arm and, glancing up, she saw that Martin was by her side. The warmth of his hand seeped through the thin material of her dress. I know how you feel, his dark blue eyes were conveying wordlessly. The beautiful woman, now twisting Fred around her little finger, must often have humiliated him too. Kate looked away from him, mortified that she had allowed him to see her upset yet grateful for his support. She would never figure him out.

"OK, folks. How about we make our way into the dining room?" he suggested.

Their procession seemed to take a natural order. Fred escorted the beautiful American divorcée while Martin and Kate were drawn along in their wake. They had been assigned a very discreet corner table. Kate was relieved to find that the big potted palms would screen them from prying eyes. When they were seated she realised that she had not yet contributed one word to the conversation. She struggled to think of something interesting and sophisticated to say. The words which came rushing out of her mouth did not qualify.

"What do you think of Ireland, Lee?"

Even seated, Lee managed the downward look. Kate shrivelled into her new dress. She may as well have said, 'D'you come here often?'.

"It's all the green and misty things I expected it to be. Does it ever stop raining though?"

"You'll have to come back during our summer season. We've plenty of sunshine then."

"Do that," Fred said. "You'll find that in the summer we use pastel-colour umbrellas to protect us from the rain whereas in the winter our brollies are more blacks and browns. That's how we mark the seasons."

They all laughed, even Kate, but her laugh was only on the outside. She felt that Fred had put her down and in the process made their country the butt of a joke. True, it rained a lot here. How else could it have all its luscious greens? But the sun shone too. Glorious days full of heat, buzzing bees, full-blown roses, the scent of furze on the breeze, carpets of daisies and clover in the fields, orange sunsets. Realising that her mind had slipped back to her childhood summers, she dragged her attention back to the Grand Hotel. The conversation was now about the effect ambient climate had on the psyche of a nation. Fred was in full flight.

"That's why Mediterranean people are so passionate. Their senses are bombarded with colour day in day out.

Intense colour. Vivid blues and reds and oranges. So they respond to that intensity."

"I see," Lee said. "So you are saying that Irish people respond to the greys of the skies and the browns of the bogs. But you're certainly not depressive as a nation, Fred, are you?"

"No, but we're cooler, more introspective, slower to react than people from warm climates. Where were you born, Lee?"

"New York. The glorious Big Apple. It may be a bit arrogant to consider it the centre of the universe but nevertheless I do."

"There you go," Martin said. "Ireland breeds introspection. The Mediterranean breeds passion. New York breeds arrogance. Your theory certainly has some merit, Fred."

There was a moment's lapse in conversation as they all absorbed Martin's comments. He had accused Lee of arrogance but yet had slipped the insult into a seemingly harmless piece of social chit-chat. What a sophisticated relationship!

Kate had been observing the divorced couple and noted that they never seemed to look directly at each other. It was as if there was a wall between them. Why was Lee here? Was it because of the child? The silence was getting uncomfortable. Kate could not stand it. Time for another standard question.

"How old is your son, Lee?"

"He's three."

"And what's his name?"

"Robert – after my father," said Martin.

Lee laughed and for the first time she looked over at her ex-husband. Obviously their son was the common ground they shared. "My father is called Chuck. Could you imagine calling your son Chuck Burke? How unfair would that be?"

Their starter course was served then, giving them all a chance to relax. Kate sipped very slowly at her wine. She did not want to make the same mistake as last night. What a spectacle she would make of herself if she staggered when she stood up! The thought of last night reminded her of the tape. The incriminating tape. What in the hell was she going to do about it?

"Penny for them, Kate. You're miles away and not very happy judging by the frown."

Kate looked across at Martin and smiled. How could she tell him that Richard Gordon was apparently involved in a tax-evasion scam, that his suspicions had been correct? Not to mention the minister's confession. Then he would have to investigate the allegation. What effect would that have on Cora's health? No. She could not even consider it until after . . . well, after Cora's health issue was resolved.

"Just thinking how lucky you are, Martin, to be living in the Grand Hotel. The food is delicious."

"It's lovely only for a while. It gets repetitive. I must get around to house-hunting."

Lee turned her attention away from Fred the instant Martin mentioned house-hunting.

"I did advise that you should be properly organised for

moving continents. At least have a place to live arranged." She leaned conspiratorially towards Kate and Fred and spoke in an exaggerated whisper. "Don't know what he was running away from but Martin hightailed it out of the States very suddenly. I wonder if he's harbouring any big, dark secrets that will catch up with him?"

Martin's lips tightened and Kate noticed a slight angry flush on his tanned skin. Lee seemed to be teasing him but yet she had planted the doubt. Had Martin Burke's mad dash to Ireland been inspired by a need to escape – something? Sick of their games, Kate took a decent mouthful of wine.

Martin turned to her. "And where were you born, Kate? Is that a soft Kerry accent I detect?"

Kate relaxed. If there was one topic she could discuss endlessly it was her beloved Kerry. She told them about her parents'farm, about the hills and fields, the rivers and heather, the furze, the sweet air and the bogs.

"Sounds like Donegal." Martin said. "Just a little softer."

"Why do you live in the city, Kate?" Lee asked. "It seems to me your heart is still in the countryside."

Kate looked over at her husband. He was the reason, the only reason why she trod the hard streets when she longed for the spring of grass beneath her feet, why she breathed traffic fumes when her lungs ached for clean air. Fred winked at her.

"Guess what, Lee? The only thing her Kerry hills don't have is an advertising agency. Anyway, Kate still owns her parents' property. She's held onto it all these years. She slips down there whenever she can. It's her retreat from the world."

Martin sat back in his chair and closed his eyes. "That sounds so idyllic. What I'd give for a fresh breeze and a head full of quiet right now!" He opened his eyes and looked directly at Kate. "How about I come down to Kerry with you the next time you're going there? Would you mind? Robert would love it too."

Before Kate had a chance to answer, Lee spoke. "You're going to turn my son into a country bumpkin, Martin Burke. You're taking him to Donegal too, aren't you?"

"Not your problem," Martin said brusquely. "At least I'm not dragging him off to an alien culture."

"Funny that," Lee replied. "I'd have thought thatched houses and bogs were as alien to a New York child as souks and sandstorms."

"I guarantee he'll have no difficulty leaving here when the time comes. Can you say the same about Saudi?"

Kate and Fred exchanged puzzled looks. If they were following this exchange properly, then Lee was going to Saudi Arabia while her son was staying here with Martin. Lee was silent but her flashing eyes spoke volumes. Somehow her quiet displeasure was as hard-hitting as a full-blown temper tantrum. Everyone at the table felt the force of her disapproval.

"Too bad for Robert that you're depriving him of such a wonderful experience. I told you the hotel has a special children's club. He'd be well catered for."

"In the children's club? For the offspring of the rich and famous? And what about the Religious Police, the Mattawa?"

"There's no reason whatsoever that we should have a

problem with them. Our villa's totally secluded. Anyway, Amir –"

"Ah! The sheikh!"

"Yes! Sheikh Amir Al Bahar. He does have a name, you know."

"But he does not and will not have my son."

A tense silence fell over the group. Kate blushed and even Fred shuffled around uncomfortably. Kate reacted to the tension like she always did. She babbled.

"Is Robert staying at the Grand Hotel too? It must be boring for a little boy. Are there any other children in the hotel?"

She tried to stop herself blurting out the questions but her tongue was running way ahead of her judgement. It was none of her business and the way it had come out it sounded disapproving. Lee jumped on it.

"Yes. Not a nice prospect for a two-year-old, is it? And unless your job description includes baby-sitting, Kate, he'll have to find a nanny too. Never one to let little details ruin the overall plan, are you, Martin?"

To everyone's relief the waiter arrived with the main course. Fred managed to keep the conversation light and flowing through to dessert. When Kate said she was tired after coffee and would like to go home, she was not making an excuse. She was exhausted from the strain of Martin Burke and his beautiful wife. They obviously still shared a lot of feelings but they were all negative and uncomfortable to be around. She shook the royal hand again. "It was very nice meeting you, Lee. How long will you be staying? Will I meet you again?"

"Likewise, Kate. Nice to put faces to the people Martin was telling me about. I doubt we'll meet again in the near future. I leave on the first leg of my journey to Saudi in the morning."

"Have a good trip then."

"She will," Martin said. "The sheikh will ensure that. Spares nothing to give Lee what she wants."

Lee shot her ex-husband an angry look. He glared back and Kate would not have been surprised if the air between them had burst into flames.

Fred to the rescue again. "Anyway, thanks for dinner. 'Twas a very nice evening. And Martin, we'll let you know the next time we're going to Kerry. No matter where your son was born, he'll love the freedom of the countryside. You'd never know, the sun might even shine!"

They were all smiling and laughing as they parted.

When Kate and Fred reached the car, Kate threw herself onto the passenger seat and gave a big sigh of relief. She kicked off her high heels and closed her eyes. What a strain!

"The sheikh's her new boyfriend," Fred said. "Their combined income must be bigger than the Irish GNP."

"Why didn't you tell me you'd met her before tonight?"

Fred shrugged his shoulders as he started up the car. "Forgot."

Kate shrugged her shoulders too and leaned back against the headrest. Fred had the right attitude. Lee Page-Burke was best forgotten.

Chapter 18

Kate woke up feeling as exhausted as if she had not slept at all. Small wonder after the strained dinner with Lee and Martin Burke, she thought as she examined her weary-looking face in the mirror. At least part of that problem was solved. Lee had jetted off by now, for sun, sea, sand and presumably loads of sex with her sheikh.

Opening the blinds she looked out on the wet, grey morning and envied Lee Page-Burke.

"I'm off, Kate!" Fred called up the stairs. "I'll ring you this afternoon. Chances are I'll be late tonight."

"Bye. Take care."

She walked slowly to the bathroom and admitted to herself that her weariness was caused by more than Lee Page-Burke and grey skies. Fred had been very withdrawn after they had come home from the Grand Hotel last night. In fact he had gone straight to bed. She had watched him sleep, wanting to wake him, needing to interact with him, yet knowing that he would be annoyed with her if she disturbed him. How many times could she ask him about having fertility testing? How many times did she need reassurance about Adele Sheehan?

"Grow up!" she told her reflection in the mirror now.

As she showered she realised that this growing-up process involved making a decision about the Dictaphone tape that now lay snugly on the top shelf of the bookcase in her lounge. Fact, as confirmed by the tape: Minister Henry Hennessey had strangled a pregnant girl and got away with it. Strong probability, Richard Gordon was involved in tax evasion. Indisputable Fact: she was going to be late for work if she did not get a move on.

The minute she set foot in the office Kate knew that Martin Burke was not in yet. The atmosphere was relaxed and casual, coffee cups in hands and feet on desks. Eileen rushed over to her.

"C'mon, Kate! Spill the beans! What's she like? What did you think of Mrs Page-Burke?"

"Coffee first!" Kate laughed but she was really giving herself a chance to think. She could hardly announce that Lee Page-Burke was a bitch. No. She could not tell the truth. Not all of it anyway.

"She's beautiful. Tall and slim. Auburn hair and very, very, expensive clothes."

The ploy worked. Eileen needed to hear every detail of Lee's appearance. She oohed and aahed over the descriptions.

"How was he with her? Do you think she and Martin might reconcile?"

Kate decided to answer that thorny question with an enigmatic smile. Anyway, who could say? There were certainly feelings of one sort or another between Lee and Martin. The only way to get Eileen off this topic now was to ask her about her own love life.

"How about you? Have you by any chance met Mr Right?"

Eileen settled onto the corner of Kate's desk and folded her arms across her chest. This was the signal that she was about to launch into a saga. Kate sat back and prepared to listen.

"Well, you remember the guy I saw in the supermarket near my flat?"

"The microwave dinner for one and Häagen Dazs ice cream?"

"The very same. I was in the Oasis Club on Monday night. That's half-price-before-twelve night. Anyway, guess who arrived in?"

"Mr Microwave Dinner For One?"

Eileen nodded. "Right! He was with another bloke and I was with my friend Terry. I decided to play it cool."

"Really?" Kate laughed.

Eileen tossed her hair and gave a little sniff. "I can be very, very cool when I want. Anyway, we were sitting at the bar and the lads were giving us the eye all the time but making no move. Then Terry and I decided to go out on the floor dancing. The two lads pounced. They were over to us in a flash. He's gorgeous. His name's Billy. He's an electrician. I could be in love, Kate!"

"How could you possibly know that after one dance?"

"Not just one dance!" Eileen said crossly. "We danced lots. And then we went away from the club. It was too noisy. We went to a pub and talked for hours and hours. By the way, I saw Fred at Oasis. I think the girl with him is his new designer. The girl with all the long blonde hair and the pierced navel. Isn't she drop-dead gorgeous? Why weren't you there too?"

Good question, Kate thought. She tried to shrug it off. "That was just a business thing. Something to do with Nigel Greenway."

"The man who owns the chain of garages?"

Kate nodded.

Eileen was frowning. "I don't remember seeing him at all, Kate. Are you sure he was there?"

"Did you see Martin and Lee?"

"Of course not! I wouldn't be asking you about her if I had already seen her for myself. Why? Were they in Oasis?"

Remembering Lee's remark about Adele being 'some gal to go', Kate nodded. If Lee had seen Fred and Adele on Monday night, then she and Martin must have been in Oasis too. Strange after a transatlantic flight but they were a strange couple.

"So you see, Eileen, you left the club too soon. If you had stayed you could've seen Lee for yourself. You missed seeing Nigel Greenway too. I hope Billy's worth it."

Judging by the dreamy look that came over Eileen's face, he was worth even more than a piece of gossip. Just as well Eileen was preoccupied or else she would have seen the flash of pure anger cross Kate's face. She was finding the reported sighting of her husband and the gorgeous, skinny, young designer very, very hard to handle.

When Martin finally arrived in, he was tired and a bit grey-looking. Kate sat at her desk and waited for the call to his office. It was not long coming. She picked up her property report. Maybe this would keep him quiet for a while. For once, he was sitting at his desk and not gazing out towards the park.

"Good morning, Kate. You're well?"

"Yes, thank you," she replied, taking his cue.

He obviously wanted to get down to business and leave all comment on last night's dinner aside. That suited her fine. After all, what was there to say? They worked steadily until twelve o'clock, when Martin had a client.

"Just leave that report you've been hiding underneath your notebook here for me, please. I'm guessing it's the property research I asked you to do. Am I to assume you haven't yet found the missing Dictaphone?"

Kate blushed. Hot and crimson, the flush spread up along her face.

Martin dropped the pen from his hand and leaned towards her, staring through her, right into the guilty centre of her being. "What's going on here, Kate? Is there a problem with the tape?"

She shifted on her seat. God! She was handling this so badly, behaving as if she had a big guilty secret, when all she had was evidence of someone else's guilt. Forget Henry Hennessey. She was not concerned about hurting him. She wanted to. She had sympathy for his wife and family though. Imagine having to live with that piece of scum, having to stand by his side and smile. She shivered. But her real problem was Cora. How could she add to the poor woman's troubles now? Bad enough being terminally ill without having to learn that your husband may be a criminal. Unless, of course, Cora already knew.

Martin was drumming his fingers impatiently on the desk. "Kate, do you have that tape or not?"

"It's no good, Martin. It's broken. In bits. I left the Dictaphone switched on, you see and –"

He put up his hand to stop her babbling explanation. He smiled and she had the uncomfortable feeling he was mocking her. "That's no problem. Bring it in. I have someone who can get it back together as good as new."

"You have?"

"Not here. In the States. I'll send it over by courier. This man has done work for me before. He's very discreet."

"What're you expecting to find, Martin? It's just an ordinary office tape."

"I expect I'll find whatever it is you're trying to hide from me. Now send in my client, please. We've already kept him waiting too long."

Kate was about to argue. She opened her mouth and then quickly shut it again. At least there was time. Cora would probably be beyond upsetting by the time the tape arrived back from the USA.

Patty smiled as she watched the children race around the

garden. The grass was still damp from the morning rain but the boys didn't care. They were running at each other, tumbling, rolling and generally being wild and rough. Clearys, she thought with satisfaction. She turned around and looked into the carrycot where Jonathan was sleeping. It would not be long before he would join his brothers in the rough and tumble. Not long. Just an endless stream of frustrating days and lonely nights.

She took a deep breath. The Molloys were not going to be met by a self-pitying wreck of a woman. She glanced around the kitchen and was satisfied that everything was in order. Taking Jonathan with her, she went to the bedroom to change her clothes. Heaven forbid that she greet the Royals in a track suit! She had just finished putting on a smart blouse and tailored pants when she heard a car pull into the driveway. Shit! No time for make-up. Pale and haggard it would have to be. When she got downstairs, Brian's parents were in the kitchen.

"You'll have to teach the boys some road sense. They almost ran under the wheels of my car."

Patty looked at her father-in-law and bit back her reply. The man had aged ten years since his son had died. She smiled at him and kissed Brian's mother on the cheek.

"You're very pale, Patty," she said. "Should you see a doctor? You must keep your strength up for the boys."

"I'm all right, thank you. Tea? Coffee?"

They had just settled themselves at the table with their steaming cups when the rest of the Molloy crew arrived. Brian's two brothers and their wives swanned in. The Molloys were prone to swanning. They sat and waited to be served, speaking amongst themselves as if this was not Patty's kitchen, as if she was not even there. They were discussing the size of the house and grounds, the cost of upkeep, the impracticality of a property this old.

"Fuckers!" Patty muttered into the plate of custard-cream biscuits. Then she turned around and faced them with a smile. "You're all welcome. A pity it took such terrible circumstances to bring us together here. Everyone got a cup of something to drink?"

"Sit down, Patty. You know well this is not a social visit."

David Molloy's stern tone stung her like a slap across the face. She wanted to scream at him, to call him an asshole, to hurt him. Instead she did as she was told. Brian's mother had taken Patty's usual place so she sat instead beside David's wife. Not a seating arrangement either of them would have chosen voluntarily.

Mr Molloy Senior cleared his throat and a respectful silence ensued.

"At the outset I want to say that I will not tolerate any bickering. That applies across the board."

"You hear that, Patty?"

Patty glared at David. How dare he? The shit! She opened her mouth to defend herself but Mr Molloy put his hand up.

"I mean you, too, David. Keep your mouth shut until I ask you to speak. Have some respect for your brother's memory."

Patty bowed her head and squeezed her eyes shut. She did not want Brian to be a memory. She wanted him to be dashing in and out of the house, demanding clean shirts, ringing to say he would be late home, leaving her at parties on her own because he had been called away. If only she could touch him now, if only she could feel his strong arms around her, she would never complain about the amount of time he spent at the hospital, about his lack of attention to her and the boys. Opening her eyes, she looked around the table and regarded his family. Grief was etched on every face, even David's.

"First of all, Patty," Mr Molloy continued, "I want you to know that Brian's mother and I are setting up a trust fund for the children's education. It'll become available to each of them in turn when they reach the age of eighteen and will be administered for college fees and books and any other ancillary expenses related to their third-level education."

"Thank you," Patty murmured, not sure whether she was meant to say anything or not. It was a huge relief to know her boys could go to college but how the hell was she supposed to get them from here to eighteen years of age?

"Now, David, since you're executor of Brian's will, would you please give us a report on the current financial situation?"

David snorted or jeered. Or maybe he laughed. Whichever, it was a mocking sound. "Where to begin? The truth is Brian's finances are in a mess. I don't believe he could have realised the situation he was in. He would never have chosen to leave himself so vulnerable."

"Or his wife and family," Patty added.

She was met with a battery of accusing stares from around the table. David sat smugly while she absorbed the animosity. When he decided she had suffered enough, he continued.

"Bottom line, he was way overstretched on his budget. I had a word with Gareth Owens, the manager at Brian's bank. You remember him, Dad – he played on the college team with Brian?"

Mr Molloy Senior nodded and his eyes got a far-away look as if mentally he was not here in the kitchen of The Rectory but back in the time when Brian had been a brilliant medical student and a powerful rugby scrum-half. He shook his head and then nodded at David to continue.

"Of course, we'll have to wait for Brian's accountant to draw up a balance sheet but I know from Owens that it is likely to make uncomfortable reading. Brian was very heavily in debt. And, unfortunately, not very well insured."

"What about the hospital?" his mother asked. "Surely he had some pension plan or insurance there?"

"Only medical practice insurance. He cashed in his pension for an investment."

"What investment?"

All eyes turned to Patty. She shrugged her shoulders. "I don't know. The first I heard of it was on the night of Gordon's party. Just before . . ."

Patty got up and put the kettle on again. Her hands were shaking. She had somehow hoped and prayed that a gaggle of Molloys would have the power to solve all her problems. Wave their golden wand over Brian's debts and make them disappear. It was obvious now that they were as much at a loss as she was. It was also plain that they were blaming her for the whole debacle.

"Stop fussing around, Patty. Sit down until we thrash this thing out."

Obediently, she sat as Brian's father had told her to do.

"You do realise that you may have to consider selling The Rectory?" he said.

Patty nodded at the old man. She'd have to do more than consider it. What else could she do? Eventually, when probate and all the legal business of winding up Brian's estate was through, the bank could be in a position to force her to sell the share of The Rectory that would rightfully be hers. And the children's. Unless there was some way of retrieving the money Brian had invested. David was staying very quiet about that. Gareth Owens must have told him more than he'd been willing to say to her. The good old boys' network again. It was worth asking anyway.

"Have you found out who Brian invested his money with?"

"How do you expect me to find out when you don't know? You've put us in a very embarrassing position, Patty."

"I have? I had nothing to do with any of this. I knew nothing about it."

"Exactly! If Brian could have spoken to you, then none of this mess would be happening. He obviously didn't have very much trust in you."

"David! Shut up! This is no time for recrimination."

Patty looked gratefully at Mr Molloy but looked away again when she saw the accusation in his eyes. He may have reprimanded David but he clearly agreed with him nonetheless. In the silence she heard the boys shouting and laughing outside. She squared her shoulders. Her children were depending on her. She turned towards David.

"If I sell The Rectory will that cover all the debts?"

He said nothing. He was forcing her to ask the question she did not want to ask.

"Will there be enough left to buy a smaller house?"

He shrugged as if it had nothing at all to do with him.

"You're the executor of Brian's will, David. You should know."

He looked down, avoiding her eyes. This was the first time Patty had ever seen David Molloy pass on an opportunity to outstare her. She soon found out why.

"I'm no longer executor. I have a right to refuse and I'm choosing to implement that right. As far as I'm concerned, Brian left everything to you. That includes his debts and the administration of his estate, such as it is. You can check this out with Martin Burke. He'll be acting on your behalf from now on. You'll find that I'm within my legal rights."

Patty's loss of self-control was so intense that she thought she heard a pop inside her head as it snapped. She was standing and leaning into David Molloy's face even before the angry torrent of words began to spill out of her mouth.

"I'm sure you're within your legal rights, you pompous

ass, but what about your moral obligation to your brother? It was his wish that you be executor of his will. Doesn't that mean anything to you?"

"Sit down and control yourself, Patty, please. This type of behaviour is not going to help anybody."

"I see what you mean," David's wife said loudly enough to her husband for everyone to hear. There was no doubt what she meant.

Sitting, as she had been ordered, tears in her eyes, Patty turned towards the woman. "Yes. He's right. I'm a passionate woman. Passionate about my family. If your husband wants to interpret that as ignorance and vulgarity, then let him. I'll fight for my children, for their sakes and for Brian's."

Brian's father and mother rose together. There was a sad dignity about the elderly, grief-stricken parents. They both walked over to Patty.

"I'll be instructing my solicitors about the trust fund for the children. They'll be in touch with Martin Burke. He'll explain it to you but basically it's a fund for the children's third-level education and will be administered at the appropriate time by the trustees. You'll not have to worry about handling it."

"You mean you've taken precautions to ensure I don't fritter it away on something frivolous like a home for my children! Your grandchildren!"

The old man shook his head. It was a confused, despairing gesture. He reached out and put his hand on her shoulder. She felt the pressure of his bony, shaking fingers. Brian's father looked at her and for one moment, the raw pain of loss was visible in the eyes that could have been Brian's. Patty put her arms around him but immediately he stiffened and pulled away from her.

"Keep in touch. If there's anything we can do for you or the children, let us know."

He and his wife turned in unison and walked away. The rest of the family followed in silence. Just like that, they walked out of her life.

Patty flopped down on her chair, surrounded by cups and saucers and plates of custard creams. She sat there for some time. It might have been seconds or it might have been minutes. Her mind had stopped working, suspending all sense of time and space. She became aware that she was holding a cup in her hand and, even more surprisingly, she was preparing to throw the cup. Her lips curved into a smile and feeling began to flood back into her body as the cup smashed against the wall. There was an explosion of sound as her good china broke into little pieces and skittered across the floor. She picked up a matching saucer and hurled it.

"Cool! Can we do that too, Mum?"

The boys were standing beside her, full of awe and admiration. She stood and lined them up behind the table. They each took turns throwing ware until the best china set lay in smithereens all over the tiled floor. Then Patty and her three eldest boys hugged each other and laughed until tears ran down their faces.

Martin left the office at four o'clock. Kate was busy organising correspondence until 4.30. Then, having finished her work, she decided to ring Patty.

"This is some kind of telepathy," Patty said. "I was just about to ring you. My brother-in-law has declined to be executor of Brian's will. I need to make an appointment to see Martin Burke."

"Of course. I'll organise that for you. But what kind of a shit is David Molloy?"

"The worst kind. The whole Molloy troop gave me the impression today that they're not going to have anything more to do with the children and me. They're going to pay the lads' college fees but how in the hell can they get the points for university if they don't have a place to live or enough to eat? I've spent the day trying to think of a sensible plan for the future but I'm afraid I'm failing dismally."

"How about I call over to you tonight and we could put our heads together? Maybe we'll come up with something."

"Would you, Kate? I'd really like that. Jonathan would be glad to see you too."

Kate looked up and saw Martin Burke come in the door. He had his son in his arms. A miniature of himself with the same haunting dark blue eyes.

"Patty, I've got to go. See you about eight. OK?"

"Thanks, Kate. See you."

Eileen, Anna and Rose were cooing over Robert. He was wary of all the attention, snuggling into his father for security. Martin called Kate over to him.

"I'd like you to meet Robert. We can call him Bobby now since his mother's not here. D'you think he looks like me?"

Kate regarded the solemn little face and imagined that was exactly how Martin had looked at three years of age. As she watched the child, she had an idea, the seed of a plan.

"Yes. No denying him. D'you think we could have a word in private, Martin?"

He looked surprised but nodded in the direction of his office.

Her new plan was well afoot by the time Kate left the office for home.

Guilty that she had been neglecting her diet again and conscious of the fact that she was due to have another iron injection the next day, Kate cooked a very nutritious dinner. She wrapped Fred's in foil and put it in the fridge. His latest excuse for being late was organising street entertainment for the opening of the new garages. How much time could it take to arrange for face-painting and stilt-walkers? She picked up the phone to ring him and then put it down again. Suppose he had his phone turned off? Suppose Adele answered it? Annoyed with herself for such negativity, she cleaned off the counter and put her ware into the dishwasher. She looked around her tidy and well-organised house, at the tasteful furnishings and state-of-the-art appliances. It was chic and fashionably understated. Kate looked past the décor and tried to feel the spirit of the house, the part of it that was home. She closed her eyes and pictured toys strewn on the floor, a buggy in the hall, a cot in the bedroom, tiny vests and sleeping suits on the line. A baby in her home, in her arms, in her heart. A tear squeezed from under her eyelid and trickled down her cheek. She opened her eyes quickly and went to get a tissue. Wiping her eyes, she metaphorically gave herself a kick in the butt. How pathetic was she, crying because she wanted a baby? Patty was the one who had the right to cry. Patty was the one with the right to sympathy. Kate tucked her self-pity away and went to The Rectory.

The three eldest Molloy boys looked like cherubs, all scrubbed and clean and ready for bed.

Patty smiled proudly. "Would you ever believe they spit and kick and curse?"

Kate laughed. Yes! She would! She had seen them in action and they were awesome. The children trooped obediently up the stairs and all was silent for two minutes. Then the pillow fights began. Patty must have traipsed up and down the stairs at least four times to settle fights and bring up drinks of water. The peace was glorious when they finally fell asleep. Only Jonathan remained downstairs now, sleeping soundly in his carrycot.

Kate put a mug of coffee in front of Patty. "Sit down and drink that. You must be exhausted."

Patty flopped onto a chair and sat back. She was smiling. "I know they're little terrors, Kate. They wipe their noses on their sleeves and they're forever dodging homework and causing chaos. But I love them. They're great guys. They'll be great men. They've got their priorities straight."

Priorities? The word echoed in Kate's head. What were her priorities? Getting to work on time, keeping the house clean, keeping herself in trim. Having a baby. She frowned in annoyance. There she was thinking about herself again. Selfish bitch! She looked at Patty, even tinier now and very pale. She felt ashamed.

"How are they coping with . . . with Brian not being here?"

"They've had good practice at getting on with their lives without their father."

Kate started at the bitterness of the words.

"That wasn't meant to be as sharp as it sounded," Patty said. "It's a bonus now. Brian was rarely here to put them to bed or to help the older boys with homework. He brought them to rugby at weekends. That's where they'll miss him most. I s'pose I'll have to start carting them off to the mucky pitches. I don't think their uncles are going to fall in for any of the caring duties. Fuck them."

"Amen to that."

They sat in silence as they both thought of the future without Brian Molloy. Kate was not so sure now that her plan was a good one. But she had started the ball rolling, hadn't she? She was just about to broach the subject when Patty spoke.

"Richard Gordon called to see me the other day. He said he and Cora were off on a trip."

"Yeah. He called to the office as well. Did he say where he was going?"

"I think he mentioned some kind of cities tour. London, Paris, Rome. That kind of holiday. And he mentioned Budapest too. Well for some."

Kate had a moment of doubt. She would love to tell

Patty why Richard was taking this trip. That everything in the Gordon garden was not as rosy as it seemed. But she had made a promise.

"I know you worked for him for a long time, Kate, but I don't like Richard Gordon. And it's not just his overbearing attitude. There's something creepy about him. He seems a bit shifty to me. I can't explain it. He was very nice to me when he called. Offering to do anything he could to help but yet I felt uncomfortable with him. I always have. He was Brian's friend, not mine. I can see that relationship with me going the way of the Molloys too."

Kate knew she would have to change the topic. For many reasons she felt uncomfortable discussing Richard Gordon.

"I told Martin Burke you want to see him. He said make an appointment for whenever suits you."

"Thanks, Kate. The sooner, the better. I tried to contact Gareth Owens again today but he wasn't available to speak to me. It's just so ridiculous. Brian dumps a bucketful of money into some get-rich-quick scheme and nobody, but nobody, seems to know what it is or where the money's gone. I asked Richard Gordon again when he was here. He still says he knew nothing about it. But somebody advised Brian. Somebody he knew and trusted."

Kate mulled Patty's words over in her head. They seemed to blend and mix with remembered snippets from that blasted Dictaphone tape. Brian had thrown what he had and what he could borrow into an investment scheme. Richard was somehow instrumental in organising a property scheme so secret that he dealt with it only himself. Richard was somebody Brian knew and trusted. Q.E.D! No! Richard would have told Patty and got Brian's money back. Unless the money had gone out of the country and was inaccessible. Anyway Brian had raised funds on his property. That would be too traceable for a tax-evasion scheme. But he could have invested other moneys that nobody knew about. Nobody outside the cartel, that is.

"Are you OK, Kate?"

She shook her head to clear it and smiled at Patty. She really must get her off the topic of Richard Gordon.

"I hope I'm not overstepping the bounds of friendship here but I assume you're going to need some source of income to tide you over?"

"Kate, I'm going to need a source of income to feed my children. This is what I was saying to you on the phone. What am I going to do? I could do a refresher course and go back nursing but who would look after my children then? I could stay at home and look after them but how would I feed them? My head is reeling from trying to find an answer."

"Well, I know a person who's looking for a childminder. They're willing to pay very well to get the right person. I recommended you, Patty. You're so good with children and it would mean earning some income without leaving home. Would you consider it?"

Patty's face lit up with the elfin grin Kate had not seen for some time. "Bloody brilliant, Katie O'Hanlon! Why didn't I think of that? And this house is –" The grin faded as Patty remembered that she was going to have to sell The Rectory. She shrugged. "Well, I was going to say this house is big enough for a dozen children but I don't know how long we'll be living here. Or where we go after this. How old is the child?"

"He's three and the position would be temporary anyway. It's just that this child's mother is away at the moment. Actually, it's Martin Burke's son."

Patty laughed. "My, my! Starting my nannying career at the top of the social ladder!"

"Well, I hope it works out. You can discuss details with Martin when you come in to see him. I'm sure you'll love Robert or Bobby as his father calls him. He's a beautiful child."

"I'm sure. But what's his mummy like? C'mon, Katie O'Hanlon! I want chapter and verse. You haven't given me any of the important details about the heiress. Botox, yes or no?"

They were still gossiping when Jonathan woke for his feed. Kate cuddled him before she went home to her very neat, very tidy, very empty house.

Chapter 19

It seemed that Kate had no sooner fallen asleep than her alarm rang. Still only half-awake, she dragged herself out of bed and into the shower. She heard Fred whistling in the kitchen as she dressed. Where did he get the energy? She was drained after one reasonably late night in Patty's house yet he seemed to be full of beans after . . . after what? What time had he come home last night? Frowning, she looked at herself critically in the mirror. She did look pasty. No wonder Fred was choosing to spend his time with the healthy, energetic blonde. That she may get fat and wrinkled, she thought. Yes, and spotty too. And develop a very painful infection in her piercing! Feeling less worthy but far happier after her tantrum, Kate went downstairs.

Fred had her breakfast ready for her. Orange juice, muesli and toast. He kissed her on the cheek and then stood back and looked at her.

"You look tired. What time did you get to bed?"

"Earlier than you anyway."

Even to her own ears, her voice seemed peevish and sulky. Why was it that every time she tried to let Fred know that she missed him, she just ended up nagging? She sat and drank her juice, thinking of another of her mother's favourite sayings. 'Least said, soonest mended.' Or should that be 'Least said, soonest parted'?

"You're very pale. I thought you were getting iron injections."

"I'm due to get one today. This evening after work."

"You need a break. Why don't you go to your parents' place at the weekend? The rest would do you good and anyway the cottage probably needs the once-over by now. It's a while since you've been there."

Kate looked up from her toast and smiled at him. Even the thought of going to Kerry cheered her up. "I'd love that. We'll go straight after work tomorrow evening. As a matter of fact, I'll take a half day and we can head off early."

Fred put up his hand. "Whoa there! Slow down. I'm not sure yet if I can go. But that needn't stop *you*."

"Are you trying to get rid of me? Why so anxious to pack me off to the other end of the country? Have you something planned for the weekend?"

Fred whirled around towards her. His face was flushed and his lip stuck out in a pout. He was very angry. "Where do you get off being suspicious, Kate? I've told you over and over, I'm at a critical juncture with my business. If I don't start to rake in the big orders soon, I may as well cut my losses and go back to being somebody else's employee. And I don't want that. I hope to be meeting some people at the weekend. Friends of Nigel Greenway –"

"How did I know he'd be involved?"

"Listen to yourself. You're like a spoiled child. These friends of Nigel's own a string of travel agencies. They're shopping around for an advertising company to handle their next campaign. Have you any idea how much that would mean to Lucas Advertising?"

That was the trouble about Fred's arguments, Kate thought. He had a great gift for always appearing to be in the right. How petty she would appear now if she asked him about Adele. Anyway, she did not have to ask. Adele Sheehan was always by his side. His prize possession. How had they got to this point?

"Are we in trouble, Fred?"

Suddenly Fred burst out laughing. Kate was hurt. She was suffering agonies of doubt and insecurity and he was laughing at her! Prick! He put his head to one side and looked at her. His little-boy pose.

"I could be in big trouble all right. I happened to meet Martin Burke last night."

"Because you just happened to be in the Grand Hotel. Yes. Go on."

"Well, the truth is I told him we'd be delighted to take him and his child to Kerry for the weekend."

"You what! Fred! How could you! He's my boss. And I'm not sure I even like him. I don't want him near me in my time off, let alone have to spend a weekend with him! Why did you do that? Is there something in it for you? A contract somewhere."

"Well, you know who his wife is."

"His ex-wife. And at the rate we're going we could

end up with an ex in our relationship too. This is the second time you've foisted him on me without even asking. I hope you told him the invitation is withdrawn if you can't make it."

"Well, no. Now that I think of it, I probably didn't. What difference does it make? You're making a big fuss about nothing."

"Fred Lucas, if you're not going to Kerry you can tell Martin Burke he's not either. Or else . . . or else . . ."

Lost for words, she jumped up from the table and grabbed her car keys, staying in the house only long enough to get the Dictaphone with the broken tape from the top shelf of the bookcase.

Kate had calmed down some by the time she reached work. She even approached normality during the intervals she managed to forget the prospect of telling Martin Burke that he and his son could not come to her parents' cottage. She knew beyond doubt that Fred would not make that call. God! Fred was a dickhead!

"Good morning, Kate. Who ate your cake?"

Kate turned around to see Eileen, disgustingly smiley. She must have met up with Billy again last night. By the ice-cream cabinet in the supermarket, no doubt. Kate did not have long to wait to hear the details.

Martin Burke seemed pretty pleased with himself too when he arrived in. The white smile was flashing all over the office. Kate began to rehearse a speech in her head as she followed him into his office. She would be very apologetic. And very disappointed, of course, but . . . but what? What could she say? That Fred was not yet sure whether he could make Kerry at the weekend? Maybe he could, or maybe not. That she could not face the thought of Martin and his son in her Kerry sanctuary, in the only spot in the whole world where she felt safe? She would think of something plausible. She would have to.

Martin sat at his desk and grinned at her. "I can't tell you how much Bobby and I are looking forward to our trip to Kerry. 'Twas really nice of you and Fred to invite us. It'll take Bobby's mind off missing his mum."

The words in her head knotted into a ball and dropped into the pit of her stomach. He had played the child card so well. Fuck! Her mouth opened but no words came out.

"Were you burning the midnight oil last night?" he asked. "Not exactly bright-eyed and bushy-tailed this morning, are you?"

Well! How dare he! He was the original morning grouch. She welcomed her hot flash of temper. Anger was far more straightforward than the doubts that were eating into her.

"Actually I was late at Patty Molloy's house last night. I went to ask her about minding Bobby."

He had the grace to look apologetic. "Sorry. I didn't mean to upset you. What did Patty say?"

"She said she'll contact you today. I'm sure you'll find that she is the ideal person to care for your son."

"The staff in the hotel crèche are good but you know yourself. Not an ideal situation."

Kate had to bite her tongue. He was chatting to her as if she herself had been through this situation. How could she know anything about crèches in five-star hotels? The man was a moron. But for the time being at least, this moron was her boss. Reaching into her bag, she pulled out the Dictaphone and handed it to him.

"If you take a look inside you'll see the tape's destroyed. Are you sure you can get it fixed?"

"I told you I've a contact. The man's a genius. Maybe you'd organise a courier for me today?"

Kate wrote down his instructions and felt a few qualms. Should she tell him now what was on the tape? But then how could she explain not handing it over earlier? Was she herself committing a crime? Suppressing evidence? Perverting the course of justice? Holy shit! No. She definitely could not tell Martin Burke, or anybody else, that she had heard the tape.

"About that property report you gave me, Kate."

She stopped writing and looked up at him.

"I've discovered that International Landform Securities and Leaf Ltd are two offshore companies. Registered in Gibraltar."

Kate could almost feel the hairs stand up on the back of her neck. That tape was going to haunt her for the rest of her days. It echoed in her head again now. 'Tax evasion. Offshore companies.' Kate frowned. She could not understand how a man as clever as Richard Gordon would have left any evidence if he had decided to commit a crime. How much did Martin Burke know?

"So? Lots of people own offshore companies. Nothing sinister in that."

"No. Of course, not. A perfectly legitimate instrument.

But it does lend itself to abuse of one sort and another."

"And is that what you suspect here? D'you think the Post-its and the notebook page add up to an international scam? Do you honestly believe Richard Gordon would have left evidence for you to find if he was involved in any illegal venture?"

"Events caught Richard unawares. The minister's trial kept him so busy that he hadn't cleared everything up before I arrived. Then I took over the office sooner than he'd expected. He didn't have the opportunity to remove everything he wanted to. Not that he's worried. Do you know what catches people out? How they give themselves away? Arrogance. Ask yourself whether Richard Gordon's an arrogant man or not."

Kate did not have to think long about that. Of course, Richard Gordon was an arrogant man. But even with the evidence of the tape, the property files and the mysterious notebook page, Kate still found it hard to believe that the man who had been her boss for seven years had been party to a fraud. Harder still to credit that he might have been the person to advise Brian Molloy to throw his family's future away. Kate remembered Patty's little face, pinched with worry, and she almost told Martin Burke about the tape. Almost.

Chapter 20

Friday traffic leaving the city was chaotic. Kate regretted not taking a half-day. She could have beaten the rush. If she had not spent the day dithering over whether to travel to Kerry or not she could have been here in daylight. It was so dark by the time she reached the turn-off for her parents' cottage that she felt rather than saw the hills.

The car bumped and rattled over the rutted laneway. Lights were still switched on in the McCarthy house. Kate smiled as she noticed the curtain on the front window part just a little. Enough for Noreen to peep through and report to her brother Phil that young Kate O'Hanlon was back on a visit. As she hooted the horn and waved, the curtain immediately closed. She would meet Noreen and Phil tomorrow, they would pretend to be surprised to see her and she would pretend to believe them.

Kate stopped the car a half mile further up the lane and got out. She was home. Stretching, she took deep breaths of the sweet air. She could not see the smoke but she knew the McCarthys had a big fire blazing because the peaty aroma of burning turf wafted up the hill.

Opening the lock she swung the gate back. She drove in and left the car lights on until she had opened the front door. The house was freezing. After she had switched on the heating, it took ten minutes to unload the stock of things she had brought with her. She flopped down on a chair and looked at the heap she had piled on the kitchen table. Four different cereals! What did three-year-olds eat for their breakfast? Specifically a three-year-old who was being catered for in the luxury of the Grand Hotel? Coco Pops sprinkled with gold dust?

Extra towels and blankets lay beside the provisions. And she had brought a whole box full of detergents, deodorisers and polishes.

She got up wearily and put on the kettle. Caffeine was urgently needed to put some energy back into her before she tackled the cleaning. Even though the air was beginning to lose its chill she still huddled into her coat and cradled the hot cup in her hands. Her gaze travelled around the kitchen from one piece of furniture to the next, from one memory to another.

The big old range had long since been replaced but if she squinted her eyes now she could see her mother sitting by the fire, knitting. Her mam had always been knitting or sewing. Her hands were never idle. She used to make Aran sweaters for a tourist shop in Killarney, fashioning twists and cables from the cream-coloured yarn, never using a pattern. A simple woman with a complex skill. Kate smiled as she remembered the excitement when a batch of sweaters had been delivered to the store and Mam had got her payment. That was treat time. New shoes or maybe a new coat. For Kate. Everything had been for Kate. She squinted again and time passed on. Her mother got stooped, her fingers bent, the knuckles knobbled with arthritis. And still she knitted. For Kate.

Hot tears burned behind her eyelids. No matter how she squinted her eyes or tilted her head, no matter how hard she imagined, all she had left of her parents was a memory. Her body, her soul, ached for the protection of their total commitment to her, for the warmth of their unconditional love. Putting her head down on the worn surface of the timber table, she cried for her parents, for the security of her childhood, for the passion of the early years of her marriage.

When she had cried so much that there were no tears left, Kate lifted her head from the table and took a deep breath. The hard lump of sadness which had been lodged in her throat for the past week had dissolved. There was nothing left inside now but the coldness of reality. Her husband had manipulated and manoeuvred so that he could spend the weekend with another woman. A young and very attractive woman. He could, and did, talk endlessly about the importance of the meetings he had with the travel-agency people, about how vital this contract was to the future of Lucas Advertising. Kate did not doubt that. What she could not accept was how Fred had so cynically packed her off to Kerry out of his way. Did he think she was a fool, so naïve that she could not see what was going on? 'Adele is brilliant. A creative genius. The leading graphic designer. Adele. Adele. Adele.' Fuck Adele! Tears came to her eyes again as Kate realised that is exactly what Fred wanted to do. Maybe they were at it now, his hands all over the young girl's tanned body.

Jumping up from the table, she ripped off her coat and rolled up her sleeves. Her head would burst if she allowed herself to think any more about Fred and Adele. The cleverest part of Fred's plan was that he had put Kate under an obligation. Martin Burke was looking forward to his trip here. More importantly, Bobby was excited about coming to see the hills and cows. She had threatened but had not had the courage to tell them they could not come. What would she have said? 'Sorry, Martin. I have to stay here and watch over my husband. I think he's having an affair. Besides, I don't feel comfortable sharing with you. Sorry your little three-year-old's going to be very disappointed.' She had attempted several times in the office today to tell Martin the weekend in Kerry was off. Each time she thought she had enough courage to say it, he just happened to mention how excited Bobby was about the trip. She had been manipulated into a corner. And a lonely place it was.

The only blessing was that Martin would be driving down himself. He had decided to buy a car. It would not be ready for him until the morning so at least that gave her time to get organised. She cleaned and scrubbed late into the night. The old cottage was gleaming by the time she fell exhausted into bed.

Kate woke with a start. There was a knock on the door. Shit! Glancing at her watch she saw that it was after ten o'clock in the morning. She had meant to be up at cockcrow, all ready to greet her guests. Martin must have left at dawn in order to be arriving here now. Throwing on her dressing-gown, she went to the door and was relieved to see her elderly neighbour, Noreen McCarthy, standing there.

"I saw your car and said I'd come and say hello. When did you arrive?"

Smiling, Kate asked the other woman in.

Noreen looked around and admired the kitchen. "You've been busy, Kate. The place is shining. I hope you don't think I've been neglecting it. If you'd let me know you were coming I'd have had it ready like I always do."

"It was a last-minute decision to come here. I would've let you know otherwise."

Noreen's "Hmm" in reply showed she clearly did not believe Kate. Ironic, since it was true. Kate had hoped up to the very last moment that Fred would ask her to stay with him, to accompany him to meet the travel agents, to be the one who stood by his side as he negotiated for the future of Lucas Advertising. That is really why she had been so late arriving here. Waiting for the reprieve that never came. Noreen coughed, reminding Kate that she was not alone. She smiled at the old lady.

"How's Phil? Well, I hope."

"Not a bit wrong with him. Doesn't stop him complaining though. Men are all the same."

As a child Kate had been terrified of Noreen's brother. She had always thought of Phil as 'the pointy man', a life-sized, evil elf. His chin, nose, even his eyebrows were pointed. He wore a perpetual frown and his collection of narrow features was topped with a bald skull that rose to a shining point. He and Noreen had been arguing for the best part of a century but yet there was no doubting their devotion to each other.

"Is Fred still in bed?"

"He's not here. He's very busy at the moment. No time to take a break."

"Pity," Noreen said. "I made his favourite soda bread. And a spotted cake for you."

Kate took the bag Noreen offered. She opened it up and the aroma of the freshly baked bread filled the kitchen. She hugged the old woman.

"You're all bones!" Noreen accused. "Sit down there. I'll cut a bit of that bread for you. Are you looking after yourself at all?"

Kate sat back and allowed Noreen to prepare breakfast. She knew it was as important for the old lady to do this as it was for her to have someone fussing over her. Carer and cared-for sat happily together in the warm kitchen.

"I'll be having guests calling later. My boss and his little boy."

Noreen digested this piece of information. Kate prepared for the barrage of questions.

"And the boss's wife?"

"She's abroad. Anyway, they're divorced."

"Will they be staying?"

When Kate nodded yes, Noreen frowned.

"Does Fred know?"

Kate was tempted to tell Noreen that Fred had organised

all this, that the whole trip had been a plan to get her out from under his feet. She looked into the aged and weather-beaten face and knew that she could never do or say anything to upset her. The very idea of Fred Lucas fucking around would be enough to send her into a tailspin. She caught Noreen's hand.

"Fred knows all about it, Noreen. He and Martin Burke are friends. They went to college together."

"I see. Well, don't forget I'm nearby if you need me."

There was no doubt about that. Noreen would make it her business to be looking out for the thirty-two-year-old woman she still considered a child. And Kate enjoyed the looked-after feeling.

When Noreen had gone Kate went into the front garden of the cottage and looked down along the lane. There was no trace of a car turning off the main road and heading up the laneway towards the hills. She did not know what type of a car Martin Burke would be driving but guessed it would be big and expensive.

It was breezy. A lovely swirling wind that caught her hair and tossed it gently around her face. She walked as far as the gate. Far below, to her left, lay the road, the access to the outside world. To her right the path got narrower and steeper as it wound up into the hills. She glanced at the mobile phone she held in her hand. Martin would surely ring to let her know he was on his way. Opening the gate, she stepped onto the lane. Her hesitation lasted only a split second. She clipped her mobile onto the belt of her jeans and began to stride uphill.

Her feet found grip on the stony path and soon she had fallen into a fast-paced walking rhythm. She had not invited Martin Burke here. Why should she waste this glorious morning, hanging around waiting for him to arrive? As the breeze strengthened and the path got steeper she continued her climb, every step bringing a fresh problem to mind. Adele Sheehan. Richard Gordon. Henry Hennessey. Nigel Greenway. Patty. She was almost to the top before she realised that at some stage during her ascent the problems had left her, carried away on the wind. She stood and looked up ahead. No point in going on. The summit was wreathed in mist. Finding a nice flat rock she sat and took a few minutes to get her breath back.

She stretched out on the rock and relaxed, noticing the clouds scudding, the river glistening in the valley below, the scent of heather on the breeze.

She woke with a start, stiff and sore where the rock had pressed into her shoulder. The mist had crept down from the hilltop. With the world veiled in moist fog, it was difficult to gauge what time it was. Peering at her watch she realised that she had slept for an hour. She pursed her lips to whistle for Shep and then laughed at herself. She was taking her nostalgic trip too far. The last Shep had died shortly before her father. That must have been Shep Mark Twenty. Their dogs had always been named Shep and had always been black and white Border collies.

After stretching to ease out her stiff muscles, she began her descent. She remembered Martin Burke. She checked her phone and saw two missed calls. Then she deliberately ignored them, let the thought go and gave herself up to the peaceful spirit of the hills.

He had bought a Volvo. A big green Volvo. It took up most of the space in front of the cottage. He had also obviously let himself in.

When Kate arrived into the kitchen she almost laughed. Martin and Bobby were seated at the table and Noreen was plying them with soda bread and her home-made strawberry jam.

"Eat up now, child," she was telling Bobby. "You'll never be a big man like your daddy if you don't finish your food."

Martin stood when he saw her. He was staring.

Kate realised then that she must look wild, her hair windswept and curly from the damp. "I'm sorry I wasn't here when you arrived. I couldn't resist a little hike uphill. How was the journey down? Any problem finding the cottage?"

Martin laughed and nodded towards Noreen. "Noreen spotted us searching for your cottage. She led us here and I must say she's been looking after us very well. It's years since I ate Spotted Dick."

"Spotted Dick!" Bobby repeated in his American accent.

Kate laughed. It had always amused her to hear people refer to the sweet white soda bread with currants as 'Spotted Dick'.

"Well, I'll leave you young people now," said Noreen. "Don't forget to bring Bobby down when Phil is milking the cows. The little American should see where the milk for his cornflakes comes from."

Kate sighed in relief. Problem solved. Bobby ate cornflakes and she had brought a big packet of them. Maybe she should set Noreen on Fred. She would not be long ferreting out the answers to the hard questions.

There was a moment's awkward silence when the old lady left. Martin was still giving her surprised looks and she was returning them. He looked absolutely stunning in a cream crew-necked sweater and jeans. Sweater and jeans were close-fitting and showed off his well-muscled body to perfection. His tan seemed deeper and his smile whiter.

"You look different, Kate. Your native environment suits you."

She laughed self-consciously. Different was one way of putting it. She put her hand to her hair and tried to smooth it.

Martin came over to her. "No. Leave it. It really suits you with all the waves and curls. More like Kate Bush in the *Wuthering Heights* video than Kate Lucas."

"And you look more Heathcliff than Martin Burke."

She bit her lip. What had possessed her to say that? He did look dark and brooding and very attractive but she had sounded like a simpering idiot. And he had managed to make her red-faced yet again. She began to tidy off the table and then remembered that she had not shown them to their rooms yet.

"I wasn't sure whether Bobby would like to sleep with you or on his own. Just in case, I got two rooms ready. You can decide yourselves. Will I show you?"

"Bobby stay with Daddy," the child piped up and the matter was decided.

Kate finished the tidying up while they brought in their overnight bags. Like any child, Bobby seemed to have an inordinate amount of luggage. The just-in-case gear, as Patty called it.

She got the dinner ready while they unpacked. By the time they were organised she had a stew on the hob and a rice pudding in the oven. The settings on the cooker were turned down low so she could forget about them for the rest of the afternoon. Martin and Bobby were wearing jackets when they came back into the kitchen.

"Are you too tired to come out again, Kate? Can't wait to get grass under my feet."

Kate gave the cooker a last check and grabbed her jacket. She could think of nothing better now than getting out of the uncomfortably intimate atmosphere of the cottage. When they reached the gate, Bobby began squealing in delight.

"Dog! Look, Daddy! Dog!"

Noreen and Phil's collie stood on the lane, wagging his tail. He was half-blind and half-deaf. Almost as ancient as his owners and every bit as good-natured. Kate noticed Martin flinch as the child reached his hand towards the dog.

"You needn't worry. That's Rex. He's very gentle. I bet Noreen sent him up for Bobby."

Martin relaxed as Rex wagged his tail and looked expectantly from one of them to the other, ready to accompany them wherever they were off to. Kate looked back up the hill. It was still misty and she did not feel like climbing again anyway.

"We could go to the ruins of the old castle. Four, maybe five fields away. How about it? Would Bobby be able for it?"

"How about it, son? Will we go to see the castle?"

The child jumped up and down with excitement.

Noreen McCarthy was smiling as she discreetly watched man, woman, child and dog set off across the fields.

Rex and Bobby went ahead, scattering birds and rabbits as they scampered excitedly though the fields.

There was something about the way Martin scaled the ditches and scanned the horizon that made Kate wonder.

"I had you pegged for a city man. Am I wrong?"

Martin stopped and looked down at her. His expression was very serious. "I'm from a farming background too. To be honest I couldn't wait to get away from it. I felt the pull of city lights from a very early age. Maybe it was the fact that I was the second son. I knew my brother would inherit the farm and that I'd have to make my future elsewhere. Now, I'm not so sure."

"So, you've got a brother. What about the rest of your family?"

They continued to walk as he told her about his brother and two sisters and his parents. The clouds were filling up and seemed to be dropping lower. Spatters of rain were falling by the time they reached the castle ruins. They took shelter under the only section of roof that remained intact.

"Shoot! I should've brought the camera," Martin said as he watched Bobby and Rex sitting on an age-smoothened block of granite, the child's chubby arms around the old dog's neck.

"I think, New Yorker or not, there are some farming genes in that boy's make-up," Kate remarked.

"Ah! New York. The Big Apple. Rotten at the core."

"That sounds very bitter, Martin."

He looked at her and she noticed that his eyes were even darker in the gloomy light. They were sad eyes, full of something that looked very like regret in the gloom of the castle walls.

"I suppose that's not fair. It's a wonderful place. So energising. So full of opportunity. So now. I could never have been as successful as I've been if I'd stayed here."

"Professionally?"

"Well, yes. And financially too. I commanded fees that would be unattainable here. That calibre customer base doesn't exist in Ireland. We don't have the population to support it."

Kate wanted to ask him why he had come back. Why had he left the land of milk and honey if he thought it impossible to build up as lucrative a practice here? Guessing the answer had nothing to do with his career, she decided to stay quiet. The rain was easing up. It was time to leave the shelter of the castle walls. Bobby ran out into the field and pointed up. The sun was struggling through the clouds and a magnificent rainbow straddled the sky.

"Let's find the pot of gold," Kate suggested and the

three of them and Rex happily set off towards the end of the rainbow.

Darkness was closing in as they arrived back at the cottage. They were welcomed by the aroma of beef stew and rice pudding. Kate turned on the ring under the pot of potatoes she had already peeled. By the time they had all dried off and dressed in warm clothes, dinner was cooked. Kate watched with interest as Martin cut up his son's meat and mashed his potatoes for him. She was seeing a softness and vulnerability about him that she had not suspected. He laughed as the child ate spoonfuls of the dinner.

"You'd never believe he was a fussy eater, would you? I'll know what to do in future when he refuses to eat."

"A whiff of mountain air's the best appetiser known to man," agreed Kate.

They had just finished when there was a tap on the door. Noreen, draped in a big oilskin, poked her head into the kitchen.

"Ready to milk the cows, Bobby?"

The child jumped up and ran to Noreen. Martin raised his eyebrow at Kate.

"You go ahead," she said. "I'll just tidy up here."

She went to the door and watched as Martin, Noreen, Bobby and Rex piled into the new Volvo. Then she laughed out loud. Imagine what Eileen and the rest of the staff in the office would say if they could see Martin Burke heading off to milk the cows! The trouble was she knew what they would say. That was why they could never be told about this trip.

When she had finished in the kitchen she went to the shed and brought in some kindling and a basket of turf. She set the fire in the sitting room, put a match to it and sat back watching the flames blaze up and then shorten and change colour as the turf caught and the heat intensified. Her eyes wandered around the room. Her mother's pride and joy. The parlour. The place where dignitaries such as the priest and the doctor had been invited to sip tea from her best china cups. It was a room full of flickering shadows and memories now, as the flames from the fire created highlights and dark corners. This was where she had seen both her parents for the last time, each in their turn laid out in their coffins, candles burning on the little table, neighbours coming to view their remains, rosary beads wound around their dead fingers.

She shook her head and stood up abruptly. These memories belonged to another age. A part of her life that was gone, buried with her parents. She dismissed the treacherous thought that she had ever been ashamed of them, embarrassed by their lack of sophistication, their uncultured accents and their elementary education. That silly phase had come and gone with her first year in college. It had not lasted long. Neither had they. She had never had the opportunity to pay them back, to give them all the things that would have made up for their lifetime of struggle.

Annoyed for thinking herself into a melancholy mood, Kate switched on the lights. She was just about to choose a disc to put on the stereo when her phone rang. She saw Fred's name come up and was very surprised to realise she had not thought about him for several hours.

"Hi, Kate. How are you? How's life in the hills?"

"Great, thanks. We had a lovely day. Wet, but we were able to get out. Bobby seems to be enjoying himself."

She had been about to add that Bobby's daddy seemed to be having a good time too but then she realised that she did not know. Martin Burke was impossible to read. Those eyes hid his reactions very efficiently. "How about you? Have you met up with the travel agents yet?"

"No. I'm just getting ready to go now. I got through a lot of work today though. Keep your fingers crossed for me. These guys could change our lives."

Kate tapped her foot in annoyance. So he wanted to change their lives, did he? She longed to ask him just what changes he wanted to make and if his future plans included a family. Instead she asked him what he was going to wear going out. If he thought that was strange, he did not say so.

"My navy suit and I think a white shirt and maybe a red tie. I must make the right impression."

"I'm sure you will. Have you eaten?"

"No. We'll be having dinner at the club."

Kate paused. Should she ask who 'we' meant? Knowing that it would include Adele, she skipped the question.

"I'll see you tomorrow night, then. Take care. And good luck."

"Is Burkey there? I'll have a word with him."

"He's gone down to Noreen and Phil with Bobby. Milking the cows."

Fred laughed. "I don't believe it. Cow shit on his

Guccis! Right then. I'd better be off. Love you. See you soon."

Just as well he had not waited for her reply. She did not know how to answer. Making a response to his glib 'love you' was getting increasingly more difficult. There seemed to be a widening gap between her definition of love and Fred's idea of what total commitment meant. She was relieved to hear the Volvo drive up the lane. At least she had something novel to worry about now. How was she going to pass the evening with Martin Burke and his son?

Kate realised how out of touch with the world of three-year-olds she was when Martin asked her if he could put on a video for Bobby before he went to bed. She mentally scanned her store of videos from *Pretty Woman* to *Saving Private Ryan*. Nothing remotely suitable for a child.

Martin grinned. "Take that scared look off your face. I've got a stock of Disney tapes. Care to watch *Bear in the Big Blue House*?"

Bobby clapped his hands at the mention of his favourite video. Kate had to quell the urge to pick him up and cuddle him. He was like a little cherub in his cosy sleeping suit. She put more turf on the fire while Martin got the tape. Then the three of them settled down to watch the video. Bobby's eyelids began to droop. He was sound asleep before the video was halfway through. Martin picked him up in his arms to carry him into bed. Kate stood to look at the child. He was the beautiful offspring of beautiful parents. So privileged, and yet here he was, in the arse end of Kerry, in a stranger's house, while his mother was off on the other side of the world. Poor little mite! How could Lee bear to leave him? Kate bent and gently kissed his forehead.

When Martin came back from the bedroom he had a bottle of wine in his hand.

"Grown-up time," he said. "Would you like a glass?"

Kate nodded. She was feeling increasingly uneasy. It felt so odd being here alone with Martin Burke. Shit, she didn't really know the man at all. Suppose he was some kind of a rapist? Maybe that was the reason he had left America in such a hurry. He could be a mass murderer, wanted in all states, a price on his head. Kate gave herself a talking to. That was a ridiculous line of thinking. If there was any suspicion about his character he could not be practising law here. Global communications had ensured there was no escape for criminals now. But she still felt uncomfortable. She jumped up from her chair.

"I'll get glasses."

She practically ran into the kitchen. When she turned around from the cupboard, Martin was standing at the kitchen door, leaning his shoulder against the frame. She dropped the glasses. They made such a loud bang she waited to hear Bobby cry. But the only sound was the crackling of the fire in the sitting room and the tick of the grandfather clock.

"I'm sorry, Kate. I'm scaring you. Do you want me to go?"

"No. No. I'm sorry. It's just that . . . well, just . . ."

"You've suddenly realised you're in a very isolated place with a man you don't really know?"

She nodded. That is exactly what she had been thinking. Except that she was also wondering how Fred could say he loved her and still put her in this position.

"Tell you what," Martin said. "You go in by the fire and sit down. I'll sweep up here and get glasses. Then I'll tell you about myself. That way I won't be such a stranger to you."

She smiled and went into her mother's precious parlour. Sitting down, she closed her eyes and said a quick prayer to her parents to watch over her. When she opened her eyes again, Martin was handing her a glass of wine. He pulled his chair over to the other side of the fire and sighed as he stretched his long legs out.

"I love the smell of a turf fire. I didn't realise I had missed it. Here's to bogs and logs!"

They raised their glasses and laughed.

"Now, Kate. I'll tell you about Martin Burke. I was born in Donegal thirty-five years ago, the second son of Gillian and Robert Burke. I went to primary and secondary school locally. I attended college in Dublin, as you know. That's where I first met Fred Lucas. After graduation I joined the law firm of Woods, King & Doherty. Two years later I took off to the States to make my fortune. There I met and married the famous Lee Page, heiress to the Page fortune. It was there too, that the selfsame Lee met and fell in love with Sheikh Al Bahar. While still married to me. And so, here I am, new owner of Richard Gordon's practice, baby-sitting my son while my ex-wife gads off with her new partner. And I'm halfway up a mountain in Kerry with my PA who is terrified that I'm about to attack her!"

Kate laughed. "That sounds more like Martin Burke in a nutcase rather than a nutshell! Anyway, you didn't really tell me anything I don't already know."

"What do you want to know?"

"Well, like why you came back from the States."

Martin leaned forward and gazed into the fire. Kate looked at the flames too. They were hypnotic, dancing and leaping and changing colour. Eventually he lifted his eyes and looked at her. She could hear the sadness in his voice.

"I was obsessed with Lee. I adored her. She was everything I thought I wanted in a woman. It took a long time for me to realise that she'd married me because her father didn't want her to. The same reason she's having a relationship with the Arab. If her father pushes her too far, she'll marry Al Bahar too. I got tired of her games, tired of her old man trying to run my life. Tired of all the old men in silk suits. I fought for custody of Bobby but I lost. No matter what, though, I'm damned if I let her take him to Saudi."

"Are you sorry now that you came back or is it too soon to say?"

"More like I'm sorry I stayed away so long. This is a great country. We're at the cutting edge of technology but yet we retain most of the old values. People like Noreen and Phil could only exist here."

"They're a dying breed. Even here."

They certainly were. The Gus Cochranes and Henry Hennesseys were beginning to hold sway. She dismissed the thought of those thugs and wondered instead if Martin still loved Lee. He was certainly hurting. Wrapped up in her own thoughts, she jumped when he spoke.

"That's me done and dusted. Now, what about you?"

Kate waved her hand around the room and smiled. "This is me. Kate O'Hanlon, only child of the late Kitty and Paudie. Local primary school. Secondary in Killarney. College in Cork. I moved to Dublin after my parents died and was introduced to Fred by a mutual friend. PA to Richard Gordon for the past seven years. Now your PA. That's about it."

Martin stood and got the bottle of wine. He reached for her glass and refilled it. He remained standing beside her, disconcerting her with his direct gaze.

"I think there are two Kates."

"Really?"

He put the bottle on the coffee table and squatted down beside her chair. He was so close that she could smell his aftershave – the subtle, expensive one. Suddenly she felt a new fear. It was a dread that she would put out her hand to touch his face. Her fingers itched to trace the outline of his lips, to feel the stubble on his chin. A film of sweat prickled the skin on her back. Desperate that this mad urge would get the better of her, she picked up her glass and cradled it in both hands.

"Yes. Really," he said softly. "There's Kate Lucas, the quietly efficient and loyal PA. She would appear to be compliant to someone who has not seen the flashes of anger in her eyes from time to time, the stubborn set of her chin when she thinks her boss is being an idiot."

She was about to deny that she had ever thought he was a fool but she saw the futility of it.

"Unsubstantiated evidence!" she laughed.

Her vain attempt to lighten the mood did not work. The atmosphere in Kitty's parlour was supercharged. She was entranced by the shadows his long eyelashes cast onto his cheekbones. When he raised his hand and gently touched her hair, she felt a shock pass though her body. He was whispering now, his voice as soft as a caress.

"Then we have Katie O'Hanlon. Wild and beautiful. At one with nature. A strong and compassionate woman but yet vulnerable. Someone who needs to be protected from the world beyond her beloved hills and fields."

Kate stared into his beautiful dark eyes, trying to see his soul as he had examined hers. There were many hidden dimensions to Martin Burke. Ambitious and successful with all the necessary ruthlessness and arrogance his level of achievement required. Yet she had seen his soft side too. The caring father, the man who respected Noreen and Phil, the man who saw beyond her veneer of cool efficiency. A perfect match for the Kate he had described. Her hands began to shake.

Afraid that she would let the glass fall again, she leaned forward to put it down. Making the glass safe had been her intention. Brushing close enough to Martin Burke to feel the heat of his body, the strength of his muscles, had not been planned. By the time she realised his arms were around her, she was beyond analysing her motives. Closing her eyes, she rested her face against his strong chest. His heart beat as strongly as hers. She knew now what he meant about being protected from the world beyond. Nothing existed in time or space except this haven of safety in his arms.

His lips brushed her neck. They were as soft as she had imagined. Turning her face up to him, their lips met in the gentlest of kisses. He slipped his hand around the back of her neck and drew her closer to him. Her lips parted under his. The sensations from her mouth rippled through her body. He pulled her to her feet and they stood together, their bodies aching for each other. His hand slipped underneath her sweater and cupped her breast. A gasp of sheer ecstasy escaped her lips. Giving in to her urgent need to explore his body, she caressed him, stroking his warm brown skin. Every nerve was alive to the pleasure of his well-muscled back, his narrow hips, his taut buttocks, his –

"Bobby have a cuddle too?"

They jumped apart. The child was standing in the doorway, his teddy bear under his arm. Kate's legs gave way underneath her and she flopped into her chair. Martin strode towards his son and picked him up. He carried him over to the fireplace.

"What do you think, Kate? May Bobby have a cuddle?"

She was stunned by his light tone. How could he be so casual two seconds after his son had caught him about to have sex with a woman who was a stranger to the child? Then it hit her that Martin was not the person cheating. He was single. Free and available. She was the one who had done the unforgivable. She was the cheat.

She tried to smile at the child. "Of course, Bobby can have a cuddle. A big one."

Bobby put his hot little arms around their necks and snuggled into them. In two minutes he was fast asleep again. Martin carried him back to bed and Kate wondered if she should run away before he came back into the sitting room. She was angry with herself, embarrassed, ashamed. Fuck! What had she done? Put her marriage, her job at risk. And for what? A quick shag! Even as the thought materialised, she knew it had been more than that. Her body still tingled from the touch of his hands on her. Unbidden, an image of Fred flashed across her mind, all curly hair and boyish appeal. She jumped up and dashed into the kitchen.

Needing to do something to banish the haunting image of her husband, she put two cups of milk in the microwave to heat. Cocoa. Her mother had always given her cocoa to help her sleep. Her mother! God! Had the spirit of Kitty been watching as her daughter groped a man? A man who was not her husband. A man she barely knew. And in the sacred parlour too! She got the packet of cocoa powder and spooned some into two mugs. She did not have to ask Martin. She knew he would like it. There were a lot of things they seemed to know instinctively about each other. Knowing how to control each other's physical passion did not seem to be one of them. The milk was heated and the cocoa ready by the time Martin came into the kitchen.

"Ah! Cocoa!" he said. "It's a lifetime ago since I had cocoa at bedtime."

Kate looked at him and felt anger replace all the nice tingly sensations. "How can you be so cool? We almost – well, we almost did something we'd both regret. And you talk about cocoa!"

"Kate, we had a kiss. Now we need to talk. Sit down."

Unable to think logically for herself, Kate did as she was told. They sat at opposite sides of the kitchen table, both making sure that there was no point of physical contact between them.

"Delicious," he said as he sipped his drink.

"For Christ's sake, Martin! Forget the damned cocoa! What're we going to do?"

"How do you mean? What do you want to do?"

"I want that scene in the sitting room to never have happened. I want to never lay eyes on you again. I want . . ." Tears welled in Kate's eyes and trickled down her cheeks.

Martin reached out his hand towards her and then drew it back again. "I'm sorry, Kate," he said softly. "It should never have happened. It was my fault."

Kate thought back over their embrace and the time leading up to it. She realised now that it had been waiting to happen. Two lonely people, isolated in the warmth and privacy of Kitty's parlour. Of course they would have to accept some responsibility. But not totally.

"It wasn't your fault, Martin. Or all mine either. Fred and Lee must share the blame. Especially Fred. He practically railroaded us into spending the weekend here together. I really don't understand him any more."

Martin frowned. When he spoke, it was as if he was carefully measuring each word. "Fred led me to believe he'd be here with us for the weekend. You should have told me he changed his mind." He paused. "He's not the man I knew before I went to the States. Of course, that was a long time ago. We were carefree students then. Maybe we all had different values."

"What do you mean?"

"Well, he was fun to be around. A good sense of humour. A team player. Someone you could call on if you were in trouble. Someone you could trust. The Fred I see now is different. People don't seem to matter that much to him any more. Nothing matters but getting Lucas Advertising off the ground."

Kate bowed her head. She could not be so disloyal as to comment on Martin's opinion. But he was right. Fred did not give a flying fuck about anyone or anything except Lucas Advertising. And maybe Adele Sheehan.

She looked up at Martin. "You're astute."

"I've been there, Kate. Marrying Lee was all part of my career plan but I didn't admit that to myself at the time. She's a very beautiful woman as you know. But bit by bit I realised that I had fallen in love with a lifestyle. Money, status, contacts. If Lee had been working behind the counter in WalMart, I probably wouldn't have given her a second glance. Bobby changed my perspective on life. Fathering a child brings you back to your childhood values. The important ones. You've never lost your way. I admire you for that."

She should have contradicted him, told him about how her rural background had embarrassed her, how she had envied the sophisticates, wheedled her way onto guest lists, copied the clothes and manners of the people she had considered to be socially superior. She stayed quiet. She had already bared too much of her soul to Martin Burke and how was that going to impinge on their employer-employee relationship?

"D'you think we'll be able to work together any more, Martin? Will it be too awkward now?"

He shrugged his shoulders. "We'll have to see how it pans out. I don't anticipate a problem. We probably shouldn't be alone together again though. We obviously share a very strong physical attraction."

Kate twisted her mug around nervously as she remembered how passionately she had clung onto this man, how her hands had travelled all over his body. Could she possibly take dictation from someone whose ass she had grabbed? The crudeness and shame of that scenario brought colour to her face. And what if the child said something?

"What about Patty? D'you think Bobby will tell her?"

Martin smiled at the mention of Patty's name. "She's some lady, isn't she? Bobby just adores her. That was an inspired idea of yours and I'm very grateful. Good for Bobby too to be part of the lively Molloy bunch. He's been rather isolated from other children up to now."

"Great but will he tell Patty? About . . ."

"What could he say? Nothing really happened. My son saw to that."

Despite the implications of what happened, or nearly happened, Kate had to smile. A night of illicit passion brought to an abrupt halt by a three-year-old. Pity she could never tell Patty. She would enjoy the farce of it. Another secret for Kate to add to her guilty arsenal. And suddenly that was one secret too many. She looked at Martin Burke. He had kissed her, had his hand on her breast. He could probably think no less of her than he already did.

"I've got something to tell you."

He drained his cup of cocoa and put it down on the table. "So! You're going to tell me about the tape at long last."

She stared at him. How could she ever have thought he was an idiot? Was it her mind alone he could read or was his eerie perception the secret weapon that had enabled him be such a successful defence lawyer? Maybe he was just making a lucky guess.

"What do you know?" she asked and held her breath for the answer.

"That you heard the tape and considered the contents too sensitive for my ears. I'm not sure if you deliberately broke it or not."

"It broke accidentally."

"I see. And who're you trying to protect? Richard Gordon?"

She shook her head. "No. It seems you were right about him. I have no wish to do anything to help him. But he's not the only one involved. I can't tell you why, Martin, because I gave my word, but I was trying to delay any controversy for a while. Until . . . well, until later."

Martin's expression changed, became sharper. He was the professional now. "Whatever was on the tape, Kate, could very well, almost certainly would be, irrelevant as far as litigation goes. I understand there was no chain of custody of that tape. Did you sign for it before you brought it home?"

"Of course, not. It was just a dictation tape. It wasn't potential evidence. At least I didn't know that at the time."

"No prosecutor would accept it. There's just your word that you didn't interfere with it. Or allow someone else to tamper with it in some way."

"So the admissions made on the tape wouldn't count for anything?"

"Admissions?"

"The ex-Minister, Henry Hennessey, was in Richard's office the evening I forgot to switch off the Dictaphone."

"Hmm . . . it gets more interesting. So he made a confession?"

"Not so much a confession as a casual admission. He was horrible. Crass and unfeeling. He threatened Richard with blackmail too."

"Why? Tax evasion?"

She nodded miserably. She felt by now that she had betrayed everybody. Her husband, her ex-employer, the man sitting across the table from her. And especially herself.

"I know you must have had a good reason for withholding information from me, Kate. I can see from that stubborn look on your face that you're not going to tell me exactly what's on the tape. I won't push you now but we must learn to trust each other."

Kate looked into his eyes, into the dark shadows. She had no option but to trust Martin Burke. She had to. He had the power to destroy what was left of her marriage and ruin her career. That was a lot of trust to put in someone you barely knew. Then she remembered the way he was with his son, remembered his hands on her, gentle and caring. She smiled at him.

"Deal. No more secrets."

But yet she went to bed without telling him of Cora Gordon's illness. Keeping that secret was the only little piece of self-respect she had left.

Chapter 21

Shouldering through the Saturday night crowd, Fred made his way to the bar in the Oasis Club. Another five minutes went by before he managed to catch the barman's eye and order his pint. By the time it was eventually served he had wormed his way to a stool at the counter. He lifted the glass and took a sip of the drink that thankfully was not blue or green. He hated the multicoloured shots that seemed to be de rigueur in the clubs. He hated the clubs – the noise, the heat, the pressure of appearing to enjoy himself.

Just as he was putting his glass on the counter, someone elbowed him in the ribs. His pint slopped over. He looked angrily around and was met by the disgusting sight of Gus Cochrane's puce face.

"She's gagging for it. Did you see how she's digging in?"

Fred conjured up a smile from somewhere. Not from within himself. He was plum out of smiles and laughs and jokes and nods of agreement. He forced the grin, the boyish one.

"Yeah. I saw. Nigel's well in there with Adele."

"I fancied my own chances but his cheque book's bigger than mine. Bet his dick's smaller though."

The coarse, vulgar laugh was swallowed up in the rhythmic din of the incessant music. Fred drained what was left of his pint and turned to the sweating lump of lard beside him.

"A drink, Gus?"

"Scotch on the rocks. Are you knocking her off too?"

Fred found a grin even harder to access. He wanted to smash this piece of shit in the face. He felt his lips pull back to bare his teeth in the parody of a smile.

"I get plenty at home, Gus. I don't need to fuck around with the staff."

"Ah! C'mon, man! Be honest. I know Kate's tasty. Wouldn't mind having a go myself. But a change of menu every now and then might help with your little problem."

"What problem?" Fred asked and he was not being disingenuous. He was choking in a thick fog of fucking problems.

"The family one. The producing the son and heir. What's it all for if you have no one to hand it on to?"

Fred looked into the piggy eyes and imagined them swollen and black and blue, the pug nose streaming with blood. He shoved his bunched-up fists into his pockets. That was what this prick wanted. It would suit him fine to have Fred thrown out of the club, out of his chance to join their little cartel. He turned his back on Gus and tried again to catch the barman's eye. By the time he had ordered new drinks, Adele and Nigel Greenway had joined them at the bar. She was very drunk. Nigel was as dapper and in control as ever even though he had drunk more than any of them this evening.

"Order for us too, Fred. There's a good chap."

When Fred felt a powerful urge to punch Nigel Greenway too he made up his mind to leave as soon as possible. If he hung around them much longer he was going to end up destroying all the grovelling groundwork he had laid down. He made an attempt at a smile again.

"I'll get whatever you want, Nigel, but I think Adele's had enough, don't you?"

"Depends on what you're talking about," Gus Cochrane sneered.

Just as Fred was about to turn towards the bar again, he noticed that Adele had suddenly gone very pale. Shit! She was going to throw up. The graphic designer he was depending on to raise the profile of Lucas Advertising was about to spew vomit all over the fastidious businessman. He grabbed her arm and tried to loosen the stranglehold she had on Nigel.

"C'mon, Adele! You need some fresh air. I'll take you outside."

She struggled against him. He had to let go her arm because people were beginning to stare.

"I want a tequila. With lemon and salt."

Her last few words were slurred and faded into a sigh as she seemed to fold up in slow motion. She landed on the floor at Nigel Greenway's feet. He tapped her prone figure with his highly polished leather shoe.

"Can't hold her drink, can she? Just as well she has so much else going for her."

Fred leaned over the counter and, shoving money into the barman's hand, gave him the drink order for the two other men.

He turned to them. "Sorry about this. I'll take her to her apartment."

"You horny old devil!" Gus jeered. "Thought you said you never played away from home!"

Fred ignored him and stooped to help Adele to her feet. She was out cold. How much alcohol had she downed? Christ! He put his arms underneath her and lifted her up.

"I'll take care of her, if you want," Nigel said and his quietly spoken words sent shivers down Fred's spine.

He had an idea how Adele would be taken care of by Greenway.

"No, thank you, Nigel. I'll take her to her apartment. I appreciate you inviting me along tonight. I had some very promising discussions with your friends from the travel agents. I think we may be able to do business with them."

Nigel waved his hand dismissively. "No problem, Fred. You don't need me to promote your company when you have a designer as talented as Ms Sheehan. Pity about her low level of alcohol tolerance though."

Fred smiled briefly and turned in the direction of the door. His arms were burning and he was going to let

Adele fall if he did not move soon. He had to battle through a mass of swaying bodies in order to reach the exit. The security men on the door stopped him to know if everything was all right. "Fine," he said through clenched teeth and staggered on past them. Idiots! He was carrying an unconscious girl and they asked him if everything was OK!

The club was surrounded by a low perimeter wall. Fred made it that far before his knees buckled. He propped Adele up against the wall and flopped down on it himself. He loosened his tie and wiped the sweat from his forehead. It was a very cold and breezy night. He turned his face into the wind and took in big lungfuls of the turbulent air. Peering at his watch he saw that it was 2.30 in the morning. What in the fuck was he doing at this hour, sitting on a wall outside a nightclub with a drunk young girl at his feet?

The crumpled figure thrown against the wall began to moan and make gurgling sounds. Then Adele threw up. She was so violently sick that Fred was afraid she might choke. The acrid smell of vomit engulfed them both. Fred held her long hair back from the seemingly never-ending stream of puke. God! What had she drunk? He handed her his handkerchief and she wiped her face.

"I think some bastard spiked my drink," she gasped.

Fred said nothing. She had been knocking back shots all night. She had no one to blame but herself.

"You'd better get yourself into bed and sleep off that lot. I'll call a cab now."

She caught his hand and hauled herself up onto the

wall, avoiding the mess on the ground. She was shivering with the cold and the shock to her system. Smiling at him, she gave that sideways glance he found so attractive.

"I'm sorry, Fred. That was terrible for you. How did I get out here? Did you carry me over your shoulder or was I thrown out by the bouncers?"

"I carried you and my arms feel about six feet long now. I'm not as fit as I thought."

"Maybe I'm not as light as you thought."

"No. You're certainly not heavy. The fault is mine." His lips tightened in anger as he said this. The fault was his. He was to blame for everything. Every fucking thing! He got out his phone and dialled for a cab. This was no time for self-analysis and he was in no condition for it anyway. They waited in silence for the car.

Fred asked the cab driver to drop Adele off first. She was asleep on the back seat, her head thrown against the headrest. She looked very young and vulnerable with her hair spread out around her.

"I hope she's not going to get sick, mate," said the cab driver. "If she does, you pay the valeting bill."

Even though he was doubtful Fred assured him anyway that she would be fine. She was very pale. He was relieved when they approached her street. Reaching into the back of the car, he shook her to wake her up. Her eyes, when she finally managed to get them open, were confused and unfocussed. When she got out of the cab, she staggered and fell against it.

"What're you doing, mate?" the driver asked as Fred

jumped out of the cab. "I'm busy. I've a stack of calls lined up. I can't hang around here all night."

Fred reached into his pocket and handed him the fare. He had enough on his hands now without adding an irate cabby to the list. He could ring for another cab when he was ready.

Adele's apartment was on the second floor. When they got there, she began poking in her bag for the key.

"Is your flatmate here?"

She looked blankly at him.

Furious now, he almost shouted at her. "Jim's sister! Is she in the apartment?"

She shook her head. The movement nearly caused her to fall over. She muttered something about her flatmate being on a weekend trip to Paris. Fred took the keys from her, opened the door and switched on the lights. It was a newly built apartment, all timber floors, white walls and a few strategically placed abstract paintings. Adele staggered towards the bathroom and he heard her vomiting again and again. Fuck! She was really sick. He put on the kettle. Coffee might help to sober her up. She must be getting dehydrated by now. He sat on the cream leather settee and added allowing Nigel Greenway to give Adele alcohol poisoning to his guilt list.

He heard water running and knew that she had now gone into the shower. Suppose she fell and hit her head? He knocked on the bathroom door. No reply. Going back to the settee he tried to stay calm by counting very slowly and breathing deeply. The higher the count went, the more panicky he got. Here he was, a married man, alone in an apartment in the early hours, with a very attractive, very young and maybe very dead girl. He could not think straight. The alcohol he had tonight was slowing down all his reasoning processes. Maybe he was overreacting. He lost his place in his count, jumped up and banged on the bathroom door.

"Adele! Are you OK? Adele!"

She must have heard because the water stopped running. Satisfied that she was still alive, he went and made coffee.

When Adele came back into the lounge she was wearing an oversized white fluffy dressing-gown. Her wet hair hung down her back and her face without make-up looked angelic. Fred stared. This innocent girl could not be the same person who had practically had intercourse with Nigel Greenway on the dance floor. She sat down beside him.

"Fred. Thank you so much. I'm sorry I put you to all this trouble."

"No trouble at all," he lied.

He began to feel hot. She smelled so clean. And warm. And damp. She crossed her legs and her dressing-gown parted. Her legs were long, lean, tanned and bare.

"I owe you," she said softly.

He was sweating like Gus Cochrane. He would not be surprised if he was leering too. Mentally, he had already stripped off her dressing-gown and was feasting his eyes on her pert little breasts. She caught his hand and an electric shock ripped through his whole body. Jesus! He wanted to fuck this girl, to bury his face in her luxuriant hair, to run his hands over her smooth skin, to kiss her breasts and belly. To kiss every inch of her.

He pulled his hand away and stood up.

"We've both had too much to drink, Adele. I'm ringing for a cab now. You should drink plenty of water before you go to sleep. You're going to have a hell of a hangover tomorrow."

"You've a hell of a hard-on now," she said, staring at his crotch.

Jesus! His fingers shook as he keyed in the cab number.

"We've a driver in your area now. He'll be with you in minutes," the base operator said and Fred felt both relief and a terrible, deep regret. It was being offered to him on a plate, as Gus Cochrane would say.

He felt safe stooping down to kiss Adele. She put her arms around his neck and stood up, moulding her body into his. Outside, the cab hooted loudly. He pulled away from her.

"Night, Adele. Sleep well."

He had reached the door when she called him. He turned around. She was lying on the settee, stark naked.

"Just wanted to show you what you're passing up."

She was beautiful, her body fuller, curvier than he had imagined. The cab driver hooted again. He could call another cab. Shit! He could stay the night. Kate was safely in Kerry. With Martin Burke. Wasn't this just the scenario he had planned from the first minute he had set eyes on Adele? She was coyly crooking her finger at him, looking askance from underneath her curling eyelashes.

No. Not like this. She was still drunk.

What a noble fucking idiot he was!

When he got to the front of the building the cab was

just about to drive away. Fred cursed as he saw the reversing lights come on. One more minute and he would have had the perfect excuse to go back up to the apartment. By the time he reached home he realised there would have been no excuse, perfect or otherwise, for going back.

Chapter 22

When Fred finally threw himself into bed he felt so exhausted he thought he would sleep forever. But his body forgot to tell his mind that it needed rest too. He tossed and turned and drifted in and out of fitful sleep. When dawn light began to seep through the curtains, he gave up any attempt at meaningful relaxation. Jumping out of bed he noticed the sour smell of vomit pervading the room. He picked up the clothes he had discarded last night. They were splashed with dried-out flecks of Adele's puke. He bundled them up and put them on to wash before making breakfast. Kate would probably wonder at his domesticity. Kate wondered about everything anyway.

He turned on the radio to catch the early morning news and turned it off very quickly when the noise sent spears of pain through his head. Sitting at the table, hunched over his cup of tea, Fred felt like he was caught in a time warp. He could be his father. Or like his father had been before he drank his veterinary practice into bankruptcy and himself to death. He closed his eyes against the intense light of morning and imagined Kate's dark eyes watching him, silently accusing him of becoming a drunk like his dad. What in the fuck did she know about it? What did anyone know about the fighting and arguing, the embarrassment, the shame?

He went to the medicine cabinet in the bathroom and found some aspirin. It would have to do. He swallowed a few tablets with water and went out into the garden. Somewhere behind the blanket of cloud, the sun had risen. Ignoring the damp, he sat on the garden bench. The throbbing in his head was easing but worries were rushing in to fill the space. The travel-agency account was up for grabs. Another nationwide, multimedia campaign. He had got on well with the agency owners. They were surprisingly nice people considering they were friends of Nigel Greenway's. But if he were to bid for this campaign, he would have to mount an impressive presentation. That would take time. And money.

The 'money' word twisted inside in his gut. What type of idiot had he been to sign that contract with Greenway? Nigel must be laughing up the sleeve of his Louis Copeland suit. Any fool knew you should read the small print. Not Fred. Not the arse-licking, yes-sir, I'll-do-anything-for-a-contract pushover he had proven himself to be. The performance-related clause was bad enough – he made profit only if Greenway did. But the part payment in shares of a property-development scheme he knew nothing about was a disaster.

"I'll deal you in for a share in this scheme. Believe me,

Fred, long term, it'll earn you more profit, tax free, than you could ever earn with your little promotions company."

Fred had listened to Nigel Greenway and worshipped at the altar of his success. He loved the idea of being involved in property development, feeling at last like one of the big boys. A mover and shaker. The realisation that he had invested without knowing what he was getting into had dawned gradually. The more questions he asked, the more dismissive Nigel Greenway's answers became.

"All you need to know is the company is named International Leaf Ltd and that the project is in Eastern Europe."

It was not until Fred had signed on the dotted line that Nigel told him he would have to supplement the investment with a large sum of money. Re-mortgage. Pledge the deeds of his house as security.

"You must understand that all the other members of this group are big players. I couldn't get your name past them without showing some collateral. We're playing for high stakes. But the eventual profits will be huge."

Fred dropped his head into his hands in shame. He had willingly signed over the deeds of the home he and Kate shared together. Without her knowledge or consent. He had reasoned that the property was his to do with as he liked. He had bought it before they married. It was his by law. Unless, of course, he intended selling the property which wasn't the case. She didn't need to know anything about the investment. Everything to do with this development was on a need-to-know basis. Obviously they thought Fred too needed to know very little. It was not until Brian Molloy had died, leaving his wife and children penniless, that the nagging worry had begun to wake up and make a persistent nuisance of itself. He had been pretty sure that Brian Molloy must have been involved in the same scheme. So sure that he had asked Nigel Greenway.

"All you need to know, son, is that you've a small stake in it. None of your business who else is involved. Pity about Brian's wife and children. Horrible accident."

Maybe he should have told Patty to talk to Nigel Greenway. But what if he was wrong? Maybe Brian Molloy had not invested in this International Leaf Ltd. Then Nigel would be furious at Fred and would probably throw him out of the syndicate.

Nevertheless, Fred had double-checked his own insurance cover. It was fine. If he died, Kate would not be left in the same situation as Patty. All he had to do now was to keep up the payments. But how in the fuck was he going to do that?

Getting up from the damp bench, he strode around the garden. No matter how fast he walked, his thoughts ran faster.

Dizzy from following his whirling thoughts in circles, Fred went inside to clear up the house before Kate came home. It was tidy, just needing a hoovering. Houses had a habit of staying tidy when there were no children around to mess them up. Fuck! His head began to throb again. Bad enough to have money worries, keeping the company running on overdraft until some cash came in but there was the promise, the hope that the cash-flow situation would ease. Not so the baby problem. The baby Kate so desperately wanted.

He went upstairs and picked his wallet up from the bedside locker. He was acting automatically, being driven by a force outside himself, a power he could not control. He did not want to see the piece of paper. He never wanted to lay eyes on it again but still his hand reached out and opened the leather wallet. The page was creased and tattered from being handled. He scanned it and his eyes focussed on the same words they always did. Low sperm count. Just three little words and some numbers. The shock hit him anew as it did each time. Christ! He had only done the test to help Kate, to let her know that he wanted a family too. It was meant to be a surprise for her. A gesture of support. Instead it had turned out to be a nightmare for him and another secret from Kate. He crumpled the paper in his fist and ran downstairs to get a box of matches. He would burn the blasted thing. Save himself the regular crucifixion of examining it. The results were not going to change no matter what the doctor said. He was a young guy, the doctor he had gone to. Not Dr Shorten, their decrepit old GP.

"This may just be a blip," the young doctor had explained breezily. "You need two more tests so that we can have a clear picture of where your count really lies."

Fred had vowed never to go back. Once was enough for that humiliation.

His hand shook as he held the match to the page. He needed a drink to steady it. He needed a drink to face the day, to face his wife. Fuck! He just needed a drink.

Kate pulled on her clothes as quickly and quietly as

possible. She crept to the kitchen and got a banana. Not much of a breakfast but it would do. Stave off the hunger until later. The house was gloomy, filled with the grey light of an overcast day. On tiptoe, she went to the hall closet to get her coat and boots. It would be cold up on the hills. When she was muffled up in her waterproofs, she breathed a sigh of relief. She was on her way. Out of here. As far away from Martin Burke as she could get. She tiptoed to the front door and turned the lock. It made a loud click. The door swung open and mist rolled in. She closed it and began to walk quickly towards the path.

Outside the gate, Kate stood and looked upwards. She saw nothing of the majestic sweep of hillside. It was obliterated by fog. It would be foolhardy and very dangerous to climb up in these conditions. She turned and faced towards the valley, not caring where she went as long as she escaped from the cottage. Her lips were burning. She wiped the back of her hand across her mouth but her lips still tingled. They felt like they were tattooed with the inscription '*Kissed by Martin Burke*'. She imagined everyone reading her lips and snickering. She imagined Fred getting angry, hurt, throwing her out, ending their marriage, going to live with Adele and fathering hordes of blonde-haired, long-legged babies who were very gifted artists.

It had been many years since she had resorted to her childhood game of whispering her troubles to a stone and then throwing it far into the hills. Picking up a stone, she wiped it across her mouth as she whispered and threw it as far as she could. It landed with a clunk somewhere on the rocky hillside. Feeling that she had now proven beyond all doubt that she was immature and on the verge of total mental breakdown, she headed downhill towards McCarthy's and the comforting sanity of Noreen and Phil.

There was no sign of Rex in the yard so Kate assumed that he was gone with Phil to collect the cows. She tapped on the back door and walked straight into the kitchen. Her hand shot up automatically to cover her mouth. Martin Burke and Bobby were seated at the table, their plates piled with soda bread. Rex was lying placidly at the child's feet.

"Good morning, Kate." Noreen smiled. "Sit yourself down. I'll make tea for you."

"Rex! Look at Rex!"

Kate did as Bobby told her. She looked at Rex and kept looking at him, not wanting to raise her eyes. She felt Martin's gaze on her. There were four tan patches on Rex's black coat and one was shaped like the map of Italy. It was no good. She drew her eyes away from the dog and looked at Martin. He was smiling.

"We snuck out this morning, didn't we, Bobby? We thought you might need a rest."

"Kate very tired," Bobby nodded.

Noreen arrived over to the table with the cup of tea. She stood in front of Kate and stared at her. "What have you been doing to yourself, Katie O'Hanlon?"

Kate looked down at the dog again but too late. The guilty blush of shame was rushing from her toes upwards.

Noreen dashed across the kitchen and came back waving a tissue like a flag of surrender. "Hold up your face to me, girlie." She rubbed vigorously on Kate's lips and then held the tissue out for inspection. "Look. Pieces of moss. Have you been telling your troubles to the stones again? It must be all of twenty years since you last did that."

"Is this a Kerry tradition?" Martin asked with interest.

Noreen winked at Kate and then went into a very long explanation of the trouble-stone tradition. It was hard not to laugh. She was a brilliant storyteller and a great liar.

"So tell me, Kate," Martin said, "what size stone did you need for your problems?"

"A boulder."

"That bad!"

"Lunch should cheer you up then," said Noreen. "Martin's invited all of us to eat out in Killarney."

"Is that OK with you, Kate?" he asked.

She nodded and smiled her thanks at him. It was more than OK. It was perfect. Noreen and Phil would enjoy the trip and she and Martin could relax with other people around them. They looked at each other and silently acknowledged that they had found a way forward.

Locking up the cottage always left Kate feeling sad. She felt a different kind of sadness this evening. She was not only saying goodbye to her home and her hills but also to a relationship that could have been. Who knows? Another time, another place, another life, maybe she and Martin could have shared something special. He stood by her side as she turned the key, locking the memory of their shared kiss into the cottage with the ghosts of Kitty and Paudie.

"Are you all right, Kate?"

She nodded assent. And she was not lying. She had come to terms with her momentary loss of control. A glitch. An aberration. Never to be repeated again. Another little secret. She smiled at Martin. He stooped and kissed her on the cheek.

"Bobby cuddle too."

Martin picked the child up in his arms. The three of them laughed and had a big hug. Kate waved them off and stood, just breathing in the pure mountain air. Then she reluctantly got into her car and headed for Dublin and whatever lay ahead. She rang Fred several times during her journey but his phone always rang out. So did the house phone. She sighed. Back to reality.

Fred had been doing some phoning too. He had rung Adele several times. Just to make sure she had survived her alcohol overdose. When her phone rang out for the third time he began to worry. Suppose she had got sick again and choked on her vomit. Or maybe she had fallen and hit her head. After the fourth call with no reply, he got in his car and drove over to her apartment. It was two o'clock on a Sunday afternoon. She should be answering her phone unless there was something wrong.

He rang her doorbell. The sound echoed through the apartment but the door remained closed. He called out her name and thought he heard a sound from inside. Putting his finger on the bell he kept it depressed. The door opened a slit and Jim Grant's sister appeared. Her hair was tousled. He had obviously woken her up.

"I'm sorry for disturbing you. Is Adele here?"

She opened the door wider and he could see that she was in her dressing-gown.

"Hello, Fred. I'm not long back. Maybe an hour or so. I've had a hectic few days in Paris. No sign of Adele since I came home."

"Are you sure? Could she be in her room?"

The girl took a step back and Fred realised that he must appear a bit strange.

"Quite the slave-driver, aren't you? It's Sunday, you know. Do you give your staff any time off?"

He shuffled his feet in embarrassment. He could hardly ask her to check if Adele was still alive but he could not go until he knew. Seeing that he was not going to leave, the girl invited him in while she went to check. She came back shaking her head.

"As I thought. She's not here. Do you want me to give her a message when she comes in?"

"No. No, thanks, and sorry for disturbing you."

He turned and left with as much dignity as he could muster. When he got back to his car he switched on the engine and then realised he did not know where to go. Certainly not back home. The empty house was making him edgy, giving him too much time to think about things he would rather forget. He could go to the office but knew he would end up going over the accounts. He was depressed enough without adding that dose of realism. Maybe if he rang Adele again? He searched his jacket, the dash, the glove pocket. No phone. He must have left it at home in his rush out to rescue Adele. He checked his watch. Kate would not be back until around teatime. Maybe later. She had sounded quite happy last night. Enjoying her time with Martin Burke. Immediately he felt the jealous twinge, Fred knew he had no right. It was he, after all, who had arranged for the returned Yank to spend the weekend in the cottage.

Putting the car in gear he drove out onto the main road. The Sunday-afternoon traffic was heavy. Droves of people headed for DIY stores. They would be returning with lengths of timber on their roof racks and flat packs sticking out of the open boots of their cars. Families whizzed past him in their four-wheel drives, Mam and Dad in front, two point two children and the dog in the back. He drove aimlessly towards town, feeling like the only person in the whole city with no purpose to his Sunday afternoon. When he parked, he had a half-formed plan about going for a walk. It just so happened that his walk led him to a pub and that one drink led to another.

The house was in darkness when Kate pulled into the driveway. Fred's car was not there. She had not expected it to be. When she went inside the first thing she noticed was his phone on the hall table. Glancing at it, she saw he had six missed calls. Four of them had been from her. At least she knew now why her calls had not been answered.

A cup of coffee later, she decided to unpack and get organised for the morning. A little shiver of dread ran through her. She was very good at hiding things from herself, at pushing memories into secret places in her mind. But did she have a space big enough and safe enough to hide her kiss with Martin Burke? Heat flashed through her body as she thought about his warm lips, his strong but gentle hands.

Grabbing her weekend bag she began to sort through laundry as if her life depended on it. It did. Clean, dirty, needs a wash, must be ironed. She rifled through clothes at a furious pace and then went into the utility room with an armful for the washing machine. She stared in amazement. The machine was full. Fred had done a wash. This was a first. His initiation into the mysteries of hot wash, cool wash, synthetics and cottons. Dropping her bundle of laundry she opened the drum and took out her husband's good navy suit, one of his best and most expensive white shirts and a silk tie. The suit was as crinkled as if it had been made from crepe, the shirt streaked with daubs of red and orange dye and the tie was shrunken and twisted like a length of coloured rope. Fuck! He must have put them into a boil wash. An expensive learning experience. And why had he wanted to clean them anyway? What was he trying to wash away? Streaks of Adele's fake tan?

She had just switched on her own wash when the phone rang. So Fred had remembered his wife, at last. She would enjoy telling him his suit was ruined. When she heard Patty's voice, she had to do an instant change of moods.

"I'm dying to know how the weekend in the wilds went. How'd the two of you get along?"

"Very well. Bobby's a lovely child."

"And Bobby's daddy?"

Kate hesitated. It would have been such a relief to

share her experience, to talk about how easily she had fallen into Martin's arms, how close she had been to betraying Fred. Patty would not judge or condemn. She knew that. Yet the habit of a lifetime stopped her. Katie O'Hanlon kept to herself. 'Least said, soonest mended.'

"He enjoyed all the fresh air and open spaces. I hadn't realised that he's from a farming background."

"Really? What other information did you screw out of him? Not literally of course!"

The breath in Kate's throat caught. Why was Patty talking like this? Did she suspect something? Then she exhaled and relaxed a little. Patty always talked like that.

"Nothing earth-shattering except that he's surprisingly good at looking after Bobby and he got on great with my elderly neighbours, the McCarthys. Charmed them to bits."

"He's a charmer all right," Patty agreed and then suddenly changed the topic. "I've made up my mind to go to an auctioneer tomorrow. The sooner The Rectory's on the market the sooner I can get my life or at least my finances sorted."

Kate did not know what to say. She was fairly sure that the answer to Patty's problems couldn't be as simple as selling The Rectory, heartbreaking as that was. It wasn't Patty's to sell. Not yet. Maybe not at all. It seemed obvious that Patty would eventually lose the home she and Brian had built together. The children's home. But maybe if she hung on . . . Maybe what? The Molloys would have a change of heart and clear Brian's debts? Not likely. She had a better chance of winning the Lottery.

"I'm sorry, Patty. I can't even begin to imagine how awful everything must be for you right now."

"It's shit. But I figure, if I go to the auctioneer myself to organise the sale, at least I have some control over who buys it. I can't bear the thought of Gareth Owens instructing an estate agent to sell our home. Prick!"

Kate didn't comment. Better leave Patty with the hope the idea of selling gave her . . . until there was good reason to say otherwise. The good old 'least said' principle again.

"How's Fred?" Patty asked and Kate's resolve broke down. Some things just had to be shared.

"To be honest, I don't know. He's not here but his phone is, so I've no way of contacting him. I think it's a case of when the cat's away."

"God, no, Kate! I hope you don't think Fred is messing around with someone else? Not Fred. He idolises you."

"I wish! I come somewhere below Lucas Advertising and Nigel Greenway in his affections. His wonderful new designer has a strong foothold there too."

"Would that girl's name be Adele Sheehan, by any chance?"

"Yes. Why?"

"I heard a rumour that Nigel Greenway's seeing quite a lot of her. Par for the course, I s'pose. She's young and blonde. I don't know how his wife puts up with it."

"Maybe she has no choice," Kate said and felt equal measures of pity for Mrs Nigel Greenway and gratitude to her cheating husband. Allelluia! It was the garage tycoon's hands roaming all over the young girl's body, his head on her pillow. Not Fred. Not Fred Lucas.

Patty interrupted her silent celebration. "Enough of the scandal. Will you call over some night during the week? I've an idea I want to run past you."

The doorbell rang. Kate quickly arranged a night with Patty and then went to answer the ring. When she saw Martin Burke on the doorstep, she froze. Jesus! Had she misinterpreted their tacit agreement? Had he come here to fire her, to tell her not to turn up for work tomorrow? He seemed uncomfortable. Guilty.

"Is there something wrong, Martin?" she asked in a little voice that did not sound like hers.

"It's Fred. He's in the car. He's a bit tipsy."

She stood there, staring foolishly at him, unable to take in what he was saying.

"He's been drinking in the Grand Hotel bar since this afternoon. I'm afraid he got into a bit of an argument. "

"Is he hurt?"

"See for yourself," he said and led the way out to his car.

Fred was sprawled across the back seat. When she leaned over him, she reeled from the smell of alcohol and vomit. She immediately understood the significance of the shrivelled suit in the boil wash. Maybe it would have been better if it had been Adele's fake tan he had been trying to eliminate. She shook his shoulder. His eyes slowly opened and gazed up at her.

"I'm sorry, Katie. Sorry about everything. You deserve better."

Together she and Martin managed to get him out of the car and into the house. He kept up a continuous stream of apologies. They sat him on a chair in the kitchen.

"Who was he arguing with? D'you know?"

"I believe he hit a barman. I'd just dropped down to the bar for a quick drink when I heard all the rumpus. I'm not exactly sure what happened."

Kate knew Martin was protecting her from the sordid details. Obviously Fred had been asked to leave and had decided to stand and fight for another drink. History repeating itself.

"His father was an alcoholic," Kate blurted out. "Drank his veterinary practice into the ground. Fred's always been very cautious around alcohol up to now. I don't know what's going on with him any more."

"Just one drink. The asshole wouldn't give me one for the road. He took my car keys too," Fred slurred.

"Do you need help getting him to bed, or would you prefer me to go?"

Fred was sprawled on the chair, muttering and mumbling, a drunken, helpless mess. She knew she could not manage him herself. His legs would probably not support him when he stood. Practicality overcame her shame and embarrassment.

"Would you mind helping, please, Martin? He's too heavy for me."

Getting Fred upstairs and into the spare bedroom took the best part of twenty minutes. He fought them every step of the way. They were both drained by the time they returned to the kitchen.

"He needs help," Martin said.

She nodded. He stooped and kissed the top of her head. She closed her eyes. When she opened them again, he had gone. She was alone with her drunken husband and her guilt.

Chapter 23

Kate showered and ate breakfast without seeing any sign of Fred. Still smarting from the disgust and embarrassment of his drunken arrival home last night, she had been glad not to lay eyes on him at first. By the time she had finished dressing she was reconsidering. He was probably lying low until he heard her leave. Ready to sneak downstairs to nurse his hangover in peace. Like hell! Lipstick and perfume on, she was ready for battle. She stormed towards the spare room and almost collided with Fred on his way out. The angry words died on her lips. He looked terrible. His skin was a ghastly grey-white and there were dark pouches underneath his eyes.

"Morning," he muttered and then stood, head hanging and lips pouted.

"You made a disgrace of yourself."

She knew she sounded more like this man's mother than his wife. He shuffled his feet, acting for his part more like her child than her husband. For a moment there was a stand-off as they regarded each other. Kate blinked first.

"Well! What've you to say? Is there any logical explanation for the condition you were in last night?"

"I'm sorry."

"And?"

He brushed past her and headed for the bathroom. She ran ahead of him and stood across the doorway, blocking his path.

"D'you think a half-hearted apology will make it all go away? I want an explanation, Fred. I want to know why my husband was brawling in a bar."

"For Christ's sake! You're such a drama queen! I wasn't brawling. That prick of a barman took my car keys. I was just trying to get my property back. Now, out of my way, please. I need to pee."

"He obviously took your keys because you were too drunk to drive. You should be grateful to him."

"I'm shit-sick of being grateful. Thank you, Nigel! Thank you, Kate! And of course, I mustn't forget, thank *you*, Mr Burke!"

"Martin deserves your thanks. You may not remember but he brought you home."

Fred shoved past her and went into the bathroom. He pushed the door almost closed and then turned to her. "I meant I should thank him for spending the weekend with you. Did he take good care of you?"

Kate stared at him in shock. What had made him say that? Did he suspect something? Had Martin dropped a hint, passed a careless remark? Fred smirked and Kate was stunned to find that she wanted to slap his face. God!

What was happening to them? She struggled for calm before she spoke. "You engineered it so that I was forced to allow Martin Burke and his son to come to Kerry. You invited them to my cottage without my permission. I would've refused except I couldn't disappoint the child. You put me in a very awkward situation. Why? Because you wanted to spend time with your precious graphic designer without me looking over your shoulder. Was that it? Tell me."

He closed the door but not before she saw a look of surprise pass across his face. Finding a vulnerable spot she could not help digging into it. Shouting through the door she passed on Patty's bit of gossip.

"You must've been devastated to find out that she's screwing Nigel Greenway. Is that why you lost your sanity, Fred? Is that why you ended up brawling in the hotel?"

The door shot open and he stood there, toothbrush in hand, even paler than before.

"What d'you mean? Who told you that? She's not sleeping with Greenway. She's not sleeping with anyone. Jesus! The girl has only just arrived here. Can't you leave her alone? What's your problem?"

Kate had passed on the scandal just to hurt Fred. Now she was the one who was hurting. The devastation on her husband's face would have upset her under different circumstances. She would have put her arms around him and held him close to her, stroked his back and rubbed his hair until he felt better, safer. Now she hated him for the sadness in his eyes. Just how deep were his feelings for that blonde little tart with the pierced navel? A treacherous voice in her head told her they were probably no deeper than her feelings for Martin Burke. Unable to look at him any more she turned and walked away. He could bloody well find his own way to the hotel to collect his car or else spend the day mooching around the house. She really did not care which.

Just to add to the frustration of an already lousy day, a lorry had broken down on the motorway and Kate had to join the queue for the one lane remaining in operation. Everyone was settled into work when she finally got into the office. Eileen was in full flight with a 'Billy said' story. She stopped talking about the electrician who liked Häagen Dazs for long enough to let Kate know that Martin was in and had been looking for her.

"He was in Kerry for the weekend. Weren't you there too? You didn't happen to come across him, did you?"

"I was in my parents' cottage," Kate answered and then congratulated herself on getting out of that one without lying. She gathered up her notepad and pen and knocked on the door of Martin's office. When she heard his "Come in" she froze. Because of her row with Fred this morning she had not considered how she was going to face Martin Burke and what she would say to him. What is the appropriate thing to say to your boss when you have kissed him passionately one night and he delivered your drunken husband to your door the next?

"Go on, Kate! Chance it!" said Len.

She pretended to laugh and opened the door. Martin was sitting at his desk, engrossed in his work. He looked up and saw her smile.

"Good morning, Kate. I'm relieved to see you in such good form. I was a bit worried when you were late."

"I'm sorry. There was a hold-up on the motorway."

"No problem. Everything OK?"

"Yes, thank you," she said as she sat and arranged her pen and notepad on the desk. Nothing in her past experience had prepared her for this situation and she did not know how to handle it. Her relationship with Richard had been very clear-cut. He was the boss, she the employee. Even if the respect had not been mutual, the line of authority had been very clear. But she and Martin had crossed that line. She could not sit here and take dictation without thanking him for bringing Fred home last night. She could not look at him without remembering how warm and soft his lips were.

"Are you all right, Kate?"

She was forced to stop fidgeting and make eye contact with him. Maybe it was because she was tired, or maybe it was just because it was all too much to hold inside, but everything came blurting out in a stream of nervous words.

"Thank you very much for looking after Fred last night. I really appreciate it and Fred will too when he gets his head together. He's not usually like this. It must be the stress of his new contract. And I'm sorry if my behaviour was inappropriate in the cottage – I –"

"Stop there."

He was holding his hand up and the expression on his face was stern. Kate began to shake. Christ! What kind of a mess had she got herself into? Sensible, level-headed

Kate, shaking like a leaf because she almost, would have, had wanted to, shag her boss. The word resign leapt into her head and she grabbed onto it. Resign. She must. She would have to. It was the only answer. As she was about to say the resign word out loud, Martin spoke.

"It seems like we've got ourselves a bit of a situation here, Kate. We'll have to talk it through, lay down some ground rules."

She nodded, not really sure what direction his conversation was about to take.

"Firstly, I want you to know that when Fred invited me to your cottage in Kerry, he led me to believe that he'd be there too. I was very surprised on arrival to discover that you were alone. So I didn't go there with the intention of taking advantage of you."

Kate blushed in embarrassment and anger. Is that what he thought of her? A vulnerable half-wit who could be taken advantage of at will unless her husband was minding her?

"I'm sorry to embarrass you like this but I think it's vital that we sort things out."

"Look, Martin, we have a huge problem and no matter how much we talk, we can't change what happened."

"I don't want to. Do you?"

She had to think very carefully about her answer. She thought of their walk across the fields to the castle ruins, his respect for Noreen and Phil, his devotion to his son, his gentleness, his passion. Then she thought about the guilt when she looked at Fred and the excruciating embarrassment and panic she was feeling now. She had no clear answer.

"We had a lovely time together, Martin. All of it, not just . . . not just the night-time. It's a nice memory to have."

"Exactly. A memory we must leave in Kerry, as we agreed. I think, I know, that you are a very good PA. I would like us to continue working together. How do you feel about that?"

At that precise moment Kate was not sure how she felt about anything. One thing was certain though. Fred seemed to be completely losing his way. How well was he controlling his business when he did not seem to be able to control himself? One of them needed a secure job. She looked across at Martin and made her decision.

"I don't want to start job-hunting, sending out my CV, going for interviews and all the other inconveniences involved in changing jobs. If you're happy for the two of us to work together, then so am I. It's just way more embarrassing than I thought it would be."

"How about we find a big stone and, what was it Noreen said, 'lay our troubles on it'? We could toss it into the Liffey. That should kill them off fairly quickly."

"Consider it done!"

He laughed and she could almost see waves of tension drift away from both of them.

"So we're agreed then," he said. "We can work together. Can we also be friends as well as colleagues? Can we manage that?"

She smiled at him although in fact she had no idea if she would ever again feel at ease in Martin Burke's company. But that was not something new. She never had really. And she had no alternative until she sorted out the mess her marriage had become.

She picked up her notebook and said, "Ready for work, sir, whenever you are."

They worked steadily for the next hour. Kate was surprised to find how easily they had slipped back into the boss-employee relationship when the decision had been made. It was as if their momentary loss of control had never happened. Denial was a useful tool.

She was at the door on her way out when he told her something that shattered her new-found peace again.

"The tape, Kate. It's arrived in the States and is being looked at as we speak. My man's pretty sure he can patch it up. We should have it back in a few days."

She just nodded and continued on her way out the door. At least she had told him what was on the tape. In outline anyway. But how long would she be able to delay his investigations? She said a quick prayer that it would be long enough for Cora Gordon to die without knowing she may have been married to a criminal.

Kate got to The Rectory just in time for Jonathan's evening bath.

"Here, Kate, you do it," Patty said. "You may as well get used to holding him. We'll have to christen this little scrap soon."

Kate was very nervous at first, clinging onto the child as he kicked his legs in the water. She eventually got enough confidence to support him with only one hand and to pick up the sponge with her other. Dipping the duck-shaped sponge in the bubbles she squeezed little rivers of lukewarm water and foam down the baby's chest and over his legs.

"He's my swimmer, I think," Patty said. "Look how he loves splashing."

Kate allowed Patty to take over when it was time for Jonathan to leave his plastic bath. She did not trust herself to transfer the slippery baby safely to the big heated towel Patty had ready. They both cooed over him until he was after his feed. Then, tummy full, he went fast asleep as soon as he was laid in his cot.

Kate made coffee for Patty and brought it over to the table for her.

"I rang an estate agent," said Patty. "Just to enquire about valuing The Rectory. I'd really love to put up a great big For Sale sign. It would make me feel I'd got one over on Gareth Owens."

Kate opened her mouth to warn Patty, to prepare her for the possibility of a long legal process ahead before she'd be in a position to make any such decisions.

"Stop looking at me like that," Patty laughed. "I've not lost my common sense entirely. I know I can't just sell the house and fix everything as if by magic. But thinking I can makes me feel a little bit in control. And at least I have one satisfaction. Martin has negotiated a deal with the bank to freeze the interest on the loan. Gives me a better chance of paying off all Brian's debts by my eightieth birthday."

"That's great news. Gareth Owens must be worried now in case there'll be an investigation from higher up about his handling of the loan."

"I hope he's scared shitless. He deserves to be. Martin also found out the name of the Development Company my husband sold his soul to. It's Leaf International or something like that and –"

Kate did not hear the rest of Patty's sentence. She had been hit by a double whammy. International Leaf, which was obviously what Patty meant, was one of the companies. One of the companies Gus Cochrane had his filthy paws stuck into. And Nigel Greenway. And Richard Gordon was somehow involved too. How could Richard swan off on holiday and leave Patty in such a bad situation? What kind of a friend was he? What kind of a prick was he? Then she remembered Cora. Of course. Richard could not be expected to worry about other people when his wife was dying.

That was the first blow. The second was that Martin had not mentioned a word of this to her. Did he not trust her?

"When did Martin find out about this company?"

"Sometime last week. He's working on trying to trace the directors. It's foreign registered. How Brian came across it, I'll never know."

"Someone must have told him," Kate suggested. "Somebody he trusted."

Patty shrugged her shoulders. "He could've found it on the Internet. Anyway, Martin is looking into it for me. Hasn't he said anything to you about it?"

"Client confidentiality," Kate said and hoped it sounded impressive enough to stop Patty asking more questions. It did not take her off the topic of Martin though.

"He's been very good to me. Extremely helpful. I can see where his son's sunny nature comes from."

"Are we talking about Martin Burke?" Kate asked. "I'd never have accused him of having a sunny nature."

Patty frowned and looked closely at Kate. She muttered a low "hmm" as if trying to decide whether Kate was being serious or not. "Don't you like him?"

Kate was getting a bit flustered. Patty was extremely shrewd. But very forthright too. If she had suspected anything about the relationship between Kate and Martin she would have said so by now.

"I suppose I do. But I don't know him well enough to be sure."

Patty laughed. "Cautious Kate! Not one to leap in with both feet, are you? Anyway, the reason I'm talking about him now is because I've had an idea."

"Yes," Kate said, glad that Patty's attention was going onto something else. "The idea you said you wanted to talk to me about."

"It's about the christening. You're godmother. Right? So who could I ask to be godfather? Not Fred because you can't really have both godparents from the same family. Certainly not one of the Molloys. Not my own family. They're too far away from me in every sense. So what would you think if I asked Martin?"

Kate had to bite her lip to stop herself shouting "No!" at Patty. Jesus! What a scenario! Kate and Martin standing side by side in the church, a baby in their arms. She could not cope with it. Absolutely not!

"But you don't even know him, Patty. How could you trust your child's moral upbringing to him?"

"Kate, you know that's all bull. Being godparent is

about being there to help the child through bad times, to be the friend they can go to when they need a shoulder to cry on, to be with them when they celebrate their achievements. I know you'll always be that kind of godparent to Jonathan and I believe Martin would be too."

Kate nodded, remembering how devoted a father he was to his own son. He seemed to be a genuinely caring man. Patty was right, of course. And she, as usual, was just being selfish, thinking about herself. She smiled and Patty's anxious expression relaxed into a grin.

"What lovely christening photos we will have! You and Martin make a handsome pair."

"You'd better ask him first. If he refuses you could always ask Gus Cochrane. Now there's a man who would give Jonathan moral guidance, a shoulder to cry on and his very own, customised waste-disposal unit."

They both laughed and relaxed, Patty happy that she had chosen a godfather for her son and Kate happy that they would now, at last, leave the subject of Martin Burke behind.

The supermarket was practically deserted. Tuesday night did not seem to be a very popular time for shopping. Kate's footsteps echoed hollowly as she pushed her trolley around the aisles. She looked uninterestedly at cereals and fruit and cleaners. What was she doing here? It wasn't as if she needed to stock up on groceries. She stood still, a packet of sugar in her hand. She was avoiding going home. Just as she had been doing for the past week.

Avoiding the empty house, the dinner for one, the lonely bed. Enough! Kate put the sugar back on the shelf, abandoned her trolley and headed home.

Fred's car was parked outside the house. Obviously he had decided on an early night for a change. Kate turned off the engine, sat in her car and stared at the darkened house. Her husband would be asleep again in the spare room. He seemed to have moved in there on a permanent basis since she had come back from Kerry. Apparently he had decided that if he could not sleep with Adele Sheehan, then he would sleep alone. He wasn't drinking. Not since Martin Burke had delivered him home. He just seemed to be wrapping himself in work and a thick blanket of impenetrable sadness.

Too restless to go straight to bed, Kate heated some milk and tried to read the paper. She put it down after a few minutes of trying to decipher blurry print. Those goddamn tears were filling up and spilling over again. She brushed them angrily away. Blasted men! They were breaking her heart. Fred, being all silent and withdrawn, pining after his little tart. Martin, nice and friendly on the surface but all the while keeping secrets from her. He had told her that Lee seemed to be enjoying Saudi. He confided his concern about his ex-wife's intention to leave her hotel and go to the Sheikh's compound. He reported endlessly on Bobby's progress and on how he was bonding with Patty and the Molloy boys. But he had not yet told her about Brian Molloy's connection with International Leaf. Hadn't he realised that Patty would tell her? Why had he not discussed it with her? She was his PA. Did he believe she was going to pass on the information to Richard? Prick!

A skin had formed on the top of her milk. Disgusted, she threw it out and rinsed her cup. She should have been in bed an hour ago. Dr Shorten had lectured her again about rest and nutrition when she had had her final iron injection last evening. Useless exercise. What was the point pumping iron into her system when her energy was being sapped by one worry after another? And keeping her temperature chart was pointless too. Where was the benefit in pinpointing her fertile days when her husband was sleeping in another room?

"Keep filling in that chart," Dr Shorten had said, "and I'll see you and Fred here in two months' time. Once we have established your ovulation pattern we can plan the way forward."

The way forward! How could she see a way forward when she was floundering in a thick fog of deceit and betrayal? Determined not to cry again, she quickly cleaned off her make-up. Too tired and depressed to read, she got into bed without turning on the light. She almost cried out in terror when she hit up against a warm body. Then she relaxed and moved towards Fred. Her arms went around him and she laid her face against his skin. The even breathing told her he was in a deep sleep. Very soon she too was sleeping peacefully. She slept so soundly that Fred was up and gone before she opened her eyes on the new day.

Chapter 24

The first sight that greeted Kate in the office the following morning was Martin Burke signing a delivery note for a package. Martin scurried away into his office, package in hand, even before the courier had left. Kate didn't need to ask any questions. She knew instinctively it was the tape. *The* tape.

Unable to concentrate on her work, she doodled on a page. He would be switching it on now, listening intently as Richard's voice filled his office, then Henry Hennessey's. She remembered her crawling sandwiches-with-mayo-on-the-side episode and the doodles got more complex. By the time he called her into his office, her page was entirely covered in frantic scribbles.

She closed the door and stood with her back to it. The Dictaphone sat on the desk in front of him like an exhibit in a trial. He was staring at her and his eyes were so shadowed they reminded her of an overcast sky before a thunderstorm. He gestured to her to sit. Her legs shook as she walked the interminable distance to the chair. Easing herself onto it, she looked down at her hands. They had taken on a life of their own, twisting, clasping and unclasping, totally out of control. The room was so quiet she imagined that Martin could hear her heart beat.

"Why didn't you tell me about this?"

"I did."

"Really? You covered yourself all right. Telling me the outline just before I heard all the sordid details for myself. Who are you trying to protect? Hardly Henry Hennessey. Richard? Is that it? Still working for him, are you? I told you we must trust each other. We can't work together otherwise."

Her whole body was shaking now but the driving force was anger, not fear. The two-faced slimebag! She stood and leaned across the desk, her face almost touching his. Beyond caring about the consequences, she vented her anger on him.

"You hypocrite! You sit there and pontificate about trust and all the while you're keeping something from me. Trust is a two-way street. Why didn't you tell me about Brian Molloy's connection to International Leaf? Still think I'm on Richard's side, do you? His skivvy? Just because I made sandwiches with mayo on the side doesn't mean I'm at his beck and call. I'm not anybody's skivvy! Not Richard Gordon's and certainly not yours. So there!"

Exhausted, she flopped onto her chair. Martin was still staring at her with his cloud-filled eyes. She tried to congratulate herself on her assertiveness, to feel relieved that she had unloaded so much of her anger and resentment.

Instead she felt the hot sting of tears behind her eyelids. Fuck! No! She mustn't! When his mouth puckered and his body began to shake, she did. He was laughing at her. The tears spilled over and one fat, salty drop plopped onto the desk.

Taking a tissue from a drawer, he handed it to her. "Come on now, Kate. No need for hysterics. I didn't tell you about Brian Molloy because I didn't have confirmation until yesterday."

"What else are you not telling me?"

He took a while before he answered. Long enough for her to realise there was a lot.

"I'm putting it together, Kate. Doing research, getting help from contacts abroad. The implications are very serious. I must be sure before I say anything."

"But you said in the beginning you needed my help. So far all you've done is ask me to look up some property files that you'd already checked anyway. That's not trust, is it? Or is it my competence you doubt?"

He took in a sharp breath and his eyes darkened even more. "Spare me your self-pity, will you? Can't you see I'm trying to protect you, not denigrate you in any way? And for the record, I'm very pleased with your standard of work."

"Protect me from what?"

"Just the sordid side of life," he said dismissively and abruptly changed the subject. "I believe we have another task to share. Patty's asked me to be Jonathan's godfather."

"And what did you answer?"

"I said yes, of course. I'm really flattered. If that baby grows up to have half the character his mother has, he'll make us very proud godparents."

"He will. He's a little fighter. He's funny too. And smart. He can –"

She stopped, pained by her outpouring about someone else's child. Remembering Martin's remark about her self-pity, she directed her thoughts back to the tape.

"So, you can't use the tape as evidence, can you?"

"I'm working on it. There are a lot of issues to consider. Chain of custody, client privilege etc, etc. We'll see. We'd better get some work done now."

They settled back into work. Somehow they managed to walk the narrow path between professional and personal without stumbling. The routine was comforting, therapeutic. She needed this job more than she needed to escape Martin Burke. For now.

As soon as Adele put on her jacket to go to lunch, Fred put his computer on standby. When she left the office building, he was just feet behind her. He trailed her as she made her way towards the main street. She stopped to look in a shop window and he had to duck into a doorway to hide. He matched his pace to hers, keeping near enough to maintain visual contact but far enough away so as not to attract her attention. All the detective movies he had watched were paying dividends now.

She took a sharp left off the main street and he ran, afraid he would lose sight of her. He rounded the corner in time to see her getting into a car. Fuck! A black Mercedes. This is where he should flag down a taxi and say "Follow that car!". He stood out on the street and looked frantically around. There was no taxi. When he looked back the Mercedes had disappeared and so had his chance of finding out where Adele was going. He jumped when an irate driver beeped at him. Stepping back onto the footpath, he put down his head and walked quickly in the direction the Mercedes had taken. The lunch-time traffic was heavy. Maybe the Merc had not gone far.

After thirty minutes' brisk walking, Fred had not found any trace of the car or Adele. There was a sudden squall of wind and it began to rain. He stopped walking and stood with the big, cold raindrops pouring on top of him. What in the hell was he doing here? He turned and faced back the way he had come.

He was almost halfway back when a Seven Series BMW pulled up beside him.

"Fred! Fred Lucas. What're you doing in this part of town?"

Gus Cochrane's outsize puce head was sticking out through the window.

"Just getting a bit of exercise, Gus. Not much of a day for walking though."

"Jump in, you silly fecker! What're you exercising for? You're like a stick anyway. I'm just going for lunch. Have you eaten?"

The thought of eating from the same trough as that pig Cochrane was more than Fred could stomach. But he had changed his mind before the refusal words were formed. Gus was an ignoramus but his wealth opened doors for him. The doors of the well-heeled and well-bred. He was a valuable friend to have and a dangerous enemy. Fred walked around to the passenger's side and got in.

"Right. Where to?"

"I always go to O'Grady's. Great steaks. You get a lot of the office girls going in there too. A bit of lunch-time entertainment."

Gus Cochrane entered O'Grady's with all the pomp of an emperor visiting his court. Hands were waved and greetings called out from every corner of the crowded bar. A vacant table miraculously appeared. Fred trailed along after him, a meteor in the wake of a supernova. He just sat there as Gus ordered from the waitress.

"Bring me two fillet steaks and a couple of pints. There's a good girl. And make it a big steak for my friend here. He needs some lead in his pencil."

Fred seethed. He had needs all right. To get the information he wanted from this tub of lard. He smiled, or made a grimace as close to a smile as he could muster.

"Well, Gus, how's business these days?"

At the mention of the word business an acquisitive glint shone in the fat man's eyes. His whole demeanour instantly changed. He was alert, poised, ready to pounce. Fred understood now how the man who appeared to be a buffoon had made millions. A very sharp, focused mind hid beneath all the layers of blubber.

"I'll tell you now, Fred, the fucking tax here! If I didn't have interests abroad, I'd be knackered. Jesus, they'll tax us for taking a leak next!"

Great. He had led straight into the topic without prompting. Fred leaned closer, afraid that he would be overheard.

"Talking of foreign business, Gus, I assume you know

I've signed up for a share in a development project. Courtesy of Nigel Greenway."

"What makes you think I'd know that?"

"Come on! Of course, you're involved in this scheme. Yourself and Greenway practically sleep together."

Gus's laugh was so loud that people turned to stare and then smirk when they heard what he had to say.

"There's no room in his bed at the minute for anyone except your hot little designer. Boy, is she some nice piece of totty! "

Another piece of the jigsaw. Adele was still Nigel's bit on the side. So who in the fuck was she sneaking off to see for the past few days? Definitely not Greenway – he was away. Adele was up to something. Long lunch-times. Finishing early. And it involved being driven off in a black Merc.

Fred stared at the pint of beer the waitress had put on the table. He had not touched a drop of alcohol since the night he had been thrown out of the Grand Hotel. The night Kate had come back from Kerry. He had vowed never again. He would not, could not, end up like his father. The yeasty aroma of the beer wafted under his nose. His hand shot out and curled around the glass. He picked it up and closed his eyes as a cool draught slid down his throat.

"Easy there, boy! Take your time. We don't want to have you thrown out of here too!"

So he had heard. They all knew. Or thought they did. Feeling calmer, Fred took another sip of beer and got back to ferreting out information.

"You know obviously that Nigel has been abroad for the past few days. I assume his trip has something to do with this scheme."

Gus shovelled some food into his mouth and then put down his fork and looked at Fred.

"Am I reading this wrong or are you trying to pump me for information about the development project?"

Fortified by alcohol, Fred casually admitted that he was.

"Well, then, you're a bigger gobshite than I'd reckoned. Why're you asking me about it? Are you saying you've invested in something you really don't know anything about? Fuck, man! How stupid can you get?"

Fred could have reeled off a list of things to prove just how stupid his decisions could be. Instead he continued to nod. The fat fucker was turning the screws.

"Why didn't you question Greenway before you committed? You're in with the big boys now, lad! What did you use as collateral? Your business?"

"Part payment for the Greenway advertising campaign and the deeds of a property. My house, actually."

Gus made a sound halfway between a grunt and a groan. He waved for a waitress and re-ordered drinks. When they were served he leaned across the table and asked in a voice that, for him, was surprisingly low.

"What d'you know about this development project. How much has he told you?"

"That it involves buying and developing properties in Eastern Europe. Buy cheap, develop and then either sell or lease. Investment capital is raised on the strength of properties held in trust by the parent company. An offshore company. And that all profits are tax free."

"Did he tell you Santa Claus is one of the directors?"

Fred got that horrible cold feeling in his stomach again. The one he got when he read his sperm-count results or saw the balance sheet for Lucas Advertising. He needed another drink. He drained the first glass and started on the second. The cold spot in the pit of his stomach was beginning to warm up. Enough to find out what in the fuck Cochrane was hinting at.

"Are you saying Greenway was lying to me?"

Gus laughed. "That prick wouldn't know how to tell the truth. But what I'm really saying is that you're in over your head. This thing is bigger than either Greenway or me. Nigel thinks he's one of the big shots but like me he's just one of the monkeys. And don't ask me who the organ-grinder is. I wouldn't tell you even if I knew."

"If you think it's that dodgy why are you in it?"

"Use your head, boy. I'm putting in money I'd only be throwing away on tax otherwise. My home isn't on the line."

Fred stared into his pint and saw nothing but swirling figures that did not add up. When he looked up there was something approaching pity in Gus Cochrane's eyes. Jesus!

"I was led to believe that this was a foolproof moneymaking scheme. Invest, sit back and wait for the profits."

Even as he spoke Fred realised how pathetic he sounded. Idiotic. Jesus! Had he ever been a pushover for Greenway! Why had it been offered to him anyway?

"I can't understand why Nigel wanted me on board. As you said, there are some very big players. I know I'm small fry. Do you know why?"

Gus mopped up the last of the gravy on his plate and sat back. His piggy eyes narrowed. He seemed to be deciding carefully how to answer. Eventually he just shrugged.

"Obviously he was following orders from above. Bringing someone new into the syndicate's a big decision. He wouldn't have the authority, or the balls, to act alone. I've no idea why though. All I can tell you is that there's an ongoing scheme in Budapest. It's the biggest we've undertaken yet. It's soaking up the money. The payback should be good when it eventually arrives. But not for some time. Can you hold out?"

Fred laughed and there was a hysterical edge to the sound. How could he be expected to forecast the future when he seemed to have so little control over the here and now? Adele was costing Lucas Advertising a fortune but her productivity had suddenly fallen through the floor. She must, she just must, get to work on the travel-agency bid and forget about whatever it was that was absorbing all her attention now. If only they had that contract in the bag, then maybe they could survive. Gus was still waiting for an answer.

"I need a big contract. I've cash-flow problems because of the agreement I made with Greenway. But the deal with the travel agency is almost in the bag. I can hold on. For a while."

Fred had believed that when he said it. He believed it

all the way back to his office. It was like a mantra in his head. *I can hold on. I can hold on.* It was so much easier to think positively with two pints in his belly. Just two pints. No more. He could control his drinking. He could win the travel-agency deal.

Everything remained very positive until he discovered Adele had not yet returned from her lunch break. Bitch! When she swanned in an hour later without even an apology, he realised he was behaving like a total fool. If Jim Grant carried on like that, he would fire him. He strode over to her desk. She looked up at him and smiled. Her eyes sparkled with fun and good humour. Her lacy bra was visible through the thin fabric of her semi-transparent top. Feeling that someone was watching, Fred dragged his eyes away from Adele's chest and looked over his shoulder. Jim Grant was glaring. He turned back to Adele and tried to make his voice stern.

"Your lunch break's an hour, Adele. Please make sure you stick to that in future."

She hung her head so that her mass of shiny blonde hair hid her face. "Sorry, Fred. I was shopping. I didn't notice the time passing."

He could not tell her he knew she was lying. There must be a law against sneaking around after your staff. But one thing was sure, whatever she had been doing in that black Mercedes, it had not been shopping and it had not been grabbing a quickie with Nigel Greenway. This girl was a maverick. A talented, sexy, very desirable pain in the butt.

"Well, don't let it happen again. Get down to work

now, please. We're way behind with the travel proposal."

Adele smiled, Jim Grant glared and Fred longed for another drink.

Kate pretended to be asleep when she heard Fred come home. She held her breath as he clambered up the stairs. The heavy tread and intermittent stumbles told her that he was very drunk. When he passed by the door of their bedroom she breathed a sigh of relief.

Chapter 25

Sunlight poured through the stained glass windows casting multi-coloured shadows on the little group around the christening font. Jonathan was awake. His eyes were focused towards the altar, drawn by the play of light. Kate swallowed the knot of sadness in her throat. It was difficult not to cry, not to rage at the horrible fate which ordained this baby be christened in the very church where his father's coffin had so recently lain.

She looked across at Patty. Beautifully made-up, her hair shining, as slim as she had been before her pregnancies, Patty seemed to be in control of herself and the situation. Kate looked beyond her friend's surface calm and saw the almost imperceptible shake in her hands, the little lines around her mouth as she tightened her lips to prevent them trembling. Fred, standing beside her, must have noticed too. Kate saw him take Patty's hand and hold it. The little gesture made Kate feel even more upset. That was the old Fred, the one she had fallen in love with and married. Kind, sensitive, caring. The antithesis of the self-obsessed person he was becoming.

A cloud must have passed over the sun because the reflected colours dimmed and the church got gloomy.

"Ready?" Martin asked as the clergyman indicated that the christening ceremony should begin.

Just as she and Martin walked towards the christening font with the baby, the three Molloy boys and Bobby rushed forward, pushing and shoving each other to get a better view. There was a loud bang as the tall holder containing the christening candle toppled. The Reverend tutted and righted the holder. Frowning, he re-lit the candle from another lighted one. Contrite, the boys formed a circle around the font. Surrounded by the little group who loved him, Jonathan Alan Molloy was christened.

After the photographs at the church they all piled into the cars and headed back to The Rectory. Kate had done her best to convince Patty to hold the christening party in a hotel. Not a party really. That would have been inappropriate because of Brian. She had wanted to take them all for a meal, give Patty a chance to relax. But Patty had been insistent.

"Jonathan won't have the privilege of growing up in The Rectory. At least his christening can be celebrated there."

So Kate had relented. She had been a little miffed though when Patty had also refused her offer of help with preparing food. "There's a surprise," she had announced and would not be drawn on it.

The 'surprise' began to unfold as they drove up the avenue. The trees were all hung with yards of white bunting and a huge bunch of white balloons hovered over the front door. Best of all, a marquee sprawled on the front lawn, the flaps fluttering in the breeze. Set free from the solemnity of the church service, the boys were racing in and out of the marquee, shouting and laughing and generally causing mayhem.

"I thought she was supposed to be broke," Fred said. "This lot must be costing a fortune."

Kate had to agree with him. Especially when she saw a woman in waitress uniform come out of the house carrying a tray of canapés. Had Patty totally lost her reason? When they got out of the car, they could see that Martin was as surprised as they were. That hit Kate's theory on the head.

"I thought maybe Martin had set this up," she whispered to Fred. "But look. He seems to be as stunned as we are."

Inside the marquee, the extravagance stepped up a gear. There were two tables laden with food. Platters of lobster, prawns, venison and beef covered one table while the table which was obviously meant for the children had mounds of chicken nuggets, burgers and chips. A trolley loaded with desserts sat by each table. The boys were already helping themselves to sweets.

"No, boys," said Patty. "We'll take some more photos before you get yourselves all covered in chocolate and ice cream."

Patty organised the group in front of the marquee. It

took some doing to marshal the over-excited children into an orderly line. And then, just when they expected her to lift her camera to take the shot, a photographer walked out through the patio doors. He took over the organising. He photographed the baby with his godparents, with his mother, with his brothers, with the whole group.

"Have you sold the story of the christening to *Hello*?" Kate asked and even though she laughed it was the only halfway logical explanation she could come up with for the extravaganza.

"I'll tell you later," Patty said. "Just enjoy it."

Kate could not stop speculating. Maybe the Molloys had softened a bit and had decided to treat Brian's youngest son to a spectacular christening.

"D'you think the Molloys stumped up for this?" she asked Fred.

He shook his head. "No way. Not their style. If they were going to give Jonathan anything it would be a set of encyclopaedia. Not this."

Kate relaxed then. If Patty was not worrying about paying for this lot, why should she? Things got a bit hectic when the children began to haul food up into their tree house. Kate smiled as she watched Bobby traipse along after the older boys. He seemed to be learning very quickly how to fight his own corner. One of them got the idea of using jelly babies as ammunition. The sweets rained down from the tree house in a shower of reds, greens and blues.

"Treat!" Patty called up to them. "But only for good boys!"

The children scrambled down from the tree and stood in front of her. All the little faces looked so innocent it was hard to believe they could cause as much destruction as a plague of locusts in a crop field. Kate had thought she was immune to any more surprises until she saw a magician and a clown come into the garden. The clown somersaulted towards the boys and they squealed with excitement. Patty walked away from them and came over to the group of gobsmacked adults. She laughed at their expressions.

"Right! You're all thinking I've lost my mind. And that may be true. But I haven't robbed a bank to pay for this lot. Nor have I borrowed. I couldn't anyway. What bank would lend me money?"

"Well, I'll have to admit, we are wondering," Kate said.

"I'll give you a hint. Rubbish."

Kate picked up on the clue immediately. "The Cochranes! I should have guessed. This catering has Sheila's fingerprints all over it."

"I didn't think you were that friendly with them," Fred remarked.

Patty shuffled her feet and seemed a bit uncomfortable. "Well, I'm not really. I wasn't. I think I may have misjudged them though. Sheila has been so kind. She insisted. I refused at first but when she pointed out that the children needed a distraction from – well, from death and loss, I agreed. And she was right. Look at them now."

They all turned to look at the little group of children huddled around the magician, their eyes huge in their faces. The entertainer was waving a blue handkerchief in the air and his audience stared in awe as it turned into a wand. Bobby clapped his chubby little hands together and the other boys cheered.

"C'mon while they're quiet," Patty ordered. "It's time for us to enjoy some of the goodies in peace in the marquee."

They followed her inside where they enjoyed platefuls of the delicious food. The waitress opened bottles of wine and poured for them. Kate was too busy eating at first to notice how much Fred was drinking but when she saw the waitress open another bottle she realised that Fred was drinking more than his fair share. He was beginning to speak quite loudly. Yet he seemed more relaxed. The frowns which were becoming a permanent feature on his face seemed to disappear as he laughed. When he and Martin began to swap college reminiscences, Patty nodded to Kate. They strolled up to the house, leaving the children with the entertainers and the men with their stories.

Patty waved to Kate to follow her. She led the way into the study. Going over to Brian's desk, she opened one of the drawers and took out a bulky envelope and handed it to Kate.

"I don't know what to do about this. What do you think?"

Kate glanced at the writing on the outside: *"For baby Jonathan on the occasion of his Christening."* Opening the envelope, she saw the bundle of notes inside and gasped.

"There must be hundreds here. Even thousands. So the Molloys are having a change of heart? They're not going to abandon you."

Patty shook her head and just looked at Kate. It was enough. She did not have to say any more.

"You mean this is from the Cochranes?"

"Yes. And it's two thousand."

"It's ten times bigger than mine," Kate said, "and I'm his godmother!"

She could have bitten her tongue off then. That sounded so crass. But true nevertheless. She had opened a savings account for Jonathan and put two hundred euro into it. Patty could use it for clothes or shoes for him, or whatever she saw fit. But this was two thousand. And Gus Cochrane did not even know the child.

"I don't understand. When did you become so friendly with the Cochranes?"

"I'm not. At least I haven't been. You know I never liked them. I thought him a vulgar bully and as for her – well, I thought she was a pathetic social climber."

"And now?"

"I don't know. They called to see me and offered to organise this party, celebration, whatever you want to call it. They were so nice, Kate. Very kind and considerate. And they don't seem to want anything in return. They wouldn't even come to the ceremony today. They said it was a family occasion and they wouldn't like to intrude."

The extravaganza in the garden must have cost another two thousand. That kind of expenditure was probably peanuts to Gus Cochrane. One lorryload of rubbish. But it left the question of why? It was not as if Brian Molloy and Gus Cochrane had been bosom buddies. Or any kind of buddies at all. Patty was looking anxiously at her, waiting for an answer. Kate folded the flap back on the envelope and handed it to her.

"I don't know. It's a lot of money. I'm not sure that they mightn't want a payback at some stage."

"What in the name of God could they want from me, Kate? Once The Rectory is sold I'd consider myself lucky to be living in a tent. They know I'm broke. That's why they're being so kind. Looking on me as a charity case, I s'pose."

"How do they know you're broke?"

"I told them, of course. No point pretending."

Or could it be that the Rubbish King had a conscience? Was he the one who told Brian about the development scheme, the one who encouraged him to re-mortgage The Rectory?

"Did you tell Martin about this – this very generous christening present?"

"No. D'you think I should?"

Kate was tempted to tell her that she suspected Gus Cochrane of being involved in the development scheme in which Brian had invested. Shit! Not suspected. She knew. But that would be dangerous. Patty would probably say something to the Cochranes and then all of the syndicate would be warned that they were being investigated. And why shouldn't Patty have the money anyway? It was only a fraction of what they had stolen from Brian. She smiled at her

"Patty, you must do what you think best but, if you want to know my opinion, I think you should take that money for the children. Cochrane has plenty of it. He won't miss it."

Patty nodded and put the envelope back into the drawer. She rubbed her hand across the top of the desk and looked at Kate.

"This was Brian's favourite room, you know. He loved the rough and tumble with the boys but he liked to escape from them too. This was his sanctuary. We all knew not to disturb him when he came in here."

Patty stood there for a while, her hand gently rubbing the polished oak of the desktop. Her eyes filled with tears.

"I miss him so much, Kate. I'm tired of being strong. I just want to lie down and sleep. But I can't, can I?"

Kate put her arms around Patty and held her while she cried.

The orchard to the back of The Rectory had first been planted at the beginning of the last century. Several different varieties of apple trees grew alongside pear, plum and cherry. There was even a section for blackcurrant and redcurrant bushes. Martin and Fred walked along the well-worn pathways.

"I'd like to see this in the spring," Martin said. "It must be spectacular when the apple and cherry trees are in blossom."

"Not long to wait now. Spring's just around the corner. In fact I'm sure I saw some buds on the south-facing trees."

"Trouble is, it'll probably be under new ownership by then. I hope whoever buys it appreciates what they're getting."

Fred looked at Martin in surprise. "Do you think The

Rectory will sell that quickly? It's top end of the market."

"It's a very unique property, you know. Anyway, nothing's really decided yet and I shouldn't be talking about it."

They stood and looked around them. Behind them a granite stone wall bounded the property and ahead, through the branches of the as yet bare trees, they could see the house itself. Despite the excited shouts of the children, there was a stillness, a peace. Martin shook his head. "It's a shame. Patty should be able to rear her children and grow old here. Criminal really."

"Yes," Fred agreed. "I can't believe Brian Molloy was so stupid. Why in the fuck didn't he have his insurance in place?"

"You could ask why he got involved in a dodgy get-rich-quick scheme. "

"Get rich quick, my arse! There's a long –"

Fred stopped mid-sentence. He had drunk too much wine and his mouth was running away with him. Anyway it was only guesswork that Brian had put his money in with Greenway's lot. What was Burke's interest in it? Fuck him!

Spotting an old paint tin sitting on a tree-stump near the wall, Fred noticed little heaps of stones scattered around it. The boys must have been using it for target practice. He pointed it out to Martin.

"Challenge! Best of six, OK? I'll beat the balls off you, Burkey!"

"We'll see about that. You're on!"

Fred stooped to pick up a stone. He almost toppled

over. Martin caught him by the arm to steady him. He looked into the face of the man who was becoming a shadow of the carefree, extrovert character he had known.

"What's going on, Lippy? Could I do anything to help?"

It was difficult to focus his eyes but Fred finally managed to get a clear view of Martin. Burkey. Always the most likely to succeed. Always the one destined for great things. Things like a glittering career and a trophy wife. But he was on a slide too, wasn't he? Wife gone and big career in the States over. What in the fuck could *he* do to help?

"It'd be very helpful if you could get me a rake of advertising contracts. And maybe you could pay the lease on my offices and my wages bill. Oh, and yes! Get back the money I shouldn't have given away."

Martin held his breath. He could not put words in Fred's mouth. The information would have to be given voluntarily.

But Fred didn't say any more.

"What money did you give away? Who did you give it to?"

Fred straightened up and the alcoholic fog cleared from his head. What in the name of Christ had he said? Martin Burke was a dangerous fucker. Richard Gordon had said so. And so had Nigel. As well as that he was Kate's boss. They probably had some very cosy little chats. He could imagine her now, all big eyes and sad face. "D'you know Fred has a low sperm count, Martin? Isn't that pathetic? And I want a baby." The sweat had begun to break out on his forehead before he remembered that his wife did not know anything about his sperm count. Or his financial difficulties. Or that he had re-mortgaged the house. He was safe! Relief flooded through him. Grabbing a stone he hurled it at the can. Bull's-eye! One down, five to go.

"Come on, Burkey! Beat that if you can."

Knowing the chance had passed, Martin picked up a stone. Pointless trying to discreetly warn Fred or to get him to talk about the mess he had got himself into. Or ask him why he had lied about going to the cottage in Kerry. That would have to wait until he was sober and a sober Fred Lucas was getting to be an endangered species.

Martin fired his stone and missed the can. Fred cheered and hollered and generally behaved like a drunken lout until Kate finally piled him into the car and drove him home.

Chapter 26

Martin saluted Eileen as he passed reception but she was too engrossed in a conversation with Rose to notice him. He smiled to himself, remembering a time, very, very long ago, when he too had loads to talk about after the weekend. He was learning to ignore Eileen's chattering. It never affected her work output. Clients liked her. She was friendly and outgoing and very helpful. So what if she was a gabby guts. She had no access to confidential information anyway.

He was a few strides past them when the name Fred Lucas caught his attention. He stopped, ostensibly to pick up his post.

"I'm not gossiping," Eileen was saying to Rose, neither woman noticing him standing there. "Everyone knows. He's always following her around. Like a lovesick boy. He practically drools when he looks at her. And no wonder. Have you seen how she dresses? Everything on display in the shop window."

Rose leaned towards Eileen and, being the more discreet of the two, spoke in a low voice. Martin had to strain his ears to hear.

"You've got the wrong end of the stick. It's not Fred Lucas she's sleeping with. I heard it's that guy who owns the Greenway chain of garages."

"Really? Fred mustn't realise he's been beaten to the post. The bedpost! Poor Kate!"

"Silly Kate! It's her own fault. She seems to be allowing him free rein. If she went out with him a bit more often she'd know what he was up to. Anyway, Eileen, enough chat. The Cranky Yank will be here soon. It's not like him to be late."

Martin picked up his post and tapped it on the desk. Both girls twirled around, shocked expressions on their faces.

"The Cranky Yank's not late. Would it be too much to ask you two to get started on some work, please?"

He left them as they scuttled red-faced off to their desks. He did not laugh until he had closed the door to his office. 'Cranky Yank' indeed! He was being nice now. Wait until they saw him in really cranky mood. They would have to upgrade his nickname to Mad Martin! At least they had solved one mystery for him. He knew now why Fred had backed out of the Kerry trip and left Kate to carry the can. Lippy must have fancied his chances with Adele for that weekend.

Flicking through his post he tried to concentrate but he gave up after a few minutes. He pushed it to one side for Kate to deal with. Poor Kate! Wasn't that exactly what

Eileen had said? It sounded from what they were saying that Fred was making a right prick of himself chasing after Adele Sheehan. Not surprising really. She had the cutest butt and the longest legs. Hadn't he almost taken the bait himself? He remembered the dinner date he had with her. He had been as proud as a peacock escorting the stunningly beautiful young girl who attracted male attention wherever she went. But long before they had reached the dessert course Martin felt that he had been interviewed for a job vacancy and that he had failed to meet the criteria. If the rumour was true, Nigel Greenway had got the job.

Getting up from his desk he walked to the window and looked out over the city. His eyes were drawn, as always, to the distant park. It reminded him of his son, of the times he had brought him to Central Park. He had missed him last night and missed seeing him this morning. Checking his watch, he decided it was not too early to ring. The phone almost rang out before it was grabbed and Patty said a breathless hello.

"Hi, Martin! We've just dropped the gang off at school. We're only back this minute."

"How's Bobby? Any problems?"

"Of course not. You know 'twas his choice to stay. He slept like a log and mucked in with the others this morning. Do you want to talk to him now?"

When Robert came on the phone he spoke in the same breathless excited tone as Patty. Martin smiled. It seemed as if his son really needed to stake his claim as a member of the Molloy household. He had cried such bitter tears last night that Martin had relented and allowed him to sleep over in The Rectory. Next he would be offering himself up for adoption.

"I'll collect him at the usual time this evening then," he told Patty before putting the phone down slowly.

No wonder Bobby wanted to stay at Molloys'. Living in a hotel with his father while his mother was off flitting around Saudi was not the ideal upbringing for any child. His hand hovered over the phone. One more try. He would give her one last chance. He dialled the international code and then Lee's number. After a series of clicks and buzzes he heard the ring. He held the receiver until it rang out.

Enough! It had been a week since he last heard from her. She could be mugged, raped, lying in a desert with her throat slit. He opened the phone book on his mobile and found Chuck Page's private number. Allowing himself no time to change his mind, he tapped in the number.

"Martin! Nice to hear from you. How're things in the Emerald Isle?"

Martin's skin crawled at the sound of his ex-father-in-law's drawl. Every syllable reminded him of battles he had fought and lost with this most arrogant of men. He took a deep breath and tried to pitch his voice to a casual tone.

"Very well, thank you. I was wondering if you've heard from Lee recently?"

Martin had to hold the phone out from his ear as Chuck gave one of famously loud laughs. "That gal is a chip off the old block! So headstrong! I suppose you want me to get her to change her mind. You know God himself couldn't do that once she has decided. What's it to you anyway? You've got all you're going to get out of this family!"

Martin allowed himself the luxury of kicking his desk. He hurt his foot and still felt like screaming at the asshole on the other end of the line. Wouldn't Chuck love that! He took a breath which was meant to be deep but ended up being a shallow gasp.

"I didn't ring you to rehash old arguments, Chuck. I just wanted to enquire about Lee. She *is* Bobby's mother."

"Ah! Robert. How is my grandson?"

"Fine. How's his mother? When did you last hear from her?"

"I was talking to her just this morning. I tried to convince her not to make the same mistake she did when she met you. She didn't listen then and she's not listening now."

Martin was beginning to get a picture here and he did not like what he was seeing.

"Are you saying she's going to marry Sheikh Al whatever his name is?"

The loud laugh split Martin's eardrum again. The old bollocks was loving this.

"You mean she hasn't told you yet? None of your business anyway. She doesn't owe you anything."

"She owes her son. Our son."

"If you think you're going to screw more money out of me by playing that card, you'd better think again, you Irish carpetbagger!"

Martin slammed down the phone. He thumped the

desk and it was his fist he hurt this time. Fuck! There was a gentle tap at the door and he shouted, "Come in!" a lot more loudly than he meant to. Kate's pale face appeared.

"Are you all right, Martin? I heard a bang."

"Of course, I'm not! I think my foot is broken and my hand is bruised."

Kate's eyes got even bigger and darker. She walked over to him and leant over to examine the hand he was rubbing. When Martin saw her concern, he regretted his outburst. Poor Kate.

"I'm fine, Kate, really. Just letting off steam. I've been on the phone to my ex-father-in-law. He brings out the worst in me."

"That's what in-laws are supposed to do. You're allowed an extra helping of violence for ex-inlaws."

Martin looked at her and frowned. She was laughing at him. He never knew where he was with Kate. Sometimes she was soft and vulnerable, making him want to protect her. And then at other times, she seemed to be strong and assertive. He would have to choose one of her stronger moments to talk to her about Fred. Give her the facts and let her deal with them. Assuming she did not already know. He was gambling a lot on that assumption.

Fred's head throbbed with pain and only part of the discomfort was caused by a hangover. His eyes were continually drawn to Adele's work area. She was late again. It was as if she was shoving two fingers up at him. The travel-agency presentation was way behind schedule and instead of putting in extra time to bring it up to date, she was coming in later and leaving earlier. She was making a complete prick of him. He should take this situation in hand. Assert his authority. The truth was Adele's nipples showing through one of her micro-tops had more influence over him than he had over her.

The post lay on his desk. He did not have the wherewithal to tackle it. Getting up, he went to the little kitchenette they called a canteen. Coffee, strong and black, should get him back on track. The kettle had just boiled when Jim Grant joined him.

"You're a bloodhound with the coffee, Jim. You always sniff it out."

Jim did not answer. He just stood there, shuffling from one foot to the other. Fred knew he was going to start complaining again. It was too much.

"You're like a hen with an egg. For fuck's sake, let me have a cup of coffee in peace!"

"Did you get the letter I left on your desk?"

There was something about the quiet way Jim spoke that made the hair stand on the back of Fred's neck. And why in the hell was he writing letters? There could only be one reason.

"No, I didn't open any post yet. And I don't think I want to open any letter you wrote. You're not serious, Jim? You couldn't do that to me?"

Jim got out a cup for himself and spooned in some coffee. He took his time adding water, sugar and milk. It was as if he knew Fred was on edge and he wanted to prolong the agony. He took a sip from his cup and looked Fred directly in the eye.

"I've given you my notice, Fred. I'm due two weeks' holidays and I'm taking them in lieu of notice. I'm leaving today."

Fred's headache, which had been abating, throbbed violently again. Fuck! What was he supposed to do here? Beg? Yes, if that's what it took. Jim Grant was invaluable. A good steady worker. How could all the small contracts be serviced without him?

"Look, we'll talk this over, Jim. If you've a problem, I'm sure we can sort it. There's no need for such drastic action."

Jim's face blazed with an anger which was totally at odds with his normally passive character. Fred could only sit and watch as Jim let rip with a tirade of pent-up resentment.

"I will not, I cannot, take any more of the treatment you've been doling out to me. You've been contemptuous towards me, personally and professionally. I'll be the first to admit that Adele Sheehan is a very innovative and original designer. That doesn't give you the right to sideline me like you've done or to let her make her own rules. To be honest, I'm just shit-sick of the whole set-up. I don't know why I've put up with it for so long and I can't wait to be gone now."

"Why didn't you tell me you felt like this? We could have talked it through."

Jim shook his head in exasperation. "I've spoken to you. Drawn your attention to the fact that Adele is coming and going as she pleases. I asked you for pay parity with her. You brushed me off every time. All she has to do is shake her tits at you and she has you eating out of her hand."

"How dare you! You'd better apologise. Immediately."

"No. I won't. It's all true. Why don't you fire me? I'd love to get you for unfair dismissal."

"Are you threatening me?"

Fred realised that was a stupid question. Of course, it was a threat. And there was some validity in Jim's complaints. Adele was on a much higher pay scale. He had to offer her that salary in order to take her from the company she had been with. And when she was working, when she was using her skills and exceptional creative ability, she was worth every penny. Jim was an average worker. Steady, conscientious but not innovative. A plodder. Exactly what was needed to keep the mundane bread-and-butter contracts rolling over. Nothing for it but to offer him more money although where in the fuck it was going to come from was a mystery.

"I've listened to what you said, Jim, and taken it on board. You know our position. We're trying to get established so the best I can offer you now is a five per cent increase. We can review that upwards when we clinch the travel agency contract."

Jim went to the sink and rinsed out his cup and dried it. Fred relaxed a little, knowing that his offer was being considered. That belief made the shock all the greater when Jim turned around and laughed in his face.

"I'm sorry to say this, Fred, but there's nothing you could offer me now that would make me stay. You're not the man I came to work for. You're letting Adele make a fool of you and when you're here, you either have a hangover or you're half-drunk. Lucas Advertising is going down the tube and I'm not going with it. You can send me on what you owe me."

Jim turned around, got his coat and walked out.

Martin found it difficult to concentrate on work. Every document he looked at seemed to have Lee's name printed on it. Bitch! Not that he cared about her any more. He had long outgrown his obsession with her status and beauty, the two things that had drawn him to her in the first place. She could marry Osama Bin Laden now for all he cared. It was his son's future he was worrying about. His gut twisted at the thought of Lee and the sheikh whisking Bobby off to live in the desert. It would be a very luxurious lifestyle no doubt. A five-star oasis. The sheikh was super rich, millions of dollars pumping out of his oil wells by the hour. But the culture was so different. Anyway the last thing Bobby needed was another change. His young life had seen too many upheavals already. Lee was obviously still playing her games. She was making him sit and wait for her call.

Checking his diary, he saw that he was finished with appointments for the day. Staying here was pointless. He needed to see Bobby, to hold him, to feel his chubby little arms around his neck. He rang Patty.

"Would you mind, Patty, if I called for Bobby a little earlier than usual? I'm finished up here now."

"Of course. I'm just putting on dinner. Are you brave enough to join the mob for something to eat?"

Martin could think of nothing more soothing to his

battered psyche than home cooking and a houseful of children. He accepted the offer gratefully.

The Rectory was several miles outside the city. Martin used the time he was stuck in traffic to try to clear his mind of Chuck Page and his daughter. And there perhaps, was the nub of their marriage breakdown. Lee had never become Martin's wife, just as she would never become Mrs Sheikh. She would always remain Chuck's daughter. If Bobby had any significance in her life it would be as her father's grandson rather than as her son.

Noticing that the inside lane was moving more quickly he found a gap and steered the nose of the Volvo towards it. He annoyed several people by doing this and horns began to hoot. Just as he had braved the road rage and managed to take his place, the inside lane stopped moving and the one he had left began to flow. His toe was still smarting from kicking the desk. He drummed the steering wheel impatiently. He was not good at waiting games. Not at waiting for the lights to change to green or for his ex-wife to ring. He turned on the radio and switched the volume up high. Better fill his head with noise rather than the buzz of questions clamouring for answers. He had tuned in midway through a discussion programme on Law Reform. He listened intently, not quite believing his ears at first. But there was no mistaking Henry Hennessey's rich-toned voice. Martin got his phone and tapped in Kate's number.

"Go to the canteen straight away and switch on the Radio One news."

Kate had been taking advantage of the boss's early exit from the office. She guiltily put down the crossword puzzle she had been engrossed in and did as she was told. When she heard Henry Hennessey fervently supporting the new proposals for legislation on money-laundering, she laughed at the sheer nerve of the man, just as Martin was laughing in his car.

"There are people out there," Henry preached, *"who consider themselves above the law. Of course, we need to catch the drug barons, to prevent them profiting from their heinous crimes. That goes without saying. But we must also tackle what we call 'white collar crime'. These fraudsters are criminals too. This is our opportunity to stop the outflow of untaxed income from all sources. We must close the loopholes –"*

When the interviewer cut him off to go to the weather forecast both Kate and Martin shook their heads in disbelief. Henry Hennessey was obviously launching his comeback campaign and it seemed like he had chosen a very interesting route to get where he wanted to go.

After dinner Bobby put on a repeat performance. Except that this evening he cried even harder than he had yesterday. It was heartbreaking to hear the sobs.

"Please, Dad! Bobby stay! Please!"

Martin cuddled him close and tried to reason with him. "What about Daddy? I'll be lonely without you."

"Daddy stay too."

Martin tried to comfort his son, to distract him, to bribe him. Nothing worked. He was crying so hard now that his breath was coming in gulps. The older children were in their pyjamas, sitting on the floor around the television. They glared at Martin, blaming him for Bobby's upset. The eldest boy came over to Patty and whispered in her ear. Realising that Bobby's crying was disturbing the other children, Martin brought the sobbing child out to the kitchen.

Patty followed and stood in front of father and son. "Martin, I don't want to interfere but my boys have asked if Bobby can stay."

"Bobby stay!" the child echoed.

"Are you sure? Five children, Patty! That's a handful. You need a break."

She opened her arms and Bobby dived into them. He snuggled his face into her neck as she rocked him. Gradually the sobbing eased.

Martin nodded.

"Do'you hear that, Bobby?" said Patty. "Daddy says you can stay with your friends."

The child lifted his head and smiled. The boys were all standing at the kitchen door, waiting for him. He wriggled, got down on the floor and happily went away with the others to sit in front of the television.

When Bobby had gone to bed, Martin should have gone back to the hotel. But he waited until the eldest boys had gone to sleep. Then he waited until Jonathan was after his feed. The peace of The Rectory was working its magic on his mind. His problems seemed to have gone to sleep too. There was no room for them here in this big old kitchen.

Patty got out a bottle of non-alcoholic wine. "One for the road? How good are you at fooling yourself?"

"Not very good, I'm afraid. I have quite a line in self-torture."

"Pretend. This is a lovely Chardonnay. 1990, I think."

He raised his glass to her. "That was a very good year. And this is very potent."

"See! We can all fool ourselves when we need to."

Martin looked at the petite woman sitting across from him and understood why his son wanted to stay here. Patty did not look the stereotypical maternal type. There were no comfortable fleshy arms and big bosoms. She was glamorous and svelte. Yet the warmth and understanding in her eyes inspired a desire to be with her, to be on her team, to be cared for by her. He shook his head and looked at his glass of fruit juice.

"Are you sure this is non-alcoholic?"

"Are you sure you're not good at pretending?"

They laughed and filled up their glasses again. Martin had an uncomfortable topic to broach and he was wondering how best to approach it when Patty said, "Just spit it out."

He did. "I want to talk to you about the accident. I'm sorry to bring it up but you need to think about making a claim against the lorry driver."

Patty twirled her glass around. Martin saw the pain in her eyes and he was so sorry to have put it there. But there was no alternative.

"I can handle it for you. I've read the police report and I know you would have a good chance of winning compensation."

Her head snapped up and he saw there were tears in her eyes.

"Compensation? You mean money. There isn't enough money in the world to compensate the children for the loss of their father, their home, their future. Or me for the loss of my husband. Why should I go through the trauma of reliving that night again in public? It's torture enough to have it burned onto my brain, day in, day out. I can't picture Brian any more without half his head missing and that blasted machine inflating his lungs."

"You won't have to appear at any hearing. I'll represent you. In fact, I suspect that the lorry driver's insurance company may settle the claim out of court. Think of the children, Patty. Unfortunately compensation for a fatality is not as sizeable as for injury but, nevertheless, you are entitled to it."

"Anyway, I thought the accident was Brian's fault. Wasn't he driving too fast?"

"It's not as clear-cut as that. Well, will I start proceedings?"

She twisted the glass nervously again for another minute. Then she nodded. "For the boys. Go ahead. Do whatever 'tis you lawyers do."

Martin sighed in relief. That was one hurdle over. Now for another. "I was talking to Lee's father today. It seems my wife is about to marry again."

"The sheikh?"

"And his oil wells. She'll be happy with them for a while at least. She's not told me herself yet so I'm not really sure of her plans. I know looking after Bobby was just a temporary arrangement but would you mind continuing on indefinitely until I have things sorted out with Lee?"

Patty reached across the table and caught his hand. "I'll look after Bobby for as long as possible. I love the little bundle and he gets on so well with the boys. He's like one of the family now. I don't even want to think about him leaving."

Martin squeezed her hand in thanks. What a mess! Here was a stranger who had more real feeling for Bobby than his mother had. The Middle East was top of Lee's agenda at present and nothing interfered with her plans, not even her three-year-old son.

"We're going to have to revise our agreement, Patty. The sum we agreed on was only for day care. It seems like Bobby wants to book himself in here full-time. How do you feel about that?"

Patty beamed. "I told you how I feel. I'd be delighted. And there's no need for more money. You pay me generously enough as it is. Anyway, I don't need it. Did Kate tell you about my windfall?"

"What windfall?"

Patty got up and left the kitchen. She came back carrying an envelope and handed it to him. He looked inside at the bundles of notes and then looked up at Patty.

"Gus Cochrane," she explained.

Jesus! Paying for the over-the-top christening had been one thing. Handing over a stack of used notes was something else altogether. Conscience money.

"Kate knows about this?"

Patty nodded. "I was going to give it back but Kate and I decided that I should keep it for the children. The Rubbish King has plenty of it."

Martin handed her back the envelope and rubbed his hands on the sides of his trousers. They felt dirty after handling the conscience money.

"You can't keep this, Patty. Why d'you think he gave it to you? He's not what you would call a soft touch, is he?"

"He and Sheila have been kind to me, Martin. You'd be amazed at the number of so-called friends who have turned their backs on me now that Brian is not here any more. I feel guilty about the way I've spoken of the Cochranes in the past."

"And don't you think they know that? Have you any idea why they feel obliged to be nice to you now?"

Patty dropped the envelope on the table and sat staring at it. Martin watched the expressions on her face change from defiance to anger to resignation. She picked up the envelope and took it away. When she came back, she went to the sink and washed her hands. Martin knew then the conclusion she had reached.

"You're right. I'll make sure he gets it back. And I'll try to find out from him why he felt he had to pay me off." She dried her hands and then laughed. "I'm glad about the christening though. Jonathan deserved it. It would've been perfect except that Fred drank too much. Fred always seems to drink too much these days."

Martin looked at his watch then and realised it was late. After going upstairs to see Bobby, he said goodnight to Patty and left The Rectory.

He dreaded facing his hotel room. No amount of luxury, convenience and service could hide the fact that he was a man in his thirties whose son was in someone else's house and whose wife was in someone else's bed.

Tomorrow, he would start looking for somewhere permanent to live. Tomorrow, he would ask Kate why she had not told him about Gus Cochrane's envelope full of used notes and what in the hell she meant by advising Patty to keep it. Tomorrow he would decide whether he could ever again trust Kate Lucas.

Chapter 27

Kate carefully filled in the new reading on her chart. Her temperature was up. She was ovulating. Her body ached with the need for procreation. It was as if the egg inside her was crying out for fertilisation. Standing in front of the mirror, she imagined her slim figure gradually filling out, breasts swelling, tummy getting more distended by the week. She put her hand over her flat stomach and her need was so great that she felt the beat of a tiny heart, the kick of miniature legs against the wall of her womb.

"Are you nearly finished there or will I go to the downstairs bathroom?"

Her hand dropped guiltily and she turned to look at her husband. The man she wanted to father her child. He was grey-faced and dishevelled, his curly hair sticking out in all directions.

"You need a haircut," she said and then wondered what had made her pass such an asinine remark. Fred obviously needed something far more radical than grooming. The weight loss, the pallor, the dark circles under his eyes were so pronounced that they could no longer be ignored. She moved towards him and reached out a hand to his face. He took a step back as if repulsed by her touch.

"Look at the time. I overslept. We'll both be late. Are you finished or will I go downstairs?"

Kate stood in front of him and decided that this time he was not going to brush her off. The man seemed haunted. He looked sick. Panic gripped her. Maybe he was about to die.

"I'm not going anywhere until you tell me what's wrong with you. You look awful, Fred. You must see a doctor."

He threw his head back and laughed. The sound bounced off the tiled walls and came back more eerie than when it had left his mouth. It was an out-of-control sound.

"You think a few blood tests and a prescription are the answer to everything. You're so naïve. A lot of help a fucking doctor would be to me now."

"Why not, for Christ's sake? You're obviously sick. And you're drinking too much. Your father –"

Fred banged his fist on the vanity unit. Bottles and jars rattled. Kate stood still in terror. She stared at the bloodshot whites of Fred's eyes and the bulging veins on his neck. This maniac was not her husband.

"Don't you ever again mention my father! You know nothing about him. It's easy for you, isn't it, with your safe little job? No responsibility. All you have to worry about is what you're going to wear to work."

"That's not fair. I'd share responsibility with you if you allowed me. But you made Lucas Advertising your domain. How can I help when I don't know what's going on?"

"For starters, Jim Grant has handed in his notice. Just fucked off and left me in the shit. The travel-agency presentation is late and I'll lose that contract if I don't produce something soon. And then, when I need your support so badly, what do I get? Abuse about my father and advice on a haircut. Just go away, Kate, and leave me alone."

He turned and stormed off, leaving Kate in shock. It was a few minutes before she could gather enough energy to move. She folded up her temperature chart and put it back into the medicine cabinet. As she closed the door, she saw her reflection in the mirror. A terrified woman looked back at her. She remembered Fred's bloodshot eyes and bulging neck veins, remembered the threat, the terror she experienced from his barely controlled anger. Opening the cabinet again she took out the chart and ripped it in shreds.

Jonathan was sleeping peacefully and Bobby was sitting happily on the kitchen floor, building a Lego house. Patty put the two envelopes on the table and made a cup of coffee. This was her only peaceful oasis in an otherwise hectic day. Soon Jonathan would need to be fed, Bobby would demand attention and the older boys would have to be collected from school.

"It's decision time, Bobby."

The child nodded without looking up from his brightly coloured bricks. Patty picked up the two envelopes, one in each hand and balanced them, as if the weight alone could be the deciding factor. Cochrane's money won out in the weight stakes. It was ten times heavier than the one-page letter from the car finance company. It was a very polite letter, couched in courteous business-speak but the threat was clear. The bank was no longer meeting the direct-debit payments on the Jeep and the company would have to reclaim the vehicle unless immediate payment was made on the overdue amount. With regret of course.

Patty sipped her coffee and waited for an answer to materialise. None came. A simple choice. Use Cochrane's money to make payments on the Jeep or else contact the finance company and throw herself on their mercy. Maybe they would agree to reduced payments. Maybe they would send a heavy gang to drag herself and her children, kicking and screaming, out of the vehicle. She thought over her conversations with Kate and Martin. Keep the dirty money. Do not touch the dirty money. Ask the Molloys to pay? Surely they would not want Brian's name smeared with bad-debtor status. She banished that thought. They had made their position clear. As far as they were concerned it was her debt, not Brian's. But suppose Martin was right. Suppose Gus Cochrane had come by this money dishonestly? She put down her cup and straightened her shoulders. She came from a family which had been poor, uneducated and regarded by many as common. But the Clearys had always been honest. Putting the envelope of money into her back pocket she strapped

Jonathan into his baby carrier, picked Bobby up from the floor and headed for the Jeep. If her integrity was all she had left, it was a valuable asset and that is what she intended telling the Cochranes.

Bobby giggled as he listened to the elaborate chimes of the Cochranes' doorbell. He liked it so much he insisted on hearing it a second time. Sheila was obviously annoyed by the constant ringing because her expression was cross when she opened the door. But her face broke into a big smile of welcome on seeing Patty and the children.

"Patty! Come in! It's so nice to see you."

As Sheila led the way towards the lounge Patty glanced around at the exquisite displays of Waterford glass, Wedgwood and Belleek.

"Would you mind if we went into the kitchen, Sheila? I'm afraid Bobby could damage your beautiful ornaments."

Before she sat down Patty took the envelope out of her pocket and handed it to the other woman.

"I really appreciate everything you and Gus have done for me. The christening party was marvellous. Thanks to you it was a very happy day for the children. But I'm returning this money. I can't keep it."

Sheila took the envelope and put it on the table. She nodded to Patty to sit down. "May I give Bobby a biscuit or do you think it would spoil his lunch?"

"A biscuit and a glass of milk for him, if you don't mind."

They sat in silence as Sheila made coffee and organised the milk and biscuits. Tension seemed to seep out of the envelope and fill the space between the two women. When Sheila poured the coffee her hands shook.

"I'm sorry if I'm upsetting you, Sheila. It's just that I can't accept so much from you. It's not right."

"You mean it's not good enough, don't you? If that money had come from one of your posh friends, you wouldn't throw it back in their face, would you?"

"Yes, I would. I've nothing left except my pride. I'm broke, yes, but I don't want charity."

"You don't want Cochrane money. You think Gus is a gangster. No matter what he does he'll always be the garbage collector to you lot."

Patty empathised with the fierce pride in the other woman. It was the same defensive pride she felt about the Clearys. She reached out and caught Sheila's hand. "I don't care what anybody says. You and Gus have been very good to me. My so-called posh friends are nowhere to be seen. They were Brian's friends. They don't want to know about his debt-ridden widow. I really appreciate your support, Sheila, but the christening party was enough. I can't take a bundle of money like that. I wouldn't take it from anybody. Do you understand?"

Sheila nodded slowly and then a smile crept across her face. "I know. I've an idea. You don't want to take a handout. I respect that. But suppose you earned the money?"

"How do you mean?"

Sheila waved her hand around to encompass the whole kitchen, centre island and all.

"Look around you, Patty. What do you see? And you needn't answer that. Our house is like a feature from *Ideal*

Home. Everything state of the art, contemporary, tasteful. And boring."

Patty opened her mouth to deny this but shut it again. Sheila was right. Except maybe about the tasteful bit. Some of the décor was over the top. Expensive but vulgar.

"I'm glad you agree," Sheila laughed. "This house is the result of years of interior designers running riot with Art Deco and Retro and Greco-Roman and whatever other styles and trends they care to give fancy names to. Sometimes I feel like I'm living in an art gallery, not a home. I want it to have the flair and originality of The Rectory. I want it to be warm and welcoming, yet classy. Just like your home. I'd like you to turn your talents to working on our home. How about it?"

Patty twisted her wedding ring around on her finger. True, this house needed to be taken in hand, to have life breathed into it. For a start the heavy drapes with the ornate pelmets should be pulled off the windows. And some of the carpets ripped up and replaced with polished floors. And the colour schemes! She stood up.

"Mind if I look around?"

Sheila led the way as Patty carried Jonathan and held Bobby firmly by the hand. They wandered from room to room, from one style to the next, from one colour scheme into another. It was like travelling through the colour blocks in a paintbox. Ideas tumbled around in Patty's head. She had not felt the same creative excitement since she had finished decorating The Rectory. When they got back to the kitchen again, Sheila made fresh coffee and then sat anxiously in front of Patty.

"Well, Patty? What d'you think? I know you did all the interior design in The Rectory yourself. You've a talent for it. I want you to do a job for me. This is not charity. I need a service that you could provide."

The more Patty thought about it, the more she wanted the job. She obviously would have a big budget and a free hand. What she did not have was the time. She shook her head regretfully.

"I'd love to, Sheila. But I can't see how I could fit it in with looking after the children. They have to be my priority. They need me."

"I'm not imposing any deadlines. Do it when you have time. When the children are at school. When they're asleep. I'm not in a hurry. Just so long as I know the makeover is ongoing." She picked up the envelope and handed it to Patty. "This is a down payment. I want to see a plan, samples of fabrics and colour schemes. Maybe some sketches. In your own time. Deal?"

Patty looked longingly at the note-filled envelope. The two thousand would pay for the Jeep for six months. Give her a chance to figure out where the next payments would come from. Or maybe she could sell the Jeep, pay off the debt and buy a cheaper car. Then she could put some money towards buying a home for the children. As the reality of her situation hit her, Patty realised Kate was right. She had to keep the money. And Sheila's proposal was allowing her to keep her pride as well. How had she ever thought this woman was an empty-headed would-be socialite? She smiled at her now.

"I'd love to undertake the job so long as you realise

that I've no formal qualifications in interior design and that it may take quite a while to complete."

"I know it'll be worth waiting for." Sheila said and Patty could have hugged her. Instead they just shook hands on the deal and Patty returned the envelope to her back pocket.

It was not until Patty was home and had lunches and homework sorted out that she realised she had never asked Sheila Cochrane the most important question. Why? Why were they being so nice to her, so generous? Why were they standing by her when everyone else except Kate and Martin had abandoned her as soon as the last sod had covered Brian's grave?

Before she could change her mind she picked up the phone and dialled Cochranes' number.

Sheila answered.

"Just one question, Sheila. I need to know why."

Sheila hesitated and Patty held her breath.

"Despite his reputation Gus is a very just man. He says your husband was cheated. And not by him, in case that's what you are thinking. I don't know anything else, Patty. Gus doesn't discuss business with me."

Patty thanked her and put down the phone. She knew Sheila Cochrane was speaking the truth. What in the hell had Brian got involved in and why did Gus Cochrane feel obliged to compensate his widow? Then she shrugged her shoulders and put the garbage man's money back into the drawer of Brian's desk. She would work hard to earn every cent of it. And it seemed that Bobby would be staying for a while longer so she would have that wage too. For the first time since Brian had died Patty began to feel a little hope for the future.

For once Eileen's chatter was getting on Kate's nerves. Because Martin was away attending the High Court there was no let-up whatsoever in the 'Billy said' sagas. To make matters worse, Eileen had started a new diet this week. *The* diet, guaranteed to help you lose two stone in two months. When lunch-time came around, Kate knew she could not face an hour of calorie-counting and lovesick stories with Eileen. She needed to escape, to have time to think.

"I won't be lunching with you today, Eileen. I've an appointment."

"An interview!" Len shouted across the office. "Kate has a job interview. Cranky Yank won't like that!"

"I'm meeting my husband actually," Kate said quickly, anxious to scotch any rumour of her leaving that might start floating around.

"Oh! Nice!" Eileen cooed. "I must ask Billy about meeting me some day for lunch. I'd like you all to get to know him."

Kate put on her coat, smiling at the thought of meeting the ice-cream man. Eileen had already told them his family background, his job history, his likes and dislikes. They even knew he had a pair of Man United boxers! What else was there to know? She left quickly, afraid that Eileen might get the idea that she should come along too.

Out on the street, Kate stopped and looked first one

direction then the other, unsure which way to go. As she was trying to decide a taxi drew up near her and people got out. On impulse she ran over and gave the driver the address of Fred's office. He nodded and she jumped in. In less than ten minutes she was standing on the street outside the building where Lucas Advertising had their offices, wondering what in the hell she was doing there. 'Trying to save your marriage, of course,' the little voice in her head told her. Unless Fred was already out to lunch by now. She took out her phone to ring him and then put it back in her bag again. Silly to ring when she could check for herself.

Lucas Advertising was on the second floor. Kate took the stairs, giving herself more time to sort out her feelings about this morning. Love and hate, fear and hope jostled for position as she read the signposts on the landing. She had only been here a few times and was not even sure exactly where to find her husband's office. Hardly the supportive wife. One point to Fred. She began to walk along the corridor, reading name plaques left and right, fairly certain Lucas Advertising was down towards the end. Just as she reached the door, it swung open and Adele came out carrying a large portfolio. The two women stood still, each surprised to see the other. Adele's coat was open and underneath she was wearing her trademark cropped top.

"You'll freeze to death," Kate said. "It's very cold out." As soon as she had said the words, Kate regretted them. She sounded like the girl's grandmother. Next she would be advising her to wear a vest.

"Hi, Kate. Don't worry about me. I don't feel the cold. Young blood, you know. You should take your husband out and cheer him up. He's a complete grump today."

With that comment she turned and walked away, her blonde hair shimmering, long legs striding out. The space she vacated seemed sucked dry of life and colour. The girl had such shining energy and was so beautiful that for one moment Kate understood how Fred had developed an obsession about her. Tough titty! Nigel Greenway had been the one to get to first base.

She pushed the door and went in. The open-plan area was empty. Passing between the desks she headed for the door on the right-hand side. She knocked and went into Fred's office. He was sitting in his chair, elbows on the desk, head in hands. From behind he could have been an old man. His shoulders were stooped and his hair was standing up in clumps, as if he had been running his hands through it. He probably had. He always did when he was worried and Fred Lucas looked like a very worried man now.

"Fred."

He jumped and instinctively put his hands over the stack of papers in front of him. He turned around to face her and she saw shock and then guilt in his eyes.

"Kate. I didn't hear you come in. What're you doing here?"

She was still wondering the same thing. This rumpled stranger sitting here, trying to hide paperwork from her, was not her Fred. Nor had she recognised the angry bully who had shouted at her this morning. When had he changed? When Adele Sheehan and her tanned midriff came into his life? Even as this thought crossed her mind, Kate had to admit that the subtle changes had begun long before that. Around the time Fred had decided to set the world of advertising alight by opening his own business. Around the time she had decided to start a family. *She* had decided. In a gut-wrenching flash of honesty Kate admitted to herself that all the initiative to have a baby had come from her. She had decided the time was right. And she had fooled herself into believing that Fred had been with her every step of the way.

"Well, Kate. Why did you come to see me?"

She forced herself to smile at him. "I thought it'd be nice if we had lunch together. Have a chat some place where we can't shout at each other."

"I'm sorry about this morning, Kate. You should know I'm very sensitive about my father's history. I admit I over-reacted. But 'twas unfair of you to use that against me."

Kate walked slowly towards him and tentatively reached out her hand to touch him, the possibility of rejection making her feel vulnerable and unsure. She rested her hand gently on his shoulder and felt the muscles knot with tension.

"I just wish you'd talk to me, Fred. We seem to be leading separate lives and it frightens me."

"I'm scared too. I was never so scared in all my life."

"Of what? The responsibility of fatherhood, the fear of infertility? Or is it the business? Is it me? Are you so scared at the thought of growing old with me that you have to turn to drink to face it?"

She dropped her hand from his shoulder as she saw the

veins on his neck bulge again. Beads of sweat appeared on his forehead and in the blink of an eye the depressed man had turned into an angry brute. He snatched the papers from the desk and threw them into a drawer but not before Kate had seen the distinctive banner of the bank on the top letter.

"Are you behind with bank payments? Is that the problem?"

"Bank payments, rent, tax. You name it, I owe it. Satisfied now? You wanted a chat, didn't you? I was trying to protect you but you had to keep sticking your nose in. Now you know."

"But how? How did you get into such a mess?"

"Because I had to borrow to set up, borrow to expand, borrow on equipment, on wages, on every fucking thing. And the payments are just too slow coming in. I must have more contracts to sort things out."

"What about the Greenway contract? And the travel agency?"

"The Greenway money is used up and the travel agents are still pending. I could grab that one if only Adele would get down to work. I can't afford to fire her and she knows it. I'm worried she'll walk out the door, just like Jim Grant did."

"What happened with Jim? I thought you and he had a good relationship?"

"Money, Kate. He wanted more money. I haven't got it to give to him. Anyway he's not worth it. I'll cover his work myself until I get a replacement."

Kate flopped down on a chair. Fred's anger seemed to sag just as she did. No longer in the grip of rage, he appeared broken and humiliated. She quelled the urge to hold him in her arms, to comfort him. He was isolated in his own private hell and she would have to wait for him to come to her.

"What about re-mortgaging the house?"

He shook his head. "Not an option."

"I've a few thousand in my savings account. You can have it if it helps."

He looked up at her and smiled. "I'm not going to raid your piggy bank to save my skin. Anyway, you came here to have lunch. C'mon, let's go."

Kate hesitated. They had barely begun to discuss all the issues they needed to bring into the open. But Fred was already at the door, waiting impatiently for her. Discussion was over. Kate had no option but to follow him. He took her to a pub two blocks away. It was clear that Fred was well known there. While Kate chose from the carvery menu Fred just ordered his 'usual'. When his order was served she was not surprised to see that it consisted of a plate of lasagne and a bottle of wine. Fred loved lasagne and he apparently could not get through his day without wine. His mood improved after the first glass. By the time Kate left him to return to work, he seemed to have regained his confidence and energy. He thanked her for coming to see him and said he appreciated her support. The type of polite, impersonal comments you would pass to any business acquaintance. She smiled and waved to him as she got into the taxi. As it drove away she sank back into the seat and tried not to cry.

The minute Martin left the court building he switched on

his mobile phone. He stood on the street, anxiously waiting as the screen flickered into life. It seemed to take an age to enter his PIN code and have it accepted. Another futile wait. No messages. Lee still had not contacted him. Bitch! Glancing at his watch, he saw that he had another hour to go before his appointment. Time enough to get some work done in the office.

The usual scurry to tidy away magazines and hide newspapers on his arrival did not amuse him today. As he swept through the office, he could sense the exchange of warning glances, the shared disappointment at the return of the Cranky Yank before finishing time. When he reached Kate's desk he nodded to her to follow him through. She looked at his face and immediately understood that his mood was much the same as her own.

Throwing his briefcase on the desk, he sat down and rubbed his hands over his eyes. He seemed weary.

"How did the hearing go?"

"Fine. We won an appeal. That's not what I wanted to talk to you about. I want to ask you a personal favour, Kate."

Kate did not like the sound of this. She had drawn a very thick line between personal and business with Martin Burke. The physical attraction to him was still strong enough for her to need to stay strictly on the business side of that line. Yet looking at him now, seeing the sad shadows in his eyes, she could hardly make an issue of her self-imposed embargo.

"Of course, Martin, if I can."

"I've an appointment with an estate agent this evening. I'm viewing several properties. I'd value a second opinion. I don't really know the various localities here and how desirable or otherwise they rate. Would you have time to come with me or are you busy?"

She did a quick preview of the evening she had planned. Dinner, *Coronation Street*, ironing, waiting for Fred to come home. Going to bed and still waiting for Fred to come home. She smiled at Martin. "No. I've nothing planned. I'd be glad to go with you. Are you looking at apartments or houses?"

"Both. My main consideration is Bobby. I want to buy an Irish home for him. A place where he can be comfortable and safe for whatever length of time he spends here."

"Any news from Lee?"

He shook his head and Kate was sorry she had asked. It was really none of her business. She headed for safe ground.

"There are phone messages for you. On your desk. You'll see that a Mr Meyers has been very anxious to contact you. He left four messages."

Martin immediately became alert at the mention of Mr Meyers. He picked up the memo pad and nodded to Kate.

"I'll see you then at 5.30. OK?"

As she closed the door behind her, he was already dialling. Mr Meyers, the man who spoke English with an attractive foreign accent, was obviously high priority on Martin Burke's call-back list. He seemed to know some very interesting people.

The estate agent accompanying them was dressed like a banker and spoke in the modulated tones of a news presenter. Top drawer. Martin was getting the big budget treatment. Kate sat in the back of the car as the auctioneer drove them from the city centre. The first property they viewed was an apartment in a dockside development. All glass and stainless steel. The agent led them out onto the roof garden to show them the view. The city sprawled out around them and the fumes of traffic and commerce rose to meet them. Martin glanced at Kate and she shook her head. This was an investment property. One that you rented out to aspiring executives, to a single person with money and ambition. It was not a home for a three-year-old.

The next apartment they were brought to was a carbon copy of the first except that it was situated by the park. This first-floor apartment had possibilities. The estate agent was intoning a litany of 'highly desirable' features but Martin's main interest was the proximity to the park. He went through the patio doors onto the terrace and stood looking across at the belt of oaks that formed a canopy over the pathways.

"Bobby would love this," he said. "Just like living in Central Park."

"Look down."

He did as Kate said and followed her gaze to the street below. Even at this hour of the evening, the traffic was heavy. There was a pedestrian crossing further up to their left but suppose, just suppose, Bobby decided to go to the park by himself? Kate shivered as she thought of the little child walking across that street, being mown down by rush-hour traffic. Not that it would happen. But it could.

"You're right," Martin said. "Not safe."

Kate noticed a subtle change in the agent's attitude towards her as they drove to the outskirts of town to view the next property. A house this time, four-bedroom detached. He had her pegged as Devil's Advocate and resented her for it. She was a threat to his fat commission. They did not spend long viewing. Detached meant six feet between houses and the whole package was claustrophobic and overpriced. As they drove towards their last viewing Kate recognised the district. She had often travelled this direction. It was leafy and quiet, a mature area.

"It's nice out here," she remarked to Martin. "Near the city, yet far enough away for peace and quiet. It's around here that –"

She stopped speaking. She could not utter another word as surprise robbed her of breath. She checked and re-checked. No mistake. There could not be. She had been here too often, had attended parties, dropped urgent documents into this house, drank coffee in this kitchen, cocktails in the lounge, eaten barbecued chicken on the patio.

"I like the feel of this place," said Martin as they drove up the tree-lined avenue.

The estate agent was droning on about mature gardens and pristine conditions.

"When did this come on the market?" asked Kate.

Both men looked at her in surprise. She knew she sounded frantic, but shit! She was.

"Just last week. The owners have emigrated. It's a highly desirable property in a mature area. It won't be on the market for long. It will be snapped up."

Martin was staring at her, noting the paleness of her face, the shock in her eyes. "Something wrong?" he asked.

They had arrived at the front of the house now and as he looked up at the building, Kate could see recognition begin to dawn on him.

"Jesus! It's Richard Gordon's house!"

"That's right," the agent agreed. "Mr Gordon has retired and he and his wife have decided to emigrate."

"Where to?"

"We don't know that. His son is handling the sale for him."

"Could I have his son's number, please? I need to contact him urgently."

The estate agent hesitated. It was obvious that he was torn between a potential sale and client instructions. He shook his head.

"I'm sorry. I can't do that. He has engaged us to transact any business for him. He would not want prospective clients disturbing him."

Kate tried to remember back to when Richard had been her boss. She must have his son's number somewhere. Yes, she had. She had numbers for both his son and daughter. Reminding them of their mother's birthday had been one of the duties Richard had given her.

She caught Martin by the arm and whispered to him. "I've the number somewhere. The daughter's too."

Martin nodded and turned to the agent. "I won't need to be shown around here. Drop us back to your office now, please, and contact me when you have something more suitable on your books."

The man tried to hide his frustration. Conversation was strained on the way back into the city. All three were glad when they arrived at the auctioneer's office.

As soon as the agent had left Martin turned to Kate.

"The bastard! Not a word."

Kate did not have to ask about whom he was talking. It seemed Richard Gordon had played his cards very close to his chest. He had given absolutely no hint, not even to his personal assistant of more than seven years that his holiday trip with his sick wife was going to evolve into full-blown emigration. Certainly not the type of decision made on the spur of the moment. Bastard indeed!

Fred knew that if the police breathalysed him he would be over the limit. A possible drink-driving charge rated very low on his list of potential disasters so he got into the car and drove over to Kate's office. The building still bore the legend Richard Gordon & Co. Kate's car was parked outside but the building was locked up. In darkness. Where in the fuck was she? He banged the steering wheel with his fist. He needed to see her. Now! Everything, from the smallest detail right up to his complete life plan was going in the wrong direction. He should have told her today when he had the chance. She had been willing to talk. To listen. Even to give him her savings. He had fucked up again. That would have been the perfect opportunity to ask her about the cottage in Kerry. It was not as if he was asking her to sell it. He just wanted her to use it as collateral to borrow. It was the only way he could climb out of the hole he had dug himself into. No. That was being too harsh on himself. They had all contributed. Kate, Jim Grant, Adele, Nigel Greenway and whoever was pulling Greenway's strings.

Fred sat up straight and drummed his fingers on the steering wheel. Greenway was back in town. He was the one who had talked him into this development scheme. He could fucking well get him out of it now. Or else guarantee him the travel-agency contract with advance payment. The more he thought of this course of action, the better it seemed. And he knew exactly where he would find the garage man. In the lounge bar of the Grand Hotel, pouring drink into Adele. The only problem would be to get her away from the old man for long enough to talk to him. Silly old fool! He must be getting Viagra intravenously. On the other hand Adele, dressed in almost nothing, was a pretty potent aphrodisiac. Even for a flagging old man like Greenway.

Fred turned the key in the car and indicated to pull out. He was driving very carefully so as not to draw the attention of the police. As he came to the intersection at the top of the street, he began to nose the car slowly into the mainstream traffic.

A green Volvo cut right across him and turned sharply down the street Fred was just leaving. The couple inside was so engrossed in conversation they did not see him. Fred jammed on the brake and looked in his rear-view mirror as the car pulled up outside the building of Richard Gordon & Co. Irate drivers began to hoot. He would have to get into the line of traffic. He was holding everyone up and causing havoc. Waving an apology to the other drivers, he continued. He had seen enough. He had seen too much. Kate and Martin Burke. Martin Burke and Kate. So enthralled by each other that they had not even seen him. Fuck! He should have seen that coming. He should have known smooth-talking Burkey would make a play for Kate. She was his type. Beautiful, intelligent, classy. But Kate was kind and gentle too. And loyal. What in the fuck was she doing with him? In his rage Fred almost forgot that he had thrown them together in the first place. Alone in a cottage in the middle of nowhere. Had he been mad?

He continued to fume and rage until he had downed two whiskeys in the Grand Hotel. Then everything began to seem better. For once Adele was not with Nigel Greenway. That gave Fred an opportunity to butter the old man up. He was well prepared by the time he got around to asking Nigel to release him from his investment in the development scheme.

"I'm a bit overdrawn at the moment. A slight cash-flow problem. What are my chances of cancelling that investment you advised me about? This is not the right time for me to tie up capital."

"You should've thought of that beforehand."

So, the old prick was going to play hardball. Fred took another gulp of drink before he continued. "You should've told me I'd have a long wait before I saw any money back from the scheme. You led me to believe that the profits would very quickly repay my borrowings."

"They will too. This scheme can't lose. Great location. Great business. Great demand for the service. But I never said you could depend on it to make your monthly repayments."

"Well, you didn't make it clear. I re-mortgaged my home and waived half the moneys due on Greenway Garages on your advice. You owe me."

Nigel Greenway narrowed his eyes. His nostrils flared. He was a small man but anger made him puff up like a bullfrog. "I owe you nothing, Fred Lucas. I gave you an opportunity to make money. Big money. It was, and is, your responsibility to know what you are getting yourself into."

"How in the fuck could I know when none of you would tell me anything? All hush hush. Top secret. Jesus, I'm beginning to think you're running drugs!"

Nigel laughed and deflated back to his normal size. He waved to the barman and ordered more drinks. When they had full glasses in front of them he looked at Fred and smiled. "I can see you're under pressure so I'll tell you a little of what the development scheme is about. Maybe you can relax then. The syndicate that you've been privileged to become a part of has been operating very successfully for ten years now. And it has nothing at all to do with drugs. The way we work is to buy properties in underdeveloped areas. In underdeveloped countries. Then we wait for progress to catch up with the area. When it does, hey presto! We're sitting on valuable real estate, which we bought for a song."

"So you sell and make a profit?"

"Sometimes. Sometimes, like now, we carry out the development ourselves."

"Commercial or residential?"

"You're asking too many questions, Fred. I've told you

enough. Your money's going into the development of a property in Eastern Europe. You'll start to see returns in about two years' time."

Fred's stomach heaved and he thought he would be sick. Two fucking years! At the rate his overdraft was climbing it would be millions by then! The little prick standing in front of him was playing with him, making a fool of him. "You should ask questions, Fred" – "You ask too many questions, Fred." His angry thoughts raced around his head until he felt his skull would burst. He raised his glass, drained it and shouted at the barman for a refill.

"We're not going to have a repeat performance, Fred, are we? If you get thrown out of here again you won't ever be allowed back in."

Fred focused his eyes on Nigel's tie. If he did not see the sneer it would be easier not to lash out. He spoke to the diagonal stripes on the silk tie. "Is it in Budapest? Gus Cochrane mentioned something about a development there."

The bullfrog puffed up again but the anger was not directed at Fred this time. "That loudmouth! I warned them not to let him in on the scheme. The man's a gangster. A low-down piece of trash. He'd no right to go shooting his mouth off."

"But I have to tell my bank manager something, for Christ's sake! I can't say, hang on, I'll have money in two years' time."

"Gareth Owens will understand."

Fred looked into his drink. He loved the golden hue.

He swirled it around, trying to give himself time to think. Was Gareth Owens one of the syndicate too? Was that why he had been so willing to allow Fred to borrow that amount of money with very little explanation about where it was going? He must have been laughing up his sleeve when Fred gave him the account number for the receiving bank. He already knew it. They were all laughing at him. Why did they need his input anyway? He dragged his eyes away from the whiskey and looked directly at Nigel Greenway.

"Why did you involve me in this? And don't bullshit me. I know I am a minnow in a pool of sharks."

"One of the big fish wanted out. It took two to replace him."

Fred knew that Nigel was telling the truth and that the other minnow was Brian Molloy. Had been Brian Molloy. For an instant he envied Brian his peaceful rest. He also knew he was not going to get any more satisfaction from Nigel on the matter of the investment. On to Plan Two.

"About your friends in the travel agents, Nigel. Could you speak to them again, persuade them to go with my company for their campaign?"

"I would, except that it would be pointless."

It was not what the little man had said, it was the way he said it, that sent Fred's heart pumping and drove sweat out through his body. He had almost spat the words out. He was gloating, sharpening the knife. Fred did not want to ask the question but he had to.

"Why would it be pointless?"

"Because as of two hours ago, Adele Sheehan is their

new advertising manager. Six-figure salary and car supplied. They're not just travel agents, you know. They own a chain of computer outlets and –"

Fred did not hear the rest. He turned and walked out of the hotel as quickly as his legs would allow. He was afraid he was going to cry so he just kept walking, concentrating on his next step. After a mile or so of guiding his faltering feet he came to an off-licence. He went in and bought a bottle of whiskey. Lovely, golden-coloured numbness. He walked some more, cradling the bottle in the brown-paper bag close to his chest. The streets were getting narrower now and the buildings dingier. He must have wandered across town without realising it. A girl stood in a doorway watching him.

"I'll give you a good time, love," she said and he laughed into her face.

Fred Lucas would never again, as long as he lived, know a good time. The good times were over. No more Lucas Advertising. No more Kate. No more house. No more. Continuing further on, he picked out his own doorway and settled in there with his bottle of whiskey. He felt he had at last found his place in life.

Sleep was impossible. Too many issues crowded Kate's head, each demanding attention. She threw back the covers and got out of bed. It was one of those nights when the moon played hide and seek with the racing clouds. Opening the curtains back fully, she stood and watched the dance of silver and black across the sky. As a child she had always associated moonlit nights with witches and ghosts. She shivered. Growing up had not changed her perception.

She tried Fred's number again. His phone was still switched off. It was quarter past three in the morning. Where in the hell was he? She went to the kitchen and got out the cocoa and milk. Spooning chocolate powder into a mug she added some cold milk and stirred. And stirred. The bottom was nearly stirred out of the mug before she realised she was taking her anger out on two hapless spoons of chocolate powder. She poured on hot milk and sat at the table, sipping her drink and for once finding no comfort in its warm sweetness.

Her marriage was over. She allowed the thought she had been suppressing all night to surface and settle. Finished. No more Kate and Fred, no more sleepy morning kisses, no more finishing each other's sentences, no more oneness. But the pretending was finished too, the ignoring of all the warning signs, the silences, the excuses. She remembered the way they had parted last afternoon, Fred thanking her profusely and she smiling and waving to him. Two strangers, playing a role they had both outgrown. She put down her mug and looked into the dregs of her drink. Undissolved powder streaked the white porcelain just like the unresolved issues which stained her life.

God damn it! Why was she sitting here being philosophical? Why wasn't she fighting for her man, for her future? She tried his number again. *"The customer you are calling is out of range or has their phone powered off."* Hating the disembodied voice, she slammed the phone down. Even if he had gone to a nightclub, he should be home by now. He had definitely found somewhere else to stay, someone else's bed in which to sleep. Images raced through her mind. Fred waking in the morning, opening his eyes to see another woman's face on the pillow beside him. He would reach out his hand then, after kissing her, of course, would switch on his phone to find that he had ten missed calls. They would giggle and then turn towards each other –

She got up from the table and began to pace the kitchen. 3.30. It was darker outside, the moon losing the race with the scudding clouds. It was not the fact that he was probably with another woman, even though she would tear the bitch to pieces if she could lay her hands on her now. She did not have the right to be outraged by Fred taking what was on offer. She had done so herself, hadn't she? Colour swept up her face as she recalled her own hot and sweaty, grasping response to Martin Burke. Her slide towards total infidelity had been halted only by the intervention of a sleepy three-year-old with a teddy bear under his arm. Even this very evening, when Martin had driven her back to the office to collect her car, there had been a moment, a heartbeat, when they had looked at each other with undisguised lust. The moment had passed and Martin had gone to The Rectory to see Bobby while she had come home to wait for Fred. That moment could so easily have become an hour, two hours, a whole night. That is why she could forgive Fred for Adele or whoever he was with tonight. Not to do so would be hypocritical. What she could not forgive was his silence, his secrecy, his coldness. Why hadn't he told her about his debts? And, more importantly, what else was he hiding from her?

Feeling trapped by the kitchen and the blackness outside the patio doors, she went into the sitting room. At least from here, she would see the car when it came up the driveway. If he was in a fit state to drive. Maybe she was wrong. He might not be with any other woman. But where was he then?

Throwing herself down on the couch she examined the last year of their life together. Bit by bit the roadmap to ruin began to unfold. And Nigel fucking Greenway appeared at every twist and turn on that road. The smarmy little git had changed Fred from being a dynamic, fun-loving, honest man into whatever it was he had become. A shadow of the Fred Lucas she had loved. She still loved. A powerful longing to see Fred, to hold him close to her, gripped Kate. Curling up on the couch she hugged a cushion to her and eventually fell into a restless sleep.

The waking up was a slow process. Fred seemed to be swimming through thick layers of blackness, finally emerging into semi-darkness. Icy coldness numbed his hands and feet. He looked around him, closed his eyes, opened them and looked again. It was still there, the narrow street with the derelict buildings and the moon flashing intermittent silver light through the broken eaves of the house opposite. Christ Almighty! Where was he and why was he here?

He dropped his head into his hands and tried to remember. Scattered images floated across his line of vision. Nigel Greenway, thin lips curled in a sneer, gladly informing him that Adele had stolen the travel-agency contract. A faceless girl in the off-licence, taking his money for a bottle of whiskey. The welcome sight of a sheltered doorway. The images stopped then. He lifted his head and looked up at the moon. He would have howled like the wounded animal he was if he could have found the strength. A gust of wind swirled into his shelter and lifted a nauseating cloud of stench. He gagged on the smell of vomit and urine. His vomit. His urine. Tears, hot and salty, oozed from his eyes onto his frozen cheeks. He had pissed himself. Jesus!

Clouds blanketed the moon. Fred sank into the blackness, looking for a place to hide. But the guilt, the shame, the embarrassment chased him and gave him no peace. How could he have done this to himself? To Kate? She had been right. He was like his father. He smelt like his father. Probably looked like his father, dishevelled and worn. Used up. It was all Nigel Greenway's fault. "Have another one, Fred!" "Invest two hundred grand, Fred!" His head began to pound with the details of a life he would rather not have lived. Holding onto the doorjamb, he hauled himself to his feet. He swayed, not with drunkenness. He was sober now but unbalanced by the weight of desperation. He had thrown it all away, all the hope, the ambition. He had destroyed his future and it had only taken him one short year to do it. The journey from launching Lucas Advertising to wallowing in his own piss had been a short one. And the worst thing, worse than his business failure, worse than the public humiliation of bankruptcy, was losing Kate. He banished her image from his mind. He could not bear the accusation, the pain, in her dark eyes. All Kate had wanted was him and their baby. He had failed her on both counts. No wonder she had turned to Martin Burke.

Moonlight silvered the street again. Fred let go the doorjamb and took a tentative step onto the pavement. He began to walk, not sure where he was headed. He lifted his wrist to check the time. His watch was gone. Standing, he checked his pockets. Wallet and phone had disappeared. He shrugged and continued on. There was a comfort in being nobody.

When he heard footsteps behind him, he did not turn around. He was too insulated by misery to register anything happening outside his private world of self-hate. Somebody tapped him on the shoulder. Fred stopped walking. A young man appeared in front of him and he sensed another standing at his back. Moonlight played on the youth's shaven head and sparkled in the dilated pupils of his eyes.

"We don't want no trouble, boss. Just hand over your money and you can be on your way."

"Fuck off!" Fred said. "I've nothing. Someone else has already fleeced me."

He felt something sharp against the back of his neck and got a whiff of breath that stank even more than his own.

"Respect, man! Show some fucking respect," a voice from behind him said.

The first shiver of fear gripped Fred. It swelled into full-blown terror as the reality of his situation hit him. He was standing in a no-go area of town, being held up by two junkies who had a knife against his neck. As the blade dug in a little further, he knew, with every fibre of his being that he did not want to die. Not before he had seen Kate again. Not before he had begged her forgiveness, felt her arms around him one last time.

"Search my pockets, fuckers. I've nothing. Go shake someone else down. Let me go."

The last thing Fred saw was the smile on the pockmarked face of the bald-headed youth. He could only imagine that the same sadistic smile had been on the lips of the youth behind him as he drew his knife-hand back and then plunged the blade. It struck Fred between the shoulders. There was no pain. Just blackness. And then nothing.

Chapter 28

Kate woke with a start. She was cold and stiff and for an instant confused. Why was she lying on the couch? The respite was short. Anger, worry and now fear came flooding back. There was still only one car on the driveway. Hers. Checking her watch, she saw that it was nearly seven o'clock in the morning. An icy feeling gripped her stomach. There was something wrong. If Fred had just been fucking around with another woman, he would have rung her. She knew it. He would have lied, of course, the working late and important meeting excuses tripping off his tongue. But he would definitely have contacted her. Unless he had been too drunk. Maybe he had staggered under a bus. Maybe he had driven his car against a wall.

Jumping up, Kate ran to the phone and dialled his number. *"The customer you are calling is out of range or has their phone powered off."* She slammed the phone down. What now? Just when she was beginning to really panic, it dawned on her that he might have got a cab home. Of course! He would have. She ran up the stairs. All the beds were empty.

Flopping onto the top step of the stairs, Kate tried to calm herself down. No news is good news. Another of her mother's sayings. She would certainly have been informed by now if he had had an accident. So what else? Her mind kept going back to her visit to his office yesterday, to her first sight of him as she had come through his door. The bowed head, the stooped shoulders, the stacks of bills he was trying to cover. A depressed man. A beaten man. The extent of her failure as a wife hit her like a slap across the face. He had been crying out for her support, her encouragement and all she had given him was a false smile and a casual wave of her hand. She had stood by, making plans for a baby, playing dangerous 'almost but not quite' games with Martin Burke, quietly getting on with her comfortable life while her husband had been sliding deeper and deeper into trouble. A little voice in her head came to her defence. He had not wanted her support. He had rejected her. He had flirted or maybe more, with Adele Sheehan and allowed alcohol to become an essential part of his day-to-day existence. She shook her head impatiently to clear it of all the noise. What was the point in picking over the bones of her marriage, allotting blame, when all she wanted was to see Fred, to know that he was safe?

She ran into the bedroom and threw on a sweater and jeans. It was ten minutes past seven when she left home to drive to Lucas Advertising. That was the last place she had seen Fred. She prayed, as she had never prayed before, that it had not been the last time.

Patty was no longer surprised to find that Brian was not beside her when she woke up. The shock factor was easing even if the pain of loss was as sharp as it had been on the night of the accident. Propping herself up on her elbow, she looked across at the cot. Jonathan was awake. Fierce, protective love filled her heart, leaving no room for any other feelings. There was a gentle patter of feet. That would be Bobby, coming in for his morning cuddle. He clambered onto the bed and Patty held him close, not allowing herself to think of the day his mother would come to take him back. The peaceful moment was shattered as the older boys woke, one after the other, each louder than the next. They clattered about, making as much din as if their slippers were hobnailed.

Patty threw back the bedcovers and taking Jonathan in one arm and Bobby in the other, went downstairs to start the routine of feeding, refereeing fights, making school lunches and ferrying tardy scholars to school. She set an extra place at the breakfast table. Martin was part of their morning routine now. Right on cue, she heard the doorbell ring.

"Would one of you let Martin in, please?"

The posse galloped into the hall as Bobby clapped his hands. "Daddy! Here's my Daddy!" Patty looked after the child as he trotted out to meet his father. What a shitty world! Man and boy loved each other so much, separating them was a crime. What sort of a hard-hearted bitch was

Lee Page Burke? She apparently did not want Bobby herself. How could she when she had left him behind to go gallivanting around the Middle East? Patty could not imagine leaving her boys like that. But Lee did not seem to want to grant custody to Martin either. Realising that she was judging a woman she had never met and a situation she really knew nothing about, Patty got on with making the breakfast.

Martin's coffee and toast were ready for him when he came in, carrying Bobby in his arms. He smiled at Patty over the child's head.

"Morning. Did he sleep all right last night?"

"No problem. As usual. He's a brave little soldier, holding his own with the Molloy mob. Any news? You know, from abroad?"

Martin shook his head and his expression said it all. It was a mixture of anger and worry. If Lee did not contact him soon, Patty imagined that he would hunt her down. He had that determined, dangerous air about him. Not a man to have as an enemy.

Chaos reigned supreme in the kitchen of The Rectory as breakfasts were eaten, shirts buttoned, ties knotted and school bags readied. Martin took over the refereeing role as Patty dashed upstairs to dress. When she came down, everyone was ready to go. They all walked out into the hall together.

"I've got a job. One I can fit in with the children," Patty told Martin. "I'll tell you all about it this evening."

Martin looked around him at the ring of shining faces and laughed.

"You're a better man than I am, Patty, if you can fit in another job with this lot."

She looked at him and wondered if he would still be laughing when he knew she would be working for Sheila Cochrane.

"I need to talk to you too, Patty, about the business Brian was involved in. I'm hoping to have some solid information later today. There's this guy named Hans Meyers –"

He stopped mid-sentence as a car sped up the avenue and screeched to a halt outside the door.

"It's Michael Schumacher!" one of the boys said, imitating the high-pitched brake sound. In one second flat the children were all driving their imaginary Formula One cars around the hall.

Patty carefully picked her way through them and opened the front door. Kate almost fell into the hall. Without saying a word Patty handed Jonathan to Martin and, catching Kate by the arm, brought her through to the kitchen and sat her down. Kate was white-faced and shaking and had obviously been crying.

"What's happened to you Kate? What's wrong?"

"It's Fred," Kate whispered. "He's missing."

"How do you mean missing? When did you see him last?"

"Lunch-time yesterday."

Patty sighed and tried not to let her annoyance at Fred show. Somehow, she was not surprised. There had been plenty of gossip about Fred and his obsession with his new graphic designer. Nothing but rumour, of course, as events had proved. Nigel Greenway had been the one to finally get his leg over that little slapper. But Fred had behaved in such a way as to invite gossip. No smoke without fire. Maybe he had been recruiting more staff last night.

"I'm sure there's an explanation, Kate. Just give me ten minutes and I'll be back. We'll sort it out then."

Kate nodded and Patty went to collect the children only to find that Martin had them loaded into his car. He handed Jonathan to her.

"I'll drop the lads to school, Patty. You stay with Kate. Is she all right? She looks dreadful."

Patty smiled at him. "You're a gent. Thanks, Martin. I think Kate'll be OK. It's just that Fred didn't come home last night. We need to have a girl talk. See if we can sort something out."

"See you soon then. I'll drop Bobby off on my way back. He doesn't want to be done out of his morning spin."

She waved them off and went back into the kitchen. Kate was sitting exactly as she had left her. Patty made Kate's coffee hot and sweet. The woman was obviously in shock. She shoved the cup in front of her.

"Drink that up. We'll go through everything step by step then and see what we can do."

Kate drank her coffee as she was told and colour began to come back into her cheeks. She put her cup on the table and looked directly at Patty. "You think I'm being hysterical. To be fair, I am a bit. But I know. I know something terrible has happened to Fred."

Patty was not about to argue with a feeling that strong. It would be pointless. But somehow she would have to get

Kate to realise she was overreacting. Fred was not missing. He was curled up somewhere nice and warm and safe. Maybe he was dealing with a hangover right now or maybe he was enjoying breakfast with a girlfriend. Either option was possible as far as Patty was concerned. Fred Lucas had changed so much. There were odd flashes of the old Fred. Like the night he had dragged her, frozen and half dead, from the banks of the river. That had been the Fred she had come to know and respect over the years. An honest, dependable and kind man. A sober man, a faithful husband. None of this speculation was helping Kate.

"Where've you checked, Kate?"

"I've been trying his phone all night. It's switched off. I went to his office. I thought he might have stayed there. It's all locked up. The security man in the building told me Fred left last night at seven o'clock and has not been back since."

"What about his friends? Did you contact them?"

"I rang Nigel Greenway. I hated letting that slimeball know my business but I had to. He was drinking with Fred in the Grand Hotel until eleven o'clock last night. He hasn't seen him since and doesn't know, or even care, where Fred went after that."

Patty began to worry now. Suppose Fred had driven the car while drunk. He could have crashed, driven over a cliff. An image of Brian's broken body flashed before her. She shivered. Kate caught her hand.

"If you're worried about a road accident, forget it. His car is still in the carpark at the hotel. Wherever he went, he walked there."

"Well, that's good news anyway. What about his staff? Have you contacted them? Maybe they know something."

Tears filled Kate's eyes and she began to shake again. His staff! His fucking deceitful, dishonest, disloyal staff! They had let him down just as badly as she had. Worse. They had destroyed Lucas Advertising. They had taken away his reason for living. She tried to explain to Patty in a sane and logical way but she knew she was being hysterical and illogical.

"Jim Grant's no longer working for Fred. He just left. He probably had his reasons but he knew 'twas the worst time. The debts are mounting and there's the travel-agents contract. But she told me herself when I rang her this morning. And she didn't even apologise. Said it was just business. Nothing personal. Bitch! "

"Stop there, Kate! Calm down! Take a deep breath and start over again."

Kate did just that. She explained how Fred had told her about his spiralling debts, how he had been desperate to get the contract for the travel agents and how Adele Sheehan had proudly admitted to Kate on the phone that she had stolen it from under his nose.

"I'll never forgive myself, Patty. He was so depressed yesterday. Really down until he had a few glasses of wine. And I just left him and went back to work. I wasn't there for him. No wonder he – no wonder he decided he'd had enough."

Patty sat there not knowing what to say. Kate was making a lot more sense now and her fears seemed more real. In the silence she heard the Volvo come up the avenue. She went to the door and gave Martin a whispered rundown on what she knew before going back into the kitchen. He followed her in and sat down, Bobby still in his arms.

"Patty has told me the story, Kate," he said. "Have you contacted the police or the hospitals?"

Kate shook her head. Her need to know what had happened to Fred was surpassed only by her fear of finding out. She had not been able to take that final step on her own.

"OK. Come on."

He handed his son to Patty and caught Kate by the hand. She felt the strength in his fingers and gladly allowed herself to be led along.

"We'll visit Accident and Emergency Departments first. If we turn nothing up there, we'll go to the police. We'll find Fred. Trust me, Kate."

Patty hugged her close.

Kate looked at both of them, Martin and Patty, and smiled. With their support she was ready to face whatever lay ahead.

Kate sat in the car and waited while Martin checked Fred's office. She could not face the security man again or the sight of the locked door with the plaque proudly announcing that Lucas Advertising operated from here. Martin was right, of course. It made sense to recheck here before traipsing around from hospital to hospital. The expression on his face when he came back told her she had been right. Fred had not appeared miraculously in the office, all dapper and ready to face a day's work.

"The girl was waiting outside the door. I told her to take the day off."

What girl? Then Kate remembered that Fred had mentioned something about taking in a girl on work experience. Somebody to answer the phone and make coffee. Cheap labour. She muttered her thanks and steeled herself for the first visit to an Accident and Emergency Department.

Kate hung back with the other patients as Martin approached the reception desk. She tried not to stare at blood-soaked bandages and sick faces. Instead she picked out the people who were only here for check-up. The plaster casts and stitched wounds. Some looked so healthy that she wondered why they were here at all. They were probably thinking the same about her. Maybe there was an epidemic of missing spouses. Martin shook his head as he returned.

"Nobody admitted in the past twelve hours matching Fred's description. One down. Come on, let's get going."

Two hospitals later, they still had not located Fred.

"This is good," Martin said. "At least it's looking like he didn't have to be hospitalised. Well, so far anyway. Where to now?"

Kate directed him south, towards the biggest Accident and Emergency department serving the city. Maybe they should have tried here first. She sat amongst the walking wounded again as Martin inquired at the desk. The conversation with the receptionist seemed to go on longer this time. The girl picked up her phone and made a call. When she spoke to Martin again, her hands were waving about as if she was giving him directions. Kate walked over to stand by his side.

"Take the lift to the second floor. Then take the third left down the corridor to 2B. The ward sister will be expecting you. OK?"

Martin thanked her and catching Kate's arm led her in the direction of the lifts. Her heart began to thump. The lift doors closed and that innocuous voice told them they were 'going up'. Thank God! Not down to where the morgue nestled, cold and lifeless, in the bowels of the building.

"You must prepare yourself, Kate," Martin said. "A man matching Fred's description was admitted here in the early hours. It may be Fred and it may not."

"Why was this man brought here? What happened to him?"

"He was stabbed."

The voice told them needlessly that the doors were opening. Kate's legs felt weak as she walked along the corridor. This man could not be Fred. How in the name of Christ could he end up with stab wounds? Knocked down, maybe. Alcohol poisoning, maybe. But stabbed? No way. This was not Fred. Another wild-goose chase.

The ward sister was waiting for them. Her face was grave. Only snippets of her conversation registered with Kate. Patient in operating theatre. Critical condition. No identification. She followed blindly on as Martin and the sister went into a cubicle. Opening a locker the nurse drew out a big plastic bag on which the words Patient Property were printed in large letters. Kate stopped shaking then. Her breathing and her heartbeat seemed to stop too. Her whole system shuddered to a halt as she stared uncomprehendingly at Fred's blue and white striped shirt in the nurse's hand. The last time she had seen that shirt it had been spotlessly clean. There had been no bloodstains, no disgusting smell. Bit by bit, in a humiliating procession, the nurse dragged out items of filthy clothing from the bag. Fred's grey suit jacket, slit down the back and covered in blood, his trousers, stained with vomit and smelling like a urinal. His boxers, for fuck's sake. His blue cotton boxers. Kate screamed then. Or maybe she just whimpered. She no longer knew or cared.

Patty answered the phone on the first ring. Her face changed colour when she heard Martin's news. This could not be happening. Please God, don't let it happen. Not Brian and Fred both. What kind of merciless cruelty was that?

"How soon will you know?" she asked in a weak voice.

"They're almost finished in the operating theatre now. Assuming he survives the surgery, he'll be in Recovery for a while before we get to see him. The doctors are going to speak to us shortly. We'll know more then."

"How's Kate taking it?"

"Very shocked. Even though she said she'd been expecting the worst, she's not taking all this in ."

"Self-preservation," Patty said and the bitterness of her personal experience was in her voice. She had not believed Brian was going to die either, not even when she heard the last hiss of air leave his lungs and saw the lines on the monitors go flat. She had got her strength that night from Kate. She looked at Jonathan asleep in his carrycot and Bobby kneeling on a chair pushing dinky cars around the table. She made up her mind.

"Martin, would you object if I got somebody to mind the two babies while I go to the hospital? I want to be with Kate."

"If you've somebody you can trust with them then I'm happy to go along with that. See you soon."

Patty hesitated before making the phone call. There would be no point in contacting Helen Long. She had made it perfectly clear she would never baby-sit again after the disastrous night when Patty fell in the river. Making up her mind, Patty dialled and explained the situation as quickly as possible to Sheila Cochrane. Sheila was around to The Rectory in the blink of an eye.

"Don't worry about the children, Patty. Take as much time as you need. I can collect the boys from school for you. The only thing is the car. You know I drive an Aston Martin. Not suitable for a gang of children. But I have open driving insurance. Have you?"

Patty nodded.

"That's fine then. Leave me the Jeep and you take the status symbol."

Patty smiled as she thanked Sheila. Then on impulse she hugged her, partly by way of gratitude and partly by way of apology for all the awful things she had ever said about this very insecure but very warm-hearted woman.

Patty and Kate did not speak. There was no need for

words as they held on tightly to each other. They did not let go until Martin came back into the relatives' room with cartons of coffee for them. Kate found herself longing for a cigarette. It had been ten years since she had last smoked but the urge to light up and inhale now was overwhelming. She sipped at her coffee and tried not to check her watch every ten seconds. They had been told the doctor would be with them shortly. That was forty-five minutes ago. Maybe Fred had died on the operating table and they did not want to tell them. Kate dismissed that silly thought from her mind. These people dealt with death and dying on a daily basis. Fred would just be a statistic to them. A failure in their life-saving skills. A disappointment. What did they care about his grey eyes with the green flecks in them, his curly blond hair that needed gel to smooth it down, his offbeat sense of humour, his grandiose schemes and plans? Why should they care about those little details when they had mattered so little to his wife that she had left him to wander off to lie in the gutter, alone, bleeding, frightened and . . .

The door opened and the surgeon walked in, followed by a retinue of solemn-faced junior staff. The senior man looked from Kate to Patty.

"Mrs Lucas?"

Kate stood and shook his outstretched hand. His grip was firm and strong. The sure hands of a surgeon.

"Well, Mrs Lucas, your husband is back in the Recovery room. We have managed to control the bleeding. But I have to warn you he is still very weak."

"When can I see him?"

"Hopefully he'll be back up here in another hour or so. We'll be putting him in the Intensive Care Unit. The next twenty-four hours will be critical."

Kate nodded. She had been going to ask a lot of questions. What injuries had Fred received, how much blood had he lost, had any of his vital organs been damaged? She did not want the answers now. The only thing she needed to know was whether her husband was going to live or die. She would not ask the surgeon to make an educated guess, to quote his percentages and trot out statistics. Instead she would put her faith in herself, in her own will to have Fred survive, to hold him again, to tell him she loved him. It was up to her now.

She thanked the doctor and when he and his team had left she sat down again, ready to continue the vigil.

Patty switched on her phone as soon as she stepped outside the hospital door. She had a text message. *"Just gone on school run. Don't want you to worry if you ring house and get no reply. Hope news at hospital is good. Babies fine. Sheila."* Patty heaved a sigh of relief. Sitting in the silence of the relatives' waiting room she had begun to worry. Sheila was a middle-aged woman. A baby and a toddler could be too much for her to handle. Needless worry, judging by the tone of that text. Anyway, she herself should soon be back home. She would just wait for Fred to be brought to Intensive Care and then drive the Aston Martin hell for leather to The Rectory. The older boys were too much to ask anybody to handle, no matter what their age.

Patty's timing was perfect. The Ward Sister was just about to usher Kate and Martin to the Intensive Care as she got back.

"Only one visitor at a time. In fact it would be better if only Mrs Lucas went in to see him now."

Martin and Patty nodded.

"And something else," the nurse added. "You may be visited by the police, Mrs Lucas. Nothing to worry about. They might ask you a few questions but it is your husband they are interested in really. They hope he may be able to identify his attacker when he wakes up."

Kate's heart began to beat more strongly, her steps get surer. Sister had said 'when' Fred woke up. Not if.

Martin felt drained when he went into the office. The intensity of the morning's search for Fred Lucas was equalled only by the shock of finding him, critically injured and clinging onto life. He knew when he and Patty were leaving the hospital that Kate was not allowing herself to admit to the gravity of her husband's condition. She was sitting by Fred's side, holding onto his hand as if she could make him survive by dint of her willpower alone. Maybe she could. There was nothing more medicine could do for him anyway.

Martin's staff were all looking at him now, anxious to know how Fred was but reluctant to ask. When he rang in earlier he had just told them in general terms that Fred had been involved in an accident and that he and Kate were at the hospital. Eileen was the one, of course, to break the silence.

"Any more news about Fred? How is he?"

Martin was not sure what he should say. Should he stick to the accident story? What would Kate want? Then he realised Kate would not care what he said. She had just one concern now.

"Fred was attacked last night and stabbed in the back. He's been operated on and has come through surgery. He's very weak. I'm afraid his condition remains critical."

"Oh! Poor Kate! Is there anything we could do to help?"

Eileen was the spokesperson but Martin could see that she spoke for all of them. Their concern for Kate was stamped on all their faces.

"Pray," Martin said and went into his office.

Messages were piled high on his desk. He flicked through them. Hans Meyers had rung several times. He put that memo aside. He could not cope with it now. Chasing Richard Gordon, trying to unravel the intricate financial scheme he and his cohorts had in place, seemed unimportant when Fred's life hung in the balance. Then his breath caught as he picked up the next memo. Lee had been trying to contact him all morning. Shit! He dialled her number straight away only to find her phone was completely dead. Shit again!

There was a tap on his door and Eileen came in carrying a cup of coffee. She placed it on his desk and smiled at him.

"Thought you might need that, Mr Burke. I know I probably don't make it the same as Kate but it will perk you up anyway. You look knackered. I mean exhausted."

Martin laughed as he gratefully took the cup of coffee. "You were right the first time. I'm knackered. It's been a very harrowing morning. Much worse for Kate, of course."

On her way to the door Eileen hesitated and then stopped. She turned around.

"Just in case you've forgotten with all the drama – your wife will be landing at about half past nine."

Martin nearly choked on his coffee. "What?"

Eileen looked alarmed. "Oh, God, didn't you know? She rang here four times. You had your mobile switched off in the hospital. I didn't tell her where you were, of course. I know how you value discretion. She just wanted to make sure you were there to meet her. Terminal B. 9.30."

"Right, Eileen. Thanks for coffee and close the door after you, please."

When she had left, Martin stood and walked to the window. He looked into the distance at the treetops in the park. The park he had dreamed he and Bobby would play football and cycle and race and laugh and do all the father-and-son things in. Fuck Lee Page Burke and her laughing hyena of a father! She could do whatever she liked, use all her stinking money but it would do her no good. He had let Bobby go once and he would not do that again.

Kate rubbed Fred's face as she whispered to him. His eyes were closed, his breathing shallow, his hands cold but she knew he could hear her. She told him things she had never told him before. Little things about her childhood, about days of turf-cutting and gathering hay. She whispered forgiveness and understanding to him and asked him for the same. She whispered love and comfort and cried tears of fear and anguish when his hands got colder and his breathing shallower. Doctors came and went. The drip was speeded up and slowed down. Fred was injected and an oxygen mask put on his face. Yet Kate still sat there, holding his hand, whispering the silly things that only lovers do.

"You should take a break, Mrs Lucas. Have a cup of coffee. I'll call you if there is any change."

Kate smiled at the nurse and shook her head. "Thank you but I'm staying here. I'm not going to leave my husband's side ever again. Never."

The nurse gently closed the door and left husband and wife together for whatever length of time they had to share.

Chapter 29

Patty drove the Aston Martin slowly up the avenue, aware that at any second one of the boys could dive out of the shrubs or jump down from a tree. There was no sign of a child anywhere. The Jeep was parked in front of the house so they had to be around somewhere. Maybe they had gone to the orchard. She had forgotten to warn Sheila about that. When they set foot in the orchard the boys suspended whatever few civilised rules they normally obeyed. Or much more likely, they were inside watching television. It would be just their style to tell Sheila that they were allowed to sit in front of the screen all day long.

Taking the spare key from underneath the big clay pot she let herself into the Rectory. It was eerily quiet. Patty began to panic. What had she done? She had left her children with a woman she did not really know and now they had disappeared. Then she heard the voice speaking softly. She followed the sound to the lounge. Standing unnoticed at the open doorway she watched and listened as Sheila read from *Harry Potter* to her enthralled audience. Bobby was sitting on her lap, Jonathan asleep in his carrier, the rest of the gang were sitting on the floor at her feet, eyes wide and mouths open. Not a kick or nudge. Not a face being pulled or a tongue being stuck out. Sheila's voice droned on, her peculiar diction a mixture of local accent overlaid with acquired rounded vowels. The boys had found a gran.

Bobby was the first to notice Patty standing there. "Story," he said. "Sheila read story!"

Sheila looked up and smiled. "That's all for now, boys. If you're all good, I'll read for you some other time. You can watch television for a while." She walked over to Patty her expression anxious. "What's the news? How is he?"

"Hanging in there. The knife missed the major organs by millimetres but he has lost a lot of blood. It's still touch and go."

"How's Kate?"

"Sitting beside him, holding his hand and not believing that he could die."

They walked together into the kitchen. Patty had not realised how hungry she was until she got the smell. She sniffed. Onions? Sheila ordered her to sit and in two minutes a plate of shepherd's pie appeared on the table in front of her.

"Eat that up now. You could do with it after the day you've been through."

Patty looked from the plate to the woman hovering anxiously over her. Tears filled her eyes. It had been so long, such a lonely time, since somebody had done something this nice for her, had recognised that she was tired of coping, tired of having the responsibility of the boys, tired of trying to plan their penniless future, tired of being alone. Sheila's arms enfolded her and she cried and cried for Brian, for Kate, for Fred and for herself. When she had finally cried herself out, she realised that Sheila was crying too.

"I'm sorry, Sheila. Sorry for breaking down like this and sorry for the times I was nasty to you. I'll never be able to thank you enough for what you've done for me."

Sheila straightened up and dried her eyes. She went to the fridge, poured out milk and brought a glass over to the table.

"Drink this with your dinner. You need it. You're like a waif. And don't thank me, Patty. I'm indebted to you. D'you know how long it's been since somebody needed me? Our children have not alone grown up. They've grown away from us. Gus and I gave them all the advantages that money could buy. Everything we didn't have ourselves when we were young. Now we're not good enough for them. They're ashamed of us."

Patty was about to contradict her when she realised how hypocritical that would have been. She too had laughed at Sheila's pretensions, at her attempts to be hostess with the mostest, at her exaggerated mannerisms and her mistaken ideas of chic. She caught the older woman's hand.

"Their loss, Sheila. You don't have to fit in with somebody else's idea of what you should be. Look how my boys love you. My God! You've civilised the little terrors!"

Sheila laughed. "They're great, Patty. A credit to you! I'll mind them whenever you want. I've plenty of time on my hands. Gus still spends every waking minute working. He could retire. He can afford to but I think he'd curl up and die if he was not wheeling and dealing."

Patty ate her shepherd's pie. It was delicious.

Sheila gathered up her bag and keys and put on her coat.

"I'll go now, Patty, but I want you to promise me that you'll call me if there's any news from the hospital. You'll probably want to be there for Kate one way or the other. So I'll baby-sit later on."

"If you're sure."

"I'm sure. And there's something else, Patty. I understand from Gus that Fred Lucas was involved in the same scheme Brian got caught up in. Gus would go absolutely mad if he thought I'd said anything but, whatever you think, he's a decent man. I told you he never discusses business with me but I do know he's very angry about Brian and Fred being drawn into this scheme. He said it was out of their league and that they were used. I'll try to find out more. Ring me when you want me to come over."

Patty sat at the kitchen table after Sheila had left. Their new-found gran had taken her calming influence on the boys with her. They were arguing over which programme to watch on television. She should go into the lounge but she wanted to sort out some things in her head. One question dominated. What had Sheila Cochrane meant by saying that Brian and Fred had been used? Who had used them and why?

The argument in the lounge reached crisis proportions. She ran and immediately slipped back into her mammy role. Intrigue would have to wait.

The shifts had changed over. The new nurse was full of bustle and efficiency. She checked Fred's charts, his vital signs, his drip and finally she turned to Kate.

"Go down to the canteen and get something to eat. You're no good to him if you collapse from hunger."

"I'm not hungry."

"You still need to eat. Take your phone with you. I'll call if you're needed."

"But I want to be here when he wakes up."

The nurse caught Kate by the arm and led her to the door. "Mrs Lucas, I guarantee you I'll call if he as much as flutters an eyelid. You must look after yourself too. Now off you go. I've got work to do."

Kate went out and looked back in through the glass partition. The nurse was pulling the covers back, moving pillows, tossing Fred around as if he were a toy. She rolled him onto his side and the theatre gown parted, exposing his bottom. Kate turned her back and walked down the corridor towards the lifts. Who planned all this? What kind of power ordained that we should be born helpless and dependent, spend our lifetime learning self-help and independence only to come full circle to die in our initial state of helplessness and dependence? She shivered. Why was she thinking about death? Hospitals were so creepy and depressing.

The smell of coffee and chips led her to the canteen.

Realising that she was suddenly hungry, she ordered curry, chips and coffee. After two mouthfuls, she felt full. She pushed the plate away and got up from the table. She would find the shop. Get something to read. The poky little hospital shop was situated on the first floor. Kate skimmed over the magazines and rejected them. She did not really care which romance had broken up or which look was the latest must-have. Picking up the evening paper she glanced at the headlines. Something drew her eye to the bottom of the page. It was her husband's name. *The victim has been named as thirty-four-year-old advertising executive, Frederick Lucas. He remains in a critical condition in . . .* She dropped the paper and ran. Too terrified to wait for the lift she raced up the stairs and sped along the corridor. She skidded to a halt by the side of Fred's bed.

"Mrs Lucas! You'll kill yourself or someone else running around like that. What's the matter?"

Kate looked from the waxen face of her husband to the plump no-nonsense nurse.

"He's critically ill. Fred's critically ill."

"That, Mrs. Lucas, is what we've been trying to tell you. Do you understand now?"

Kate nodded. She understood at last. She understood too well.

Martin closed the door gratefully after the last client. By now he had managed to see most of the clients he had intended seeing today, and the rest Eileen had managed to reschedule. He had been a less-than-sympathetic legal adviser this afternoon. In fact at the moment he did not give a damn about his clients' petty crimes, their claims for personal injuries, their wills and house deeds. How important was any of it? Look how Fred had given everything to building up his business and now he was struggling for his very existence. There was a tap on his door. Eileen backed in. Martin smiled. She had yet more coffee for him and this time she had brought biscuits as well.

"You're spoiling me, Eileen."

Her face went pink as she put the tray down on his desk. "I know you're old friends with Fred Lucas. It must be hard for you having to work and not knowing . . . well, not knowing what's going on at the hospital."

"I'll be going there later. Just dropping by for a few minutes."

"Tell Kate we're all praying, will you? And, of course, if there's anything we can do. Poor Kate!"

Martin nodded, remembering Kate's shocked and pale face, her shaking hands. Where was she going to find the strength to cope with whatever fate had in store?

"Good night, Mr Burke. Don't forget. Terminal B. 9.30."

Martin smiled at her as she went out. Then as soon as he heard the click of the door closing he dropped his head in his hands. Fuck! Bad enough to have one of his oldest friends hovering on the verge of death but he had to cope with Lee as well. She could flaunt her wealth and the sheikh's oil dollars all she wanted. She was not getting her hands on Bobby. Unless, of course, that is what Bobby wanted. And there was the great imponderable. Which way would Bobby choose and where in the hell was the justice in putting a three-year-old in that position anyway?

Unsettled, upset, angry and afraid, Martin was unable to concentrate on work. Picking up his brief-case, he threw some papers into it. He had court tomorrow. He could look over his notes later on. After he had collected Lee from the airport and strangled her! He was just ready to go when he noticed the memo about Hans Meyers. He sat down again with a sigh. Here was another mess that needed to be sorted. He dialled and waited as the phone rang. Hans always let his phone ring six times before answering. He pretended it was some type of safety precaution but Martin knew it was superstition. Hans thought the number six was very lucky for him. He picked up on cue.

"Hello, Hans. Martin Burke here. Sorry I couldn't get back to you earlier. Things are a bit hectic today."

"Bet they were quiet and ordered before you arrived. You always stir things up."

Martin smiled. Hans was not joking. He never joked. The man had no sense of humour. Zilch. Every word out of his mouth was grave and solemn. Maybe that was what made him such a good detective. He took everything seriously, even the bizarre.

"Well, how's the search going, Hans? Have you made progress?"

"You will not like what I have to tell you. What do you know about Nauru?"

Martin had to think. He knew the name. It was an island. Yes. "It's an island just south of the Equator. I think perhaps the smallest republic in the world. It used to be a huge exporter of phosphates but their mines are almost worked out now."

"If you know that much, Martin, you must know what their replacement industry is."

Jesus! Yes, he did. He should have remembered straight away. Nauru had been central to the Bank of New York scandal. Facilitating money-laundering, setting up and selling shell banks, the republic of Nauru shoved two fingers up to the world of high finance. Their banking system was not open to inspection, not bound by any of the international rules of transparency or disclosure. You paid your money for your shell bank and then whatever you did with it was your own business. Fifty thousand dollars could buy you a lot of privacy on Nauru.

"So you see, Martin, the news is bad. The trail on your people ends in Nauru. They bought a shell bank there. I can tell you that bank is named DYBRYN International. And that's as far as I can go. Absolutely no way of finding out what funds are entering or leaving it. "

Martin was silent. How much more bad news was there going to be? The syndicate had spread its wings very far. One thousand two hundred miles east of New Guinea to be exact.

"There is one other thing."

"Yeah," Martin said, not really wanting to hear. The way things were going it could not be good news.

"The Gibralter-registered companies you asked me to investigate. Leaf International and Landform Securities. They buy and sell properties, as you already know. They are profitable but the turnover is slow. Or at least it would be slow without the sideline."

"What sideline?"

"Prostitution."

"Bloody hell!"

Martin's first reaction was to ask Hans if he was sure, if he could have made a mistake. But Hans did not make errors. If he said the syndicate was involved in prostitution, then it was. And Mr Meyers did not take kindly to his information being questioned or to having his reports interrupted.

"Sorry Hans. Go on."

"They operate the buildings as brothels. When an area is developed, they just sell the building, at a profit, of course, and move onto their next investment site. It's a win-win situation for them. Appreciation on the building and regular income until the price is right to sell. The brothel earnings are obviously channelled through the shell bank, although that has to remain speculation since we cannot prove it."

Martin had heard enough. Any other time, he would have debated with Hans, tried to figure out a way through this maze of deceit and criminality. Tonight, he was tired and worried and just plain depressed. Throwing prostitution into the mix was more than he could take.

"Hans, thank you for that. I've got to go now. I'll ring you within the next day or two. We can talk more about it then."

"Sure. I've only given you the outline anyway. There is a whole network of companies. They are very clever, your friends. I'll let you know if I find anything else."

As Martin put the phone down, he wondered what else there could be to find out. No wonder Richard Gordon had taken off. He could afford to on his immoral earnings. Martin kicked his desk and this time he almost broke his foot. What a stupid habit! He would try being grown up when he had the time to practise.

Maybe it was Sheila's influence or maybe it was just that the children sensed her upset, but whatever the reason the Famous Five were unusually well behaved and obedient this evening. Just as well, since a big part of Patty's attention was taken up with worrying about Kate and Fred and listening out for the phone to ring. Martin was late arriving and when he did he seemed cross and distracted.

"Dinner? Lasagne. The baby-sitter made it. It's delicious."

He shook his head and sat down at the table, Bobby in his arms. He kissed the top of the child's head and told him go watch television for a few minutes.

"I must talk to Patty. Grown-up talk. OK?"

"K", the child said and trotted off.

As soon as he had disappeared Patty sat down opposite Martin. Her hands were shaking. This was bad news. The worst.

"Fred?" she asked, needing to know yet not wanting to hear the answer.

"No. Lee."

"Oh, my God! Has something happened to her? Has she had an accident?"

Martin laughed, the sound harsh and bitter. "Accidents don't happen to Lee. They wouldn't dare. She's here. At least, she will be at 9.30. Flying in on her boyfriend's private jet."

The momentary relief at knowing that Fred was still alive was gone. Patty reached across the table, caught Martin's hand and clung onto it.

"No! She couldn't! She mustn't! He's happy here. Oh, shit! Sorry. It's none of my business. But I love Bobby so much. It'll break my heart to see him go."

"His too. He's settled here so well. He thinks he's part of the Molloy family."

"He is."

Patty could not bear the pain she saw in Martin's face. She got up from the table and put on the kettle.

"You must have coffee, even if you don't feel like eating."

"I'm going to fight her. I know I did before and I lost. But that was different. She was in the States and Bobby's home was there. I'm not letting her take him into a culture that is totally alien to everything he has known. She can't keep moving him around as she goes from one relationship to the next."

Patty put his coffee down in front of him and had to resist the urge to put her arms around him. His pain was so visible in his dark eyes that her maternal instinct urged her to comfort him, to kiss away the hurt. Walking around the table, she sat in her own place, a safe distance from him. Bobby came back into the kitchen and crawled up onto Martin's knee.

"Talk to Bobby now, Daddy!"

Patty and Martin exchanged glances. The decision

would have to be Martin's. The sooner the child knew, the better prepared he would be but how could you tell a three-year-old that he was going to lose not only his father but all his new friends, his brothers, for Christ's sake! Martin held his son close as he spoke to him.

"I have something to tell you, Bobby. It's very good news. Mummy phoned today. She's coming to see you."

"Mummy!"

"Yes. Tomorrow. When you wake up. You can show her the tree house and the orchard. She'll like that."

Bobby looked from his father's solemn face to Patty's tear-filled eyes. A frown creased the silky baby skin on his forehead. "Daddy sad? Patty sad?"

Looking from the agonised eyes of the father to the bewildered eyes of the son, Patty found the strength to lie.

"We're just a little bit upset, Bobby. Our friend is sick in hospital. Daddy will put you to bed now and when you're asleep Sheila will come here to mind you while we go to see our friend."

Bobby threw his chubby little arms around Martin's neck. "Say good night to boys. Piggy-back upstairs." Hoisted up on his father's shoulders, the happy smile was back again. Martin bent his knees so that Patty could kiss his son goodnight. She brushed her lips against Bobby's warm, baby cheek and had to choke back a sob. The doorbell rang and she practically ran to open the door for Sheila. There were only so many goodbyes the human soul could tolerate.

Having driven at breakneck speed to the hospital, Patty

now found that she could only stroll. She hated the thought of going to the Intensive Care Unit. Hated all the tubes and monitors and paraphernalia of death. She had put her faith in medical technology but it had failed Brian and now she had no belief that it could save Fred. A lift arrived but she remained standing in the lobby, the plate of food Sheila had made for Kate balanced on her hand. She frowned, remembering how curt Martin had been with Sheila. Even rude. Of course, he was upset but that was nothing to do with Sheila. He had said he was calling here to the hospital when he left The Rectory. Maybe he was up there now. At least his sombre mood would be fitting in Intensive Care. She heard another lift descending and, taking a deep breath, stepped forward. Time to stop dithering and go to see Kate. And hopefully Fred.

The doors opened and Martin got out.

"Well? How is he?" Patty asked eagerly. "Any change?"

"No. Still the same. And what in the hell do you mean by having a gangster's moll looking after the children? I trusted you, Patty, to have some sense of responsibility. I'd expect the baby-sitter to be at least decent!"

"What are you talking about? How dare you insult Sheila like that! And you've offended me too. I trust her with my children. Is she not good enough for your child?"

Martin caught her by the elbow and brought her over to a quiet corner of the lobby.

"I'm sorry if I have upset you, Patty, but I discovered today that the syndicate is not just about property development. Gus Cochrane is up to his ears in criminality and I don't really want his wife baby-sitting my son."

The plate of food seemed to be getting uncomfortably heavy. Patty changed it from one hand to the other. She craned her neck to look up at Martin. She was so angry she felt as tall as he did.

"I see. So Gus Cochrane is a gangster, is he? And since my husband was part of the same syndicate, if only for a short while, does that make me a gangster's widow? I s'pose you have some Americanised, judgemental name for me too!"

Martin looked at her in surprise. Then he laughed. "Can't say I looked at it like that."

"Well, that's how it is. I spent long enough getting to know the real Sheila Cochrane. She's a true lady. She's my friend, someone I trust with my children. And my family includes Bobby."

Martin dropped his head and Patty hoped he was ashamed of himself. What in the hell was he talking about anyway? What did he mean by 'criminality'?

He looked up and put his hand on her shoulder. "I'm sorry, Patty. There's some stuff going on with this syndicate we'll have to talk about. But, of course, you're right. Sheila Cochrane has no more to do with it than you have, or Kate or Cora Gordon. I'll take it up with her husband and leave her out of it. If you say she's kosher, then so be it. Bobby likes her too."

"He's a better judge of character than his father."

"True. I married Lee, didn't I? Which reminds me, I'd better head for the airport. I'll bring her to see Bobby tomorrow, if that's all right with you?"

On impulse Patty stood on tiptoe and kissed him on

the cheek. Carefully holding Sheila's plate she went towards the lifts, heading for Ward 2B.

Kate looked up when the door opened and smiled when she saw Patty. "What're you doing here? You've enough to deal with at home as it is."

"Of course, I want to be here with you. Any change. How is he?"

Kate shook her head and tears welled in her eyes. Patty could see that Kate's strength was beginning to ebb. She pushed the plate towards her.

"Here. Sheila made this for you. Said it would help to keep you going."

"Sheila Cochrane?"

"Yes, Sheila Cochrane," Patty said firmly, not wanting to have to defend Sheila for the second time tonight.

"That's very nice of her. In fact, I am hungry now. Put the plate on the tray there, please. I'll just let go Fred's hand."

But as Kate went to pull her hand away from Fred, his pale fingers flexed and gripped onto her. She tugged again, afraid to believe what she had just felt. His eyelids flickered and she cried out.

"Fred! I'm here, Fred. You're all right! Oh, I love you, Fred!"

His eyes opened. He looked up into Kate's face and smiled. Then the lids dropped again on his beautiful grey eyes with the green flecks in them. Kate kept calling his name as Patty ran out into the corridor to get help. The Ward Sister, monitoring from her desk, had seen what was happening on screen. She brushed past Patty and dashed to Fred's side. Picking up Fred's wrist, she put her fingers on his pulse and counted. She dropped his hand and checked the monitors. Then she turned to Kate.

"He's turned the corner, Mrs Lucas. His pulse and heartbeat are returning to normal. His blood pressure is climbing too. He's just sleeping now. Rest is what he needs. And so do you."

The nurse was wrong. Kate did not need rest. She needed to eat the smoked salmon platter Sheila Cochrane had so kindly prepared and then she needed to sit by her husband's side and wait for him to wake up again.

Chapter 30

Martin could not stop himself looking in the rear-view mirror as he drove towards The Rectory, his eyes drawn to the limousine following behind. He would have laughed if it had not been so pathetic. His ex-wife had arrived in Ireland last night by private jet and this morning she was being chauffeured around Dublin in the biggest, longest car oil-money could buy. The sheikh is only protecting his investment, Martin thought bitterly, remembering the rock-sized diamond on Lee's finger. He hated Sheikh Amir Al Bahar. Not because he was jealous but because he had to spend last night listening to Lee rattle on endlessly about the sheikh's wells, his hotels, his shopping malls. She was in love with an empire and she and the billions seemed to be a good match. In fact she was so anxious to sing her fiancé's praises that it had been a full hour after meeting Martin before she enquired about their son.

Martin had been hesitant in telling her about the child-care arrangement he had made with Patty. He explained so cautiously that even to his own ears it sounded as if he had something to hide. Lee had put her hand out and stared admiringly at the play of light on her big share of the Kimberly diamond mine. Eventually she just put her hand down and said, "I see," in such a way that left Martin wondering whether she approved or disapproved.

And so this morning, her driver was following Martin's car to The Rectory, filling his rear-view mirror with acres of shiny black metal.

Martin parked near the front door and waited for the limousine to pull in behind him. The chauffeur parked, jumped out and opened Lee's door in one fluid movement. Lee executed one of her near-perfect exits from the car. The one which showed her long legs to the best advantage. She and Martin walked to the front door and stood together waiting for Patty to answer the ring. When the door opened, Patty was holding Bobby in her arms. The child's face lit up and he reached his arms out to Martin.

"Daddy!"

Martin took his son, kissed him and then turned him to face his mother. "Look who I've brought to see you. Mummy's here."

Bobby looked solemnly at Lee with eyes as smoky and dark as his father's.

"My! I do believe you've grown, Robert! You're such a big boy. Come to Mummy. I must have a hug."

A slow smile crept across the child's face. He reached out his hand and touched Lee's face, almost as if the memory of her features was in his fingertips. The smile widened but when Martin moved to hand him over he turned suddenly and buried his face in his father's neck.

Patty held out her hand to the tall beautiful woman. "Nice to meet you, Lee. Welcome to The Rectory."

Before Lee could say anything, the boys came rushing out to the hall, shot past her and dived down the steps, pushing and shoving each other in a race to get to the stretch limo.

Lee raised an eyebrow and smiled at Patty. "When Martin told me Robert had company here, I didn't think he meant a full baseball team. I assume you're Patty."

"Yes. Come in, please."

Lee went into the hall, glancing through open doors, looking up to examine cornices, down to inspect floor rugs.

"I like your house, Patty. Very quaint."

Patty led them into the kitchen and offered them tea or coffee, which they refused. When Lee sat she seemed to pour onto the chair. She was the most elegant, beautiful woman Patty had ever seen. Her movements were fluid, ballerina-like. Patty could not help staring at the source of Lee's special sparkle. The gigantic diamond on her engagement finger must be worth more than The Rectory.

"Congratulations, Lee. Martin told me you've got engaged."

Lee smiled and for the first time there was some animation in the beautiful features. "Thank you. Amir and I are very happy. You must meet him some time."

Patty nodded and stole a glance at Martin and Bobby. The child was still cuddled into his father. He was sucking his thumb. She dragged her eyes away from Bobby. She would cry again if she kept looking at him. She felt like screaming at his parents. What in the hell were they doing to their child? Could they not see how confused he was? She was confused. Were they taking their son away or not? The silence was uncomfortable. Lee seemed to have taken charge and she had decided not to talk. Patty could not stand it another second. She got to her feet.

"I'd better check on the boys. They're probably bothering your driver, Lee."

Bobby clambered down from his father's arms and ran after her. "Me too! Go with Patty!"

Patty stooped down and hugged him close to her, breathing in his baby scent. His soft cheek resting against hers, she whispered into his ear. "Mummy has come a long way to see you, Bobby. She loves you very much. You should give her a big hug now. And always remember that Patty and the boys love you too."

He tightened his arms around her neck and Patty had to fight the urge to snatch him and run away with him. To a place where his feuding parents could never again use him as a pawn. She picked him up, carried him over to his mother and put him sitting on her linen skirt. The fine fabric would crease. Good! Mother and child remained sitting straight, together but not re-united. Patty stooped and kissed Bobby. She looked into the baby eyes that were clouded with grown-up sadness. Patty turned to Martin.

"I'm taking the boys to school and then I'm going to collect Kate from the hospital. Bobby's packing is done. His things are in his room."

She shook Lee's hand. "Enjoy your stay, Lee."

In her dash from the kitchen Patty almost forgot Jonathan. She grabbed the baby carrier and ran through the hall. She had no idea whether she would ever again see Bobby or not. Maybe Lee would whisk him off today to live the life of a billionaire child. But Patty knew one thing for certain. Wherever Lee took her son, Bobby Burke would always live on in Patty Molloy's heart. She thought she heard Bobby cry but maybe it was just the sound of her own sobs.

Sheila Cochrane heaped extra sausages and rashers onto Gus's plate this morning. His cholesterol was high. The doctor had told him no more fries but Gus as usual made his own rules. "What do those fuckers know? They can't cure themselves, can they?" had been his reaction to his GP's warnings. Sheila had been surreptitiously reducing the amount of grease Gus was consuming but this morning she needed a favour and nothing worked on her volatile husband's mood like a plateful of sausages and rashers for breakfast. He slapped her on the backside as she placed the dish in front of him.

"That's my girl! Real food for a real man! They can pick at their muesli all they want. Fucking wimps! Give me my sausages. Any time."

Sheila sat down opposite Gus as he wolfed down his breakfast. His muscles had long since fallen into fat but underneath the layers of blubber she could still see the young man with whom she had fallen in love. They had travelled a long road together. It had brought them from penury to the comfortable position they now occupied. Seeing that he was ready for more tea she got up and poured him a cup. As she stood behind him, she noticed the roll of fat over his collar. She impulsively dropped a kiss on it.

"Are you getting skittish in your old age, woman?"

She smiled at him and sat down again. "We've been lucky, Gus, haven't we?"

"'Twasn't luck, you dozy mare. 'Twas hard fucking work."

She nodded in agreement. Nobody had ever worked as hard as her husband had. Nobody had started off with so little and made so much of himself against all the odds. Along the route to prosperity they had outgrown their roots and had never since found a place that was as welcoming and comfortable. The price of success.

"I want to ask you a question, Gus."

His eyes narrowed and he looked at her in that way that saw right into her head.

"How do I know this is about Patty Molloy?"

She laughed. He was right as usual.

"I'm not asking you to tell me anything you would prefer keep to yourself. I just want to know if there's anything you could do for her."

"I tried, didn't I? She won't take our money. Feisty little thing."

"She's a proud woman, Gus. She doesn't want handouts. She just wants what's hers."

Gus heaped butter onto his brown bread, the only concession he made to healthy eating. When he had finished plastering he looked up at his wife.

"Did she put you up to this?"

Sheila had to bite her tongue. There was no point getting angry with Gus. He could out-shout God Himself. She smiled at him.

"No. I just remember you saying that Fred Lucas and Brian Molloy were cheated. I'm not a fool, Gus. I know you bend the rules. Sometimes you even write your own. But I also know you're the most decent, just, man I ever met. You might cut corners here and there but you'd never take the roof from over a man's head. Or his widow's. The girl's in dire straits and she has a houseful of children to support. And look at poor Kate Lucas. It'll be a long time before her husband can do a day's work again. "

Sheila got up from the table and began to tidy up. She knew her man. She had said enough. All she had to do now was keep his bed warm and his plate full of rashers and sausages. And wait.

Patty was amazed to see Fred sitting up in bed, free of drips and wires. She kissed him on the cheek.

"Fred! I can't believe you look so well. We didn't give tuppence for your chances yesterday. Very bad of you to give us all such a fright."

He laughed but it was a weak sound. Patty guessed that he looked a lot healthier than he actually was.

"I'm in better shape than my poor wife. Are you going to take her away from here? I've told her umpteen times to take a break."

Patty looked at Kate and decided Fred was right. She looked ghastly.

"Anyway," Fred added. "My folks will be here soon. It's not as if I'm going to be alone."

"His brother has flown in from England," Kate explained, "and his sister and mother are on their way up from Killarney."

Jonathan began to whinge. He was hungry. Patty caught Kate by the arm.

"C'mon, lady. I didn't bring Jonathan's bottle with me so I've got to go. I'll drive you back to The Rectory to collect your car. You can go home then and have a sleep. Your in-laws can't see you like this."

Kate looked down at her crumpled clothes. The sweater and jeans she had thrown on yesterday morning. She was exhausted. So tired that she had forgotten her car was still at The Rectory.

"Go on," Fred urged. "I'll be fine. Talk to the doctors if you like. You know they'll say all I need now is rest. Look after yourself, Kate."

"I'll just freshen up and get the things you need. Pyjamas, wash-bag. Anything else?"

Fred looked at her as if he wished she would go away. She understood how badly he needed to sleep. She kissed him and waved goodbye.

It was not until they reached The Rectory that Kate noticed how drawn Patty looked. Her eyes were puffy.

"Have you been crying, Patty? Has visiting the hospital been too painful for you?"

Patty shook her head. "It's Bobby."

In stops and starts she explained to Kate about Lee's visit.

"I was so mad, Kate. Neither of them had the courtesy

to tell me what was going on. I don't know if I'll ever see Bobby again. He could be flying off to Saudi bloody Arabia now for all I know."

Kate was surprised. That was so unlike Martin. She had expected more consideration from him. He knew how much Patty loved his son.

"Maybe they'd not decided."

"You mean *she* had not decided. Spoiled bitch!"

Kate did not have the energy or the will to disagree with that. She got her car keys and left as quickly as possible. She had things to do. Important things.

Kate fitted the key the security man had given her into the lock of Fred's office door and turned it. She hesitated before opening up. It had only been two days since she had last been here but it felt like a whole lifetime ago. She crept in, almost as if she was afraid of waking the sleeping ghosts. Standing in the middle of the open-plan area she looked around and tried to imagine what it had been like when Jim and Adele had been busily working at their desks and Fred had been supervising, planning, building his dream. She ran a finger over one of the computers. Already a thin layer of dust lay on the top. Just like Fred's dreams. Dust.

Walking across the room her footsteps echoed in the empty space. The door to Fred's office was open. Bills were stacked on the desk. Taking a deep breath, she picked them up and began to read. She searched in a drawer and finding a calculator, began to tot up. Finally she wrote a figure on a page and sat back to wait.

It was not long before she heard footsteps on the tiled

floor of the corridor outside. There was a tap on the door.

"It's open. Come in!" she called and was surprised and pleased at how strong her voice sounded. There was a pause and then the footsteps travelled towards Fred's office. Kate straightened her shoulders and sat up as tall and straight as she could. She knew she looked a complete mess in her crumpled jeans and sweater but her appearance didn't matter now. Her visitor stood in the doorway, a briefcase in her hand and a superior look on her face.

"This isn't my fault, you know," the girl said defiantly. "Fred had lost the plot long before I got the travel-agency contract."

"Shut up, Adele, and sit down. I want to make this as quick as possible. I hate talking to you, hate having to deal with someone as cold and calculating as you are. The sooner we finish our business here the better. Now have you thought about what we discussed on the phone?"

Adele sat down and put her briefcase on the floor. She leaned her elbows on the desk and stared at Kate. There was steel in the gaze.

"Why should I bail out Fred Lucas? He got himself into this mess. Do you seriously think I owe him anything? Have you any idea how disgusting it was to have him continuously leering at me?"

"Maybe you should try behaving less like a tart if you want respect, Adele. Look, I don't have time to waste on trading insults. I've got to get back to the hospital. You're looking for premises. I'm offering you the lease on this one. Included in the package is equipment and also the smaller contracts. The ones you didn't steal."

Adele tossed her hair back and laughed. "I'm not interested in those piddling little fliers and newsletters. I only –"

"I'm not going to bargain with you. This is what I want. Take it or leave it."

Kate shoved the piece of paper she had written on across the desk to Adele. Then she sat back and prayed. She had added up all the outstanding sums. Lease, rental on office equipment, rates and taxes. It was a fair exchange. Adele would get an office already set up, a list of contacts and no matter how she pretended to sneer at the small contracts, Kate knew they were essential. She also knew that Adele needed premises in which to base her business. Jim Grant's sister had told her that on the phone this morning. She had also informed her that Adele had been given a budget by the travel agents to finance her set-up. In time, she would cheat on them too but that was their problem. Justice would be done if the travel-agency money now paid off Fred's debts. If Adele paid them off. The bitch had almost cost him his life.

Adele had her laptop open and was busily tapping away. Kate looked at the curtain of blonde hair hiding the girl's face and tried with all her strength to will her to say yes. Adele finished tapping and turned the screen towards Kate.

"That's my offer," she said.

Kate picked up her bag and stood. "I told you I wasn't here to bargain with you. You know my price. I'll have no problem getting it elsewhere. Now get out of my husband's office."

"Oh, sit down, Kate! Don't be as stupid as your husband. We both know you can only sell the goodwill of this business, pathetic as it is, to another advertising agency. How many of them do you think are queuing up to buy Lucas Advertising? If you want a quick sale, you deal with me."

At that minute Kate would rather deal with the devil than Adele Sheehan but the girl was speaking the truth. And the difference between the price offered and asked was minimal. It was more a matter of principle now. Kate sat and looked across at the person opposite, so beautiful on the outside and so ugly inside.

"I'll take what you offer but I'll not allow you to keep the fixtures and fittings. I'll sell them separately."

"For heaven's sake!" Adele said in exasperation and took out her cheque-book. She filled in a cheque and threw it across the desk. Kate put out her hand and caught it. She did not care how it had arrived so long as she had it in her hand. She glanced at it. It was for the full amount.

"See Martin Burke about the lease. I'll instruct him to change it to your name. I'm sorry I can't find it in my heart to wish you luck, Adele."

"No need, Kate. I make my own. Now, would you please leave my office."

Kate opened a drawer in the desk and took out the stack of bills she had hidden there. She put them into her bag with the cheque. Then she left the office that still bore the name Lucas Advertising on the door.

Martin had to call on his wealth of experience in court

procedures. He was running on autopilot. His mind continuously wandered away from the courtroom and back to his son. He kept seeing the tear-stained little face peering out of that ostentatious car as it left The Rectory this morning. And Patty's grief-stricken face as she had dashed from the kitchen, knowing that she might probably never see Bobby again.

"All rise now."

At last. Session over. Martin grabbed his brief-case and stuffed papers into it. He glanced at his watch. Perfect timing. He would be waiting for Bobby and Lee when they arrived.

He walked. It was quicker. As he entered the hotel lobby he was surprised to see they were already there. Bobby ran to meet him and jumped up into his arms.

"We were at the zoo, Daddy. Saw elephants and monkeys. Monkeys are funny."

He kissed the child, glad to see the morning's tears were forgotten. Lee walked over to join them.

"Ready for lunch?"

Martin nodded.

Lee led the way into the dining area, pretending not to notice admiring glances as she sashayed along. Every floor was a catwalk to Lee, every venue a stage, her ex-husband and son support players in her production. Martin held tightly onto Bobby and took a deep breath. He would have to keep control. Stay calm.

Waiters fluttered around them. Seating them and taking their lunch order became another Lee Page-Burke, soon to be Lee Page-Burke-Al Bahar, production. To observers, and there were quite a few of them, they must have seemed like the perfect family.

Martin looked at his son and forced himself to smile. "So what else did you see at the Zoo Bobby?"

"Giraffe! He was eating a tree. I go home to Patty now."

Martin glanced at Lee. She was admiring that vulgar ring again. His resolve wavered. How self-obsessed could the woman be? Could she see anything beyond her own wants and needs, whatever they were? He took a deep breath.

"Did you enjoy the morning, Lee? How did it go?"

She reluctantly dragged her attention back. "Yes. Of course we had a good time. You know how much I love zoos."

The sarcasm in her voice was cutting. Martin was grateful that his son was as yet too young to appreciate his mother's talent for the ultimate put-down. She had won. Let her gloat.

"All right, Lee. Enough of this fencing. What do you intend doing? I need to know now."

"About what? You don't have any right to know my plans, Martin. Or have you forgotten that we're divorced?"

"I don't care what you do with your life. I don't care if you go to Timbuktu and never come back. I want to know about my son."

"*My* son. I won custody. Remember?"

Bobby looked from one to the other of his parents and his bottom lip began to quiver. "Go home to Patty now."

"You're upsetting him," Lee accused but she made no

attempt to comfort the child. Martin picked him up and held him close.

"I'm leaving this evening, Martin. Amir has been doing some business in London. I'm flying over to meet him and Robert's coming with me." She leaned towards the child. "You'll have a lovely spin on the plane, Robert. Your very own plane."

Bobby looked distressed. "Go home to Patty now. Must play with my dinkies."

"Congratulations, Martin. You've managed to brainwash him very well."

"For Christ's sake, Lee! He's a three-year-old child, not a political prisoner. I only want what's best for him. I'm going to fight you on this. You're not taking him to Saudi."

Lee smiled coolly and spread her napkin over her linen skirt. "You're right. I'm not. I'm taking him back to the States. My father's going to be his guardian."

"And you're going to Saudi with Amir?"

"Of course. He's the man I love. I'd follow him to the ends of the earth."

Martin's mind raced through remembered family law from the States. Lee changing her domicile would strengthen his case. For however long that would last. But he would have to battle through the courts for years, fighting not just the system but also Chuck Page's millions as well. He kissed the top of Bobby's head and tried not to transmit his heartbreak to the child.

"I don't want to upset Bobby any more than is necessary, Lee. Can we meet before you go, just the two of us, and discuss this like adults?"

Always aware that frowns would ruin her skin, Lee never allowed her feelings to show on her face. She shrugged. "I must get some shopping done."

"Good God! Would you stop playing games? This is our child's life we're talking about, his future, his happiness. Forget about us and whatever has gone on between us."

"No need for you to worry on that score. You're completely eradicated from my memory."

Martin felt helpless. He would beg, he'd even crawl to Lee and her loud-mouthed father, if he thought they would grant him custody but he knew the more he'd beg the more they would refuse. Bobby was Page property and nobody messed with the Pages. He saw Bobby's lips begin to quiver again and he had to make one last attempt to appeal to whatever little selflessness was in Lee.

"You saw for youself how happy Bobby is here. If you leave him with your father, he'll be brought up by staff. Good professional people, I admit, but hired help just the same. Your father's a busy man and not a very affectionate one as you well know."

"You mean the way I was brought up? You don't think that was good enough?"

"This isn't about you. It's about Bobby."

"My son's name is Robert."

"I want to see Patty! Now! And the boys!" Bobby cried and big tears began to roll down his cheeks.

People were beginning to look at them and this time the glances were more curious than admiring.

Lee stood up and held her hand out to Bobby. The child turned his face into his father.

"Come on, Robert," she said. "We must go shopping. Mummy's going to buy you some nice new clothes. "

Seeing that Bobby was still clinging onto his father, she upped the stakes.

"I'm going to buy you lots of toys too. What would you like?"

Bobby was more interested now. He gradually turned his face to look at his mother.

"A rugby ball?"

"I'll get you football boots too. How about that?"

Bobby got down off Martin's knee and took Lee's hand. She smiled at Martin, a gloating smile, ugly on the beautiful face.

"You can come to the airport to see us off if you like, Martin. Eight o'clock."

She turned then and led Bobby away, his little legs struggling to keep up with her long stride. At the door they both paused and looked back at Martin, Lee cool and unruffled, Bobby's face still tear-stained but his eyes glittering now in anticipation of getting his very own rugby ball. The child lifted his hand and waved at his father. Martin tried to smile as he waved back but he was not able.

Nor was he able to move from the table for a long time afterwards. He was weighed down by sorrow, paralysed by guilt and grief, immobilised by the feeling that he had let his son down. He tried to reason that the child would have every advantage money could buy, that it was right he should be in his mother's custody, that a protracted court case would be damaging to Bobby and probably pointless anyway. All the reasoning in the world could not shift the pain of parting or lessen the fears for his son's future. This was the little boy who had laughed as he milked the cows with Phil McCarthy in Kerry, who screamed with laugher as he joined in the rough and tumble of Molloy family life. Martin believed that Bobby would never laugh like that again and he knew that it would be a long and lonely time before Bobby's father would ever smile again.

Gareth Owens hated having his routine disturbed. He was very organised, one of the qualities which had made him such a successful bank manager. But then, as he admitted grudgingly to himself, his business with this man was never routine anyway. He would just have to go on a later lunch break. He checked his watch impatiently. Bad enough having to deal with the rag-and-bone man without being forced to wait for him. He was already two minutes late. A loud rumble outside the office signalled Gus Cochrane's arrival. The receptionist ushered him in and made a very quick escape. Gareth wondered if the Neanderthal now sitting in front of him ever questioned why he saw far more backs walking away from him than faces coming towards him. He probably did not care anyway.

"Hello, Gareth. I won't keep you long. I know you're anxious to go to your lunch."

"No rush at all, Gus. What can I do for you?"

"You can tell me what in the fuck kind of a knack you and your buddies pulled on Brian Molloy and Fred Lucas."

Gareth tugged at the cuffs of his shirt and cleared his throat. He needed time to think. What was this about? Why was the bin-man asking these questions?

"I don't know what you mean, Gus. There was no 'knack' as you call it. They bought into the syndicate. Money for shares. That's how these things work."

"Don't patronise me, you pathetic excuse for a man! I know how it fucking works. Grease the palm of a crooked banker like you or a twisted politician like Hennessey and then everything goes as smooth as a baby's ass. Now I'm asking you again, why were those two men dragged into this? How come we needed their input?"

Gareth relaxed. The bin-man was just fishing. "They were hardly dragged in kicking and screaming. Both gladly accepted the offers made."

Gus put his elbows on the desk and leaned towards the prissy banker. He smiled as he noticed Gareth unconsciously lean back an equivalent distance. Just to intimidate him more, Gus narrowed his eyes. Experience had taught him that eye-narrowing could be very effective.

"D'you remember the last trip we all took together, Gareth? To visit the development in Bucharest?"

Gareth nodded. He certainly remembered Cochrane on that trip. He had been rowdily drunk most of the time.

"Well," Gus continued, "in case you've forgotten any of it, I made a video. I can lend it to you. Your wife might like to see just how much you enjoyed yourself. Especially the bit in our whorehouse. Jesus! You're a dark horse, Owens!"

Gareth went pale and began to tug frantically at the

cuffs of his shirt. "You bastard! You spied on me!" he muttered between clenched teeth.

Gus laughed and banged his huge fist on the desk. "Now, quit pissing about, you fucking pervert, and tell me what I need to know!"

White with shock, Gareth just sat there attacking his shirt cuffs. Gus reached into his inside pocket and pulled out a videotape. He waved it in front of the other man's nose. It acted like smelling salts. The words began to pour from between the clenched teeth.

"Richard Gordon wanted out. He wanted to liquidate his assets. He's going away. When his share was paid out we were short one million to finish development of the Budapest project. We raised that between Brian Molloy and Fred Lucas. Three quarters from Brian Molloy and a quarter from Lucas. Now are you going to give me that video?"

Gus held the video up, just out of the other man's reach. "Not so fast, you little prick! What do you mean Richard Gordon's going away? I thought he was just on holiday."

"He's not coming back. He tidied up all the legal paperwork before he went. We have nothing to worry about."

"I haven't. You can't say the same. You're totally fucked if this ever comes to light. We could never have done it without your double entries or whatever it is you do to square the books. You'd better pray hard that Gordon tied everything up tight. I wonder why he decided to sneak off like that?"

"He just wanted to retire and enjoy his money."

"My arse! There's something else going on there."

Gareth Owens squirmed around on his seat. It was obvious he was considering whether he should reveal some information or not. Gus waved the videotape a bit more to help him decide.

"It could have something to do with the new legislation pending. The Money Laundering Bill. He could have been warned. Maybe by Henry Hennessey."

Gus thought about that and dismissed it. There was a raft of money-laundering legislation already in existence. The bills were always being amended. They had to be. As soon as one loophole was plugged, another appeared. Besides, the syndicate's scheme was too complex. They would all be six foot under by the time anyone had the trail of companies unwound. Anyway DYBRYN International was a firewall. No one could ever discover what moneys moved into and out of that shell company or even who was moving them. The Nauruan banking laws guaranteed total privacy – secrecy. No. Richard Gordon had some other reason for pulling out now. Fuck him!

"You used the deeds of Brian Molloy's home, and Fred Lucas's too, as collateral. Right?"

Gareth nodded. "Straightforward re-mortgaging on both properties. Plus their cash lodgements."

"So just straightforwardly undo both re-mortgages and return the money to Fred Lucas and Brian Molloy's widow."

"I can't just return the money. This isn't garbage collection. This is banking for Christ's sake! What do you think I can do? Just conjure up a million and wipe out their debt?"

Gus tapped the video on the desk. Barely out of the other man's reach. He could see the beautifully manicured fingers clasp and unclasp as Gareth Owens thought about making a grab for the videotape.

"I have copies, you know. They could end up anywhere. I might even get very careless and send one to your head office by mistake. Or maybe they'd prefer the one I made last summer in Kiev. Very entertaining, that."

Gareth Owens was visibly shaking now. Gus knew he was ready to cooperate.

"I'll try to contact Richard Gordon," said Gareth. "See if he would be willing to release some of his equity."

Gus put the videotape back into his pocket and stood up.

"You do that, you little shit! Gordon must have cleaned up on this deal. He has plenty. And don't ever, ever again, make any decisions affecting the syndicate without consulting me. Richard Gordon had no right to withdraw without everyone's agreement. Including mine. If my money is fucking good enough for you, then so am I."

"Nobody knew. He just decided. He only told me because he had to. He made me promise –"

"Oh, shut up, you snivelling freak! Just get working on it. If I don't hear from you soon, I'll be back with my picture show. And this time I'll be ready to use it."

Gus banged the door on the way out. He thought it was a nice effect. In the car, he put the videotape carefully into the glove pocket. Sheila would be furious if he misplaced her video of the *EastEnders Omnibus*. It was her favourite soap.

Kate was looking forward to meeting up with Fred's family. His brother she did not know very well. He had left for England straight after college. A vet, like his father, he practised in the Yorkshire Dales. Annette, his sister, was married and living outside Killarney, within walking distance of their home place. It was Fred's mother, Beth, whom Kate felt closest to. She was a quiet woman, softly spoken, yet with a wicked sense of fun. Worry lines on her face were equally matched with laughter lines. It was a well-balanced face Kate thought as she kissed it now and hugged Beth Lucas.

"The police called," Fred told her. "They've arrested the two yobbos."

Kate smiled with satisfaction. Today seemed to be the day for tying up loose ends. The creditors would have their money and the thugs who stabbed Fred would get their come-uppance. She allowed her mind to drift away from the hospital room as Fred and his family chatted happily, reminiscing about people and places she did not know. For the first time a niggle of doubt began to tarnish the shine on the deal she had done with Adele Sheehan. She had assumed Fred would be pleased. Glad to be rid of the debts that had driven him over the edge. What if she was wrong? He might be angry with her, furious that she had sold what was left of his business to his arch-enemy. Thirty pieces of silver. She jumped as she realised her mother-in-law had been trying to catch her attention.

"You should be at home in bed, child," Beth said. "You're exhausted. We're off to get something to eat now. We won't be long. You can toddle off as soon as we come back."

Kate waited until the door had closed. Then she pulled her chair closer to Fred and took the cheque out of her bag. She handed it to him.

"I've a surprise for you, Fred. This completely clears your debts. All you have to worry about now is getting better."

He stared at the piece of paper in his hand. She saw him flinch as he read the signature on the cheque. For an instant Kate thought he was going to rip it up. He handed it back to her and turned his face away. She was silent, realising now the depth of his humiliation. She should have been more sensitive. Not alone had he mismanaged his business but his wife and the girl who had treated him so treacherously had rescued him. Kate straightened her shoulders. Tough titty! It was reality time.

"I'll manage the payments on the mortgage, just about, until you are well enough to work again. You'll have no problem getting a job, Fred. We'll be fine."

He slowly turned to face her. "I'm sorry, Katie. Really sorry. You deserve better."

She opened her mouth to utter something consoling but he gently placed his hand on her lips.

"Let me talk. The least I owe you now is the truth. I've messed everything up. Every single fucking thing has gone wrong. I can't keep deceiving you. The business debt was only part of what I owe. Nigel Greenway railroaded me into joining a syndicate with some of his friends. Property development. In Eastern Europe. It's a sure bet. A big money-spinner."

Kate's heart began to race. Not Richard Gordon's syndicate! "International Leaf ?" she whispered.

He nodded. Kate grabbed her bag and began to throw the contents out on the bed. Right down in a bottom corner, she found it. She straightened the crumpled piece of paper, read it and then dropped her head in her hands. The scribbled page of nonsense letters and numbers. She should have known, should have figured all this out long ago. Martin Burke must have. He probably knew. The letters were abbreviations for the occupations of the syndicate. GO: garage owner. Not Gareth Owens as she had thought. HS: heart surgeon. And stuck in the middle of them was AA. Advertising agent. How could she not have known? BM of course would be Gareth Owens, the bank manager. The others she could figure out later. Now, she would have to ask Fred the most important question of all.

"How much?"

"I re-mortgaged the house for two hundred thousand. The rest was in lieu of payment for the Greenway contract."

Fuck! Two hundred thousand on top of a mortgage that was already stretching them to their limits. Jesus!

"There's no way I can repay that on my salary," she said. "What're we going to do?"

"You could sell your cottage. It's not as if you need it."

That was how little he knew her. She could not survive without her home on the hills. It was the only place she could breathe, the only place she felt safe. Fuck him! Fuck the syndicate and the bank! Kitty and Paudi's home was not for sale. Her past was not up for grabs. She shook her head.

"Sell your own house if you must, Fred. Leave the cottage out of it."

He lay back on his pillows. Kate almost relented when she saw how pale, how sick he looked. Then she remembered the hills, the fields, Kitty's parlour with her good china, the sweet air, the smell of turf. It was all hers. It was her.

"There's something else," Fred whispered. His voice was so low she had to bend closer to him in order to hear. "I believe I may be discharged tomorrow. When I leave here, I've made arrangements to go to a convalescent home. Our health insurance will cover the cost. Then I'm going . . . going to a rehabilitation centre, a place that can help me cope with my drink problem. I need to get myself together."

Kate was stunned, speechless for a while. Of course, she had seen that Fred had been drinking too much recently. And she had confronted him with his father's history of alcoholism on several very angry occasions but she had never really believed that her husband's drinking was a serious problem. He was not an alcoholic. Not Fred. He was just stressed because of the business. Under pressure because of financial worries. And Kate's need to have a baby. She bowed her head now and remembered Fred's hurtful words to her. He had told her she was selfish. It seemed now he was right. He had needed her help but she had been too self-absorbed to see that. Too busy groping and being groped by Martin Burke. When she got her voice back, it was full of contrition and concern.

"Fred! I'm so sorry. I've let you down. I didn't realise . . . I didn't know you were . . . I know I accused you of being like your father but I didn't mean it. I did at the time but not –"

"Kate, stop apologising. I'm the one who should be doing that. I've made some very unwise decisions lately and the more I drank the more reckless my decisions became. I'm facing the problem now."

Kate grabbed his pale hand which seemed to have shrunk in the past few days.

"I'll be there with you every step of the way. We'll fight this battle together, Fred. And we'll win!"

He pulled his hand away from her and lay back against the pillows. He looked exhausted. Kate lifted her hand and brushed his hair back from his forehead. Even his curls were tired and limp. He turned his eyes to her and there were tears in them.

"You don't understand, Kate. This is my battle. It's my addiction. You can't help me. I must do this on my own."

"I love you, Fred. I never realised how much until I thought I was going to lose you. I want to help. I want to be there for you. We'll get through this together."

His lips shaped into a Fred pout and Kate smiled. That lovely boyish, petulant pout which was so much part of Fred. She leaned forward to kiss him.

He pulled away from her. "Please try to understand, Kate. I need to be on my own. I feel ashamed and stupid and weak. I can blame my genes, Nigel Greenway, even you, but I know some day I'll have to look in the mirror and blame myself for the mess I've made of my life and yours. That's a journey I need to take alone."

Feeling hurt and rejected now, Kate felt a surge of bitter words begin to form in her head. She silenced them before they could leave her mouth and cause even more hurt. She stood and paced, then sat again. She twined her fingers together for comfort and took a deep breath for composure. Calmer now, she smiled at her husband.

"You're still weak Fred. Too weak to be making all these big decisions. Why don't you come home? I'll get some time off work until you feel stronger and then we'll go together to this rehab place and talk to them. You may just need counselling. We can –"

"Not we. Me. This is my problem. My addiction. My way of coping with it. Leave me alone, Kate. Let me get on with it and you get on with your life."

Fred's words seemed to Kate to hang in the air for an endless minute and then they swooped, sharp and lethal into her very soul. Her breath caught in her throat as their meaning hit her with all the force of a fatal blow. He was sending her away, rejecting her, telling her that they had no future together. There could be no other meaning to the horrible collection of vowels and consonants which had just left Fred's lips. That's what he had been trying to say more gently before now. Get lost, Kate. Go away. I don't need you.

"You don't mean this, Fred," she whispered.

"I do. It's the only way."

"But what about us? What about our future, our marriage? Our children."

Fred closed his eyes. He was so still and pale he could have been dead. Kate remembered her desperation of last night, the pledges and promises she had whispered to his comatose body. How could she keep those promises if he would not let her be by his side? She peered at him, not knowing whether he was asleep or not.

"Fred?"

His eyelids fluttered. He was awake but he did not answer. It was as if he was willing her to go away. Hurt piled on shock. She suddenly needed to make him feel what she was feeling now, to know the hurt of rejection.

"So it was all right for me to clear up the mess of your business, to carry you to bed when you were drunk, to lie in bed listening for the sound of your key in the door while you were out making a fool of yourself with Adele Sheehan? That was fine. That's what Kate was for. But now, when we have a chance to start again, you decide you don't want me any more. Would you be behaving like this if I had said you can sell the cottage? Is that it?"

He opened his eyes and looked at her. She saw sadness and determination there.

"I have no future unless I control my drinking," he said, so softly that she had to bend her head close to him to hear. "I must look inside myself, learn to live with what I find. I'm not asking you to wait for me, Kate. I don't want you to. Go now, please. I'm tired."

Kate stood. She walked slowly to the door, waiting for Fred to call her back, to say sorry, bad joke, I love you,

Kate, and whatever problems we have we'll fight them together. She heard nothing but the busy sounds of a hospital going about the business of curing ills and saving lives. She put her hand on the handle and pushed. Still no sound from Fred. The door opened and the outside noise bombarded Kate.

She stood, afraid that Fred was calling her back and she could not hear him. Glancing over her shoulder she saw that he was asleep. Kate took a step out onto the corridor.

There was a very final feel about the click of the door as it shut behind her.

Coming here had not been a plan. Martin found himself driving in the direction of The Rectory without being conscious of turning off the motorway. Where else could he go? Who else would understand the pain that twisted sharp and sour through his gut? The children were in the tree house. He saw the three faces peer down at him as he passed. Patty greeted him wordlessly. He had caught the hopeful look that crossed her face when she first saw him and then the flash of disappointment when she realised he did not have Bobby with him. She led the way into the kitchen and did not speak until they were both sitting.

"She's taking him away, isn't she? When are they going?"

He looked at his watch. It was almost six o'clock. "Two hours' time."

They sat in silence, Patty's obvious upset making Martin feel even worse.

"I had to let him go," he explained. "She has custody."

Patty nodded and silently slipped her hand across the table to touch his.

"You've got to believe I've done everything possible to gain custody of Bobby," he said. "At least she's not taking him to Saudi. She's pawning him off on her father. Or rather on the child-care her father hires."

"So, he's going to America. How does he get along with his grandad?"

"Fine, when he sees him. He barely knows the man."

"Shit! Shit! Shit!"

"My sentiments entirely. To be fair to Lee, she loves Bobby as much as she can. It's just that she loves herself so much, there's not much left over for anybody else."

"Even the sheikh?"

Martin shrugged. He was the last person to pass an opinion on the likelihood of Lee's latest relationship lasting the course. He had proven that he really did not understand the workings of her mind, let alone have any idea on the state of her emotions. She loved Bobby. In her own way. He was sure of that. But Bobby deserved far more in life than his mother's cold and distant brand of loving.

"D'you think he will settle? Will he be all right?"

Martin did not answer the question and Patty had not expected a reply. They sat in silence, both feeling a desperate longing to hold the warm little boy in their arms, both trying to banish the image of confusion and hurt in his dark eyes. Both feeling guilty that they had somehow failed Bobby.

The doorbell rang and Patty was glad to leave the

emotional cauldron of the kitchen. Her relief was shortlived. Kate stood on the doorstep, tears streaming down her face, crying so hard that her breath was coming in gasps.

"Fred? Is it Fred?"

Kate nodded. Patty threw her arms around her and held her friend while she cried. How had this happened? He had looked so much better this morning. As Patty rubbed Kate's shaking back, she raged at fate. Their little group didn't deserve to be visited by so much grief. So many goodbyes. So much pain.

"Not Fred! It couldn't be."

Patty turned to see that Martin had come into the hall. His face reflected shock upon shock. She nodded to him and the pain she saw in his eyes reminded her that Fred and Martin had gone to college together.

"I'm so sorry, Kate," he whispered.

Kate's sobs suddenly stopped. She raised her head and looked from Patty to Martin. As she saw their grief-stricken faces, her expression began to change from total devastation to realisation.

"He's not dead," she said. "I'm sorry if I gave you the wrong impression. He's leaving me. Leaving me with his bloody debts!"

Patty dropped her hands from Kate's shoulders and caught her by the arm. "Come on. Don't say any more until we have coffee. Strong and black."

As the two women walked into the kitchen, Martin stood at the front door. He looked at his watch, looked at Patty's retreating back, looked outside at the children in the tree house. For an instant he thought he heard Bobby's hearty chuckle as he played with the Molloy children he had come to regard as his brothers. Then Martin drove to the airport to say goodbye to his son.

The airport was very busy. Martin stood in the departure lounge and cursed himself for not getting exact details from Lee. Where would he find them now? Just as he was about to ring her, he heard his name announced. At the information desk he was told Mrs Lee Page was expecting him in the VIP lounge.

Under other circumstances he would have been amused at the fact that she had dropped Burke from her name. He was led to the VIP area by a ground hostess.

As soon as the door was opened Bobby ran to him and leaped into his arms.

Lee smiled at Martin. "I was hoping you'd come."

"You knew I would. You had a message announced for me."

"I don't want to argue," she said. "We've done too much of that."

Bobby was wriggling in his father's arms, anxious to get down and run away again. Martin felt a lump in his throat and for an instant he was afraid he would cry. Bobby was gone from him already, anxious to be getting on with his own little life, running around VIP lounges and flying away in private jets. He felt guilty at his selfish rush of emotion. It was good that Bobby for once seemed to be happy in his mother's care.

He nodded to Lee. "You're right," he agreed. "We

argued our marriage away and nobody won in the end. Isn't that sad?"

"It was but not any more. I've found someone I really love and you will too. Besides, we produced a fine son between us. Don't you agree?"

Martin looked across the lounge to where Bobby was struggling with a huge cardboard box, trying to drag it over to where Lee and Martin were standing. Martin smiled at the determined little boy and felt fierce pride in him.

"You'll make sure he's OK, Lee, won't you? I'll try to see him as often as I can but you know how awkward your father can be and he doesn't give a damn about court orders."

"He's a mule," Lee agreed and when she smiled Martin remembered why he had been attracted to her in the first place.

"Help me, Daddy, please!" Bobby shouted, his face red from trying to pull the box which was three times bigger than himself.

As Martin moved to help the child, Lee put her hand on his arm.

"I do love Robert, you know, and I want the best for him."

"We both do. At least we can't argue about that."

"I asked him if he wanted to live with Granddad Chuck who would give him anything he asked for even his own pony. Or to stay with you."

Bobby was shouting louder for his father's help. In fact he was on the way to having a tantrum. For once, Martin ignored his son.

"What did he say?" he asked Lee.

"You must know. Go and see what he has in the box. That will answer your question."

Martin rushed over to the now very frustrated child.

"Let me help you, Bobby. What do you have in this big box?"

"Rugby balls an' jerseys an' boots for all boys! You play too, Daddy?"

Martin scooped his son up into his arms and hugged him close. His head was spinning. He was afraid to trust the hope that was filling his heart now. It would be too cruel if Lee was playing another game. Putting the child down, he dragged the box over to where Lee was standing.

"What are you telling me, Lee? Can he stay?"

"Only if you agree to the same visiting rights you were granted under my custody order. I'll want to be consulted about his education and any other important decisions and I'll want him to spend some of his summer holidays with me. Are you agreeable to that?"

At that point in time, Martin forgot all his legal training and he would have agreed to any conditions as long as he could keep his son by his side.

Lee offered him her hand. "Shake on it?"

He grasped her hand so firmly that she pulled away quickly, rubbing her fingers where that rock of diamond had squeezed against her skin.

"I take it that's yes," she said. "My attorney will be in touch. I'll say goodbye to Robert now. My flight is ready to take off."

Lee stooped and kissed her son on the cheek. He

raised his hand and stroked her face, running his soft little fingers over her smooth skin. Then he smiled at her, a shy, dimpled smile.

"You be a good boy, Robert, and I'll have a nice present for you when I see you again." She stood and turned to Martin. There were tears in her eyes. "He's a fine boy, Martin. I know you'll help him become a fine man."

Then she was gone, walking her model walk across the VIP lounge. She didn't look back but this time Martin knew it wasn't because she didn't care. He waited until she had disappeared from sight, then he picked up his child and the huge cardboard box and headed triumphantly for The Rectory.

Chapter 31

Gus was already seated when Martin reached O'Grady's pub. Two whole days of calls and messages it had taken to pin Cochrane down to a meeting. Martin walked over to join him and arrived at the table the same time as the waitress.

"Whatever Mr Burke is having and my usual," Gus said to the girl. "And bring us two steaks with our drinks. There's a good lass!"

Martin looked at the man he had come to meet, at the sharp eyes peering out from underneath the bushy brows, at the purple-hued jowls and the beads of sweat gathered below the hairline. A volcano waiting to erupt. Both men were silent, weighing each other up. The waitress came back and sensing their mood, wordlessly served up their food and drinks and left as quickly as possible.

Gus picked up his knife but just before cutting into his sirloin, he looked at Martin. "What d'you want, Burke? You're not here for my company. Stop pissing around and tell me."

"Suits me. You want straight talk, I'll give it to you. I know about the syndicate. About International Leaf, Landform Securities and the myriad other offshore companies you and your friends have set up. I even know about your shell bank. Very clever."

Gus put down his knife and stared. "Richard Gordon swore he'd not tell you a word about it. The fucker is full of surprises."

"He didn't tell me," Martin said and sat back to wait for a reaction. It was not long coming.

"What's this about? Are you threatening me? Do you want a share of the action, is that it?"

"I wouldn't touch your filthy scheme even if I was down to my last penny. Brothels! For Christ's sake, man! Your syndicate is scum."

"Don't you look down your nose at me, you prick! All the girls in our establishments are well looked after, medically and financially. We don't run dosshouses. None of them are forced to work there, none of them are under-age. They're all adult women who choose to charge for a fuck. They provide a service and I don't see anything wrong with that."

"You evade tax by setting up offshore companies, you run brothels and channel the immoral earnings through a shell bank, you con two ordinary people into investing in your scheme. Do you see anything wrong in that or are you so corrupt that you don't have any decency left?"

Gus Cochrane's skin turned a deeper shade, the purple infused with bright red. Beads of sweat developed into full-blown droplets and began to trickle down his forehead. He leaned towards Martin, his voice hoarse with anger.

"I'll tell you, you patronising fucker, what corrupt is! It's little girls walking the streets of Dublin or Cork, servicing their clients in doorways, on the back seats of cars and in dingy rooms! It's dirty old fuckers, pillars of the community by day, street prowlers by night, using and abusing these girls. And boys too. No health checks, no protection. A slapper gets beaten up. So what? A john brings gonorrhoea home to his wife. Tough. It's all right so long as we don't talk about it. Turn a blind eye. Fuck! That's corrupt."

"Well, I think –"

"Shut up! I'm not finished. Then there's the grabbing shower in the Revenue Commissioners. Those fuckers would leave you penniless if they could. You work your arse off, for what? To hand nearly half of it back to them. Now tell me that's not wrong!"

Martin nodded. Not that he agreed but he understood the point of view. There was no doubt that Gus was sincere. He was not trying to excuse or explain what he had done. He was just telling the truth as he saw it. He was still yapping away, his jowls wobbling with every word.

"I pay my fair share. I'm not a man to shirk his dues. But they take the mickey altogether. Jesus! Look at the money they waste! They're forever going on trips here and there. If you want to pay for their junkets, elocution lessons and fucking makeovers, off you go. I don't. Let them earn it, like I did. Where in the fuck were they when my wife was out scrubbing floors to help me with the repayments on my first tipper truck? They didn't want to know Gus Cochrane then and I don't want to know them now!"

The man was apoplectic. Martin thought he had better ask the question he had come to ask before Gus keeled over or blew up.

"I need to contact Richard Gordon. Where is he?"

Gus picked up his knife again and nodded his head at Martin. "Eat your lunch. It'll be going cold."

They ate in silence. Martin decided to let the other man fill his belly in peace. He would probably be easier to deal with on a full stomach and a less purple face. When Gus had nothing left on his plate but the pattern, he returned his attention to his lunch partner.

"So why d' you want to contact Gordon? Has he fleeced you too?"

"He's landed friends of mine in hot water and I want to talk to him about it. Hell! I want to twist his bloody neck!"

"These friends of yours? Would one of them be recently widowed and the other your PA?

"They might be."

"Don't fuck around with me. I asked you a question. Are you talking about Patty Molloy and Fred Lucas's wife?"

Martin nodded. Somehow, despite all his preconceptions about the waste-disposal man, he was beginning to warm to him. Rough, vulgar and outspoken. Yes, definitely. Not a man you would introduce to your maiden aunt. But he had an intrinsic honesty, an integrity that shone through all the bluster. A true pearl in a pigsty. Even his voice had lost some of its harsh edge when he spoke again.

"Before I answer your question, Martin, I want you to know that I had nothing to do with bringing your friends into our syndicate. I'm not one of the insiders. Like, for instance, Nigel Greenway. They take my money but they don't confide in me. Brian Molloy and Fred Lucas could not afford to gamble their homes. I would never have allowed them to."

On impulse Martin stretched out his hand. "I'm sorry if I was a bit judgmental, Gus. I still think you're a gangster but a well-meaning one."

The glasses on the table shook as the fat man laughed. "That's fair enough. And I think you're a pompous ass but a decent bloke at heart. We'll shake on that?"

They shook hands then and before they left O'Grady's, Gus Cochrane passed on the information he had blackmailed out of Gareth Owens. Including Richard Gordon's whereabouts.

Kate slipped over the lock on the toilet door, pulled down the seat and sat. She needed to escape the pitying glances and curious stares of her workmates. Of course the whole office must think it peculiar that Fred was going to a nursing home in Killarney to recover. What would they say if they knew where he was going as soon as he was strong enough? What they did not realise, Kate thought angrily, was that 'looking after' was not nearly enough for Fred. He needed to open old wounds, pick at festering sores. To face his father's demons as well as his own. He needed to 'find himself'. And to his way of self-pitying thinking 'finding himself' involved losing his wife. For fuck's sake! There was a tap on the door.

"Are you all right, Kate?" Eileen called.

"Fine, thank you."

Kate stood up and flushed the loo for effect. Jesus! Eileen meant well but she would not allow her a minute's peace. Looking at her watch, she saw that it was 2.30 in the afternoon. Fred had been due to be discharged at two o'clock. She could have got the time off. Martin would have given it to her. She had chosen not to be there, not to see Fred being discharged into someone else's care. He had made his choice. She had gone back to see him the night before. For hours she had pleaded and begged for him to allow her help in his recovery. She told him Martin Burke knew about the syndicate and was hopeful of sorting something out. She had tried to explain that he was blaming his father for heavy drinking that was totally his own responsibility, blaming business colleagues for decisions that were of his own making, blaming his wife for the cold state of their marriage – and distancing himself from her wasn't going to cure it.

When Kate opened the door, Eileen was standing there waiting for her. She attempted a smile as she went to the sink to wash her hands.

"Sure you're OK?"

"Great, thanks," said Kate abruptly. "Just busy."

As she walked out of the bathroom she caught a glimpse of the hurt on Eileen's face. Shit! She had not meant to be snappy but how in the hell could she be all pleasant when

Fred was fucking off to psychoanalyse himself, leaving her with his goddamn debts? Sitting at her desk, she continued typing the letter that was taking her an inordinate amount of time to get through.

Martin came striding in and gestured to her to follow him through to his office. He threw his brief-case on the desk.

"I had lunch with Gus Cochrane."

"And you survived. Congratulations."

"Don't be sarcastic, Kate. I know he's a wheeler-dealer. But he's also a sort of Robin Hood."

"Why should he rob the rich to pay the poor? He's one of the rich."

"OK, OK. But just believe me, he's not all bad. He told me where Richard Gordon is. At least where he will be for the next two days. He's moving about quite a bit."

"Did he say how Cora is?"

"No. Why should he?"

Kate just shrugged. Even now, even since she discovered that Richard had been one of the people involved in facilitating the re-mortgaging of the home she and Fred shared, she felt she could not break the secret he had entrusted to her. Anyway, it was Cora's secret not Richard's. If Cora did not want anybody to know she was terminally ill, so be it.

But Martin was not going to let it go.

"Cora must be in good form to be tearing around the world like she is. Anyway, her children didn't say there was anything wrong with her when I spoke to them."

"I didn't say there was either. From what I recall,

Richard's family said nothing at all. They were very reticent. As if they'd been told stay quiet."

That was true. They had inherited their father's gift of building polite word-shelters around information they wished to hide. It had been impossible to gauge from Richard's son and daughter whether they knew about their mother's illness or their father's whereabouts. Maybe not. They certainly did not seem to care.

"That's beside the point now," Martin said. "What we do know is that Richard Gordon will be arriving in Budapest in the morning. He has been contacted about releasing Brian Molloy and Fred from their commitment to the syndicate."

"My God! Have you been talking to him?"

Martin shook his head. "No. Gareth Owens has. It's a long story. I'll fill you in later. Get on the Internet now, Kate, and book us a flight to Budapest and accommodation in the Vari Hotel. We'll have a little surprise for Richard Gordon when he arrives to collect his pay-off."

"*We* will?"

"Yes. I'll need someone to witness documents. Anyway you'll want to see his face when he discovers the present we have for him. You will be able to come, won't you? You did say that Fred's going to a nursing home?"

Kate nodded and wondered if she should tell Martin that Fred would be going to a rehabilitation institute when he was strong enough to leave the nursing home. Then she shrugged her shoulders. What did it matter to Martin Burke where Fred was going? That was her business, her problem, her heartbreak. She smiled at Martin.

"Yes. Of course I'll go with you. Fred will be in good hands. Besides, you're right. I really need to see the look of shock on Richard Gordon's face."

Martin stood up and went to the wall safe. He punched in the number combination and when the lock opened, he took out the tape which had been broken, repaired, broken again and finally patched together in the States.

Kate nodded, understanding now.

Before she logged onto the Internet, Kate rang Fred. His phone was switched off. She closed her eyes for a second and prayed that her husband would find healing for the wounds which were deeper, and more life-threatening, than his stab injuries.

Chapter 32

Budapest's Ferihegy International Airport was bright, clean, modern and sparkling in the morning sunlight. Kate stood guard over the luggage as Martin organised a taxi to their hotel. There was not much to take care of. Two small suitcases and their overnight bags. Martin appeared, a taxi driver in tow. Five minutes later they were driving through an industrialised section of Budapest, on their way to the Vari Hotel. Kate looked out on pipelines and factories.

"This is not what I was expecting," she remarked. "I had the idea that Budapest was old and beautiful."

"It is," Martin replied. "You'll see."

He was right. Soon they left the grim tower blocks and the paraphernalia of industry behind and the beautiful old city of Kate's expectations came into view. Wide streets were bordered by magnificent buildings, the history of the cultured Hungarian nation written in the different architectural styles. The ambience was cosmopolitan and at the same time uniquely Hungarian. Passing St Stephen's

Basilica, Kate craned her neck to view the neo-classical building.

"You get one of the best views of the city from that dome," Martin told her. "We might try to fit it in before we leave."

Kate looked askance at the man sitting beside her. How could he casually chat about sightseeing when they were here to confront the person who had played games with all their lives? Martin was an enigma. So was Richard Gordon. And the biggest enigma of them all was her husband. She banished the thought of Fred. She could not cope with all that hurt and rejection now.

The marbled lobby of the Vari was luxurious. Kate booked them in and was given the swipe cards for their rooms. The concierge spoke very good English. When Kate explained to him that she thought friends of hers were visiting, he confirmed that Mr and Mrs Richard Gordon were indeed guests of the hotel and asked if she wanted to leave a message for them.

"No, thank you. I'd like to surprise them. What room number are they?"

"I'm sorry. I cannot give you that information but I can tell you they've gone out. They booked tickets for The Gellért Baths at the desk here this morning."

She was just about to thank the concierge when Martin grabbed her arm.

"Quick. We'll just dump our bags and head out," he said.

The concierge frowned. That was not how things were done in his hotel.

They had to wait while a receptionist accompanied

them to the lifts and a porter collected their bags. The girl opened the door of first one room and then the other with a flourish. Martin hopped impatiently from one foot to the other as she intoned the list of facilities. When she eventually left, Martin whipped off his shirt.

Kate was stunned and took a step back. What in the fuck did he think he was doing?

"I must put on a fresh shirt, Kate. I feel all clammy after the journey. We can leave both cases in this room and decide later which room we each want. Are you ready to go? Do you need to change?"

She laughed in relief. Martin looked at her and then laughed too.

"God! I didn't think, Kate. Sorry. You must have thought I was going to attack you!"

She had embarrassed both of them now. Martin self-consciously turned his back to her and began to search his suitcase for a shirt. His tan was all over. At least it went as far as his waistline anyway. His shoulders were even broader than they appeared when he was dressed. Kate started. Jesus! She was ogling him! She dragged her eyes quickly away from his well-muscled torso.

"I'll just hop into the other room and throw on a light sweater. I'll meet you in the corridor."

Grabbing her suitcase and bag she almost ran from his room. Safely inside the room she was now calling her own, she gave herself a stern talking-to. She was here to try to save Patty's home from being sold, her husband's house from repossession, and her marriage from disaster. No matter what happened she would never again look at

Martin Burke in that way, never again allow herself to think about the maybes and what-ifs.

Kate did not have time to absorb any of the sights of Budapest as she struggled to keep up with Martin's long stride. They were on their way to catch the Number 47 tram, which would drop them outside the famous Gellért Baths. He got tired of looking behind to see if she was keeping up so he grabbed her hand and hauled her along at his pace. They arrived at the stop just as the tram pulled up. Martin bought their tickets from the dispenser and they hopped on board.

"You seem to know your way around pretty well, Martin. You've obviously been here before."

"Honeymoon," he said and turned his head away to look out the window. His one-word reply told Kate a lot about how much his visit to Budapest with Lee had meant to him and how the memory of it still hurt.

Catching her first glimpse of the Danube and the wooded Buda hills, she forgot his sadness and almost forgot her own. The symmetry and beauty of the sweep of land toward the majestic river, the bridges straddling the water, elegantly connecting Buda to Pest, the Royal Palace and Citadel keeping their stony watch over the city, filled her with the sense of harmony and peace she had only ever experienced before on her beloved Kerry hills.

Martin tugged at her arm. "Get ready to jump. The next stop is ours."

At the stop directly in front of the Gellért Hotel, they joined the throng leaving the tram. Kate tried to remember the details from the guidebook she had read on the plane. The Gellért Baths were amongst the most famous in a city renowned for the curative powers of its thermal mineral-water springs. It must be one of the classiest. Richard Gordon would never dip a toe in anything less than the best. Bastard!

"We cross here," Martin said, catching her hand to lead her across the pedestrian sector.

She had just put a foot on the crossing when she stopped still. She squinted her eyes to see better. Yes. She was right. It was them.

Martin tugged impatiently. "C'mon, Kate! Don't hang about! We must catch up with them as soon as possible. The element of surprise is –"

"They're over there! Look! Heading towards the bridge."

Martin followed her gaze and saw Richard and Cora, walking towards the Liberty Bridge. They both looked tanned, fit and relaxed. Martin immediately headed off in that direction, hauling Kate along in his wake. She looked back regretfully at the Gellért. Her tired body was aching for the healing waters.

Whichever illness Cora Gordon was suffering from, it did not seem to be affecting her fitness level. The Gordons were striding ahead, arms swinging, covering ground at an amazing pace. Martin and Kate were puffing by now. They were both thirty years younger than the Gordons but were thirty times less fit.

"Just keep your eyes peeled," Martin gasped.

Kate nodded, saving what breath she had left for staying upright and, hopefully, maintaining her forward motion without falling on her face. The wide pavements were crowded with pedestrians. It would be easy to lose sight of the two senior citizens who were running them into the ground. Sweat began to trickle down Kate's face and dribble into her eyes. She was seeing Cora's pink and white top now through a watery haze.

Suddenly Martin stopped walking and swore. "Fuck! They're splitting up. He's getting into a car. Kate, you stay with her. Get her back to the Vari. Keep your phone switched on. Take care."

He stooped and kissed her on the cheek. Then he was gone, frantically flagging down a taxi and jumping in. Kate watched him disappear into the stream of traffic. Jesus! She was all alone in a strange city, gasping for breath, hunting down a woman who was supposedly dying, worrying about the welfare of a man who was not her husband. Blinking her eyes to clear them, she allowed herself one brief plea to her mother. Her lips shaped the words, "Help me, Mam!". When she opened her eyes again she felt she had more strength, more breath and clearer vision. Kitty had never let her down.

Cora was standing at a tram stop, just another tourist in this city which attracted visitors in their thousands. Kate approached her from behind and tapped her gently on the shoulder. The older woman registered shock and then recognition. Finally a welcoming smile lit her face.

"Kate Lucas! What a surprise! I can't believe this. What're you doing here? On holiday, are you? Where's Fred?"

Kate was startled for a moment. Fred seemed another world, another lifetime away. "No, no, my visit is . . . work-related. Fred's not very well at the moment, Cora. He was mugged. Stabbed and left for dead."

Cora's hand flew to her mouth and genuine sympathy shone in her eyes. "My God! I'm so sorry, Kate. That's awful. Is he in hospital?"

"He's in a nursing home. It's a long story, Cora. Will we go for a coffee and chat?"

"Actually, I'm just on my way to The West End Shopping Centre. Have you been there?"

Kate shook her head. "I've just arrived. I haven't been anywhere really. I'll tag along with you."

Kate took out her purse and began to peel off one of the unfamiliar forint notes.

Cora pushed a ticket into her hand. "Here. Use Richard's travel pass. He's just gone to see to some business."

Before Kate could ask any questions about Richard's business, the tram arrived. They got on and sat together. To casual observers they just seemed like tourists, maybe mother and daughter, looking forward to a shopping spree in one of Europe's biggest retail outlets. It would have taken a much closer study to notice the tension in their raised shoulders, the slight frowns on both their faces, the wariness with which they eyed each other. Still maintaining a united front, they went into the shopping mall and stood to admire the cascading waterfall feature before finding a café. It was not until they sat facing each other over their cappuccinos, that guards were dropped and real conversation began where obligatory politeness left off.

Martin's taxi driver seemed to be enjoying this job, getting into the spirit of the chase. He had kept pace with Richard's car all the way from the Liberty Bridge. The streets were getting narrower, the buildings taller, the endemic graffiti less artistic and more threatening. Martin tried to read street signs but they blurred as he sped past. The car ahead slowed down, then took a right turn at the next intersection. The right-hand side of the street was bordered by buildings, some of which appeared to be commercial and some residential, but all of them in disrepair. The left-hand side, the whole length of it, was a building site. Above the hoarding running parallel to the pavement, Martin saw scaffolding rise into the air. This was a huge development, and from what he could see of the upper sections of the buildings, almost near completion.

"What's going on here?" he asked the taxi driver.

The man shrugged.

The car ahead stopped suddenly. Richard got out.

Martin quickly paid his driver and jumped onto the pavement.

"I wait for you?" the driver called.

Martin told the man to go. The least Richard Burke owed him was a lift back to the Vari Hotel.

Richard walked in through a gap in the hoarding. Martin ran. He caught up with the older man just as he was about to enter a Portakabin, which was presumably the headquarters of this operation.

Richard stood and looked at Martin. There was no surprise, no fear, no shame evident in his steady gaze.

"Welcome to the International Leaf Development, Martin. I expected some such confrontation since I got a garbled phone message from Gareth Owens. But how in the hell did you put it all together? Your reputation is well deserved."

"Yours is not," Martin said, just before he punched Richard Gordon on the point of his jaw.

Richard staggered back, rubbing his chin. Two men came rushing out of the Portakabin but Richard waved them away.

"For fuck's sake, Burke! I'd have expected better than thuggish behaviour from you!"

"That was for Patty Molloy! I'd love to give you one for each of her children too."

"Quite the hero, aren't you? Chasing halfway across the continent in defence of the little lady. Why?"

"It's not just Patty, is it? You dragged Fred Lucas into this too."

"I didn't force anybody to do anything against their will. Greed. Unadulterated greed motivated Brian Molloy and Fred Lucas. They were so anxious to grab money, big money, that they jumped in 'feet first' when I dangled the carrot. Or in Fred's case, when Nigel Greenway did the carrot-dangling for me. They didn't take much coaxing."

"Fuck it, man, you knew they couldn't afford it. And that they trusted you. Why did you hit on them, of all people? They were supposed to be your friends."

"Come on, Martin. I thought you had all the answers. I wanted to get out of the syndicate. I needed my pay-out. But each of us had to make a final investment of one million to finish this project. The syndicate boss insisted I find a new investor to take my place or else no divvies for me. I found not one but two replacements. What would you have done? Sacrificed your pay-out?"

"I wouldn't have dragged friends into this mess. That's for sure."

Richard smiled and shrugged his shoulders. "'Twas the easiest answer to my problem. I knew both Brian Molloy and Fred Lucas dealt with Gareth Owens's bank. Gareth diverted their bank loans through our usual channels. A clean swop. Richard Gordon out, Lucas and Molloy in. They both got valuable shares in a property development, the syndicate got the million it needed and I get my profits."

"So, between them they paid a million into the syndicate. Money you would have had to come up with if you didn't find some suckers to do it for you."

"That's about the size of it. Brian and Fred met that obligation for me. Pity the way it worked out. Not my fault though. Brian should've been insured. But Fred Lucas stands to make a hefty profit when this place gets on its feet."

"Fred Lucas has lost his business and nearly lost his life."

For the first time Richard's face showed some emotion. "How's Kate?"

"You can ask her yourself. She's waiting for you back at your hotel. Keeping Cora company."

An instant of panic flashed across Richard's face. It passed quickly and he relaxed back into his casual demeanour. Then he suggested that Martin get the grand tour. An army of workers swarmed around the site.

Richard proudly led him through the complex, from the basement parking lot to the retail units on the ground floor, the rooms on the second floor and finally the apartments on the third floor. Work had already begun on interior decoration. Even without furnishings, the units had style. Top-grade fixtures and fittings everywhere, expert plastering and paintwork. Martin tried to estimate the investment here but could not even guess.

"I'm not surprised that you had to plough so much money into this," he remarked. "It's state-of-the-art, isn't it? Are all your developments this high class?"

Richard beamed proudly like a father whose child had been singled out for praise. "This is our first really big scheme. Our flagship. Right time, right place. We can consolidate everything here, legally and above board. As an offshore company we will only have to pay four per cent tax. That's on what we declare, of course."

Martin glared at the older man and noticed the red mark on his chin where the blow had landed. Ashamed, he looked away and turned his attention back to the building.

"The second floor? Are they office spaces?"

Richard laughed. "You could say that. They're the rooms where the girls will be bringing their clients. The upstairs apartments are for the big spenders. The people who want to spend a ransom on a girl for the night."

"This is all one big brothel? Jesus!"

"One big and classy entertainment centre, you mean. We'll cater to every fantasy here. Sex toys, videos and whatever else in the retail units. We've an area dedicated to massage, sauna, and treatments. Then our rooms, by the hour or by the night."

"And the girls?"

"Medically certified, adult and willing. And before you say anything else or even hit me again, the whole operation is legal. Or at least it will be by the time it opens."

Martin stood and looked around him at the busy scene. It was a slick and highly professional operation. Just as Gus Cochrane had described it. Which only deepened the mystery. Why did Richard Gordon need so badly to cut his ties, especially since this project was almost certain to be a money-spinner?

"You're here to collect your final pay-off, aren't you? I assume DYBRYN International Bank is situated for now in the Portakabin?"

"You're good, Martin. Yes. The syndicate is finally ready to pay me over my share of the accumulated profits. All that took some figuring out. How did you do it?"

"You think you're very clever, setting up this intricate plan but it's been done before and no doubt will be done again. I worked on a similar case in the States. And if I figured it out, someone else will too."

Richard smiled at him and shrugged. The grin was so smug that Martin had to clasp his hands behind his back in order not to punch the old man again.

"Doesn't matter. Nobody, not even a hotshot lawyer like you, could prove anything. I don't have to labour that point. You wouldn't be standing here now if you could have had us arrested on any charge. You'd be getting the law to do your dirty work for you. True?"

He was right, of course, but Martin would not give him the satisfaction of agreeing. He just stood there and waited for Richard to continue.

"Most of our scheme operates in the grey area, uses loopholes, flits in and out of legitimate investment. The network is so complicated at this stage, that sometimes we nearly lose track ourselves. And, of course, our little Nauruan shell bank is an insurance. It can operate anywhere but all its secrets are buried safely underneath the Nauruan non-disclosure policy. So fuck you and any other prick who thinks they can stick their noses into the business we've built. Now excuse me, I've business to attend to."

Martin stood in front of Richard and blocked his path.

"Not so quick, Richard. I think you should come back to the hotel with me now. I've something to show you. Something for you to listen to. It'll wipe the smug look off your face. Save me the trouble."

Richard glared at Martin. He was at last losing his calm, superior attitude. A nerve underneath his eye began to twitch as he moved to push Martin out of his way. "Look, Burke, shove off out of here. I've had Gareth Owens on the phone whingeing because that animal Cochrane is turning the screws on him. Now I've got you here shouting the odds at me. I am not, do you hear, *not*, paying off Molloy's or Lucas's debts. They were stupid, both of them. I'm not paying the price for their stupidity."

"Why did you involve them in the first place, Richard? That's what I can't understand. You could have sold your share for a hell of a lot more in the murky underground where you operate. What was your hurry?"

Richard's lips tightened and he just stood there, glaring at the younger man. Martin reached into his pocket and took out his phone. He punched in a number and kept watching Richard as he waited for a reply. When Kate answered he told her to talk to her ex-boss, to tell him about the tape. He handed the phone across to Richard. His face got paler as he listened to Kate. This time there was no argument. Martin and Richard left immediately for the hotel.

Both women were very subdued as they made their way back to the Vari, each thinking about the confidences they had exchanged over the past hour. Kate continuously glanced at her companion, each time wondering anew at her strength and equanimity. There was not a trace of self-pity in Cora, not one 'why me?'or 'not fair'. She just expressed gratitude for the life she had been privileged to live and pragmatically laid out her plans for the dignified end she planned to that life.

"Of course, the diagnosis was a shock," she had confided. "I felt so well. Still do. Just a few headaches. A couple of dizzy spells. Who could believe that this tumour is growing away, spreading its tentacles all over my brain and there's sweet damn all anyone can do to stop it? Two to three months I've left. Maybe, with a bit of luck, six."

Sitting in the West End Centre, the crowds milling around them, the splash of the water-features in their ears, they had spoken of death, of the sudden, violent ending of Brian Molloy's life, of Fred's fight to survive and of Cora's acceptance of her terminal diagnosis.

"I'm so lucky. I've been given the chance to do things I always wanted but never got around to. I was at Ayers Rock last week, Kate. And I'm going to Vienna, to Rome, to Nepal. And when I can no longer travel, I'm making my final journey to the clinic in Holland. I've already decided the place and, when it is necessary, I will decide the time."

Kate had caught her hand and held it. Words would have been inadequate. Which words could have expressed their feelings?

They had sat there, silently supporting each other, until Martin had rung. Then Kate watched the surprise and anger on Cora's face as the details of the tape were related to Richard.

"You'd better explain to me how and why you're blackmailing my husband!" Cora had said angrily.

Kate had told her the whole story of the much damaged and much-patched-together tape. Cora had listened with the same calmness as she dealt with her illness. When Kate finished speaking, they both rose, left the lights and energy of the retail outlet behind them and headed for the hotel. They were much more in control of themselves and their situation than the two agitated men who greeted them in the lobby of the Vari.

Because the tape and the necessary papers were in Martin's room, that is where the four of them gathered.

"Do you want to hear the tape?" Martin asked.

Richard shook his head. "Kate told me enough."

"And me," Cora said, turning to her husband. "The

point is, Richard, they cannot do anything with this tape. You know that better than I do. It's not admissible, impossible to authenticate. As evidence it's rubbish. Martin knows that very well too. But it could still damage you. You did, in effect, withhold evidence, protect and defend a man you knew to be guilty. There are also some nasty allegations of tax evasion."

Richard was standing there, head bowed, carefully listening to every word his wife spoke. Kate and Martin exchanged glances, aware that the Gordons were following a procedure familiar to them. Rules of engagement. And it appeared that Cora laid down the rules and Richard obeyed.

"I believe, Richard, that it's payback time. And not because of this ham-fisted attempt at blackmail. We could fight that if we wanted to. No, do as they ask but do it because you are an honourable man. "

Richard raised his hand and stroked his wife's cheek. There were tears in his eyes. "Are you sure, Cora? There's the clinic in Arizona. The laser surgery –"

"Stop, Richard. Enough! I don't want any more traipsing around from one experimental centre to the other. I'm happy with the arrangements I've made in Holland. You must face it. I am dying and no amount of money is going to change that."

Martin gasped and looked to Kate for confirmation. She nodded.

"My God!" he said. "I'm so sorry, Cora. I didn't know."

Cora rounded on Martin, and all the love for her husband and the anger at his detractors shone in her eyes.

"It may surprise you to find out there are a lot of things you don't know, Martin Burke. You've no right to judge my husband. When he sold his practice, his business interests and his house, it was for me. I've learned to accept my illness. He has not. Richard believed he could buy a cure. The best doctors, the best hospitals, the newest treatments. He did it for me."

Martin sat down on his bed and dropped his head onto his hands. Now he knew why Richard Gordon had needed so much money so quickly. He respected him for trying to help his dying wife but yet he could not condone the way he had gone about it. Cora's illness did not justify using Brian Molloy and Fred Lucas so cynically. Fuck! Richard Gordon had destroyed so many lives in his effort to save his wife's. Cora was right. It was payback time. He opened his brief-case and took out the documents he had prepared.

"I truly regret upsetting you, Cora, but, as you realise, some wrongs have been done and now is the time to right them." He held the papers out to Richard. "Read through these. When you sign, as you must, you are in effect buying back your share in International Leaf. You can make your own arrangements with them. Take a million less in profits. Whatever. I don't care how you handle that but I have to insist the investments made by Brian Molloy and Fred Lucas be returned. Their obligations to your syndicate end here and now."

"And the tape?"

"You may get it when the money is back in the Molloy and Lucas accounts and the deeds of their properties are freed of any lien to International Leaf. I haven't decided yet."

Richard stood in front of Martin, his face flushed with anger, no trace of the vulnerability of only a minute ago.

"No tape. No deal."

"What are you so afraid of? I thought you said the tape could not harm you? Are you still trying to protect Henry Hennessey?"

Cora handed Richard a pen. "Sign," she said in a low voice.

Richard flicked through the pages. Kate watched as his eyes skimmed over the document and she knew he was assimilating every detail. He was a superb speed-reader. He placed the papers on the bureau, signed and wordlessly handed the pen to Kate to witness his signature.

"When are you leaving here, Burke?"

"Tomorrow. Early afternoon."

"It will be arranged by the morning. Ring Gareth Owens for confirmation. Then I want that tape and any copies you have made."

Martin hesitated. The tape, tenuous evidence that it was, was all he had if he was to bring the syndicate to justice, if he was to try to overturn Hennessey's Not Guilty verdict.

Richard obviously read his mind. "Forget about any more investigations," he said. "You would only end up looking like a fool. Gareth Owens and I have everything covered as tight as a drum. You can leave Henry Hennessey to me. The courts cannot deliver justice to him now. I'm not proud of my part in that. I know how to use the tape to redress the balance. Will you trust me on that?"

Martin looked at Kate. At the sadness and despair in her eyes. The very same expression he saw every day in Patty Molloy's face. The sadness was theirs to bear and come to terms with but the despair could be dispelled. All it would take was a nod of the head in Richard Gordon's direction. Letting him off the hook, allowing the syndicate go scot-free. There was no reason to doubt what the older man had said. By now all trace of any illegal investment would have disappeared. That thought was easier to bear than seeing Henry Hennessey go unpunished. Could Richard Gordon right that wrong? Did he have any trace of morality left? Martin took a deep breath and looked up at the man he had had once admired and honoured.

"Deal," he said softly.

Like synchronised swimmers, Cora and Richard turned together and, in step, walked out of the room.

Kate tried to feel triumph. She searched deep in her psyche. The elation must be in there somewhere. She and Martin had managed to save The Rectory for Patty and the children, to remove the threat of re-possession from the Lucas home. But they had got no justice for Henry Hennessey's mistress. And they had upset a dying woman. Triumph and elation did not sit easy with failure and guilt.

Without even looking at Martin, Kate left his room and walked quickly to her own. She needed to be alone with her failure and guilt.

Kate heard the knock on her door through layers of sleep. Sitting up on the bed, she looked around at her unfamiliar surroundings. It took a few sleepy seconds to acclimatise. She was in Budapest. Cora Gordon had maybe only two months to live. Richard had signed the release document. The knock sounded again, louder this time. Swinging her legs onto the floor, she smoothed her hair and clothes before opening the door. Martin Burke was standing there, tickets in his hand.

"Come on, sleepy-head! We owe ourselves a little celebration. We're going to enjoy some music tonight."

"We are?"

"For sure. I've booked tickets for the Operetta ship. Music, dancing, food and the Danube at night. You'll love it."

Kate smiled at him. She had seen the beautiful long white river-buses moored along the banks of the Danube and had wondered what it would be like to board and stand on deck. A night sailing would be spectacular. Her smile faded as she thought of the contents of her suitcase. She had brought smart but workaday clothes – all well creased by now. Not good enough for the sophisticated-sounding Operetta ship.

She shook her head. "That sounds very glamorous, Martin, but I've nothing suitable to wear – I didn't bring –"

"No problem!" Stuffing the tickets into his pocket, Martin grabbed her hand. "We're going shopping. Now!"

Kate hesitated for an instant but then she got caught up in the excitement, in the need to do something that was not tragic or depressing. She ran back into the room and got her handbag, checking to be sure her credit card was in it. Then she followed Martin's long strides out of the hotel and along a series of narrow streets. In less than ten minutes they arrived on a wide boulevard, lined with shops representing every international store-name known to fashion. Kate took a deep breath and plunged into a shopping spree as intense and enjoyable as the one she'd had on her first pay packet. Martin relaxed in a café with a glass of wine as she flitted from shop to shop, fitting on, twirling in front of mirrors, matching accessories, even buying a set of silky, extravagantly priced underwear. Laden with bags, she arrived back at the café to meet Martin. Glancing at his watch, he drained the last of his wine and stood.

"Better get a move on. The show starts at eight."

After showering and slipping into her silky undies, Kate towel-dried her hair, applied make-up and put on her new dress. It was the pinky purple of heather. Her colour and her style. Simply cut and close-fitting. Fastening on the chunky beads and her new strappy high heels, she stood in front of the full-length mirror. The sleeveless V-necked dress fitted her like a second skin. For once Kate looked at her own image and liked what she saw. When Martin tapped on her door, she unwrapped the cream cashmere pashmina on which she had spent a disgraceful amount of money and draped it over her shoulders. He stood back when she opened the door and his eyes swept from her dark shiny hair to her spiky sandals.

"You look beautiful, Kate," he said, offering her his arm.

She linked him, and arm in arm they strolled to the nearby Vigado ter district where the Operetta ship, lights blazing and gangplank down, was waiting to welcome them aboard.

Magic, with all the connotations of illusion and distortion of reality that word evoked, was the only way Kate could describe her feelings as the Operetta ship cruised along the dark ribbon of the Danube. Their candlelit table was by a window and she watched in wonder as she drifted past the night-lights of Buda and Pest. The banks were close, yet they seemed an age apart. They belonged to the world of trade and commerce, the world where people triumphed or failed, where every day was a challenge, the world where you were judged and called to account. Here on the Operetta, Kate felt safe, cosseted in a timeless place of elegance and grace, her senses soothed by the beautiful sights and the soothing strains of violin music.

"Are you enjoying it, Kate?" Martin asked.

She just nodded. Her shining eyes were answer enough. Folk dancers came on stage whirling and stamping to stirring gypsy music, then some Lehár and Strauss, followed by a cabaret artist. The programme aroused and soothed, gently teasing the senses. Food was served below decks. A huge array of tasty meats and salads, breads and soups. Then more music, more entertainment, more twinkling lights and buildings on distant hills lit up like castles in the sky. As the show drew to a close, Kate got to her feet with the rest of the audience to clap and cheer the cast. Her blood was racing to the rhythm of the music. She did not want the show to end or the ship to dock. As she felt it bump against the quay wall, she turned to Martin and kissed him on the cheek.

"Thank you. That was just wonderful."

He put his hand on her shoulder. She felt the warmth of his skin through the thin fabric of her dress.

"You're welcome, Kate," he said. "Such a pity this night has to end."

They held hands as they left the ship, as they retraced their path to the hotel, as they rode the lift to their rooms. They were still holding hands when Martin inserted the swipe card and pushed open the door to his room.

Kate walked in ahead of him, violin music still echoing in her head, gypsy music coursing through her veins. Feeling, reckless and free, she twirled around the room to the rhythm of her music. And then, just as they had known would happen, she danced into his arms.

Their lips met. It was not the gentle touch of their kiss in the Kerry hills. It was a passionate meeting of lips, of tongues, of hot writhing bodies, of lonely souls. He kissed her neck, her shoulders, her back, as he slowly undressed her. Then gently picking her up he laid her on the bed. She opened his shirt buttons as he lay beside her. The smell of Martin, that clean sweet smell, assailed her senses. She buried her face in his broad chest, kissing, licking, touching. He took her nipple in his mouth and licked and sucked until her body arched in a spasm of desire. He stood up then and removed his clothes. When he lay beside her again, they were no longer two lonely people in a strange town. They were a song, an aria, a magnificent opus, rising and falling, soft and raucous, moving to the rhythm of the music in their souls. It was their magic night.

Chapter 33

Kate had travelled the road to Killarney so often in the past three months that her concentration lapsed. She almost drove through a red light. Jamming on the brakes at the last minute, she sat glaring ahead of her. She was very angry. Angry at Fred, at fate, at herself. The lights changed and she tried to concentrate on the traffic as she drove towards the outskirts of Killarney. Towards Fred's homeplace. Towards Fred.

Fred's mother must have been keeping watch. She opened the front door as soon as Kate drove through the gates.

Beth Lucas stood on the doorstep, a welcoming smile on her face. Kate got out of the car and walked towards her. Daughter-in-law and mother-in-law embraced warmly.

"How is he?" Kate asked.

Beth shook her head and Kate saw all the despair of a mother helplessly watching her child's suffering reflected in the older woman's eyes.

"'Tis hard on him, Kate. He's struggling."

Beth led the way through the hall into the kitchen. The house that had once seemed so grand to Kate now looked a little worn and shabby. The walls needed painting and the carpets were bare in patches.

"It's too big for me to manage now," Beth said.

Kate blushed in shame. Her opinion on the condition of the house must have shown on her face. She had not meant to hurt Beth's feelings. She had never meant to hurt anybody's feelings.

"I'm going to sell it and buy a smaller place." Beth added. "As soon as . . . as soon as Fred's on his feet again."

Kate did not answer. Her eyes were riveted on the frail figure in the back garden. She walked closer to the window and watched as Fred dug a trench. Like a robot he bent, dug, emptied the loaded shovel and started all over again. His T-shirt hung loosely on his body and Kate could see the sharp angles of his shoulder blades through the thin fabric. He was a shadow of the big man he had been.

"He's setting some vegetables for me," Beth explained as she tapped on the window to attract his attention.

Fred looked up and immediately saw Kate inside the window. He smiled and for an instant the old Fred was back. The laughing, good-humoured man with the grey-green eyes.

Kate sat down at the table and gladly accepted Beth's offer of a cup of coffee. She heard the yard tap running as Fred washed off his boots and hands. When the back door opened, she did not know what to do. How does one greet an estranged husband? What is the protocol? A peck on the cheek, a handshake, a slap across the face? Her questions were answered when Fred came to her and hugged her. She hugged him back, feeling all the impact of her loneliness and lost dreams in the bony embrace.

"I've a bit of shopping to do," Beth said. "I'll leave you two for a little while."

Neither Kate nor Fred noticed that Beth had left. They sat at opposite sides of the table, each reading the past in the other's eyes and trying to see the future through the shadows of hurt.

"How are you feeling?" Kate asked at last.

"I'm not drinking, if that's what you mean. Not today. Not ever again, I hope."

"Good," Kate muttered and then sat in silence. The man in front of her was Fred and yet he was a stranger. He was at once the man who had made her laugh, made love to her, had given her life focus but at the same time he was the man who had re-mortgaged their home without telling her, had lusted after Adele Sheehan and had finally rejected Kate when she had wanted to help him recover.

"And you, Kate. How are you ?"

She took a while to answer. She was not sure. She was lonely. Hurt. Lost. Scared. "I don't know. I don't know where we're going. If anywhere. I can't get on with my life, look to the future. It's decision time, Fred. We can't go on like this. It's three months now since you left hospital. You've been through rehab. Are you going to come back home? Back to me? The house is sorted out now, thanks to Martin. You can get a job. We could start over. "

He bowed his head and Kate felt an overwhelming

urge to touch his hair, to wind her fingers through the curls. He looked up suddenly and her breath caught in her chest when she saw the tears in his eyes.

"I can't go back. The city almost destroyed me. It destroyed us. It's not who we are, Kate. It's not where I want to be."

"What're you saying? You don't want the city or is it that you don't want me?"

He stood up and walked around to her side of the table. Stooping down, he caught both her hands in his and held them tightly. "I love you, Katie. I always will. I want, more than anything in the world for us to be together for the rest of our lives. But there's something I have to tell you. Something that makes me ashamed. You'll probably hate me when you know."

Kate looked into his face and prepared for him to confess his obsession with Adele Sheehan. Maybe he had slept with her, just as she had slept with Martin Burke. Should she confess too? Was this the time for honesty? It was. But she was not prepared for the cruel honesty of Fred's next statement.

"I have a low sperm count. It's unlikely that we can have children. Not naturally anyway."

Kate withdrew her hands from his and stared at him in shock. "How d'you know? When did you find out?"

"I went to a doctor when you first started talking about having a family. Not Dr Shorten, your bothered old GP. I visited a young man. I wanted a family as much as you, whatever you believe. I thought that having this test would convince you of that. The results devastated me. I just couldn't tell you. I couldn't bear the thought of losing you."

"You let me go on believing that I'd get pregnant if only my problem could be sorted and all the while the problem was yours? How could you?"

He just shook his head in reply. He could find no words to excuse the deceit. Seeing the anger flash in Kate's eyes now, Fred knew that he had lost her.

"Did it ever dawn on you that we could have coped with it together?" she shouted at him in fury. "How low is the count? How many tests did you have?"

"Once was enough to go through that humiliating experience."

"Didn't the doctor tell you to have another test? It could change, you know. Why didn't you do that? Did you think I would turn my back on you just because of a test result? You don't know me at all, do you?"

Yes, he did. He knew his beloved Katie O'Hanlon very well. She was born to be a mother, to carry and nurture children, to guide and love them. And he loved her too much to deny her that. He stood up and took a step back from her.

"I'm so sorry, Katie. I've let you down very badly. I've lied and cheated and made you very unhappy. I hope you'll find the person you deserve."

Kate stood up. She did not want to hear any more. She looked away from him, afraid that the sight of his beautiful eyes and curly hair would have her begging him to stay with her, throwing herself at his feet.

"What do you want to do about the house?" she asked and was surprised at the coolness of her voice.

"Whatever you want. You decide."

She walked to the kitchen door, opened it and then turned to take one last look at him. An image to take with her, to console her in the emptiness that lay ahead.

Chapter 34

Jonathan was beginning to sit up and take notice. At five months old he was showing all the signs of becoming another beefy, rugby-playing Molloy. Kate followed his gaze to the stained-glass window. A ray of sunshine was piercing through an intricate panel, throwing a cascade of colour onto the chapel floor.

Kate held him more closely in her arms, remembering Jonathan Alan's christening in this very place, remembering his father's funeral. She looked around her at the congregation. At Patty, surrounded by her brood which now seemed to include Bobby Burke. At Martin, tall and handsome, more at ease, less driven than he had been. Both Cochranes were here, newly included in all the social events. Henry Hennessey sat in the front row, appropriately dressed in his funeral suit and mourning expression. He was not accompanied by his wife. She did not appear in public with him any more. Adele Sheehan sat side by side with Nigel Greenway, her gold navel-ring glinting in the sun. Success had not brought her any class.

A murmur went through the congregation as the priest announced that the deceased's husband would like to say a few words. A stooped and white-faced old man made his way slowly to the lectern. Richard Gordon was a dilapidated parody of the vigorous man he had been. It was as if his spirit had gone with Cora, and the shell left behind was cold and empty. He took some notes from his pocket and laid them on the book rest. Then he just stood there. The man whose genius with words had earned him many triumphs and a peerless reputation, seemed bereft of any utterance.

People began to shift uncomfortably in their seats. His son and daughter exchanged glances, as if unsure whether to lead their silent father off the altar or not. Kate focused her eyes on the dappled pool of light on the floor. She could not bear the raw pain on Richard's face.

Someone coughed. The throaty sound seemed to drag Richard back from his silent communion with his grief. His voice was low, an echo of his strong and confident delivery.

"I would like to thank you all for coming here to my wife's Memorial Service. I could, and maybe should, talk about the kind of woman Cora was, about her kindness, her understanding, her intelligence, her humour. But you all knew those qualities. What you may not have known about was her strength. I was privileged to be with her as she bore her illness and when she departed this life. I stand here in awe of her dignity and courage. Her passing has left an empty space in my life, in our family and in her wide circle of friends. It was her wish that she be cremated in Holland where she died and that her life would be celebrated here in Ireland, where she lived. Cora wanted you all to remember her today, but not with sadness. You are invited to the home Cora and I shared to raise a glass to one of the greatest people I have ever known."

He dropped his head and stood there, a lost and lonely old man. Somebody clapped and then a ripple of applause went through the chapel. He picked up his unused notes and began to leave the altar. Remembering something, he went back to the microphone.

"Forgive me. I forgot to thank Martin Burke for generously allowing us to have the celebration in the house that was home to Cora and me for so long. As you may know, Martin bought our property. I wish him many years of happiness there."

The organist began to play as Richard went back to take his place beside his son and daughter. Jonathan stirred restlessly in Kate's arms. She stood up and walked out onto the aisle. Both she and her godson needed some light and air. She squinted as she walked out of the gloom of the church into the sunlight. Someone tapped her on the shoulder. She jumped and Jonathan did too.

"I'm sorry. I didn't mean to frighten you."

Kate stared at Fred. It had been a whole month since she had last seen him in Killarney. He looked stronger now, his eyes and skin clearer. He seemed older, as if at last outgrowing his boyishness. Questions pounded around in her head, clamouring for answers. Why was he here? Did he want to apply for divorce? Did he know she had slept with her boss? She cradled the child close to her as if his innocence could hide her guilt.

"I've just come to sympathise with Richard," Fred explained. "I'll be leaving as soon as I've seen him."

She nodded, still unable to talk, still afraid the chaos in her head would escape in a torrent of words. People began to stream out the door, murmurs turning to chatter as the congregation was released from the solemnity of the service. Fred leaned towards Kate and kissed her on the cheek. She closed her eyes and savoured the touch of his lips.

"We must talk, Katie," he whispered.

When she opened her eyes, he was staring intently at her. She shifted Jonathan's weight on her hip and then lowered her eyes in discomfort as Fred continued to examine her face. It was as if he was trying to memorise every feature.

"Are you still with your mother?" she asked.

"For the time being. I start work again next week. Did Gus Cochrane tell you he's opening a new waste-management branch in Killarney? I'm going to manage the plant for him."

Kate held her breath as she waited for him to tell her that he was better, that the past few months had just been a feverish dream, that Kate and Fred were waking to a new day, a new life.

"I'll ring you," he announced.

Kate's grip on Jonathan tightened. She needed the comforting warmth of the tiny little body to counteract the coldness of Fred's announcement. So! He would ring, would he? Only the fact that they were standing in a churchyard prevented her from screaming at the man standing in front of her. This stranger who used to be her husband. The man with whom she had wanted to have a baby. He turned his back on her and her hurt and walked away.

Patty and her football team came to join her.

"We'd better get going, Kate. This lot have been suspiciously well behaved. I'd better remove them before they return to normal. By the way, is that Fred I see over there?"

Fred was talking to Richard, his hand on the older man's shoulder. Then he turned and walked towards the gate. Kate watched until her husband disappeared from view. She turned to Patty.

"It was," she said.

Patty opened her mouth as if to say something and then changed her mind. Instead she gave Kate a quick hug. Good choice.

The party in what used to be the Gordons' home was surreal. Inhibitions loosened by alcohol, people laughed and cried more easily. Every conversation, maudlin or merry, was about Cora, about her life, about her death. The Molloy children ran around in the huge garden, very much at ease in Martin and Bobby's new home. Patty's prediction had been right. The boys had returned to normal. One of them had managed to find the garden hose and turn on the tap. Luckily Martin stepped in before they had the chance to do too much water damage.

Kate was sitting on the patio, Jonathan sleeping peacefully in her arms, a glass of wine on the table. Sheila Cochrane sat down beside her and kicked off her high heels.

"This is a beautiful house, isn't it?"

Kate agreed. It was. Although she remembered now that she had always felt slightly uneasy visiting here when it had been Cora and Richard's home. Maybe it was that Richard had, at times, been an intimidating boss, impatient and even arrogant. But he had been different when at home. In this house, Cora had softened the edges of his harshness. She had seemed to bring out the best in the man she had lived with and in whose arms she had eventually died.

"What does any of it matter now?" Sheila asked.

Kate knew what she meant. Cora had been a wonderful wife and mother, a trusty friend and a very charitable woman. She had also been an inveterate snob with very definite ideas about who was 'suitable' and who was not. The Cochranes had never made it onto Cora's 'suitable' list. And never would have, had she lived another fifty years. But as Sheila so wisely said, none of it mattered now.

"Listen to that!" Sheila laughed, digging Kate in the ribs. "Gus Cochrane will be in trouble again!"

Kate looked to where Sheila was pointing. Martin and Patty were stooping down beside Bobby who was clutching a rugby ball into his chest. The pout on his face made Kate smile. It reminded her of Fred.

"It's Bobby's ball! Mine! Fuck off!"

Sheila put her hand up to her mouth and tittered. "Gus

loves those kids. As you can hear from Bobby's vocabulary, my husband's spending a lot of time with them."

Martin had his face close to his son's. A battle of wills was in progress.

"You must not use that bad word, Bobby. Your tongue will go all black."

"But Uncle Gus's tongue is not black and he says fuck, fuck, fuck!"

Patty and Martin stood up and turned their backs to the child. They looked at each other and laughed. Bobby took the opportunity to run away and join the other children. Martin and Patty did not notice. Nor did they notice that Kate and Sheila were watching them. Sheila slowly moved her hand across to Kate's arm, as if afraid that any sudden or unexpected move would spoil the moment.

"Well, well! I didn't see that one coming, did you? But now that I see how much they mean to each other, it just seems right, doesn't it?"

Martin and Patty were still staring into each other's eyes. Obviously they had not seen it coming either. Kate smiled and nodded her head. How perfect! She could almost believe that Cora had a hand in opening Martin's eyes and Patty's heart.

It would be a long time yet. A long time before Patty would feel right about saying a final goodbye to Brian. A long time before Martin would be able to let go his bitter regrets about Lee. But that was a road they would travel together. Ironic too, that Patty should discover her new love here in Gordon's garden, the very place where she had said her last goodbye to her old one. Maybe Brian and Cora had teamed up.

"Yes. It's obviously meant to be," Kate said to Sheila and both women smiled.

They had not noticed Bobby coming up to join them. He pulled on Kate's sleeve.

"Can Bobby hold the fucking baby, Auntie Kate?"

Sheila and Kate laughed until tears ran down their faces. Not all the tears were from laughter.

Kate's arms felt empty and cold when Patty took Jonathan home. Bobby went to bed as soon as the boys were gone, worn out from practising his new curses. Kate felt restless and uneasy. People were getting a bit drunk. Gus Cochrane was trying to organise a singsong and Sheila was trying to take him home. Cora's farewell party was beginning to fray around the edges. Kate decided to say goodbye to Richard and go home. There was no sign of him in the garden or the lounge. She knocked on the door of the study, knowing that she would find him in the peace and solitude of what had been his favourite room. Except that, when she opened the door, the atmosphere was anything but peaceful. Richard was sitting in his leather armchair, the one Cora had had specially made for him. Henry Hennessey was standing over him, his face flushed. Kate hesitated, not knowing whether Richard needed rescuing or privacy. He waved her in.

"Henry and I are just discussing the wonders of technology, Kate. Isn't it miraculous the way special moments can live forever?"

The politician took a step forward and Kate thought he was going to injure Richard.

"It's only out of respect for your wife that I'm not knocking your brains out, you vicious old man!"

Richard looked up at Henry Hennessey and his eyes held all his trademark disdain and contempt. "You blustering fool, Hennessey, sit down and listen! Cora supported and encouraged me in everything I did. She was my partner, in every sense. Except one. She never agreed that I should defend you. I regret to say that I went against her wishes. I wanted to go out in a blaze of glory. You were to be my last big case and I was determined to win. So determined that discovering your guilt was only a minor annoyance."

Henry Hennessey swivelled his head in Kate's direction, panic on every feature. Richard laughed. "Don't worry about Kate. She made the tape. She's already put it to good use, haven't you?"

Kate just nodded her head, not really sure what was going on here.

"So I promised Cora that I would try to right the wrong. It's too late now to give justice to the girl you murdered. And yes, Kate, her baby too. But I swear, Hennessey, you will never, ever, stand for public office again. I'll see to that."

Henry Hennessey straightened himself up. Kate watched in fascination as an array of emotions from anger, to fear and finally defiance crossed his face. He walked towards the door and then turned back to face them both.

"You're bluffing, Gordon. You'd have to compromise yourself and your professional standing. All the shit about your little tax-evasion scheme would come out too. You're too proud, too self-obsessed to allow that to happen. You think you're a god. You're nothing more than a crooked lawyer. I'm not afraid of you or your tape."

"I have two big advantages over you, Henry. The first is that our syndicate has more brains in their little fingers than you have in your entire idiotic body. Did you think we were going to leave ourselves in any way exposed? There's not a shred of evidence to prove that we ever did anything other than invest legitimately in property development abroad. Even Martin Burke and his team of sleuths admit that. Isn't that true, Kate?"

Kate nodded agreement. It was partly true anyway, if you could call Hans Meyers a team of sleuths. He had used all his expertise and experience to investigate the syndicate. Not even he could provide any evidence that would stand up to official investigation let alone prosecution.

"Fuck you, Richard!" Henry shouted. "I know! Too many people know!"

"You thick-head, Hennessey! Knowing is not enough. Proof, man! Proof is what is needed and there's none against the syndicate. Thanks to Gareth Owens and me, every single operation we are involved in can be legitimised on paper from funding to completion. We're really grateful to you for your help. We got great benefit from some of the financial legislation you negotiated."

Henry Hennessey bared his teeth and snarled. Kate was shocked as she looked at his handsome face distorted with rage. Out of control. This must have been how his girlfriend had seen him before he squeezed the life out of her. She took a step back, wondering if she should call for help. Richard seemed calm, in charge. He spoke quietly to the feral creature now drooling saliva from his open mouth.

"Here's the deal, Hennessey. I give a snippet of this tape to your leader. The part where you so graphically talk about your mistress. Want me to remind you? 'I had to shut the bitch up. She was going to go to my wife, to the papers. She would have ruined me. I had to do it.' How do you think your revered leader will react to that? Do you think for one minute that he will stop to ask for authentication? That he will give you the benefit of the doubt? All he'll see is the party's percentage dropping in the polls. He'll hang you out to dry to save his own ass. He'll know, even if you don't, that my next move is to release it to the press."

The politician moved slowly across the room, flopping onto a chair as if his legs had given way underneath him. The man who had strangled a girl without compunction was now devastated by the thought of his leader's anger. He sat like an outclassed boxer in his corner between rounds, head bowed, hands hanging between his knees.

"The deal is?" he asked softly.

"You hand in your resignation and I'll put the tape in storage. Gareth Owens will keep it safely in the bank vault. You've twenty-four hours to decide."

"And you lot get away scot-free? I want that tape. You're not playing fair, Richard. If I lose everything I've worked for while you and your cronies never get your just desserts, the least I deserve is to be allowed to destroy that fucking tape!"

"Stop whingeing, you pathetic piece of shit! We just did a bit of creative accounting. You took a life. Two lives. Being allowed to fade quietly into anonymity is more than you deserve. And you may as well know now that the syndicate has sold out to a Russian conglomerate. Lock, stock and brothels. We're no longer associated with it and no evidence exists that we ever did."

Henry raised his head and looked from Richard to Kate. He seemed to accept defeat, to even be glad that he could control the manner of his resignation. Kate knew that he would spin a good story, one that garnered public sympathy. He might even say he wanted to spend more time with his wife and family.

"You said you had two advantages over me," he said to Richard "One is that you have sanitised your corrupt syndicate. What's the other?"

Richard leaned back in his chair and closed his eyes. "I have nothing to lose any more. Cora was my reason for existing, for plotting and planning, for getting up in the morning and looking forward to the day. Unlike you, I don't care what happens to me now. A priceless weapon against an egocentric prick like you."

Henry Hennessy brushed against Kate on his way out the door. She shivered. She went and sat beside Richard. He seemed to shrivel as his anger left him. For the first time since she had met him, Kate saw vulnerability in her old boss.

"Do you really believe he will resign, Richard?"

"Yes. He knows he's lucky to get away so lightly. I've left instructions for the tape to be released to the Press if he ever tries for public office again. Defending that bastard has been the biggest regret of my life. And of course, on reflection, I should never have involved Brian Molloy and Fred in the syndicate. I wouldn't have except I was desperate at the time to buy more time for Cora. "

"I'm so, so sorry about Cora, Richard. What're you going to do now?"

He shrugged. "Go away. Wander around. Spread Cora's ashes on the Nile. That's what she wanted. Just bide my time until I can be with her again. And you?"

"I haven't decided yet. To be honest, my life's a mess."

"Funny thing, that's exactly what Fred said to me. Seems like you two should talk."

"And that's exactly what he said to me." Kate laughed. "We'll see."

"Don't wait too long to decide, Kate. Life doesn't stand still."

Kate then did something she would never have believed she could do. She kissed Richard on the cheek and hugged him.

She stood and looked at him before she left the room, a shadow of the man who had inspired admiration, fear and respect. She committed the image to memory. A shrunken old man in the leather chair his deceased wife had commissioned especially for him. Kate knew this was the last time she would ever lay eyes on Richard Gordon.

Kate had to check her desk calendar to find out what day it was. It was Friday. She felt her days were losing their definition, one being much the same as the next. Work, home. Home, work, with the odd visit to Patty or Sheila thrown in to relieve the monotony. It had only been a week since Cora Gordon's Memorial Service, only two days since Henry Hennessey had announced his surprise resignation, but the events already felt clouded in time. Just seven days since that fleeting conversation with Fred in the church grounds.

"You seem a bit down, Kate. Want a cup of coffee? Cranky Yank won't be in for a while yet."

"Why not!" Kate said and walked into the little canteen with Eileen. Listening to a stream of Billy anecdotes was preferable to hearing the endless buzz of unanswered questions in her own head.

"He's not so cranky any more, is he? Ever since that trip he made to Budapest. Maybe you should take him on another outing."

Kate looked suspiciously at Eileen but did not see any malice in the girl's face. How could she know? How could anyone know? There had been no witnesses to that night of torrid passion in the Vari.

"It's just that he is more content since he has bought a home here and has Bobby settled. Who cares as long as he's not stalking around the place, demanding everything yesterday!"

"True," Eileen agreed and noticing that the kettle had boiled got up to fill their two mugs with water.

She handed Kate her coffee and sat down across from her.

"Kate, I want to ask you a question. A personal one."

Kate's heart skipped a beat. What the fuck! Had she

underestimated Eileen's shrewdness? Did she know? Did the whole world know that Kate Lucas was an easy lay? Some music and good food and she was yours.

"Ask," she said quietly.

"Billy has suggested I move in with him. I don't know what to do. I thought it was exactly what I wanted until he said the words. Now I'm not sure if I should make the commitment. How would I know? What should I do, Kate?"

Kate threw her head back and laughed. Then she noticed the girl's hurt expression. "I'm sorry, Eileen. I'm not laughing at you. I'm laughing at me. God! Could you have picked anyone less qualified to advise you? My husband has gone to find peace and quiet. I'm living here in limbo. I've miscalculated and misjudged all along the line. I can't sort my own life. Anyway, if there's one thing I've learned, it's that you should follow your own heart. If it feels right, it is. Simple."

"So it feels right for you to be here and for Fred to be somewhere else, does it?"

Kate winced at the sharpness of the question.

"It's complicated."

"Relationships usually are," Eileen said.

Kate realised there had been a shift in the conversation. She was now the person getting, not giving, advice. She smiled at the girl sitting across from her. "It sounds very clichéd but life is short. Take a chance. Your relationship with Billy may not last. But it may be the best experience of your life. Put both your shopping in the one basket. "

Eileen laughed. "As easy as that. Häagen Dazs for two."

Kate stood up and washed her cup. By the time she was back at her desk her decision was made. As easy as that.

If Martin was surprised by her decision he did not say so. He put her letter of resignation on the desk and leaned towards her.

"Are you really sure about this, Kate? It's a big step."

"I'm sure. I've never enjoyed living in Dublin. You've been in Kerry with me, Martin. You've seen my home there. I miss it. I feel so constrained by the concrete and confined spaces of the city. I stayed here just for Fred. And now . . ."

She could not finish the sentence. And now what? Fred had left her? Their marriage was over? They would never have the baby she so longed for, never again laugh together at the silly jokes they had both enjoyed. Before Lucas Advertising. Before Adele Sheehan. Before Martin Burke.

"Kate?"

She looked up to see Martin fiddling with a pen, for once seeming unsure of himself.

"Does your decision have anything to do with Budapest? You know, our time together there. I know we agreed not to discuss it, to just forget it ever happened. But that's not easy, is it?"

Kate smiled at him and reached her hand across the desk. "I don't want to forget it, Martin. It was wonderful. A magic night. I'll always treasure the memory. I hope you will too. But it's not my reason for going back to Kerry.

In fact, if you had an office in Killarney, I'd happily work for you there."

"And where are you going to work? Do you have anything arranged?"

"I'll take a couple of weeks to sort myself out and then look for work. I've some savings to live on in the meantime."

Kate stood up and walked around the desk to Martin.

"I hope you and Bobby will be very happy. I'm sure you will. I'll miss you, Cranky Yank."

Martin raised an eyebrow and to Kate's amusement he blushed.

He stood up and held out his arms. Kate went to him, leaned her face against his broad chest and breathed in the aroma of Martin Burke. For a moment she heard the strains of wild gypsy music. Then she turned and walked out of the office, out of the building and out of the city.

Chapter 35

Phil McCarthy was mending a fence in the lower meadow as Kate drove past. She waved and smiled, knowing that he would drop his work and go to tell Noreen to bake some bread for Katie O'Hanlon.

When she parked her car in front of the cottage Kate was stiff from the long drive. She got out and stretched, taking in deep breaths of pure air. She needed a warm drink and something to eat. Taking out her bag of groceries, she unlocked the door of the cottage and went inside. She dropped her shopping on the kitchen table and just stood there, eyes closed, absorbing the smells, the little creaky sounds, the warmth and security of Kitty and Paudie's house. Of her home.

As she waited for the kettle to boil, she made herself some sandwiches. It was almost five o'clock now. She had made good time from Dublin. It was still bright enough to take a quick hike in the hills. After her meal, she took out her walking boots and laced them up. Rex was waiting for her when she went out. She patted him and together they headed up the stony path. Her muscles ached, her boots felt heavy, but her heart got lighter with every step. Each foot she climbed, each stony yard she crossed, raised her higher and higher above the turbulence of her life.

She stopped and looked up at the summit. This had been a mountain to her when she was a child. Growing up had diminished her perception of its size but not its beauty or the healing powers of the heather-clad slopes. Picking up a stone, she raised it to her lips and whispered. She told it about her marriage, how she and Fred had failed each other, how she had slept with another man, the ultimate betrayal. How Fred had lied and cheated and then turned his back on her. Then she whispered about the job she had just abandoned, the friends she had left behind, the life in Dublin that was no more. The stone sat in her hand, round and smooth, cold and hard and full of her whisperings. She drew back her arm and threw her Trouble Stone with all her might. It bounced along the stony path and then disappeared into the heather. Kate smiled. Cleansed now, she turned her face to the summit. Then she climbed to the top of the hill that was not as high as she had once imagined. When she reached the top she took off her jacket, folded it and placed it on the ground. There she sat and surveyed her kingdom.

Rex noticed before she did. He pricked up his ears and his tail began to wag. Kate leaned forward and squinted. Far below, at the start of the stony path, a lone figure was beginning the climb. Kate cried and laughed at the same time. Getting up, she put on her jacket and began her descent.

Noreen McCarthy dropped the net curtain on the dormer window and carefully made her way down the narrow stairway. She was cold and stiff from sitting in her perch, keeping watch over the narrow mountain path. Her brother was sitting by the fire. She tapped him on the shoulder.

"He went up the hill after her but I don't know what's going on now," she grumbled. "It's getting too dark to see."

Phil took his pipe out of his mouth and glared at his sister. "You're a very nosey old woman. They don't need you spying on them."

Then Phil spat on the fire and sat back to enjoy the hiss and sizzle of the spit on the burning turf. Noreen began to prepare their tea. Their lips moved as both of them prayed silently and separately for the young couple on the hill.

Kate skidded and slipped her way down the hillside. He was running too, covering the uphill climb with long, easy strides. They stopped when they were only feet apart, their momentum suddenly halted by the enormity of the questions they had to answer.

"Do you think you could forgive me, Kate?" he asked.

She looked at him and saw the traces of his suffering on his face. She knew she was about to add to his pain but she had to do it.

"I slept with Martin Burke."

Her words seemed to echo around the hills, accusing, taunting.

He stood very still. She noticed his shoulders droop a little, his lips tighten.

"Do you love him?"

"No. Do you love Adele Sheehan?"

He took a step towards her. They stood, looking at each other, not touching.

"No, Kate. I don't love Adele Sheehan. I never did. She was just part of what went wrong with my life. With our lives. Part of that out-of-control nightmare time."

"Is the nightmare over?"

He reached out and gently raised her chin so that she had to look into the grey-green eyes she had known so well.

"Can we talk, Kate?

She nodded and together they trudged back to the cottage. When the fire was lighting in Kitty's parlour, they sat and talked. And talked.

The night turned cold and windy. Clouds filled and then emptied, the wind rose and swirled and whipped away the smoke from the chimney. Kate and Fred talked.

The sky lightened, the sun rose, the air warmed, the blazing sods of turf turned to ashes in Kitty's parlour. Kate and Fred still talked.

The sun sank low on the western horizon and brought closure to the day. The talking was all done. Only the hurt lived on in the silence.

Epilogue

2 years later

"Do you think this will be enough?" Noreen asked as she heaped mountains of queen cakes onto plates.

Kate laughed and hugged the old lady. "Noreen, this lot would feed an army. All this baking's too much for you. You should be taking care of yourself."

"It's not me that needs taking care of," Noreen said huffily. "You're the one in the family way!"

Kate smiled and her hand automatically went to her distended belly. What a nice way to phrase it! In the family way! A family. Kate and Fred and their baby.

"I hope that Cochrane man won't be here too."

Noreen nurtured a great dislike of Gus Cochrane. She found his bluntness and coarseness hard to handle. Gus knew this and always tried to win her over when they met. A charm offensive by Gus Cochrane was an awesome spectacle.

"No, Noreen. He's not coming today. But I wish you'd

just try to get to know him. He really is a very kind man. Fred and I owe him a lot."

"I know. I know he gave Fred a job. And you too but . . ."

"He did more than that. No matter what he says, I know Gus Cochrane opened a branch of his waste-disposal company in Killarney just to give Fred a chance."

Noreen shrugged her shoulders. "Fred's a great manager," she said sulkily. "He makes loads of money for Cochrane. Fred's under no compliment."

Knowing from experience that this was a battle lost, Kate let the subject of Gus Cochrane drop. Glancing at her watch, she saw that the day was moving on. Time to drag Fred away from his obsession. Leaving Noreen in the kitchen, Kate waddled through the cottage to the new extension. Standing at the door of the room that would be the nursery, she watched as Fred carefully applied pale lemon paint to the walls, the floors, his hands, his hair.

"Patty and Martin and their hordes of children will be here soon," she said. "You'd better make yourself decent."

He turned around to face her and his boyish smile lit his face. "I thought I'd already done that," he laughed.

Kate went to him and put her arms around him. They stood there, in the pale lemon nursery, their baby safely cradled between them, lemon paint now staining them both. Kate closed her eyes and allowed the images of their past to flicker through her mind. Images of loneliness and struggle, of unfaithfulness and addiction, of greed and deceit. She looked at the memories and no longer felt the pain. They were the building blocks of a love that was profoundly accepting and forgiving. No recriminations. No bitterness. No pretence.

Noreen McCarthy turned and crept silently away from the door of the nursery. She smiled.

Katie O'Hanlon was home at last.

The End

If you enjoyed reading *As Easy As That*, don't miss out on Mary O'Sullivan's debut novel, *Parting Company*, also published by Poolbeg.com

Here is a sneak preview of Chapter one . . .

Parting Company

Mary O'Sullivan

POOLBEG

Chapter One

Brendan looked back. He knew Claire would be standing there, a small, dark oasis of gloom in the bustling airport. He waved to her and then continued on through passport control. As soon as he was seated on the plane he opened his brief-case and took out his reports. The pages lay unread. His mind lingered on his wife, on the clinging feel of her, on her draining intensity. He closed his eyes and took a deep breath. Three days. He was going to have three whole days without her. When he opened his eyes again, the Irish coastline was shrinking away. He smiled at the hostess as she offered him breakfast.

* * *

A wave of light and heat hit him as he stepped off the plane. Düsseldorf was warm and sunny. He shrugged off his coat as he crossed the tarmac. A few people glanced at him. Brendan Hearn, tall, dark-haired and broad-shouldered, was the type who attracted glances.

Checking his watch, he calculated that if the train connection to Bonn went smoothly he should have plenty of time to relax before his meeting. Thanks to German efficiency, he was soon collecting his case from the carousel. He stood for a moment in the Arrivals area to get his bearings.

"Excuse me. Mr Hearn of Dashern Chemical Company?"

Brendan looked in surprise at the man standing before him. He had not expected to be met.

The man offered his hand. "Klaus Haussmann. I am your driver."

"Oh!" Brendan said in surprise. "I didn't think the Conference package included transport."

"Nor does it," Klaus answered in his very correct English. "I have been sent to meet you by Mr Jacques Rondel of RTTI."

Brendan picked up his case. He should have guessed. RTTI was not a company to leave anything to chance. He followed Klaus to the waiting Mercedes.

For the first ten kilometres Brendan sat on the edge of his seat, conscious of hurtling along on what felt like the wrong side of the motorway. Eventually he relaxed into the luxury of the soft leather seats and let the Brahms from the stereo wash over him. He thought about Jacques Rondel. He felt he knew the man. They had spoken so often on the phone and had exchanged so many emails and faxes that their communications had developed an easy familiarity. But now that they were about to meet face to face, Brendan felt slightly uneasy. A bit like the new boy being introduced to the team captain.

"The Rhine," Klaus said proudly as if he was personally responsible for the great expanse of river coming into view.

Scores of barges furrowed white drills as they ploughed over and back and up and down the Rhine. It was a very crowded waterway. The suburbs of Bonn sloped gently back from the banks of the river and rose in forested waves towards the towering peaks of the Drachenfels. The Mercedes smoothly joined the traffic travelling through the suburbs of Bad Godesberg and headed towards the Konstantin Hotel.

* * *

When he arrived at the reception desk in the glass-domed lobby of the Konstantin, Brendan produced his booking form and asked for the key to his room. The receptionist waved the paperwork away and handed him a swipe card for Suite 134.

"No – no," Brendan insisted. "I ordered a single room. I made the booking myself."

"Mr Hearn," the receptionist repeated patiently, "you will be staying in Suite 134. It has been arranged."

Brendan suddenly understood. He glanced around and saw that there were people behind him waiting to check in. They were all trying to appear uninterested in his dilemma.

Leaning towards the receptionist he whispered as discreetly as possible: "RTTI?"

She nodded and beckoned for a porter to take his case.

Anger and embarrassment flushed his face. He took the swipe card and followed the porter, turning his back on the curious stares of the other guests.

* * *

The bed in Suite 134 looked big enough to sleep four. Brendan threw his luggage angrily onto the white quilt and went in search of the drinks cabinet. A stiff brandy later, he began to calm down. He deliberately slowed his breathing, poured another drink and sank back into the comfort of the cream leather couch. So! Rondel wanted to play hardball, did he? Wanted to show the little Irishman who was pulling the strings. Wanted to patronise him.

"Fuck him," he said out loud and then wondered if RTTI forward planning had extended to bugging the suite.

Just as he was getting out of the shower the phone rang. He picked it up, hoping that whoever was on the other end spoke English.

"Welcome to Germany, Brendan."

Jacques Rondel! Brendan took a deep breath.

"Thank you, Jacques. And thank you for sending a car to meet me. Very considerate. But the room I had booked for myself would have been adequate. I don't mean to sound ungrateful but I feel a little uncomfortable with this preferential treatment. I don't want to be under any obligation to –"

"Don't be silly," Jacques interrupted. "RTTI just wants to ensure you enjoy your visit here. Now, let's arrange a meeting place. Would the bistro on the ground floor suit you? In fifteen minutes?" His tone was businesslike. The warm camaraderie of email and phone seemed subtly changed.

"Fine," Brendan agreed. "See you in fifteen."

Tie knotted and hair smoothed into place, Brendan stood in front of the full-length mirror. Pulling in his already flat stomach, he squared his shoulders. He smiled at the tall, well-muscled reflection, liking the way his pale blue shirt emphasised his tan.

He was ready to meet Jacques Rondel.

* * *

By the time Brendan reached the bistro, he had decided on a wait-and-see strategy with Rondel. A waiter met him at the door and led him through the crowded restaurant to a table in an alcove. Jacques Rondel was seated facing the entrance. Brendan knew that he had been under observation since he had walked in the door.

Jacques rose and offered his hand. As the men shook hands, they assessed each other. The Frenchman's handshake was strong, his silver hair perfectly groomed, the radar sweep of the blue eyes not missing a detail.

He waved Brendan to the seat opposite him.

"Is your suite to your satisfaction?" he asked as they both settled themselves into their seats.

Brendan hesitated for a moment. Was Jacques challenging him or was he just being polite? "Yes. It's very comfortable, thank you."

"*Bien,*" Jacques said and the muttered word brushed over Brendan like a patronising pat on the head.

"I hadn't expected such a big crowd," Brendan remarked, looking around the packed restaurant. "Are all these people here for the herbal medicine conference?"

"Yes, certainly. We are not the only people who see a future in herbal medicine. Phytochemistry is 'hot', as you might say."

"And profitable, as *you* might say," Brendan shot back.

Jacques raised an eyebrow just a shade. He held up his hand and a waiter appeared at the table with a bottle of wine. "I have chosen the wine. I hope you approve. It is one of the best local wines from the Ahr Valley."

As the waiter poured some of the red Spätburgunder, Brendan noticed a third place set at the table. "Are we expecting company?" he asked.

Jacques smiled. "Our Public Relations Manager is joining us. I think you will both get on well. You have a lot in common."

"Is that so?"

"Judge for yourself." Jacques nodded his head in the direction of the entrance.

Brendan resisted the temptation to turn around and

allowed himself one moment of gloating. The Public Relations Manager! They *were* giving him the treatment!

"Ah! Yvette!" Jacques said as he stood and pulled out the third chair.

Brendan first became aware of a waft of perfume. Curious, he stood and turned around to look into the most beautiful eyes he had ever seen. They were amber, almond-shaped and fringed by long, dark lashes. He realised that other people were looking at this stunning woman, that he was staring like an awestruck adolescent, that Jacques was introducing her – but yet he could not look away from her warm, honey gaze.

She reached out her hand to him. "Yvette Previn. It is so nice to meet you, Brendan."

She had a really short haircut, emphasising the bone structure of her face. Her voice was husky, her fingers slender and her skin silky and warm. She was a warm woman. Warm eyes, warm skin. With a start Brendan realised that all these warm thoughts were generating heat in his crotch area. He released Yvette's hand and quickly sat before his gaucheness became too apparent.

The waiter arrived with the menus and Brendan was glad of the few minutes they spent poring over the extensive selection of dishes. By the time he had chosen melon for starter and veal for main course, he felt more in control.

"Is this your first visit to Germany, Brendan?" Yvette asked.

"It is indeed."

"Then you could not have chosen a nicer city to start

with than Bonn. It is so historic and so very beautiful. We must show him around, Jacques."

Jacques raised his glass. "Here's to new experiences, new friendships and new beginnings!"

"To the future!" Yvette said as the three glasses clinked together.

"To the future!" Brendan echoed and for the first time he allowed himself to really believe that RTTI International could be part of his future.

* * *

Brendan had been awake long before his morning call. As the dark of night gave way to the grey light of dawn he had lain in bed thinking over strategies. His plans for the future of Dashern Chemicals. He was more convinced now than ever that RTTI should be involved. Rest was not helped, either, by the knowledge that the stunningly beautiful RTTI Public Relations Manager was sleeping in the adjoining suite. His heart raced each time he recalled her amber eyes and honey-toned skin. She was, without doubt, the most fascinating woman he had ever met. He had learned with interest last night that she was to give a lecture this morning: 'Herbal Medicine and the Media'. She had spoken on the topic over dinner and he had been impressed by her knowledge of international legislation and regulations. He had been even more impressed by the outline of her breasts underneath her silk blouse.

He dressed carefully, choosing navy suit and white

shirt, navy and blue tie. The tie had been a gift from Claire. From his dark-eyed, solemn little wife. It reflected Claire's personality. He ripped it off and chose a red tie instead.

Checking his watch he saw that there were two hours to go before his meeting with Jacques. Two hours to study his proposition for RTTI. He opened his laptop and scrolled through the menu. Clicking on Projections, he checked and rechecked figures, tried to second-guess market trends. His conclusion was the same as it had been for the past year. Dashern Chemicals was heading for trouble. Evidence of the company's falling profits flicked across the monitor. Competition was eating up Dashern's share of the detergent market. Why could the old man not see it? Why wouldn't the bull-headed bastard listen? Brendan's knuckles whitened as he thought of his father-in-law. The great Frank Dawson. The man who had built up a thriving detergent manufacturing industry from nothing. The man who was wallowing in the shallows of past glories while the tide of progress was lapping against the foundations of his little empire. Closing off the projections, Brendan went straight to his proposal document and read through it point by point. He got up, poured some coffee and read it again. There was nothing more he could add.

He shut down his computer and checked the time. Still an hour to spare. He rode the panoramic elevator down to the lobby and headed for the Conference Centre.

The main hall was lined with display stands promoting different products and producers. Brendan stood near the entrance, watching the crowds milling around the stands and listening to the vibrant buzz of conversations in so many different languages. There was so much to see, so many companies, so much research, so much to learn. A large banner caught his eye: *St John's Wort – Food Supplement or Drug?* As he started towards that stand, he noticed a signpost for the lecture theatre. An unbidden image of Yvette's nipples pushing against the silk of her blouse sent a shiver through him. St John's Wort suddenly lost its appeal.

Leaving the hall he followed the signpost until he came to the double doors leading into the lecture theatre. He stood outside and listened. The husky voice of the speaker could only belong to Yvette Previn.

He pushed open the doors and slipped quietly into a seat at the back. Yvette was speaking in French, the musical language enhanced by her rich intonation. He gave up trying to understand and just let the sound and the sight of her tease his senses. This morning she was wearing a beige-coloured suit, the jacket tailored so that it fitted snugly. It would have been an ordinary business suit on anyone else. Fitted as it was to the contours of Yvette's body, Brendan thought it a work of art. When she finished lecturing, she opened the floor to questions. He was impressed yet again as she slipped with ease from French to German to English in order to facilitate her audience. She seemed to effortlessly attract and hold attention.

He left reluctantly to keep his appointment with Jacques Rondel.

* * *

He had to fight the urge to pace the floor while Jacques read through his proposal. The Frenchman's face was inscrutable as he turned page after page. Eventually he put the pages down, sat back and turned the Rondel stare on full power.

Like a game of who blinks first, Brendan thought.

If it was a game, Brendan lost. He could not stand the silence any longer.

"Well, Jacques? Your reaction? Do we have a deal?"

Jacques laughed and the sound hit Brendan like a splash of cold water. The prick was laughing at him! Mocking him. Testing him? He took a deep breath.

"Do I take it you find my proposals amusing?"

Jacques leaned forward and the blue gaze knifed through Brendan. "Let me point out a few issues you do not seem to have properly grasped. Number one, RTTI is a global multibillion-dollar pharmaceutical company. We do not barter with low-tech detergent plants. Number two, if we do decide to have discussions with you, it will be on our terms. You will not presume to tell us how we should conduct our business. And –"

"What the bloody hell is all this about then?" Brendan cut in, sweeping his arm around to indicate the luxury suite. "Why the chauffeur-driven car? All the emails and phone calls? Don't fuck around with me, Jacques. You have spent time and effort communicating with me. You're interested in getting a foothold in Ireland and your best way of doing that is by merging with Dashern."

"What makes you think Dashern is our only Irish option, Brendan? What makes you think we want to go to Ireland at all? Remember it was you who contacted me first. RTTI never went after you and we are not about to do so now."

Brendan was caught off guard. He needed to control his anger to think this out. He rose and walked towards the drink cabinet.

"Drink, Jacques?"

"Mineral water, please," Jacques answered calmly. "Still."

As he put ice and lemon into the two glasses, Brendan took stock. Rondel was bullshitting. He was almost certain of that. Almost. He took a steadying breath before handing the Frenchman his drink.

"OK," he said, placing his own glass of water on the table between them. "Let's stop trying to score points off each other. Yes. I made the initial contact after your article appeared in *New Scientist*. But why *did* you publish that article, Jacques?"

"Because I was asked to write a feature on the production and application of herbal extract, of course. Why else do you think I would do it?"

"Cut the crap. You published that article precisely because RTTI needed somebody like me to follow it up. Your company is a giant, a vast industrial and financial power, but your environmental reputation stinks. How could you seriously market a product that is supposed to be natural and clean? I read between the lines of your well-phrased article. You were offering profits in exchange for a clean image behind which to hide."

Jacques smiled. "Interesting interpretation. Now let us talk about Dashern Chemicals."

Brendan relaxed a little. It seemed as if talks were about to start. Jacques took a sip from his drink and opened a folder in front of him. He flicked through some pages and then fixed Brendan in his radar sights. His voice was as flat and cold as his stare.

"Dashern Chemicals is going to lose two major contracts during the coming year. You could struggle on with reduced staffing levels but you will not be able to compete with the increasingly competitive international market. You could diversify into another area but you can't afford the huge investment that would involve. You can't look for financing because –"

Brendan threw his hands up in the air, palms towards Jacques in surrender. "OK! OK! Enough! We've all obviously done our background research. But RTTI still needs a respectable front as badly as Dashern needs a wealthy backer. We have a supply-and-demand situation here. What's the problem?"

Jacques smiled at first and then he laughed. A deep, hearty laugh that seemed totally at odds with this sophisticated, controlled man. He held out his hand to Brendan.

"I admire your style. We have a lot of things to discuss yet but we *will* talk."

Brendan took the Frenchman's hand and solemnly shook it. The moment was complete when Jacques told him they were to meet Yvette for lunch.

* * *

Interesting as the conference on herbal medicine had been, or phytochemistry as the industry preferred to call it, after two days Brendan felt saturated. He had lost count of the number of lectures, slide shows and presentations he had attended. Despite all the research he had done beforehand, he had underestimated the potential for this branch of medicine. An industry in its infancy, it was so full of untapped potential that even his stubborn father-in-law would have to be interested.

But best of all, each day had been touched by the unique magic of Yvette Previn. Like a moth to the flame, Brendan was drawn to the golden light of her beauty, snatching glimpses as she went from meeting to meeting, looking forward to the meals shared with her and the urbane Jacques Rondel.

When Jacques suggested that the three of them take an afternoon trip on the Rhine, Brendan had tried to accept the invitation casually. He was fairly certain his quickened breath and the slight tremor in his hand had gone unnoticed. Even by Jacques Rondel.

* * *

They sat on the top deck of a waterbus as it sliced

through the blue-green waters of the Rhine. Yvette, seated opposite Brendan, had her eyes closed and her face turned up to the sun.

"And this is the famous Bridge at Remagen. Perhaps you have seen the film?"

Brendan became aware that Jacques was talking to him and that he expected a reply.

"George Segal, Robert Vaughan, Ben Gazarra," Yvette murmured without opening her eyes. "Directed by John Guillerman, 1969."

As the waterbus approached Remagen, the remains of the bombed-out Ludendorff Bridge loomed dark and sinister on either side of the river, a monument to an era of powerful evil and evil power. Brendan shivered, chilled in the heat of the sun by the dark shadow of history. He turned his eyes away and looked downstream, towards the forested banks and sloping vineyards.

"Not long before we reach Linz now," Jacques said. "I promise you are going to love it, Brendan. It is a special place. Is it not, Yvette?"

She opened her eyes and sat up straight. The sun touched her short auburn hair with copper highlights. Brendan knew her hair would be soft to touch. Silky. Like her skin. He focused on the bare area between the bottom of her cropped blouse and the hip-band of her low-cut jeans. Her navel was small and neat. He needed to kiss it, to run his tongue over her honey-coloured belly.

"Claire would love Linz too. You must bring her

here sometime," she said.

"Claire?" Brendan echoed in surprise.

"Your wife," laughed Yvette. "I know you have been very busy for a few days with the conference and with us but you cannot have forgotten your wife of three years already!"

"Yvette does her research thoroughly," Jacques remarked. "Just as your wife does. But while Claire's field is biochemistry, Yvette's is personal history. She knows your deepest, darkest secrets by now."

Brendan laughed with them but he felt more puzzled than amused. He was surprised that Yvette knew his wife's name. But then Claire had a certain standing in the area of biochemistry. She had published some well-received papers in the past. What shocked him was the realisation that for the past three days he *had* forgotten his wife, forgotten her depressing darkness and her accusing sadness. Forgotten to ring her! The old man would be furious if she complained to him. But Claire would not complain. She would just let him read the hurt in her tragic brown eyes. Shit! He took out his phone and tapped in a quick message: *C U 2morrow nite. Luv B.* He pressed *Send* and forgot her again.

People shuffled towards the lower deck as the ferry approached the dock. The gates of the walled town were a short walk from where they disembarked. Jacques's phone rang just as they reached the beautiful old stone walls. While he took his call, Brendan and Yvette read the high tide records carved into the stone.

This town had been battered by floodwaters for many centuries. They were talking about global warming and rising tides when Jacques joined them, a very annoyed expression on his face.

"I'm sorry. I've got to return on the next ferry."

"Something wrong?" Yvette asked anxiously.

"Just some papers I need to sign for someone who is going home today. I must catch him before he leaves."

Yvette nodded.

She obviously knew what this was about. Brendan wished *he* did. Could RTTI double-cross him at this late stage? Rondel had been careful not to make any firm commitments. Nothing on paper. It would appear that RTTI was interested in a merger with Dashern but, under the polished exterior, Jacques Rondel was probably a ruthless bastard.

Brendan smiled at the Frenchman. "Never mind, Jacques. We can do this another time."

"No. No. No. Do not let me spoil your afternoon. This is the only time off you have had. I want you to see something of the scenery. You two young people enjoy Linz. I will see you back in the Konstantin tonight."

Before they could say anything he had turned and walked in the direction of the ferry. Yvette and Brendan looked at each other and laughed.

"Come on, youngster," she said, taking his hand and leading him through the stone arch onto the cobbled streets of Linz.

* * *

Brendan was tall. Six feet two inches. He felt at least four feet taller as he strolled through Linz with this beautiful woman by his side. He noticed people noticing them as they sat at the fountain in the square eating ice cream, as they explored the little shops, as they admired the ornate facia on the buildings. By the time they had climbed the hill leading to the top of the town, they were hot and thirsty. Finding a café, they sat outside in the sun sipping their drinks. They were silent for a while, lulled by the heat of the sun and the quiet beauty of this secret little town behind the big stone walls.

"Wouldn't it be so easy to believe that life begins and ends here in Linz?" Yvette remarked.

Brendan knew what she meant. The calm and sense of timelessness had touched him too. It was as if they had always been here and they always would be.

She leaned towards him. "Talking about beginnings, Brendan, I want to know all about you. I want to know about your childhood, your family and your history. Talk!"

"Didn't Jacques say you knew everybody's secrets? *You* tell *me*."

She settled back in her chair and fixed her amber eyes on his face. "You were born in County Waterford, Ireland, in a seaside town called Tramore. You went to high school, or 'secondary school' as you call it, in Waterford City. Being a clever little fellow, you won a scholarship to University College Dublin, where you got a Masters Degree in Analytical Science. After working for three years with a pharmaceutical company in England, you returned to Ireland as Chief Chemist with a meat-processing plant in Wexford. How am I doing so far?"

Jesus! Jacques had not been joking. Yvette Previn was either very inquisitive or else a damned good detective.

"Go on," he said, wondering what more of his history she had managed to dig up.

"You took a course in Production Management and applied for the position of Production Manager with Dawson Chemicals. You not only got the job, you landed a wife and a one-third share in Dawson Chemicals too. Soon after your marriage to Claire Dawson, the company was renamed Dashern Chemicals. And now, it seems you would like to change the name of the company again. How did I do?"

Brendan raised his glass to her. "You're good. *Salut!*"

"Public record," she said dismissively. "I want to know about *you,* Brendan, about what makes you tick."

"On condition you then tell me about Yvette Previn, about what makes *her* tick."

She offered him her hand and he held it as he began to talk. The sun slanted westward, shadows lengthened and still they talked. She told him about her nomadic childhood as her family followed her diplomat father from posting to posting. Beirut, Rome, London, Bahrain, Washington. The Previn family had moved from one diplomatic enclave to another, making new friends and learning new cultures and languages, only to leave them and start all over again somewhere else.

Brendan told her about his childhood, about the loneliness and isolation of being an only child. He had not thought about his dead parents for a long time. Now memories of the tight-lipped, ambitious woman who had been his mother came flooding back, shadowed as in her lifetime by the image of the gruff, silent man who had been his father.

"My father was a carpenter," he explained to Yvette. "He was a big, awkward man. Inarticulate. Insensitive. Until he held a piece of timber in his hands. Then he was a master craftsman. An artist."

"And your mother?"

"A typical Irish mother," Brendan laughed. "She pushed me out of nappies into school. Out of school into college. She planned my life and then made me think I planned it for myself."

Yvette leaned forward and stroked his cheek. "Do you miss them, Brendan?"

Brendan glanced around him. He lifted his eyes to the beautiful carvings adorning the top storeys of the buildings around them. His father would have admired them. And how his mother would have loved the flowers that trailed swathes of colour from window boxes and pots. Did he miss them? He looked back at Yvette.

"Yes," he said simply. "I miss them."

He was uncomfortable with the depth of feeling in his reply. He had not realised there was still a corner in his psyche that needed his father's silent approval and his mother's encouragement. In fact he had never known. Bollocks to this amateur psychology! He stood up.

"We'd better think about getting back to the ferry."

"Are you afraid of being locked into the magic little town? With the Big Bad Witch?"

"You *are* a witch," he accused. "You've made me remember things I didn't really want to think about."

"Maybe you need to talk more," she said as she stood on tiptoe and kissed his cheek.

She turned quickly and started to walk down the hill, hips swaying. Brendan was startled when she broke into a run but then she turned back and laughed. He chased after her. They raced to the ferry and arrived together at the pier, laughing and out of breath.

They climbed to the top deck again and stood close together as Linz became smaller and smaller and finally disappeared from view.

* * *

Jacques announced at dinner that he would be leaving early in the morning.

"You'll be coming with me, Yvette. I'm afraid it's back to Zurich for us."

"Oh, well," Yvette answered, "this conference is practically over anyway. Tomorrow is just the wind-down. When are you leaving, Brendan?"

"Tomorrow afternoon."

Brendan swirled the wine in his glass. It was Spätburgunder again. He had developed a taste for this earthy red wine in the past few days. He had also developed a taste for dining with this beautiful woman, for talking to her, for laughing with her, for seeing her amber eyes sparkle, for touching her whenever he could. He did not want to think about tomorrow.

"So. What do you say, Brendan?"

Shit! He had missed that. He had not been listening. "Could you run that by me again, Jacques?"

"I knew you were miles away. I asked if you could organise things from your end for an RTTI visit to Dashern?"

Brendan's heart skipped a beat. They were going for it! The might and money of RTTI were going to be poured into Dashern!

"Of course. No problem. When?" he asked, hoping he didn't sound too eager.

Jacques stood up and offered his hand to Brendan. "I will let you know when we can fit Dashern into our schedule. I have a few people to see now, so I will excuse myself. I look forward to visiting your plant."

Brendan stood and shook Jacques' hand, resisting the urge to hug him.

Jacques went over to Yvette and kissed her on both cheeks. Then he turned back to Brendan.

"You will have your father-in-law and your wife on side, won't you? Make sure they understand our interest in Dashern includes your wife's department. Research and Development, after all, is our area of expertise. We would expect her to share her findings with us."

"Absolutely. No problem. You have my word on that."

Brendan stared at the Frenchman's retreating back. Claire's research? How could it possibly be of interest to RTTI? He had no idea what she spent her time on in that little lab but he doubted that it could be anything of significance. He and Claire never spoke about it. They rarely spoke. He turned back to Yvette.

"Would you like a walk?" he asked impulsively.

In reply she stood up and took his arm. They strolled side by side in the pine-scented air of nearby Rheinaue Park until the last vestiges of light left the sky. Yvette shivered in the cool darkness. Brendan put his arm around her shoulder and drew her close. He could feel her hip brushing against his, smell the rose-scented aroma that was uniquely hers. When they reached the grounds of the hotel, he stopped and turned her to face him. She looked up at him, her amber eyes glittering in the moonlight. There was so much he wanted to tell her. So much he wanted to know. So little time.

"Is there someone special in your life, Yvette?" he blurted out. He had not meant to sound so desperate, so blunt.

She nodded.

He knew he had no right to feel jealous but he could not help the wave of envy that swept through him. "Tell me about him. Is he French? Is he in RTTI? Does he deserve you?"

Yvette took a step closer. He could feel the heat from her body and the touch of her sweet breath on his face.

"My man is very special to me. I want him to be

happy but I see sadness in his eyes and in the little lines at the corners of his mouth. I would like to kiss the sadness away. I would like to hold him and love him until the smile reaches his eyes. But there is a problem."

She reached her hand up to his face and her fingers traced the lines at the corners of his mouth. Brendan closed his eyes. She moved even closer to him and he could feel her breasts, soft and full, against his chest.

"What's the problem?" he whispered into the silkiness of her hair.

Yvette stepped back and took her hand away from his face. "The problem is that he is married. The decision must be his."

Reaching into her bag she handed him something and, turning, walked away towards the hotel. He stared after her, confused and frustrated. Then he looked at what she had given him. He held it up in the moonlight to make sure. *Yes! Yes!* He put the swipe card to Suite 133 into his pocket and ran after her.

Yvette was almost at the entrance to the hotel when he caught up with her. Together they walked through the busy lobby and rode the elevator upstairs. Brendan took the swipe card out of his pocket and opened the door to her suite. He followed her inside and watched as she flicked on the lamps. She waved him towards the couch and went to the drinks cabinet. Picking up a bottle of Scotch, she raised an eyebrow in enquiry. He nodded. She poured two glasses, handed him one and came to sit down beside him.

He began to feel awkward. What next? If he

followed the demands of his body, he would rip her clothes off now, fill his mouth with her breasts and fill her with him. Wham! Bang! The bulge in his trousers strained uncomfortably against the fabric. He looked around the suite, trying to gain some control. It was the same design as his. Only the colour scheme was different. He counted the lamps. Six. He breathed deeply. Better now. More control.

"Are you sure, Brendan? I know you must think of Claire."

The 'Claire' word hung in the air between them. It slowed his thumping heart, cooled his throbbing penis, focused his mind. She was right. What if Claire found out? What if his father-in-law found out? What if Jacques found out? There was so much to lose.

He looked at Yvette. She had removed her jacket to reveal a white top. He could see the dark outline of her nipples through the lacy material. Her breasts rose and fell in the same quickened rhythm as his breathing.

They had no choice. They reached for each other.

Their first coupling was there, on the couch. A desperate sating of tingling nerve-ends, a release for tensed-up muscles. It was over quickly. Then they started again. From lounge to bedroom, from head to toe, they kissed and licked, sucked and caressed. Dawn was lightening the night sky before they fell into an exhausted sleep.